W9-CEJ-497

A
MATTER OF
HONOR

A Matter of Honor

Eugene Izzi

AVON BOOKS  NEW YORK

This a work of fiction. Names, characters, places, and incidents either are the product of the author's imagination or are used fictiously. Any resemblance to actual events, locales, organizations, or persons, living or dead, is entirely coincidental and beyond the intent of either the author or the publisher.

AVON BOOKS
A division of
The Hearst Corporation
1350 Avenue of the Americas
New York, New York 10019

Copyright © 1997 by Eugene Izzi
Interior design by Kellan Peck
Visit our website at **http://AvonBooks.com**
ISBN: 0-380-97342-1

Library of Congress Cataloging in Publication Data:

Izzi, Eugene.
   A matter of honor / Eugene Izzi.
      p.   cm.
   I. Title.
PS35559.Z9M3   1997   96-46830
813'.54—dc21   CIP

First Avon Books Printing: May 1997

Printed in the U.S.A.

FIRST EDITION

QP   10   9   8   7   6   5   4   3   2   1

For my beloved Theresa

A MATTER OF
HONOR

VIOLENT
ORCHESTRATIONS

CHAPTER

1

It was getting late, and Marshall Del Greco was comfortably aware that he was about half-drunk. He was all right with that; he could afford to cut loose once every ten years or so. The last time he'd even had a beer was when his brother-in-law had gotten married, some seven years before. Tonight was a party, a special occasion. Marshall was surprised at how good the drinks tasted.

It was a sweltering Friday in mid-July; the start of a rare, full weekend off for him. Del Greco had worked the day shift, then he and his wife had driven out here to New Buffalo, Michigan, to spend the weekend at his in-laws' palatial summer home, the sort of place that only the very rich could afford to maintain. The house had its own private beach and a boating dock, soft sand leading into Lake Michigan's lapping shores. Marshall had spent the late afternoon and the early evening enjoying himself, lounging in the temperature-controlled pool, drinking light rum drinks which his mother-in-law had personally prepared, and which she had poured into coconuts that she'd sawed the tops off of. Marshall had sipped his drinks through a colored straw, feeling as if he were on the vacation that he and Rachel had never taken. There'd been little umbrellas floating around on top of the liquor. One of the many things Marshall loved about his mother-in-law was her high, grand sense of style.

He could get used to this.

There were no servants here at the Michigan summer home, although their house in Chicago's northern suburbs had a full-time staff of three—it was what his in-laws jokingly referred to as "roughing it." There were no televisions in the summer home, either, though a large-screen monitor had been hooked up to a VCR, for viewing movies. No newspapers were delivered to this house. When the family was in residence, the outside world and all of its troubles could not touch them, was not allowed to invade.

Now, after midnight, nearly all of the people in the room were pleasantly high, and even the two nondrinkers in the family were enjoying themselves. All of the adults were still awake, and were gathered around the large gaming table in the family room, sitting in comfortable chairs that had holders in the arms for their drinks. The family patriarch, Paul Berstein, had covered the table's green felt with a cheap plastic tablecloth.

Marshall, with his elbows on the plastic, listened to the conversation as it drifted around him, enjoying the rare, alcoholic buzz as much as the relaxed company, his belly full, feeling oddly detached, while at the same time feeling himself to be a strong, important part of something so good that the mere knowledge that it would soon be over made him feel nearly sad. He wondered if he felt that way because of all the rum he'd drunk. A quiet man by nature, when he was drinking, he became a stone.

Marshall looked across the table at his wife, at Rachel. He nodded his head at her, smiling secretly, and Rachel smiled back. There was a sudden lump in Marshall's throat, which he quickly swallowed down, and he was surprised by it, by the fact that it had occurred. Marshall Del Greco was not a man easily given to displays of emotion. He told himself that it was all right to feel emotion in this place, because he wasn't in public; he was in the bosom of his family, though he was blood-related to none of them.

Still, it was what he had, at last—a family—one he had chosen, one that had accepted him in return.

He looked around at them, at all his in-laws, at the wives of his wife's brothers. Due to the nature of his work, he didn't make it to many of these family gatherings; he was often working even during the holy days. He knew the boys quite well, and two of the wives. He had only a passing acquaintance with Peter's young second wife, Tina. She seemed friendly enough, though a little shy. The family had thought the same thing about Marshall, fifteen years ago. It had taken him a couple of years to prove that he was quite the opposite, was in fact very secure, but the type of man who would prefer to set himself afire before he would sit around bragging on the things that he'd accomplished.

Paul had pronounced at a birthday party that Marshall had balance, and that had been the end of the second-guessing; everyone always took Paul at his word.

Marshall looked back at Rachel. She didn't seem to have taken her eyes off him, and those eyes were shining with her love for him. A doctor, who loved him, though she hadn't been one when they'd met. Marshall sat there wondering if he had ever before felt so safe. He had spent a good deal of his life completely unaware that such a feeling of safety was attainable. The people in this room had taught him that it was, that for some, it was even pretty damn easy to come by.

All the siblings of the family had made their speeches, toasting their mother and father on the night of their thirty-fifth wedding anniversary. Rachel, the only daughter and the eldest child, had spoken first. It was understood that Marshall would not be making a speech. His in-laws knew how he felt about them; he didn't have to say the words, he'd repeatedly proven his love and loyalty to them over the course of the fifteen years that he'd been married to Rachel.

"How long 'till you're eligible to retire, Marshall?" his brother-in-law Leslie asked him, almost startling Marshall.

"Three years? Four?" Marshall laughed at himself. "I'm not sure." Marshall joined easily in the general laughter around him, and he quickly added up the years that had passed since he'd joined the police department, then said, "Three," with a firm nod of his head.

"You'll be what, in your early forties? You'll still be a relatively young man. You gonna come to work with us, right?" Again, Marshall laughed. It felt good to laugh. He made up his mind that in the future he would find the time to get together with these people more often.

"I'll be too old to break concrete, but thanks for the offer."

"Wouldn't have to go to the gym as much as you do, if you worked for a living." That was Johnny's wife, Esthel. Marshall didn't bother to explain to her that he didn't go to the gym as often as he did merely for the exercise. Instead he simply smiled, becoming uncomfortable with suddenly being the center of the family's attention.

Lawrence's wife, Bonnie, asked, "Those casinos still trying to get you to go out West, run their security for them?"

Rachel, finely tuned to her husband's mood, so aware of his discomfort—and never one to pass up an opportunity to brag about him—said, "The casinos call; entire *cities* call. Philadelphia wants Marshall to come out and be their chief of police."

Marshall, embarrassed, said, "They call, but there's no chance."

"Why not?" Bonnie turned to Rachel. "They don't need doctors in Las Vegas, or Philadelphia?"

"They've got kids everywhere, I think." Rachel smiled. "It's not my decision to make, it's Marshall's. If he wants to go, I'll go with him."

Marshall shook his head. He would never say it in front of such a large crowd, but the reason he wouldn't consider the offers was that if he did, he might then consider accepting one of them, and such an acceptance

5

would drag Rachel away from this family. He knew what that would do to her. Knew what it would do to him, too.

"I'm serious," Leslie said, and Marshall looked over at him. "I'm talking about inside work. A partner." Marshall looked over at his father-in-law. If such an offer were really being made, it would have to have been the old man's idea, and it was just like Paul not to offer Marshall the job himself, to ask one of his sons to drop it casually into conversation. Paul Berstein was beaming at him, and he nodded. The offer was legitimate.

"The sign already says Berstein and Sons, Construction," Joanie Berstein, Marshall's mother-in-law, said, and Marshall found that he had to swallow again.

He did not like this feeling. Coping mechanisms that had long ago been implanted within him were fighting with emotions that he had always tried to deny.

"You honor me, Ma," Marshall looked over at Paul, and nodded. "Pa." The words flowed easily from his lips, and he was glad. It had taken him years to be able to think of the two titles without rancor.

Paul understood Marshall well enough to take him off the hook by saying, "When'd any of you ever see Marshall drinking?" Paul said it as if he were surprised, but the old man was grinning at Marshall, knowing that there weren't a lot of people in the world whom Marshall would ever relax with; the guard was up with everyone else.

Around him, the conversation flowed again, and Marshall was once more glad. He was uncomfortable with a lot of words; with attention, with a crowd. The Berstein sons and their wives were enjoying themselves while their children slept upstairs, all played out and exhausted from a hot day at poolside, awaiting the arrival of their working fathers, with mothers who had been conditioned to stay home and raise the children. Rachel was the only woman at the table who had a successful career outside of the home.

Joanie would get up very early, to care for the children and to cook them breakfast. Rachel would be there, too. She was also the only woman at the table who didn't have kids of her own.

For the longest time, Marshall refused to believe that this family was real, had patiently watched, waiting for the ugly side, the brutal side, to surface. He had expected to discover that Paul beat his wife, or that one of the sons had a drinking problem; he kept waiting for their deep, dark secret to emerge.

But to his surprise, it never had. They were exactly what they appeared to be: a tightly knit, loving Jewish family, loyal and honest, as fun loving as they were hardworking.

Marshall Del Greco knew what he would have said if he'd gotten up to make a speech. And although he hadn't said it aloud when they'd all been gathered around the table, he spoke the words freely to his wife, Rachel, after they'd finally gone off to Rachel's old bedroom, the last door down the hall, on the first floor of the three-story residence.

Lying naked in the bed with his hands behind his head, hair still wet from the shower, Marshall said, "You have the family everybody else wishes they had."

Rachel was undressing, light skin burned red from an afternoon in the sun. Marshall watched her in the bright moonlight that streamed in through the windows. There were white marks on her body where the bathing suit had covered her skin. Rachel was glowing. With pride, with love for him and for her family.

"It's so good to see you enjoying yourself."

"I had a good time," Marshall said, nearly surprised. "The kids are scared of me, though."

"You're the only one in the family who's quiet; they're not used to that in adults."

In the semidarkness, quiet Marshall smiled.

When he thought of his parents, he thought of his father as nothing more than a sperm donor; his mother as merely an incubator. The only thing they'd ever given him was life, and they'd nearly taken that away from him. It wasn't lack of trying that had stopped them from doing it; it was the state of Illinois, foster homes, and later, the love and compassion of his older brother.

Marshall had spent more than half of his childhood in places other than his family home, and he carried a lot of baggage.

When he was with Rachel, he could set the weight down.

He wondered now, not for the first time, and without a hint of self-pity, what it must have been like for her, growing up with four younger brothers who respected her, parents who loved her without condition and who protected her from all harm.

He was still smiling when Rachel, now naked, came over to him, stood before him with her hands on her hips. Marshall looked up at her, bemused and surprised, enjoying, as he always did, the wonder of her body. He was constantly amazed that a woman such as Rachel had chosen to share her life and her body with a man such as himself.

But he'd never articulated these feelings to Rachel, and he didn't do so now. He widened his eyes and said, "Doctor Del *Greco,* are you trying to se*duce* me?"

"You remember how we denied ourselves when I was in medical school, and interning? We've got a lot of catching up to do, Ace."

Later, Rachel, with her head on Del Greco's broad chest, said, "I used to dream I'd find a man like you. I'd lie right here in this room in the summertime, with the high school boys calling on me every night, sitting

7

out in the family room, trying to impress my mother with their courtesy and maturity. She'd look at them the way she does, you know, with her head cocked to the side? Tells you right off she doesn't believe a word you're saying." Rachel fake-shivered. "The woman's a walking lie detector. I think that's why she liked you so much, you never tried to lie to her.

"I'd come back from a boring date with one of those kids, and I'd lie here and I'd think to myself, 'He's got to be out there *somewhere*.' "

"That's me; Mr. Right."

"Oh, Marshall, you are. You're my whole life."

If Marshall had still believed in God, he would have said a prayer of thanks.

But he didn't, so he said, "You know, I come here, and all I can think about is what a wonderful family you have." Marshall was quiet for a moment before saying, "There was only my brother and me. And when he went to prison . . ."

"Shh . . ." Rachel held a finger to his lips; this was not a time for Marshall to be strolling down a memory lane filled with atrocities.

"This is all I've wanted my whole life, Rachel."

"And you've got it." Marshall felt the breath from her nose tickling the hairs on his chest. He smelled the freshness of her hair. He nodded his head in the semidarkness, wondering how he'd ever gotten so lucky.

Seeking safer ground, he said, "It's nice to have a weekend off."

"And we can spend most of it here, alone in this big old mansion. Run around naked if we want to. Isn't that a nice idea, Marshall? Everyone else is going home tomorrow afternoon, even Mom and Dad. They have to go to the ceremony early Sunday morning, they're renewing their vows."

Marshall hadn't known that. It came as a pleasant surprise. But he still said, "You should go with them."

"They understand our beliefs."

"It's the ceremony, the respect, the honor involved, that's all. It's not a religious thing."

"I don't go if you don't go."

"I'm not going." He'd spoken the words too quickly, and he regretted it.

But Rachel didn't seem to have noticed. She said, "Then it's settled. Besides, do you know how long it's been since we've had a weekend off at the same time?" She giggled. Thirty-four years old, a pediatrician, and she could still giggle, thinking of what they'd do, alone together in this large summerhouse, while her parents were away. Running around naked, she'd said.

Marshall wasn't even aware that he'd tightened the arm that was holding her close.

"What time is it?" Rachel held up her arm, squinted at her watch in the moonlight from the window. Even with the windows shut tight, Mar-

8

shall could smell the lake. He thought that this might be his favorite place to be in the whole, entire world.

"My God, it's almost two."

"Been a long day."

"It was a good day, wasn't it Marshall?"

Marshall Del Greco had spent most of it hunting down the murderer of a sixteen-year-old kid who'd had the misfortune of pitching a beanball at a tough guy during a baseball game in a public park down in Hege-wisch. The tough guy had gone to his car, gotten his gun, come back, and blown a hole through the pitcher's head.

To Rachel, Marshall only said, "It's been a great day." He wasn't smil-ing anymore in the semidarkness, as he lay staring up at the ceiling.

CHAPTER

2

The record-breaking heat wave was devastating to Anthony Silver's personal financial status; times were tough for beggars. The older people who lived in Chicago and who had the money to escape for the weekend had done so much earlier in the day, while the affluent suburbanites were staying home in droves, safely locked inside their houses, with the air-conditioning turned up high. It was usually those two types—wealthy, middle-aged Chicagoans, and their suburban counterparts—who dropped bills into Anthony's outstretched wax cup, alleviating their guilt over their own good fortune by throwing a dollar or two at a panhandler.

What such people saw as pocket change—tip money—was enough to keep Anthony going for another day.

Anthony needed a minimum of twenty dollars a day to make it. Which didn't take into account such secondary considerations as food, a rented room, or clean clothing; he would only attend to those needs after other, vastly more important requirements had been met. He didn't care about air-conditioning, nor was he on the lookout for a homeless shelter; Anthony knew where most of them were, had been to plenty of them in the three years that he'd been living on the street. The winter, mostly, was when he'd use them, when he had the choice between going into a shelter and praying, pretending to give his soul to Jesus, or freezing to death in an empty lot, or in a public park, or under somebody's front porch. For Anthony, that was no choice. He had gotten to the point where he could shout hallelujah with the best of them, even when all he got for his efforts was a bowl of weak soup, a hot dog, and a three-inch, plastic-covered mattress to sleep on in a room the size of a gymnasium that was filled with thieves and perverts.

As far as Anthony was concerned, the only good thing about winter was, when it was bitterly cold outside, most white people were a lot more generous to black folks like himself.

Strangely enough, though, it was the summertime when Anthony's existence was in its greatest jeopardy. White people figured that in the summer, you could sleep in the park, under the night sky, with God's blanket of stars for your night-light. People with homes, money and jobs could afford to have those kind of bullshit, romantic thoughts. They were tight with a buck in the summer, white people were. On most hot days, Anthony could just barely beg up his indispensable twenty dollars. Even on days such as today, when he had worked for ten long, humiliating hours.

Which was why he rarely showered in the summertime, or had a room for the night; why he ate out of garbage cans from the time the weather broke warm until the time it got cold again, and why Anthony generally had to rely on the kindness of strangers for the occasional hustled cigarette. On a Friday night such as this one—even one that had started out so promising—there didn't seem to be enough hours in the day for Anthony to get his twenty dollars.

What Anthony needed the twenty dollars for was crack. That amount would pay for four rocks—enough to get him through the night in a state of relative normality.

But these Friday night streets were dead. It was one of the infrequent summer weekends when there wasn't some sort of convention in town.

Anthony had begged in front of the Metra station on Michigan Avenue at the beginning of the rush hour, and had been greatly encouraged by the fact that he had taken in seventeen dollars. Five of that had paid for his first rock. Floating from that, and feeling overly optimistic about the evening's prospects, Anthony had spent five more dollars for a pint of Four Roses whiskey. Wasted from both the cocaine and the whiskey, Anthony had decided to really splurge; he'd gone into the White Hen and paid $3.15 for a box of Marlboros.

But now, closing in on two in the morning, with the effects of both mind-altering substances having long worn off, and with just a couple of dollars in the one good pocket of his shiny, filthy trousers, Anthony was beginning to feel the onset of high anxiety.

He held his wax soft drink cup in one hand, and he rattled the change on the bottom at passersby, Anthony growing more and more apprehensive and afraid as he was roundly ignored by the few young pedestrians who had braved the heat and were wandering the city streets, seeking a continuation of their Friday night parties. They did not seem to want to

11

even acknowledge Anthony's existence, and their aversion to him, their apathy toward his plight, filled Anthony with rage.

Part of their disgust was due to his appearance, and his smell. Anthony hadn't taken a shower in days, and he was sensitive enough to notice the way the clean, perfumed white people wrinkled their noses at him as they passed him by at the spot he'd staked out on LaSalle Street. Anthony was wise to the ways of the street, and he knew the rules: you had the right to stand there, and you had the right to beg, but you did not have the right to block other pedestrians' egress; you couldn't stand in their way.

But it was very late, and Anthony Silver was growing desperate, and desperation knows no caution.

Suffering the pangs of early withdrawal, knowing from experience that those pangs would only grow worse as the night progressed, reckless due to his great need, Anthony began to step into people's way, risking insult, risking assault, risking arrest at the hands of the white police who constantly patrolled rich tourist spots like this one; police who were always looking to reassure the people with money that they were safe from the people who had none.

Earlier in the evening, Anthony had been diffident, had shyly asked for spare change while looking down at his shoes. Now, with his heart racing, with his need to feed his hunger right there in the front of his mind, Anthony began to step right up into people's paths, blocking them, making them walk around him, Anthony screaming, begging for money.

And sure enough, some white son of a bitch pushed Anthony against a wall. He bounced off the stone, and didn't even look at whoever had shoved him, just walked quickly up the street until he came to the next rare pedestrian, Anthony's cup dropped and forgotten now, Anthony holding both hands out, crying, shaking with despair.

A white male walking hand in hand with his girlfriend tried to pass, but Anthony cut him off, going right, then left, ignoring the harshly spat out, condescending *"Excuse me!,"* trying to make his case and mumbling words that the couple could not understand.

The white man hit Anthony with the palm of his hand, hard, right on the bridge of Anthony's nose, and Anthony reeled backward, lost his balance and fell. Anthony felt the back of his head split open as it cracked hard against the sidewalk. He heard the concerned, frightened words of the woman, opened his eyes and saw her.

"Are you all right?" she was touching him, shaking him.

"Help me out," Anthony whispered. He had bitten his tongue badly, could taste the blood in his mouth. He saw the woman pulled roughly, quickly from his view, heard the anxious words of her companion as he shouted something about getting the hell out of there before the cops showed up. Did she want him to get sued by some useless fucking bum?

A MATTER OF HONOR

Anthony got to his knees, shaking his head, then slowly, carefully, he staggered to his feet, then shook his head, angry and confused. Why had he bought the whiskey? Why had he wasted his goddamn precious money on a useless pack of cigarettes? Why weren't there any *black* people on LaSalle tonight?

She came out of Michael Jordan's restaurant like an answer to Anthony's prayers, the fine, thin black woman in the skimpy white see-through dress. Anthony began to make his way toward her, then saw her white companion as the man followed her out of the place, and Anthony stopped. The two of them were walking toward Anthony now, the muscular white man who was holding her arm suddenly letting go of her and moving to her other side, so he would be the one to pass Anthony.

Anthony held both hands out at his side, palms open imploringly, Anthony crying now, bleeding from his nose and mouth, feeling blood running down the back of his neck, as well. The white man hadn't taken his eyes off Anthony since coming out of the restaurant, and those eyes weren't kind.

Still, Anthony had to try.

"*Please* help me, sister." Anthony saw her look of concern, saw her hesitate, saw her open her mouth, but it was her companion who responded.

"She ain't your sister, nigger." Anthony didn't even look at the man, just stared at the beautiful young black woman. Hadn't she heard what her boyfriend had called him?

The woman blurted out a nervous laugh, and Anthony's jaw fell.

The two of them passed by Anthony. The woman had put her hand to her mouth, was trying to hide her amusement. The man was snickering, his lips twisted into a cruel, vicious smirk.

"White man's *bitch!*" Anthony screamed, and the man stopped, turned toward him, and Anthony, frightened now, staggered back a few steps, out of reach.

"Come on, Lenny, let it go." The woman was pulling on Lenny's arm. Lenny was wearing a loose, shortsleeve, oversized white shirt, the tails of which had been pulled out of his pants and were now hanging down almost to Lenny's knees. Anthony looked at them, at the two of them standing there, the man outraged, wanting to hit Anthony, the woman holding onto the man's arm, pulling at him.

"These people all got AIDS," the woman said, and Anthony lost all caution, took one step toward them, got just close enough, then spat bloody saliva onto the front of the woman's white dress.

He saw her look of repulsed outrage, but Anthony didn't have the time to relish it, because Lenny was pushing one side of his shirt out of the way, and Anthony was able to see the star of the Chicago Police Depart-

13

ment badge, clipped in a leather holder to Lenny's belt, the star right in front of what the man was reaching for: a big, blue-barreled, automatic pistol.

Anthony stepped back quickly, tripped over his own feet, and fell against the wall. He was unaware of the fact that he was standing directly under a painting of the most famous black man on the entire planet, under a picture of Michael Jordan, captured in full hang-time stretch, Michael dunking a basketball with an angelic look on his face.

Anthony, another black man, but one without any athletic skill and having a desperate, crying need within him, was cringing as the white man, Lenny, rapidly, determinedly approached him.

Anthony saw the gun in Lenny's hand go back, saw it coming toward him. He felt a dull thud as it slapped against the side of his head, and he was aware on some distant level that the white man had grabbed the front of his shirt so that Anthony couldn't fall down.

Anthony suddenly couldn't see out of his left eye; the entire left side of his head felt numb and bloated. He screamed something, and through his right eye saw the gun going back again, saw the ugly, hateful look on Lenny's face, heard the shouted racial epithet that Lenny screamed into his face.

Then there was a flash of bright light, and Anthony didn't see anything.

CHAPTER

3

A s Anthony Silver lay dead in front of Michael Jordan's restaurant, and while the man who had shot him was attempting to escape, two other men were meeting, sitting down together at a round oak conference table, twisting the lid off of bottles of expensive, imported beer. In another setting, viewed by outsiders, they might have passed for athletes, as teammates, even. The younger man, Gerald Podgourney, would have been the rookie defensive lineman. The older man, Arthur L. Horwitz, would have been the aging, veteran wide receiver; one who would have to rely these days more on wile and experience than on his once-great but now deteriorating speed.

It was Horwitz's office, a conference room at his law firm. The two of them were hunched over the table, speaking in low, serious voices. Both men had been drinking this night, but neither man was drunk. Podgourney took a sip of his beer, then set the bottle down on the table, both hands wrapped around it. If this was some sort of setup, he would smash the bottle into Horwitz's face before anything else went down.

"I want you to do a job for me," Horwitz said to Podgourney, and the younger man opened his hands around the bottle as if he'd already figured that one out for himself. He had long ago grown used to the lawyer's pretentious, self-important manner—Horwitz had called him up at one-thirty in the morning to come to a meeting that could have waited until they'd both had a full night's sleep. Podgourney wasn't in the mood to listen to a lot of mumbo jumbo from the man—his fellow Aryan Christian Kinsmen members were already on his ass about associating with Jews.

"What?" he said, and Horwitz pinned him with a glare.

"I'm not sure you can handle this."

"I was getting laid, Artie, when you called."

Horwitz shook his head impatiently, pursed his lips in distaste.

"That's what I mean, it's another sign of your immaturity. I get you out of jail, give you a job, introduce you around, and what do you do? You start banging the help. That's no good, Gerald." The lawyer paused. "You might be too shallow for this."

"You'd be amazed how deep my waters run if there's enough money involved."

Horwitz reached into the breast pocket of his jacket, and Podgourney sat back, smiling and shaking his head. He had taken his hands off the beer bottle.

He said, "You're the only man I've seen all week wearing a three-piece suit." Podgourney chuckled. "And at two in the morning, yet."

Horwitz's glare quieted Podgourney. He wanted to pretend he was Don Corleone? Podgourney would play along. His current "wife," Amy, was waiting for him, and Gerald wanted to get this foolishness over with. Besides, the manila envelope that Horwitz was now holding in his hand looked thick, stuffed with bills. Podgourney's eyes widened, and Horwitz favored him with the patented, superior, Jew-lawyer smile.

"You need some new acquaintances, too." Gerald looked at him, enjoying and appreciating the man's sense of timing. Horwitz knew who and what Gerald was, knew that he had joined the Aryan Christian Kinsmen while in jail awaiting trial for crimes that he'd wound up beating due to the lack of complaining witnesses. Horwitz had handled both cases for him pro bono, as a favor to a friend of a friend, who was also a friend of Gerald's; it was how the two of them had met. Gerald, however, had made even better friends within the Kinsmen. Better friends than Horwitz could ever hope to be, or ever have.

Now Horwitz was holding the envelope out, waving it back and forth, as if bargaining with Gerald, getting ready to cut his deal.

But Gerald intuitively understood that the man wasn't bargaining from a position of strength. If he had been, he wouldn't have called Gerald in the middle of the night. He would have called him during the day, made this seem more of a casual encounter, rather than the desperation move that it appeared to Gerald to be. Gerald shook his head, slowly, back and forth, just once, then locked eyes with the lawyer, and saw some of the arrogance go out of the man's expression.

"Let me tell you something, Artie. I pick my friends. I pick who I fuck. And I pick what work I do, and who I do it for." Gerald spread his hands open again, telling Horwitz that part of the conversation was over. He saw the flash of irritation cross the man's face; saw it quickly disappear.

The lawyer sighed, shaking his head, almost sadly. "You're incorrigible, Gerald."

Horwitz tossed the envelope to Podgourney, then sat back in his chair, silently watching. Podgourney opened it, looked inside, then smiled, and looked up at the lawyer.

"Who do I got to kill?" he asked, and Arthur L. Horwitz told him.

When Horwitz told him, Gerald was smiling broadly, knowing exactly who he'd go to to get the job done, appreciating the way he'd seen through all the possible problems, and had come to a solution before Artie had even finished speaking. Gerald could send this off down a road that could never twist back toward him, no matter who might be sitting behind the wheel of the investigation.

"It's got to look like an accident," Horwitz said. "That's not negotiable."

Gerald rose to his feet and lied, as was his practice whenever he was engaged in conversation with the enemy. "I already got the perfect accident planned."

"Don't tell me about it!" Horwitz held both hands up, as if physically preventing Gerald from going any further with it while in his royal presence.

"How soon does it have to be done?"

"As soon as possible, without any fuckups."

"There won't be any fuckups," Gerald said, and left the room to go take care of his business; his girlfriend—his "wife"—would just have to wait.

As soon as Gerald was gone, the lawyer walked over to the coffee table in the corner. He stood staring quizzically for a moment at the round clock hanging on the wall.

Even though he knew that the camera was there, he couldn't see it, nothing seemed out of place.

Horwitz nodded his head in approval, then leaned down, opened the balsa wood doors, shut off the VCR, and popped the cassette out of the machine, already thinking about how he could edit it so that he himself would not be implicated by what was indelibly printed on the video. He put the tape in its cardboard case, carefully marked the time, date, and the name of the subject on the side, then carried the tape back to the desk and put it inside his briefcase, closed the case, and locked it tight. If anyone tried to take the briefcase away from him before he got it home, they would be zapped with 100,000 volts that would be set off by the little transmitter attached to Horwitz's keychain, a transmitter that also functioned as the remote disarming device for the alarm in Horwitz's brand-new car. Artie Horwitz liked his toys.

Once he was done with the editing, the tape would go with all the others, in a safe-deposit box at FirstChicago bank, a box that hadn't been rented under Horwitz's name. If anything untoward ever happened to Arthur L. Horwitz, the guilty party would be brought to justice, one way or another. He didn't plan to ever have to use the tapes—as sometimes, no matter how well they were edited, they incriminated him as well— but his life experience had taught him to be a very careful man, and, though no one who knew him would ever guess it, a very frightened man. One who always felt that, when dealing with scum, it was always best to cover all the available bases.

Horwitz picked up his briefcase, walked out of the conference room, walked unhurriedly down the hall, set the alarm at the office's front door, and made sure that both locks were secure before he left the place for the night.

CHAPTER

4

The jangle of the telephone awakened Alderman Billy Charge, and he lunged up quickly in his bed, sweating, hyperventilating, his hand automatically reaching for the pistol that wasn't under his pillow. Twenty-five years ago, Billy Charge had been a Black Panther, and the pigs had stormed a supposed safe house he'd been in and had assassinated four members of the Party, shot them down in cold blood, while they slept. Charge had escaped by jumping naked through a second-story window. They'd arrested him on the street, where he'd lain with a broken leg and multiple, serious cuts and abrasions, and they'd beaten him beyond recognition, but they hadn't been able to put a bullet in his head, not with half the neighborhood watching.

He'd been chained to his hospital bed, under twenty-four-hour police guard for three days, before anyone bothered to inform him that one of the people the pigs had killed had been Billy's live-in old lady.

These late-night calls always brought those goddamn memories back, in color.

Charge located the weapon, which had somehow slipped halfway down the mattress, patted it, and left it where it was. It took him a few more seconds to collect his thoughts, and he shook himself like a wet dog before he grabbed for the phone, grateful that his wife slept in another bedroom and had her own personal phone lines. His late-night calls would never bother her.

The truth was, Charge himself rarely bothered her anymore, except every four years, at election time, when he'd parade her out in front of his constituents, stand on platforms and go on and on about their devotion toward each other, and their commitment to family values. In quiet moments of solitude, Charge sometimes wondered how things had gotten so bad between them. He would wonder about it, then put it out of his mind; he had other, more important things to worry about than the status of his marriage.

"What!" Charge's voice was low and angry. He listened for a moment, still vaguely afraid and half-asleep, but he was brought fully awake by the words his caller was speaking excitedly into his ear.

Charge said, "Listen up, this is important. You're *certain* this was a white, off-duty cop?" He paused again, listening, then said, "Crocodile, this could do it, this could be just what we need. What was the dead brother's name again? *Silver?* A *Jew's* name? Rally all the troops you can get ahold of, my brother, then you meet me outside the Minister's home at"—he squinted at the bright red numerals of the digital clock on the dresser—"six A.M."

Charge paused again, as Crocodile expressed his awe at what the alderman had said to him.

Then he said, "You heard me right, Croc, I said the *Minister's* home. We're bringing the Man himself into this one. Between the three of us, and the people we can mobilize? We'll bring those goddamn white supremacists down to their motherfucking *knees.*"

CHAPTER

5

"This better be good," Edmund said, in his East Tennessee drawl, as he opened the back door of the dilapidated house and beckoned Gerald Podgourney inside. Gerald fought his resentment. There had been a time when Edmund had always seemed happy to see him, would welcome Gerald into his home at any hour of the day with a handshake and a smile.

Not anymore.

Now there was no "hello," no "how are you," no "kiss my ass," just "This better be good." Gerald was glad that he'd already taken three-quarters of the money out of the envelope Horwitz had given him.

The house they were in belonged to Edmund's father, free and clear. Should he decide to sell it, Gerald thought the old bastard could probably get ten, maybe fifteen thousand dollars for the place. If he got lucky. In the heart of the Uptown neighborhood, this house was as run-down and useless as any still freestanding; Gerald could probably have it condemned, if he dropped a dime to the Housing Department.

Gentrification had not yet reached Edmund's block, and on this block—with Yuppies invading from all sides—Uptown's nature remained as it had traditionally always been: poor, mean, drunken, white, and southern.

As always, Gerald smelled the place as soon as he walked inside, the staleness, the age, the cigarette smoke; alcohol and ancient sweat; a million TV dinners warmed up in an old, near useless oven. Surprisingly enough, considering the house's many obvious signs of neglect, there was a computer hooked up in the living room, its screen saver dancing in the

21

darkness, forming shadows; the only light in the entire downstairs section of the house. There was a fax machine, too, Gerald knew. As far as he could tell, these were Edmund's only extravagances, and they were used solely for the spreading of the Aryan Christian Kinsmen message.

As Edmund led the way up the bare, creaking stairs of a shack that had never seen air-conditioning, he said, "You woke up Daddy. This ain't Kinsmen business, Gerald, we're both gonna be pissed."

"It's business," Gerald said, smelling Edmund. He began to breathe through his mouth. He had been unable to keep the anger out of his voice. He had to feel his way up the stairs, Gerald near cringing as his hand touched the wall, or the frail, scarred, wooden bannister. The wall felt greasy, slimy, as if it hadn't been washed since the house had been built. He reached out for Edmund's shoulder, so Edmund could lead him down the hallway. Gerald had no idea why they couldn't just turn on a light; the old man's bedroom door was closed, and besides, the bare wood hall floor made loud, shrieking noises with every step they took—the sound of nails being pulled out of wood—a little light wouldn't bother anyone.

But Gerald didn't complain. Edmund was the leader of the Chicago chapter, the Man for the Aryan Christian Kinsmen for the entire city of Chicago. He was in charge of and responsible for more than a hundred men, and almost every man had a "wife" who had been united to him by Edmund's father, a self-proclaimed Christian Kinsmen preacher, who insisted that the men call him Adolph. The thinking was that any Christian male who wasn't married couldn't plant that pure white seed, thereby creating more Caucasian warriors who would fight the future battles for America's salvation. Further motivation for ACK members to marry was the fact that a white warrior without a wife might be suspected of being homosexual, which was justification for a death sentence within the ACK: on the Kinsmen's measuring scale, a homosexual was just one rung above the nigger, who was one rung above the Jew.

For Gerald, though, it wasn't a bad deal. Adolph not only performed ACK marriages, he presided over divorces within the organization, as well. Twenty dollars for either service; Adolph had given his blessing to four of Gerald's "marriages," and he had written up the divorce decree for Gerald on three separate occasions. Amy, Gerald's current wife, had been as drunk as Gerald when they'd gone down into the basement with Adolph to take their vows. Gerald had to hide his smile when he thought about Amy's later questions; her abhorrence over the Kinsmen's feeling, their stance toward women. It was in the best interest of all parties involved—particularly Gerald's—that Amy be totally separated from any of Gerald's connections within the ACK.

Now Edmund led Gerald down the dark hallway and into his bedroom, closed the door behind them, grabbed the pull-cord, and turned on the light. Gerald noticed that it was even hotter up here than it was downstairs, if that was possible. He felt like he was burning up. A bare, high-wattage bulb came to life, the bulb hanging from a frayed cord that was attached to the center of the ceiling.

How could the man live like this? Gerald wondered. Over a hundred men served under Edmund, and he got a piece of all the crimes they committed, and still, he lived worse than a nigger, in squalor, in a filthy room without a rug, sleeping on an Army cot.

Gerald knew that Edmund sent along most of the money he received from his troops' crimes to his superiors in the Kinsmen, which they supposedly used to further the Aryan Christian Kinsmen cause. Gerald suspected that was probably more of a con game than anything else. The big shots probably used the money to buy mountaintop retreats for themselves and their loved ones, then stocked them with canned food and that freeze-dried shit you had to pour water on before you could eat it. Filled their quarter-million-dollar three-story log cabins with the latest technological breakthroughs in pistols, rifles, and rounds, waiting for the economic collapse of what they called "the Jew-nited States of America," while they tooled around in their fifty-thousand-dollar pickup trucks, refusing to pay taxes, and daring the entity they referred to as ZOG—the Zionist Occupational Government—to come and call their bluff.

They were, in Gerald's opinion, misguided fools. Edmund was a fool as well, but he was an intelligent fool. In Gerald's opinion, Edmund was a master at the planning of criminal activity that could be made to look as if it had been committed by someone other than the criminal; Kinsmen crimes that Edmund planned were usually blamed on niggers. He could live like a pig if he wanted to—Gerald wasn't here to pick up pointers about personal hygiene. Still, for Gerald, who, since childhood, had consistently sought a higher standard of living, the sight of this room was enough to turn his stomach.

Though the wallpaper wasn't bad.

Cracked plaster was covered over with hundreds of posters, posed portraits, a large Nazi flag, and snapshot pictures of Aryan warriors: a shouting Bobby Matthews facing down a liberal protestor—his finger in the communist's face, his own face twisted into a mask of self-righteous anger—during a rally in Spokane, Washington, for the Reverend Paul Butler's Aryan Nations; White Aryan Resistance Youth, decked out in full Nazi regalia, giving the Heil Hitler salute, their commitment and pride stamped all over their youthful faces; four skinheads in a Polaroid snapshot, standing over the body of a black man they had beaten into merciful oblivion, the men grinning self-consciously at the camera, as if aware and somewhat ashamed of the meagerness of their offering.

23

Gerald looked around the room, hiding his disapproval, as Edmund lit three candles with a long wooden kitchen match; one on either side, and the third directly in front of, a silver-framed eight-by-ten photo of a stern-faced Adolph Hitler. The frame was the only thing in the room that seemed to have ever been dusted; Edmund no doubt regularly polished the silver, lovingly. Edmund used the same match to light up a Camel non-filter. He threw the match on the floor. He sat down on the Army cot, settling himself onto stained sheets, then motioned for Gerald to take the chair next to the small table that would have been more at place in a homeless shelter, but which Edmund called his desk.

Gerald sat down, looking briefly at the tattered cover on Edmund's copy of *The Turner Diaries;* the amateurish artwork on the front of the book had been almost worn away by Edmund's grubby fingerprints. This book was the neo-Nazi bible; The Order—and dozens of other white supremacy groups—took their every marching order from this book, and Gerald had spent countless hours—in the county jail, as well as in Edmund's dirt-floor basement—listening to near-verbatim statements from it; how the white man was being held down by the Jew; how the niggers were being manipulated to do the Jews' bidding; how the race traitors would swing from their necks from lampposts when the day of racial judgment finally arrived. Gerald had tried to read it once, but the Dear Diary style it was written in had given him a headache. Adolph had refused to refund the twenty dollars that Gerald had paid for it, too. "You snooze, you lose," Adolph had said, without a smile. It was the sort of phrase the old man used all the time, clichés that had, in Adolph's mind, multiple sinister meanings.

Edmund ran one hand across the stubble on his head, then looked up quickly, pinned Gerald with a glare. "So?" he said. "You're here; I'm awake. What do you want?"

Gerald thought, To know your real name, asshole, and your daddy's too, for that matter. But he said, "I got a—thing—lined up, and I need your help." Edmund was eyeing him warily. Gerald said, "It's got to be fast, and it's got to look like an accident. I want you to help me figure out the best way to do it."

Edmund squinted at him through the smoke that swirled around his head, taking Gerald's measure. There was something in the look that made Gerald highly uncomfortable. He calmed himself by remembering that he'd just called and woke the man up; maybe this was the way Edmund always acted when he got dragged from his bed in the middle of the night. The Camel was in the corner of Edmund's mouth; both hands were on knobby knees. Edmund was leaning forward, his elbows stuck out at angles, like triangles drawn onto the sides of a stick man in a child's crayon picture. He was wearing a pair of boxer shorts, with nothing on top, showing off his scrawny, hairless chest. Showing off about a hundred tattoos as well; swastikas and crudely drawn thunderbolts, a couple of insignias from the dreaded SS, stuck into Edmund by the pins of different artists, or by one artist who'd been trying to change his style; rough jailhouse lettering pronouncing him to be a member of the Aryan Christian Kinsmen. Atop one shoulder was the word FUCK; atop the other, NIGGERS, written in large, black letters. Edmund had had them put on when he'd been just a child, when he was filled with hatred and zeal and a racial pride that he had no interest in concealing; back then, he'd seen them as proud signs of his political affiliations and beliefs; he'd matured enough to understand that they were also distinguishing characteristics, things that witnesses could use to identify Edmund to the cops, that could get his ass thrown in prison. Edmund had told Gerald once that if he had it to do all over again, he'd never have had the tattoos put on to begin with. Gerald believed him. Edmund's politics might be all fucked up, but Gerald knew that he was as smart as any man Gerald had ever met, and he'd never seen anyone—white *or* black—whip a crowd of men up the way Edmund could, when he gave one of his inspirational speeches. Edmund could spend hours whispering about the lost tribes of Israel, shouting heatedly about racial purity, or talk in longing tones about the misty mountains of Tennessee, and tears would well up in the eyes of grown men before Edmund was half through talking.

Gerald had a hard time admitting it to himself, but he was a little afraid of Edmund, and was wary of him, too; the misgivings ran both ways.

"You got a hit lined up?" Edmund asked, clearly pleased to hear it, just as clearly doubting that it was true. Edmund now had one eye fully closed, as if it was an easier thing for him to do than to move the cigarette from his mouth. He would suck in a deep drag, then blow the smoke out around the butt. Edmund did this because he was missing several teeth, and was somewhat self-conscious about it. The ash was about to fall into his lap. Gerald noticed a number of scars on Edmund's knees, legs, and chest which he'd never had the chance to see before. Edmund didn't seem at all self-conscious about his lack of clothing, seemed confident in and almost proud of his scrawny, toneless body. What was he, thirty-six or seven, at the outside? Getting up there, but still too young to let himself go the way he had.

Gerald tried not to choke on the stench of the smoke that was filling up the small, nasty room. He wondered what hanging around with Edmund might be doing to his lungs. He decided that the smoke was more pleasant smelling than the stench it was covering up. Gerald smiled.

"I got a hit lined up," he said.

"You sure? You ain't just handing me more of your usual Gerald Podgore-ney bullshit, are ya? Wantin' us to do all the work, while you spend all the money." Edmund's hand was now under his pillow; it was the only thing that kept Gerald from going for Edmund's throat. Gerald kept his smile, shook his head, as if he knew that Edmund had just been joking around.

"Listen, it's an easy score. Horwitz—"

"You want us to do a hit for a *Jew*—"

"—already paid me twenty-five hundred dollars—"

"I wouldn't hit a *dog* for twenty-five hundred—"

"—for an easy contract on some—"

"You want *us* to take care of it, you gotta get him to come up with more money!"

"Goddamnit, Edmund, would you let me—"

There was a pounding on the wall; Adolph in the next bedroom, upset at the disturbance of his sleep.

Edmund raised his voice and said, "Sorry, Daddy," then turned back to Gerald. His hand came out several inches from under the pillow. Gerald could see Edmund's wrist; he could see the butt of the Mauser. Gerald kept his mouth shut, hearing Adolph in the next room, muttering complaints. Gerald heard the old man speaking his name, but couldn't hear what else he was saying. Whatever it was, it wasn't pleasant.

Edmund shook his head, as if what he was about to say was against his better judgment.

"There are a number of people within the rank and file of the Kinsmen who're concerned about your commitment, Gerald." Edmund paused and squinted across the room at him, but Gerald did not respond. "Daddy had a vision; said you weren't no good." Gerald did not know what to say to this; Adolph was always having visions, getting his way by telling people that Hitler spoke to him in his dreams.

Edmund grunted at what he no doubt thought to be Gerald's cowardice, then, after a long minute, he said, "Tell me who you want done, and when, and I'll tell you the way to do it that will best serve our Kinsmen. And that's *all* I'll do."

"You're pissed about that money I stole from the polacks, aren't you?" Gerald reached quickly into his pocket. Edmund pulled the weapon out from under the pillow.

"That's far enough," Edmund said.

Gerald froze. "I was only reaching for my money, I was gonna try and make things right."

"Keep your money. That dough from the polacks wasn't the only money you didn't share with us, and don't think we don't know about the rest of it! We know more than you might suspect."

Gerald looked at Edmund, nodding. They didn't know anything; it was just the way they acted. Cops had been trying to pull that number on him for as long as Gerald could remember. Pretend you know more than you do, and see how the other guy acts. Gerald had used the strategy a time or two himself. Now he slowly took his hand out of his pocket, keeping his expression neutral, but feeling the sweat dripping more freely; feeling it sting his eyes and darken his shirt, his pants where they met the skin. Edmund could order his death as quickly—and with as much thought—as he might a pizza. Gerald put his hands in his lap; Edmund put the gun back under the pillow.

Gerald said, "Edmund, I'm here to ask for your help."

"And I'll give it, 'zactly as I said I would." Edmund paused, smiling his slick, hillbilly smile, then said, "And I'll do it for five hundred dollars."

"Five hundred—"

"Shh. Get holt of yourself, Gerald. Daddy bangs on that wall again, he's gonna 'spect me to whup your ass."

Gerald thought that in a one-on-one match, even with the gun, it would be close. Still, Edmund was the Man, and he was paranoid, thought that everyone he knew was plotting against him. He might have made a call, or written something down; someone else beside Edmund and Adolph might know that Gerald had come over. He calmed himself, took a deep breath, then let it out through pursed lips, his cheeks puffed out in exasperation.

Edmund smiled again. "And you *will* tell me what else you got cookin'. Moneywise, I mean."

"Me? I've been nearly starving to death. I ain't paid my July's rent." Edmund wasn't buying it. He used his free hand to crush the Camel out in an ashtray on the nightstand that must have been hidden behind Hitler's portrait. Backtracking, Gerald said, "Just that thing with the kid, his granny . . ."

"Take somebody with you." Without the cigarette for his prop, Edmund now spoke with his lips nearly closed.

"I can handle it by myself."

Edmund's voice was instructional as he said, "Take somebody with you."

"Why don't *you* come with me?"

Edmund quickly turned his head, glared hard at Gerald. "That a dare? You darin' me?" he said, in a neighborhood where many men had died for less of a challenge to their courage.

"You don't trust me?" Gerald said quickly. "You think I wouldn't cut you in on your share?"

Edmund responded just as quickly. "You ain't never cut any of us in on our rightful shares. Y'all thinks we's dumb. And *we's* starting to think you're only using us for what you can get from us. Listen, it wasn't for us, you'd have never even *met* Ronzo, let alone got the boy to tell you his secrets."

Gerald said, "Then come with me, we'll do it together."

"All right, I will." Edmund was petulant now, lighting another cigarette. Using both hands, too. Gerald thought about jumping him, kicking his ass, taking the gun, and doing both him and his shitheaded, hillbilly, preacher daddy. He might have taken the huge risk and done just that, too, if Edmund had already told him the best way to do the contract, the way that would bring the least heat down on Gerald's own head.

Though it now was clear the guy wasn't going to go out and kill someone, was going to make Gerald do it all by himself. Not the way Gerald had planned it—he had never murdered anyone before, and had been planning on Edmund jumping at the prospect of making a quick twelve-five—but still, Gerald could do it if he had to, if he had no other choice.

As it turned out, he wouldn't have to, because, as Gerald had known all along, Edmund wasn't near as dumb as he looked.

CHAPTER

6

Homicide detective Sergeant Cheryl Laney had been sleeping when the phone rang, but the late-night phone call didn't surprise her; as the youngest female sergeant in the homicide unit, she had grown used to them. Laney's husband Daniel didn't even bother to stir; he had grown accustomed to the calls, as well, and knew his wife—technically his superior officer—would wake him if it was a callout for his SWAT team unit.

She listened as the senior detective from the crime scene gave her the specifics of the case, Laney growing angry now, thinking he was just yanking her chain and calling her in the middle of the night because he had a personal problem with female officers in general, and with female supervisors specifically. The department was filled with men like that, and that sort of thing happened to her all the time, and there wasn't a thing Laney could do to put a stop to it. When confronted with such charges, the detective would plead ignorance, throw up his hands and ask what the hell was he supposed to have done; she was the boss, he wasn't sure what he was supposed to do and needed a supervisor's opinion, and wasn't it incumbent upon him to call the sarge and ask?

Now she said, "Wait a minute—no, *wait* a minute. And don't interrupt me again." Cheryl Laney rubbed her eyes, trying to rub the anger away, too. Had this imbecile actually called her seeking help into his investigation of the death of a *wino?*

Impatiently, she said, "You got the shooter's plates?"

"Got 'em? From three independent witnesses, we got 'em. And then we ran 'em," the detective said, dragging it out, no doubt to ensure that Cheryl would be fully awake and alert before he hung up.

She had to prod him. "Who'd they come back to?"

"Leonard Brazovik."

"Am I supposed to know that name?"

"He's one of us, Cheryl."

"He's a *cop?*"

"Three years. Works out of the Shakespeare District."

"Dear Christ."

"Yeah, that's why I called you. I know the regs say I'm supposed to call OPS and the Rat Patrol, but I thought you might want to come down, see if there was anything you could do."

Laney, stunned by the remark, took a moment to compose herself before she said, "Let me ask you something. You said you had three independent witnesses?"

"We got six, but three got the plate numbers."

"And they all told you the same thing? This Brazovik was pistol-whipping the wino, and the gun went off?"

"That's the gist of it. Put a round through the side of his head. Tore out both eyes before exiting through the right temple. But we also heard there were some mitigating factors; the guy cussed at our man, spat on his girlfriend."

"The witnesses all *agree* on all of this?"

"You know how they usually are, you got half a dozen witnesses, you get half a dozen stories, but not this time. They all basically saw the same thing."

"Then screw him. Best-case scenario, with a good lawyer, he's looking at voluntary manslaughter. Call in the Rats, and OPS. Wake his civilian ass up, let him see how it feels. And don't throw away your investigative and interview notes. I know how you guys are when the Rat Patrol gets involved."

"So you want to play hardball? Throw him to the snakes?"

"He jumped into the pit when he shot an unarmed man."

There was a click in her ear, and Lancy shook her head as she hung up the phone. A cold-blooded killing, and a detective who'd sworn to uphold the law had been angling to get her to come down and see if there was something she could do for the killer. Which, when you cut through the code words, meant that the officer wanted her to get involved in a departmental cover-up. Wanted her to risk her own career to save that of some genius who'd had a bad night, mixing high levels of alcohol with an overabundance of testosterone.

As her resentment settled, though, Laney could see the officer's point. With the way the department had been under fire lately, she couldn't really blame the detective. Police officers were the only people in this city who were willing to give the benefit of the doubt to another cop; they were the only people who understood what a cop had to live with every day, who weren't right there with knee-jerk responses, judging fifteen thousand people due to the behavior of a single member of their ranks.

Cheryl paused, somewhat bewildered. She'd just thought the same sort of thing that she'd always rejected out of hand when she'd heard it spoken aloud by members of other minorities.

"Son of a bitch," she said out loud, and Daniel, in his sleep, said, "Hmm?"

"Not you, Daniel, a *different* son of a bitch." Her husband stirred, adjusted his pillow, and within seconds began to snore. But it took Sergeant Laney some time before she could fall back to sleep.

Half an hour after leaving Edmund's house, Gerald Podgourney parked his car in a lot across the street from a building on West Polk Street, got out and looked around. A black kid was standing next to a Lexus, staring at Gerald in astonishment. Gerald smiled at him, waved. Edmund's plan had made a lot more sense in a small bedroom of a run-down Uptown shanty. Here, where everything was real, Gerald was afraid.

But he kept the fear out of his voice and attitude as he said, "How you doin', broham?" and the kid, as confused at the sight of this white man as he was surprised by the greeting, nodded his head in acknowledgement. Gerald let his gaze wander past the young man, looking at the buildings, at the graffiti, at the obvious signs of abject, chronic poverty.

It was like being in the county jail, without the bars.

The building on the corner had the worst of it, was marked all in black spray paint, from street level to about seven feet up, letters drawn huge, spelling BREED, NIGGAZ. Gerald had seen a number of similar spray-painted writings as he'd driven west, heading over here. Most of the streetlights in this part of town had either burned out, or had been shot out. The Department of Streets and Sanitation would not be in any hurry to send crews out to this part of the city to repair broken streetlamps.

Gerald wasn't surprised by the crude, painted sentiment, either. It was the exact sort of statement that you live and died by at the ACK meetings, though couched in slightly different terms. You couldn't go to a meeting anymore without hearing someone preaching about having to "plant that pure white seed," in order to create more strong, dedicated Aryan warriors. It was the principal reason that Adolph kept marrying people—and divorcing them when an immediate pregnancy did not occur. You were supposed to have the kids, then raise them in adherence to the Kinsmen's

31

ideology—another sign of how dumb the leaders were; kids didn't listen to their parents anymore.

Although, to Gerald's way of thinking, fucking was never a bad idea, no matter how political the terms with which you surrounded the act. The more people, the more warriors, the more voters. Personally, he'd prefer to just keep getting married and divorced. It kept things simple, and he got plenty of pussy.

Even as limited as he was, Gerald understood that if the messages were taken seriously—by the sort of people who attended the ACK meetings, as well as by those who secured their personal philosophies off the graffiti spray-painted on the walls of ghetto buildings—it wouldn't take very long before the entire nation was overflowing with the children of the poor, uneducated, and ignorant. Gerald smiled at the thought.

He had long ago figured out that people with money, the well-bred and educated—the type of people whose children would have all the opportunities—practiced birth control, had their two-point-three kids, then called it quits. Those people spent the rest of their lives fucking for fun, for the pleasure of it, or under the pretension that it was a physical manifestation of their "love." The self-proclaimed jailhouse shrinks in the County had been big on preaching that poor people used fucking for the same reasons they used drugs: as an alternative to the brutal reality of their lives; as a way to briefly take themselves away from all this shit. The nigger babies were nothing more than a secondary consideration. And BREED NIGGAZ, along with Plant that Pure White Seed, made it all a sacrifice, as if fucking then having kids you couldn't take care of was really doing something for your people.

The thinking around the Kinsmen was that the white man had to start playing catchup, or he'd be overwhelmed by the nigger swarm.

But none of that was Gerald's problem. Gerald wouldn't be around to see it, and besides, he didn't take any of that political foolishness seriously. Edmund had been exactly right in his earlier assessment: Gerald just used the Kinsmen for the clout they had, for what they could do for him. Being in a gang was not a bad idea in an urban area; it kept people from fucking with you. And if he ever had to go back to the County, or, worse, to the joint, the warriors of the Kinsmen would be there for Gerald.

And if anyone ever killed Gerald, he could expect posthumous retaliation, for all the good it would do him. The Kinsmen might have to start right here, tonight. Gerald had no business being in this sort of place.

Most of the buildings on the block were single story, but there was a larger one, four or five stories tall, right there, across the street from the parking lot. Gerald could see a bunch of jiggling silhouettes in the top-floor window, people dancing around in front of mini-blinds; he could hear the driving bass of some militant nigger rap song, coming down to the street even through the closed, locked windows. The tall building didn't have a single spray-painted word on the front.

Gerald decided that he'd found the right place.

He turned to the kid, who was now slowly, carefully, approaching him, and he widened his eyes at the skinny little boy in his tight, white, dago T-shirt, wearing comically oversized, fancy, expensive blue jeans pulled down low, way past the halfway mark of his designer boxer shorts. He looked like a trainee for some rodeo clown school. The kid had his hand around back, as if holding the butt of a weapon. Podgourney did what he'd learned to do in the county jail: he hid his fear and smiled at the boy, showing him nothing but toughness.

Gerald said, "I'm here in peace. I want to see King Youngy."

"No you don't. What you want to do, is, you want to get back in your car, my man, and get your white ass away from around here. *That's* what you want to do." The kid stopped, as if wary of a white man who was crazy enough to drive around this neighborhood, alone and unarmed, before dawn on a wild party Friday night. Edmund had had a good idea; it was too bad he hadn't decided to execute it himself. Gerald fought to keep his expression neutral in the face of such pure human ignorance.

He said, "Somebody in there'll know me. Shorty Dee around? How about Dre'? Andre Tate or Reginald Ballard, they all know who I am." The boy's eyes widened when Gerald spoke the names of King Youngy's upper echelon as if they were intimate friends of his. Gerald began to think that Edmund's plan might have merit.

"I was in the County last year with enough of you. Tell them my name's Mister Franklin." Gerald smiled. "They called me Gerry P. I was in the max section, Division Eleven."

"Gerry P . . ." Gerald watched the boy's lips moving, as he repeated the name under his breath.

Impatient, Gerald said, "You watching for the Man?"

"For whoever come along don't belong."

"Tell you what. Let me watch things for you, while you go tell the King I'm here. Go ahead, man, he'll thank you for it."

Gerald watched the young man vacillate, turning his head from side to side, as if he were a scientist in some mentally deficient parallel world, checking out a never-before-seen specimen on a slide. Gerald raised his eyebrows again, spread his hands open—generally a sign of confrontation, but now utilized as a gesture of appeal—and slowly, as if he could not believe that he was actually doing it, the skinny kid turned, shaking his nappy, dreadlocked head, and sauntered back to the car he'd been resting in when Gerald had driven up. As soon as the boy's back was turned, Gerald closed his eyes in relief.

Then he opened them. He wasn't out of the woods yet. He still had to be careful. He cursed Edmund. He should have just done the job himself. Or taken Horwitz's money and then not done the job. What was Horwitz going to do, kick Gerald's ass?

Gerald watched the boy as the kid spoke on a cellular phone, never taking his eyes off Gerald, ready to shoot out the window of the car if need be, if Gerald made a move that the boy did not approve of. Gerald wiped his brow with the back of his hand, and thought that it would be a shame to let all that nice air-conditioning out, on a hot night like this. Gerald wondered if the kid would think about that, would take the time to open the door first and take good aim, if he decided to shoot Gerald down. It would give Gerald time to try to get at his own pistol, which he'd been smart enough to leave under the seat of his car. A cowboy like this kid might have already shot him, had Gerald been obviously packing as he'd stepped out of the vehicle.

After a couple of minutes, the kid got off the phone. He chicken-walked his way over to Gerald and said, "You the stupidest white man I ever seen. Nobody upstairs ever heard of no Mr. Franklin, or no—what was that other name you gived me?"

Gerald, stunned, did not answer. He had been certain that someone from the gang would have remembered him from the County. Edmund had been certain, too. There had been enough brawls among the two gangs; Gerald surely hadn't forgotten. For one frightening moment, Gerald thought he was about to die, but then the boy smiled at him, shaking his head at the white man's audacity.

"But the King say he want to come down and talk with you anyway. Say he ain't never seen a white boy in this hood before wasn't a strung-out junkie looking to get high." The kid grinned. "You lucky. The King in a happy party mood tonight."

CHAPTER

7

The rally was held outside of City Hall, on a broiling Saturday afternoon. Saturday is a traditionally slow news day, and the media had swarmed to the event, were now buzzing around with their cameras and microphones, tripping over their competitors' wires, falling over one another in their haste for an exclusive interview with the Man Who Would Be Congressman.

Alderman Billy Charge watched with a studied look of concern as an ambulance drove away from the scene, the paramedics working on the shattered hip of an elderly cameraman who'd been shoved to the sidewalk after getting too close to some of Crocodile Berkley's boys. Charge wondered if there was video footage of the "accident." He sincerely hoped there wasn't.

Crocodile Berkley had done the best he could in rallying the troops on short notice. More than one hundred young blacks, most of them affiliated in one way or another with Berkley's Gangster Apostle Nation, Chicago's most notorious street gang, now paraded on the sidewalk in front of City Hall, marching in a wide, orderly circle, carrying signs, chanting slogans, and looking crazy at the television cameras as they passed in front of them.

Charge knew that if the killing hadn't occurred on a Friday night, there would have been a lot more bodies showing up for the cameras. If Charge knew Berkley, and he believed he did, there would be a price to pay for those who hadn't answered the call.

Charge also knew that he'd have to be cautious in his dealings with

Crocodile. The younger man had lost his own well-organized, well-financed, aldermanic bid during the last citywide elections, and he had never gotten over the defeat. Crocodile blamed the loss on the white media's portrayal of him as a brutal gang enforcer—which is precisely what he'd been in his younger days—and on white racism, even though the entire ward he'd sought to represent had been black. Even though an entrenched politician, a black woman, had beaten him by a three-to-one margin, after an initial forced primary runoff.

Charge knew that everything in Crocodile's world was defined in terms of race. To him, every thought and action was performed due to the politics of hatred and fear. He had tried to explain that to the media on the night of his electoral loss.

Standing tall before the cameras, he'd announced, "That's right, y'all been right: I *am* a member of the Gangster Apostles, okay? I'm an *enforcer* for them, okay? You happy now?" The glare he'd then given the cameras had been broadcast throughout the city and to dozens of suburbs not only on that night, but repeatedly during the following week, as the political organization Crocodile had begun came under such fierce attack from the media that it had almost been destroyed. Crocodile had paused after giving the cameras his glare, and then he'd said, "And fuck *all* of you white, racist motherfuckers who tried to force this strong black man to bow down in front of you."

It was almost the same verbiage he had used after being convicted of a bogus murder charge, nearly twenty years before. In the years since his conviction had been overturned, Crocodile had convinced the authorities that he'd gone straight, and that he was a positive force in the community. He'd been so good at his persuasion that his other crimes had been forgiven; his burglary and assault convictions had been cleared by a gubernatorial pardon. He'd been so good at his persuasion that he'd been invited to the White House, and he had a picture of himself shaking hands with the president, a picture that now hung prominently on the Year Two Thousand Political Action Party's wall, framed and signed, right next to the door, where anyone who walked into the offices would have to see it.

Crocodile had used a Magic Marker to blacken out half of the president's teeth, and he'd drawn horns and a tail on the man he saw to be the leader of the devil's white, earthbound army. It was the sort of thing that held Crocodile back, his unwillingness to compromise, his hatred for all whites.

Which was a real shame; the brother was bright, and educated. He'd stood with presidents, he'd been consulted by the mayor, and he was the leader of his own political action party, but until just that morning, Minister Africaan had never deigned to meet with the Crocodile. Charge had set it up, had been able to fulfill Crocodile's greatest dream. Now he had to keep the man grateful, let him know that Billy Charge was the only man in a position of power who still appreciated him, who understood how he'd suffered. It shouldn't be hard to do; Berkley was one of the smartest brothers Charge had ever known, but he was also one of the most needy. Charge was in the business of fulfilling emotional needs, or pretending to.

Charge knew that with just a little more stealth and cunning, Crocodile would have won the race, and would now be Alderman Billy Charge's city council colleague. There was a lingering resentment there that Crocodile wore on his shoulder, a deep thread of it that was as much a part of him as the color of his skin. Another reason why Charge had to watch his step.

Crocodile was the most dangerous form of human being in Charge's orbit: a bright, violent man who could think for himself, and who could convince others that his thinking was right. Such a man wielded great power on the streets.

Berkley's emotion-driven need for acceptance was the main reason that Charge had invited him to the meeting with the Minister. That, and to thank him for calling Charge with the news about the shooting in the first place. There were plenty of other black aldermen who would have been happy to take Berkley's call, although few of them would admit it to reporters, and none would have the nerve to join forces with Berkley in public, as Charge was now doing. Charge had hoped, and his hope had been confirmed, that Crocodile's meeting such a controversial, powerful, and venerated figure as Africaan would force some humility on the rage-filled gang leader.

Charge needed Berkley if he was going to win the congressional seat. Crocodile was indispensable when it came to recruiting new supporters within the gang's ranks, to getting young black bodies legally registered to vote, and he could organize behind the scenes through fear and intimidation as well as anyone Charge had ever worked with.

But before he could use Berkley, Charge knew, he had to first control him. Introducing him to Africaan had been the beginning of that process. Charge would further that process by keeping Crocodile as far from the press as he could. As bright as he was, the man had never learned how to keep his mouth shut when the TV cameras were rolling.

Charge, on the other hand, considered himself an expert at handling—and manipulating—the media.

Which was what he was doing now, and just as well as he ever had when he had a righteous cause such as this one to exploit. Charge was speaking softly but with force, with just the right touch of reasoned outrage in his tone, as the young men and women behind him shouted out their indignation as emphasis to his words. Charge didn't look at any of the individual cameras that were trained upon him—he maintained direct eye contact with whatever reporter it was who had asked him the last question.

In this case, it was a young white girl, who seemed as thrilled by the size of the crowd and the importance of the assignment as she was frazzled by the great, wilting heat. Charge watched her makeup running down her face as she shoved her microphone under his nose.

"Is there any truth to the rumor that Minister Africaan is holding a rally to show his support of the late Anthony Silver tomorrow night, at his South Side church, er, mosque?" It was the way these people talked; they couldn't speak a proper sentence that hadn't been formulated in advance for them by someone else, then printed onto a TelePrompTer for them to read as they sat at a desk.

But Billy Charge did not allow his disdain for her to show—in fact, he seemed deeply reflective for a moment before he said, "I have had personal contact with the Holy Reverend Minister Africaan concerning this murder, and he is as saddened by the repeated, genocidal, systematic murder of our people as I am. He *will* be holding a meeting Sunday night, to discuss the young dead brother, Anthony Silver, and to try to find a peaceful, spirituality based solution to this horrific case of first degree murder, perpetrated on a homeless black man by yet another drunken, armed, white, racist policeman."

"But isn't it, at worst, manslaughter?"

"Ex*act*ly, young lady. Let's take a closer look at that word." Charge held his hands up together. "Man," he said, then separated his hands, spread them open, "*slaughter*. The slaughter of man. Only thing is, nobody cares when a homeless, desperate, destitute, young black man is slaughtered on the street like a foaming-mouthed dog." Charge looked out at the media horde, wondering if he'd gone too far. He decided to leave the inflamed, shouted rhetoric to the Minister. His had to be the voice of reason, and it wouldn't serve his purpose to say that no one cared while every media outlet in the city had sent a representative to cover the protest. In the interest of balance, though, in their need to appear not to be racists, none of the reporters was likely to point out the alderman's mistake. Still, he couldn't make too many of them, or someone in the studio would notice it; unflattering editorials could be written. Charge had to keep his mind focused when he dealt with the white media, had to watch his every word.

He kept his voice calm and informational as he said, "Three years ago this winter, after our beloved mayor Lucille Watkins was shot down by a white, racist sniper, this city was rocked by the greatest civil uprising since the one in Los Angeles after the verdict in the Rodney King beating. We had over thirty dead, entire neighborhoods burned to the ground, and untold millions of dollars in damage, but still, in all that time, the powers that be in this city haven't learned one single thing about race relations." Charge put a look of confusion on his face. He said, "Doesn't Chicago belong to *all* of us? Aren't the laws supposed to apply to us all? What will it take to make them wake up? How many of our people will have to die before they pull their heads out of the sand?

"This is the *second* time in as many years that an unarmed black man has been shot down in that exact same neighborhood by a white police-man. The *second* time the killer walked out of jail with a nominal bail. Can you blame us for thinking that somebody's out to *get* us? Isn't it time for the Nazi-like slaughter to stop? The time has come for all of this city's politicians, from the mayor to the local alderman, to not only go in front of your cameras and renounce the senseless killings—which is all they've done in the past—but, more importantly, to take the appropriate measures to prevent such atrocities from ever occurring again in the future."

"How?"

"How? You ask me *how?*" Charge felt the power flowing through him, felt his heart pounding in his chest; this was the moment his entire life had prepared him for. He widened his eyes, having the world as his audience, and launched into an impromptu speech that electrified his listeners.

"Brother Mike Tyson served three years for a so-called crime that wasn't anything more than an extortion demand that got way out of hand. Brother O. J. Simpson gets acquitted by a jury after three hours of deliber-ation, after spending fifteen months locked up like an animal in the white jailer's zoo, and every white human being in his neighborhood demanded that he leave the country!" Charge paused for breath, glaring at the report-ers with controlled fury. He turned to face the cameras, appealing to the people now, rather than speaking to a specific reporter.

"Congressman Mel Reynolds had *phone sex* with a young woman who admitted to being no innocent child, skipping through the daisies, and *that* proud, democratically elected black brother wound up in the white man's zoo, while baby-rapers and drug dealers run wild through our streets."

Charge lowered the tone of his voice, hoping again to sound like the voice of reason as he said, "How long do you think we as a people will be able to remain peaceful? How can you expect us to continue to *only* peacefully protest, when a married white man comes into a neighborhood with a black woman—who is not his wife—gets drunk, stays in a bar until closing time, and then, just for sport, shoots down an indigent black man on the city's streets! And *you* ask *me* how to stop it?"

Charge stopped, shook his head in disgust at the woman's ignorance.

Behind him, Berkley muttered a curse. Good man. Stay in the background, leave the speechifying to the experts.

Charge said, "If you need even ask that question, young lady, you would never understand the answer."

Crocodile Berkley chimed in just at that moment with, "Maybe if we *show* y'all the answer, we'll get your attention."

The man was learning, Charge decided. Knowing a good exit line when he heard one, he turned to Berkley, put his arm around the man's shoulder in a gesture of conciliation and understanding, then they turned their backs on the media and, fully aware that the media hadn't turned their backs on them, marched over to join the rest of the protesters.

CHAPTER

8

Ellis Turner was dressed in a manner that would have been cause for unceasing torment in the homicide division if any of his fellow officers had happened to see him that afternoon. None of his colleagues had ever seen Turner when he wasn't dressed to kill, not since he'd been promoted to detective, ten years earlier.

This afternoon he was wearing a pair of oversized white shorts, and an ancient, faded white tank top that had once had a full-color picture of Aretha Franklin stenciled on the front. There wasn't a whole lot left of Aretha on the shirt now, just a blur in the middle, which from a distance looked more like dirt than a human being. Ellis wasn't wearing any shoes or socks. He had his feet up on a hassock that matched his favorite chair. A million men were wearing similar outfits today, but not many of them were forced to wear a suit and tie on the job, no matter the time of year, no matter the weather prediction. Fewer still dressed for work with the style and panache of Ellis Turner.

Turner was sitting in his overstuffed upholstered chair in the living room of his comfortable South Side home, with the central air blasting through the vents, watching the news with his thirteen-year-old son and his seven-year-old daughter.

He and Claudette had argued about the wisdom of exposing their young daughter to the news, but Ellis didn't believe in keeping what was happening in the world away from either of his children; he wanted them to be aware that it was a highly dangerous place. Claudette was out with a couple of her friends. She'd asked Ellis if he'd wanted to go out to the

41

movies with her, and he hadn't had to say a word; his hangdog expression had sent her to the phone to make other arrangements.

Turner wasn't pleased about that—his two days off per week rarely fell on consecutive days, and when they did, those two precious days didn't fall on a weekend more than three or four times a year—but he'd rather feel guilty about not wanting to go out with his wife than to *be* out with her on a Sunday afternoon, with the temperature hovering at a hundred degrees, and rising.

"Did the police kill that man, Daddy?" his daughter Anne asked, as they looked at a high school yearbook photo of Anthony Silver on the screen. Ellis nodded, seeing her next question coming and trying to find a way to answer it before it was asked.

His son Quentin was carefully watching him.

"Why'd they do that, Daddy?" Anne asked.

"There was no 'they.' There was only one guy, and he was off duty and drinking. He might have been showing off for his girlfriend, or he might have had good reason to pull his weapon. It's been less than two days; we don't know what happened." Anne seemed happy with the answer, but Quentin was nearly smirking.

Looking at Anne, but speaking for Quentin's sake, Ellis said, "There're rotten eggs in every police department, just like there're rotten eggs in your school, or living on our block." He looked over at his son. "I bet there're even some rotten eggs in the St. Ignatius Academy." Quentin would be starting his freshman year at the exclusive college prep school in a little more than a month. He had passed the entrance exams with flying colors, had been accepted to the place due to his own intellectual proficiency; his father surely wasn't an alumnus of such a prestigious high school.

But Quentin didn't want to go there, he wanted to go to the local public high school, which most of his lifelong friends would be attending. Ellis Turner wasn't about to let that happen, and it was causing some friction between the two of them. Three of them, to be exact, as Claudette wasn't certain that she wanted her son attending a school that was predominantly Caucasian. Claudette was not as tolerant of white people as Ellis, was more concerned about their motivations—or lack of them—while Ellis cared more about conduct than he did about motive; in other words, as long as white people didn't bother him, he wouldn't bother them.

Ellis was very careful as to what he said around his son these days. Having never known his own father, he was feeling his way through the dark when it came to father-son relations, and he did not want to ever say anything around the boy that could cause an irreparable rift. He had always thought that his lack of knowledge as to the "rules" of parenting, and his uncertainty as to what a good daddy was, didn't really matter, because Ellis loved Quentin, and loved him dearly. Now he sometimes wondered if love alone was enough.

He said, "We won't know what happened until after the officer's been questioned, until there's a hearing, until all the significant facts of the case come out."

"*I* got thrown against the wall of the Walgreen's once by a cop, and I hadn't done nothing wrong."

"Anything—you hadn't done *anything* wrong, Quentin."

"Any way you say it, man still threw me against a wall."

Ellis saw red for a second as he remembered that afternoon. The police officer who had done it would not soon forget Turner's name, or his temper, or Turner's personal promises to the man, and he wasn't liable to ever bother Turner's son again unless he had enough probable cause to effect a legal search. Which wouldn't stop the ignorant son of a bitch from doing the same thing to another black man's son.

When the rage passed, Turner calmly said, "And three different bangers tried to recruit you into the Gangster Apostle Nation last year. At a *public* junior high, remember that? Does that mean all black teenagers are gang recruiters?"

Quentin, stymied, fell silent a minute, watching TV, and as soon as he saw his opening, he said, "You hear that? The woman on the TV says if the cop ain't put in jail, there'll be a riot."

"Quentin, let's not have any more of this; you know better. I don't want to hear 'ain't' out of your mouth again, son."

"*You* say 'ain't,' Daddy," Anne said, and Ellis sighed.

"Would you get me another Pepsi please, sweetie? Your poor old daddy's too tired and beat up to even get out of his chair."

"I wish I was as old and tired and beat up as you," Quentin said. He was looking at his father's muscular arms, at the broad shoulders, the deep, wide chest. Quentin was on the skinny side, at that awkward stage, making his uneasy way through puberty. Growing hair in places he'd never had it, hormones kicking in, he was noticing girls, wanting to build big muscles, and from time to time feeling the urge to challenge his father's authority.

"When you're sixteen, you'll make me look like a toothpick."

"You think so?" Quentin perked up. He'd wanted to run with his friends that afternoon, and Ellis had asked him to stay home with him. He was certain of the good character of all of Quentin's friends; it was just that in this heat, drive-bys were happening everywhere, and no young black man was safe, anywhere, at any time. The gangbangers were even doing pedal-bys now, little kids no older than Quentin, driving up to people on bicycles, killing them dead and pedaling away. Or walk-ups, blasting their enemies face-to-face, as if it took some extra measure of courage to kill an unarmed kid in that manner. These were not unusual occurrences, but the heat only made things worse. Ellis thought that this off-duty cop's killing of the panhandler up in River North was going to make the city hotter than any hand cruel old Mother Nature could deal out.

With some trepidation, Quentin asked, "You think there's going to be another race riot, Dad?" The one three years ago had horribly upset Quentin. Chicago had finally voted in another black mayor, a strong, proud woman who'd wanted to bring the city together, and when she'd been assassinated it had broken Quentin's heart. The riot that had followed Mayor Watkins's assassination had served to even further polarize a city that was already carrying more than its share of racial animosity, ignorance-based bigotry, and well-planned out, color-oriented segregation. It had been just after the riot that the other kids had started calling Quentin "white boy" because he sustained an A average at school.

Still, Ellis didn't believe in lying to his kids. He said, "I don't know. Riots are generally spontaneous, happen right after a particular event." Ellis paused, then said, "Still, there might be one, Quentin, if the media keeps hyping it up. It's what's called a self-fulfilling prophesy."

"I like the Big Lie theory better."

Ellis shook his head. "Big Lie is when people tell the same distortions often enough and loud enough that everyone starts believing it. Africaan does it better than anyone else. A self-fulfilling prophesy is a lot easier to pull off. It's when you state that something's going to happen, then behave in a manner that leaves no other option than your prophesy's fulfillment."

"Loudly, Dad," Quentin said.

"Pardon me?" Ellis said.

"Here's your Coke, Daddy," Anne said.

"It's a Pepsi," Quentin said.

Ellis said, "What did you say, Quentin? Loudly?"

"All right, *Pepsi.*" Anne hated to be corrected.

Ellis first heard the key in the lock, then the sound of the front door opening and closing. He was surprised to feel the lifting of an unease he hadn't known he was feeling. His wife was home, and safe.

"You said 'loud enough.' It's 'loudly enough.'"

Claudette said, "Sweet *God* it's hot out," as she leaned over the back of the chair and kissed the top of her husband's head.

"Claudette, is it 'loud enough,' or '*loudly* enough?'"

"Depends on the preceding phrase."

"I said when a lie is told often enough, and loud enough—"

"Then 'loudly' would be correct."

"Thank you," Quentin said, self-righteously.

"It doesn't hurt to have an English teacher for a mother."

"She's a pro*fess*or," Quentin said, proudly.

Claudette came around the front of the chair, stood in front of Ellis as she said, "Professors teach, so you're both right." She waved a finger in Quentin's direction, and said, "No bickering, you two," jokingly. Ellis sat smiling, nodding his head, looking quickly from one loved one to another as they spoke. Locked in his secure home, with the air-conditioning on, with both his kids and his wife in the same room with him, Anthony Silver's death was the furthest thing from his mind.

"Did you have a good time, Mommy?" Anne asked.

Ellis said, "Quentin? I just have a *public* high school diploma. That's why I *occas*ionally screw things up when I talk."

Quentin lowered his voice to a parody of his father's. "I don't want to hear 'loud' come out of your mouth again, Father."

Ellis laughed, loudly. "Funny young man you raised, Claudette. Regular Richard Pryor."

"Who's Richard Pryor?" Anne looked confused.

Claudette said, "You had more to do with his sarcasm than I did. I've been meaning to talk to both of you about that."

Quentin and Ellis both said, "Woe," dragging the word out and raising their hands in the air in anticipation of their being in serious trouble with the boss.

Anne said, "I got Daddy a Coke and got the lid off myself."

"That's good, Anne." Claudette glanced at the TV, and then said to Ellis, "Is that more about that shooting in front of Jordan's restaurant? The radio said he got out after posting only a hundred-dollar bond." Her tone told Ellis how she felt about a lot more than the low bail; the silence following informed him that she would have said a lot more if the kids weren't in the room.

"What's the bond for *drunk driving,* Dad?" Quentin asked.

Ellis sighed. "They'll raise it after he's indicted. Do we have to keep talking about homicides on my day off?"

"*You're* the one who has it on; *I* just got home. And no, we don't have to talk about homicides on your day off. We *could* be talking about the movie we just saw. Or we could be at the beach, talking about how nice the breeze feels."

"There hasn't been a breeze for over a week, honey."

"Still . . ."

"Wait, there's Billy Charge." Billy Charge was one of Quentin's role models. Ellis and Claudette exchanged a worried look. The boy wasn't old enough to be told the truth of the situation yet. Maybe he never would be; he was bright enough and inquisitive enough to figure things out for himself. But in Turner's mind, and Claudette's, Charge was an opportunist who would stop at nothing to further his own agenda. The boy would probably come around; Quentin had already seen through Crocodile Berkley's game. They'd discussed Berkley at length, the three of them, one night earlier this summer after Anne had been put to bed. Berkley had made the TV news after getting himself evicted from a luxury downtown high-rise, due to nonpayment of rent. The common "adult" conversations between the three of them were often lively, as Claudette was far more of a radical than Ellis, and was far better educated, as well. Turner could tell that their son was leaning more toward his mother's more radical views than toward Ellis's middle ground.

"So what did you do today, hon?" Turner said, not wanting to watch the tape of the politician, when the phone rang, and Anne shouted that she'd get it, and ran over to the little phone table that was set up next to the couch. Claudette eased herself down onto her husband's lap. Ellis could feel the heat of her, could smell her. Claudette felt as if she'd just stepped out of a hot tub. She kissed at his ear, then whispered into it.

"I found a boyfriend who likes to go to the movies."

Ellis, knowing Claudette, laughed aloud at the thought.

Anne hollered, "Daddy, it's for you." Claudette got off his lap. Shaking his head, still laughing, Ellis walked over to the couch, flopped down on it, reached for his pack of cigarettes with one hand as he put the phone to his ear with the other.

"Hello?"

"Something funny?" Sergeant Cheryl Laney said, and Ellis lost his good humor and became a hard, cold professional.

"Sergeant Laney," he said, and waited, lighting his cigarette, until Laney at last seemed to figure out that he wasn't going to share any aspect of his private life with her.

"I know it's your day off—"

"Sergeant—"

"Please don't interrupt!" Laney's harsh, abrupt anger bit away a small part of Ellis's pleasant frame of mind. He waited, sucking on the cigarette, thinking, Fuck you, lady.

Laney said, "I've been ordered to ask you to work the Africaan rally this evening."

Ellis's tone was weary as he said, "Sergeant, there'll be a dozen cops there. I've done it. He's good for a time, even compelling. But it gets old after the first couple of hours."

"I'm not asking you to go for entertainment purposes, Ellis. A murder's been committed, and it's the reason for the meeting. The press isn't invited, so we won't be able to get a tape."

"You told me once you believe we live in a color-blind society. So why don't you go yourself?"

A MATTER OF HONOR

"Africaan doesn't believe we live in a color-blind society. And besides, women aren't invited, either." It was a good answer, and quick. Better than he'd expected from her. "So can I tell the lieutenant you'll be attending?"

"It's my day off." Laney didn't respond. Ellis saw Claudette watching him. Quentin was watching him, too.

He said, "If it's a request, then no, I'm not going. If it's an order, and I have no choice, I'll be there."

Ellis waited a long time before Laney said, "Ellis, we really need you there."

"That doesn't tell me what I need to know, Sergeant."

"I can't order you to go. I'd appreciate it if you would."

Ellis sighed. In today's climate, with doctors and lawyers and bosses all worried about lawsuits, it was impossible to get a straight answer out of anyone. He said, "I'll go. Can the report wait until morning, at least?"

"We need it tonight, Ellis. The meeting'll be at—"

"I know where it'll be," Turner said, cutting her off on purpose, knowing how much she'd hate that, then he hung up the phone before Laney could chastise him for interrupting her.

The second the phone conversation ended, Ellis Turner turned into a loving husband and father again.

He smiled, put the cigarette between his lips, got up off the couch as he rubbed his hands together, smiled, and said, "Daddy got called in to work tonight; we've got about three hours. Mommy, you're melting. Why don't you hop in the shower and cool off, and we'll decide what video to watch while you're gone."

"*Original Gangstas!*" Quentin said.

"No." Ellis spat out the word, as if he were still arguing with his boss rather than refusing a request from his son.

"*Meteorman!*" Anne said.

Claudette said, "How about *The Color Purple?* We haven't watched that in years." Quentin sighed, and Anne looked at them blankly—she'd never seen the movie before. "Whoopie Goldberg and Oprah Winfrey are in it." Anne's eyes widened.

Ellis said, "I'll make the popcorn while you take a shower."

"Ellis, would you mind smoking that thing in the kitchen? You know how I worry about the kids . . ."

Anne said, "Daddy's been smoking in here all day, Mommy."

"Snitcher," Ellis whispered, as if Claudette couldn't hear him. Over his shoulder, he jokingly said, "Where's that stool? We have to get the stool for the stool pigeon," as he walked into the kitchen, knowing there was more to his wife's request than her concern about Ellis's smoking. He went over to the stove and turned on the hooded fan, as much to keep the kids from hearing their conversation as to suck the smoke out of the air. He took a last drag off the butt, blew the smoke at the fan, doused the cigarette under the faucet, and threw it into the garbage.

He said, "I hope we're not going to have an argument—"

"Did you get a chance to talk to Quentin?"

"We talked most of the afternoon."

"You talked, but did you *talk*?"

"He doesn't want to go to St. Ignatius, it's as simple as that. He says there's a lot of white kids go there, and he's always gone to all-black schools."

Claudette's silence was eloquent.

It was with a bit of an attitude that Ellis said, "I won't let him use that as an excuse not to face his fear. He doesn't want to go, but he *will*. He took the test, and he aced it. He could have flunked it on purpose if he'd wanted to, and we wouldn't ever have known."

"He's got too much pride to purposely flunk a test." Claudette paused, then said, "He seems—I don't know—different, lately."

Ellis knew what had brought this on: Quentin's quick desire to watch a violent gangster movie. There were aspects of that lifestyle that appealed to Quentin, Ellis knew, as they would appeal to every young black male who'd been roughed up by the police for no better reason than the color of his skin. But he also knew—Ellis hoped and prayed—that his son was too well adjusted to ever fall into such a lifestyle.

Wasn't he?

Ellis thought of his son's remark earlier, how he'd admired his father's physique, how he'd joked about Ellis's ungrammatical expression. Throughout the day they'd kidded each other back and forth, with just a few bumpy moments in an otherwise pleasant afternoon. Ellis thought about the young boys Quentin's age and younger, boys who were out there banging in the streets, selling and ingesting drugs, shooting each other for no reason.

Then he thought of himself at Quentin's age, alone and afraid, living in the Robert Taylor housing projects, spending his summers gazing longingly out the window when he wasn't in the Baptist church down the street.

He said, "Quentin's going to be fine. He's a man-child, the worst part of a kid's life. Don't worry about him, sweetheart."

Claudette, though seemingly relieved, said, "Today, we were downtown, ready to go into the Esquire theater? Three white conventioneers asked LaVella if she was looking for a date."

"They say anything to you?" Ellis's eyes were hard and dry, he had to fight to keep his voice steady.

"No. But what if Anne had been with us?" Ellis wasn't certain he believed her. Claudette said, "The way things have gotten . . . Sometimes I think we should have never had children."

"Don't say that!" The anger in Ellis's tone shocked Claudette, and her hurt quieted her for a moment. But only for a moment.

"All well-dressed black women have to be call girls; all black young men have to be gangbangers."

"That's media hype. There's nobody with any sense who believes it."

"Tell that to the conventioneers."

"And most black boys *aren't* in gangs. Overwhelming majority aren't, thank God."

Angrily, Claudette said, "If they had feathers or fur, instead of black skin, they'd be shielded by the Endangered Species Act. But they're young men, and they're only killing each other, so who the hell cares."

Ellis looked at her, saw her pain, and took her into his arms. He had to fight down another wave of red-hot anger before saying, "*I* care. *You* care. Quentin cares, too, and he's going to be just fine. I'd know by now if he wasn't, Claudette. He's going to be just fine." Having lived through days of hope for racial harmony, then having had those hopes destroyed, Ellis buried his rage as his wife subsumed her fear, the two of them holding onto each other tightly, each the other's lifeline, both hoping that Ellis Turner's words would turn out to be the truth—a self-fulfilling prophesy.

CHAPTER

9

He could hear them out there, calling for him, shouting his name in unison, black men's voices raised in happy screams and rapturous bellows, feet stomping, hands clapping. He felt the building shaking beneath him, felt the sweet tingle of their love as they called his name, as they hollered for him. The Holy Minister Reverend Africaan smiled, thinking of the seizures his Seeds of Africa would be having out there right about now. He knew that none of the Seeds would dare come into the wings where he was standing and ask him to hurry his entrance. They thought he was God, and God did what He wanted to, in His own sweet time.

Africaan knew that he wasn't God. He knew that he was nothing more than God's humble messenger; His prophet.

The message is often obscured by the messenger. Nobody knew that better than Minister Africaan. Delivering the message had caused him to spend two long, hard years in the Snake's 20th Century version of the plantation—the penitentiary—locked up underground, in a one-man cell in the federal prison in Marion. Africaan had accepted two million dollars from an Islamic zealot who described himself as the "president and spiritual master for life" of an oil-rich nation that was dedicated to the downfall of the United States of America, and Africaan hadn't declared that two million as income, had lied to a federal grand jury about it when questioned, and had continued to lie to them, even when presented with tapes of conversations between himself and his fellow demagogue, during the course of which Africaan had pledged to use part of the money to blow up a federal building. Africaan had been arrested, charged, and convicted of income tax evasion, perjury, and treason. The government only kept the worst of the worst in Marion. It was a twenty-four-hour lockdown facility. For a portion of his sentence, Africaan had been locked in the cell—which were referred to by the oppressor as "units"—next to John Gotti.

His preconviction popularity had been incredibly high among, but nevertheless generally restricted to, poverty-stricken blacks—particularly those who lived within the nation's big city ghettos—where he had recruited the first hard-core members to his Nation, men who had served time in various penitentiaries, and who viewed Africaan's main competition, the Nation of Islam, as being too centralized, too middle-of-the-road for themselves. But during the years of his incarceration, his popularity had vastly grown outside of the ghetto. The newspapers and magazines had written about him, huge posters with his picture on them and the words "Free The Minister" had been plastered across buildings nationwide. His case had generated national headlines, even among the conservative press, as it further demonstrated the great divide among black and whites in America, and then it had expanded beyond national boundaries, as people of other nations demanded that Africaan be freed. He had become *the* cause celebre, the topic of hundreds of hours of radio and TV shows. His picture had appeared on the covers of both *Newsweek* and *Time* magazines during the same week. His own organization had done a computer search which determined that, in the course of two years, more than a million words had been published about him in the free world, and beyond.

William Kunstler had argued Africaan's case before the Supreme Court, which had overturned Africaan's conviction, claiming he had been merely exercising his right to free speech. It also proclaimed that Africaan was the head of an established, if unorthodox, religion, and that the money he'd accepted had been a religious contribution, exempt from American taxation.

In the three years that had now passed since his release from Marion, Africaan had come to believe himself to be what the CIA had long ago termed "unindictable." If the government were to attempt to lock him up, the already burning fuse that was attached to the powder keg of race would explode and expand beyond its original limitation; it would escalate into a blast that would be nothing less than thermonuclear. Still, that wouldn't stop the white puppeteers from trying to get him.

Africaan had proof of this; the American government had tried it yet again. He would talk about that tonight.

He did more than discuss the government's conspiracies before his flock. Every six months or so, Africaan would plant stories about the conspiracy to kill him, would write personal articles in the Nation's paper—which he himself published—revealing how only the attentive, quick-thinking of his crack Seeds of Africa security force had once more averted just such a tragedy, and that that averting had been narrow.

There were now over twenty thousand dues-paying members of the Nation of Africaan, who were charged twenty dollars a month for the privilege of inclusion. For their money, they received a monthly issue of the *Africaan Declares* newspaper and bimonthly newsletters that updated them on events which Africaan believed were of importance unfolding from across the nation. In the newsletters he did what he did best; planted seeds of distrust and discord among his people through the spreading of rumors and lies, while giving them plenty of seemingly benign information as to how they themselves could help to rectify the situation.

One such article stated: "When a Brother is called a *nigger,* be it on the *street,* in the *schools,* or at a *sporting* event—whether he is merely a spectator at that event, or the main participant—then that Brother has the *right,* nay, the *obligation,* to defend his Blackness and his manhood through the means of physical force." Within days of its mailing, physical assaults by blacks upon white teachers, sporting officials, and strangers had increased by hundreds of percentage points across the country, and in each case, the young black men arrested for the crimes had claimed that the white man he'd assaulted had initiated the confrontation by calling him a nigger.

In his gated, secure, highly fortified palace on Chicago's near South Side, Africaan had read the reports as they'd come in, and he'd sat back in his chair and smiled.

Power was everything. Africaan knew that he held that power. Besides the twenty thousand dues-paying members of his Nation, there were thousands of others who sympathized with him, agreed with him, believed in what he said, but still had chosen, for whatever reason, not to accept him as their spiritual leader. It was a position he understood. Although aware that he was the Prophet of God, he was also acutely aware that it would take more than the years he would be on earth to break the slave mentality of those who had been the white man's lackey for hundreds of years. Many of these good Christians sent him money for his battle, and they came and filled the football stadiums when Africaan toured the country, speaking publicly in their cities.

There was a ten-dollar-per-man cover charge to get through the door of the rallies, and books, videotapes, T-shirts, and pamphlets were for sale, laid out on tables which were located at every stadium entrance. Also for sale were Africaan's own brand of herbal remedies, guaranteed to cure everything from poor eyesight to sickle-cell anemia; from minor arthritis to AIDS. The cure *always* worked if, in addition to the herbs, you prayed to the One Great Black Jesus hard enough and long enough.

A MATTER OF HONOR

They were shouting his name now as they did at the rallies, and Africaan reveled in it, enjoyed it for just a moment more. His eyes closed, his head raised toward the ceiling, he listened to his name as he thanked God for all he'd been given, with a beatific smile on his face, Africaan's hands open, at his side, as if he were about to ascend into heaven.

CHAPTER

10

He had descended into hell, Ellis Turner thought, sweating like a pig in his nice, new, shiny blue suit, fifteen hundred dollars at Barneys, and it wasn't even on their VIP rack. Turner's tie was knotted, was pushed all the way up to his neck. It was a regular tie, not the yellow string type that many in the audience wore in imitation of their spiritual leader, Africaan. The top button of Turner's shirt was fastened. He would think that with all the millions of dollars that Africaan pulled in from his believers every year in "love offerings," he would have popped to air-condition the mosque.

Turner sat, sweating and seething. His anger, he knew, was merely a cover for his fear. At the moment, Turner knew terror, but it wasn't Africaan who was making him so afraid. Africaan frightened him, certainly—madness had always frightened Turner. But what truly terrified him was the prospect that thousands upon thousands of other black men believed what the man said, believed in the hate-filled lies that Africaan so easily spewed.

Turner understood black rage as well as anyone in the room. He had faced bigotry, ignorance, and racial prejudice from the first day that he'd stepped out of the all-black housing projects and had entered the working world. He'd feel that rage every time some asshole pinned a racist, hand-drawn cartoon to a bulletin board, which happened more often in the city's police department than most white people would like to believe; he felt it every time a cab passed him by, then stopped a few feet up the street, for a white man. He had experienced that rage—and vented it—

when white officers had belittled his fast rise to detective as a result of affirmative action, rather than a product of Turner's hard work and dedication. He'd made his feelings clear about white bigotry when he'd first been promoted to the most prestigious job in the department: Homicide. Turner had posted a letter of his own on the bulletin board, stating his feelings, stating also that if anyone had any problems with his promotion, they should grow a set of balls big enough to allow them to state their objections directly to Ellis Turner's face.

Oh, he knew black rage, all right. Understood it as well as anyone.

And he had felt a little sting of it just an hour ago, directed toward the Seeds of Africa, who had made him walk through a metal detector and then *still* had felt the need to run a handheld, wand metal detector up and down his body. The Seeds apologized to each man as they searched him, explaining that they should blame the white Snake for the indignity, the Snake who was not above sending in an undercover, hanky-headed Uncle Tom to try and assassinate the Prophet. They explained that they'd caught more than one such man in the process of attempting to carry out an assassination upon the Prophet. Most of the men around Turner had acted as if they'd believed the justification. Turner had kept his face blank, but had felt the anger rising inside him. Turner's weapon was locked in the trunk of his car. He understood black rage, and he understood the frustration of a black man in today's world. He'd understood it all his life, had even let it loose a time or two.

What he didn't understand was how so many otherwise intelligent men would allow a demagogue to speak for them, tell them how to dress, how to act, tell them how much money they had to send in every month in order to be guaranteed a spot in Heaven. Africaan had seen his opportunities and had seized them. But what were these men's excuses?

Turner calmed himself with reason; there were a minimum of thirty million blacks in America today, there was no need to panic because a thousand of them were inside a mosque, preparing to listen to the ravings of a madman. This group represented a minuscule percentage of American blacks. Even if Africaan were correct, and he had twenty thousand hard-core followers (which Ellis Turner seriously doubted), that was still only a tiny percentage of African-Americans, nothing to worry about.

Or was it?

Turner felt first ashamed of, then angry at, the Minister's followers. Africaan called for the destruction of the white race. Wasn't that as racist as anything Adolph Hitler had said? Or any recorded statement made by that jagoff out in Los Angeles, the rogue cop from the Simpson trial, Fuhrman? Turner would like to spend five minutes, alone and unarmed, in a locked room with Mark Fuhrman. He'd also like five minutes, alone and unarmed, in a locked room with Africaan.

Africaan, who did not preach brotherhood, but hate. Africaan, who did not call for conciliation, but for destruction. Africaan, who preached that it was understandable for black men to have sex with anything that moved, that it was not your fault if you chose to shoot deadly drugs into your veins, because you needed to do these things in order to alleviate the mental anguish that the white man had forced upon you in the six hundred and sixty-six years of first physical, and now mental, slavery. Africaan, who kept a well-maintained shrine to Tawanah Brawley in the vestibule of the palace in which he lived, a statue which—he readily explained to visitors and the very few curious black journalists who were allowed into the house to interview him—symbolized the continued rape of the great Black Woman, and the breadth of the conspiracies that were entered into to ensure Her silence when one Brave Woman dared to protest the indignities perpetrated upon Her by all those white policemen.

Africaan, who was now striding across the stage, to the rising screams and cheers of the sheep who followed him, the mass of black humanity whose proud energy was undeniable, even to Turner, who, fighting his terror, got to his feet along with them, and clapped his hands as hard as anyone until the Minister waved for the congregation to be seated.

"My dear brothers, my *dear,* dear brothers," Africaan said, shaking his head, as if he were filled with sadness. "How long can we be expected to take this? How many of us have to die before we are justified in fighting *back*?" He'd been going on this way for twenty minutes, working the crowd into a frenzy of bloodlust, then calming them down, then calling them to battle. He was in a passive phase now; a man of peace. Behind him, Seeds of Africa guards in suits and baseball caps exhorted him with cheers of "Go 'head," and "Tell it."

Turner knew a setup when he saw one, and he was seeing one now. He thought that within a matter of minutes, Africaan would speak the name of a man who he felt was responsible for the plight of the black man, and someone in the crowd, some enthusiastic extremist, would latch onto that name, and make it his business to go out and kill in the name of the beloved Minister. Turner was betting that the name would be that of Leonard Brazovik, the copper who had shot Anthony Silver Friday night. Turner knew the name of the man who was responsible for Ellis Turner's plight. That name was Ellis Turner. He would not even consider any option other than that; to do so would be to put his fate in the hands of another man—a white man—and that was something Ellis Turner was not prepared to allow.

But there were plenty of men in this room who thought otherwise, and Turner knew it. Men who blamed the white man for AIDS, along with every other scourge in the community. Even though just the slightest research at even the most barren public library would teach them that AIDS had first been discovered in Africa, not far from the site where a group of black *and* white scientists, working together, had found the remains of what historians now believed to be the first human being to ever walk the planet Earth; the remains of a black woman.

But try telling that to the men who filled this mosque. Those here were exclusively black; exclusively male. Half of the race had been excluded from attendance, and Turner resented this, not only on behalf of his college educated, intelligent, well-employed black wife, but also on behalf of his daughter Anne, who was seven years old and already facing exclusion by tens of thousands of males because of her gender, an accident of birth.

"HIS NAME IS LEONARD BRAZOVIK!" Africaan's booming shout caused Ellis to jump in his seat, and some of the men around him looked at him oddly; he heard someone mumble, "Sissy." He looked straight ahead as someone else whispered, "He a faggot?" Turner listened as one of the Seeds of Africa that were roaming the aisles shushed the men who'd been talking. Turner felt an unexpected flash of pleasure, as if he were back in school and the teacher had chastised someone for messing with him.

Africaan was saying, "I implore every black man in this room to do *all* in your power to keep Mr. Brazovik safe, secure, and alive! I want you all to promise me tonight that none of you will harm him! If any harm should come to him, who will the Snake blame? Who will be arrested, tried and convicted, and put to death for killing the killer? A *black man,* that's who!

"The fires of *hell* will consume Leonard Brazovik, sooner or later! When the time comes, Brazovik will *burn*! His flesh melting from his bones, as God Himself, my Father, your Brother, pours even more heavenly gasoline over the all-consuming flames." He closed his eyes, wiped his face with a silk handkerchief, and stood there for a moment, allowing his words to sink in. Then Africaan, eyes still closed, said, "Imagine it, brothers. Close your eyes and think about it. Envision Leonard Brazovik, the cold-blooded murderer of our poor, dead brother, Anthony Silver, lying in a pool of flames, screaming with every breath. And when that Snake sucks in air, trying to breathe, the fire will be sucked down into his murderous lungs!" Africaan opened his eyes and said, "Awaken now, brothers, and let God handle Leonard Brazovik. Let God handle the punishment of all the Snakes, even the black ones! My own trusted aide, a man I love and trusted like my brother, Minister Mallik, has betrayed me, as he has betrayed all who love me, and who love our Nation. Mallik even used phony audio tapes"—the Minister chuckled—"he found an Africaan *impersonator* to call and try to entrap me, to blame me for the riots in this city three years ago, after our beloved Lucille Watkins was shot down in the street by a *white* man . . ."

Turner sat through an hour and fifteen minutes more of the Minister's lecture, hearing about how the hook-nosed, bagel-eating, *Jew*elry-wearing member of the *Jews* media was doing everything in its considerable power to destroy him. Africaan then gave an exhibition of his bizarre dogma of numerology, taking the number of letters in Leonard Brazovik's name and somehow transposing them into the name of Satan, the Betrayer. Finally, his kidneys bursting, his ears ringing, his head heavy and his body soaking wet with sweat, Turner was on his feet with the rest of the crowd, cheering loudly as the Minister was led off the stage by his Seeds.

Turner's report was finished, signed and filed an hour and a half later, and immediately thereafter Leonard Brazovik, his wife, and his two young children were taken into protective custody and housed in a Holiday Inn in the south suburban village of Matteson. Brazovik would be arraigned early Monday morning. The police officers who provided his protection were—as a precaution—all white.

While Ellis dreamed uneasy dreams beside the form of his beloved Claudette, Leonard Brazovik's home was destroyed by a fire, and a white man in search of drugs three blocks from the Gresham District police station was pulled out of his car, doused with lighter fluid, and set aflame by a group of teenage blacks. The white man died six excruciating hours later, in the burn unit at Cook County Hospital.

CHAPTER

11

Edmund was fighting a horrendous headache, waiting for a friend of his to tap lightly on his door. He sat at his computer terminal as he waited, in the dead of night, mostly relaxed, composed. He was vaguely aware that Daddy was moaning loudly upstairs, no doubt in the grip of another vision. All the lights in the house were turned off. Edmund barely noticed the heat.

Daddy would go off sometimes, would scream like mad as God allowed him to see what was going to happen in the world, and from time to time that screaming got on Edmund's nerves, but there wasn't much Edmund could do about it; after all, it was his daddy. Still, his head felt like it was afire.

Edmund was so antidrug he would not even take an aspirin. Nicotine didn't count, nor did caffeine. Both were extracted from God-grown leaves and bushes, so according to the Bible he was allowed to use them to steady his nerves. Edmund lit a cigarette, then watched the smoke swirl around the computer screen in a ghostly manner. Upstairs, Daddy screamed like a banshee, and Edmund involuntarily winced.

He was trying to read a Bulletin Board posting from a lawyer in Tallahassee, Florida, who claimed to have indisputable proof that the Sixteenth Amendment—which allowed income tax collection—had never been ratified, as the Constitution demanded of all amendments, and therefore was not legal. Edmund had heard that before, but never with such documentation. He downloaded the file, smoked his cigarette, and set his printer to make a hundred copies of the document.

If only the sheep knew what was really going on . . . Edmund's job was to teach them. Let them know that the White European Male was the true heir to Israel; that they were members of the Twelve Tribes of Israel, which sprang from the seed of Jacob, whom God had anointed as the patriarch; the first true Israelite. It was his mission to let the people know that the term Jew did not even appear in the Bible until 2 Kings 15:5-6.

Sheeple, he called them—they had more sheep in them than they had people—were led astray by elected officials who'd spent millions of dollars to buy their positions. Edmund didn't think you needed a degree from Harvard to figure out why someone would spend millions to get a job that only paid thousands. He'd give a broad hint to anyone who doubted him: the professional politicians didn't do it to serve their country.

It was all there, in writing, for anyone who cared to look. The sheeple who went so haughtily about their lives, pretending they were safe and thinking no one could ever hurt them—particularly not their police, or their sworn elected officials! They paid their taxes on time, and a lot of them cheated. But pay they did, with fear in their hearts of an audit, carefully documenting every dime they owed, never knowing that the massive computer beneath the Pentagon had a record of every penny that came in and went out of their pockets. ZOG would let them live in peace, as long as they didn't get too greedy. When they did, the Beast would grab them, make an example out of one of them—usually around April 15th—with blaring headlines and attendant television coverage, so the rest of the sheeple would fall in line. Edmund often imagined ZOG—a bunch of hook-nosed, money-grubbing fat Jews, smoking cigars—huddling in their bomb shelters, rubbing their hands together and chortling over what they were doing to America. Trying to think of even more ways to tax the working man into bankruptcy. During times of desperation, Edmund thought that the sheeple deserved whatever happened to them.

They were all hooked into the Internet, but they wouldn't read the postings, they didn't care about their country; all they wanted to do was download dirty pictures, go into a private chat room with some harlot and pretend they were young and virile. The word was getting out, though, and minds were being changed.

Type in a few letters, and there it was, the sworn testimony of one of their own FBI agents, a patriot who had risked his life to inform the world that the Oklahoma City bombing had been plotted and carried out by the men who controlled the U.S. government. The problem was that a lot of The Truth on the Internet was written by patriotic white people who were preaching to the converted. Still, it was good to know that anyone with access to a computer could punch up The Truth. The Truth was that the Jewnited States was on its way to hell. He could show the sheeple more than typed words on a computer screen. He didn't even have to count on them putting their trust in periodicals that had been written by patriots. Edmund could show them actual, published books.

Like *The Turner Diaries.* He could show them an authentic copy of the *Protocols of the Learned Elders of Zion.* He could hand them a copy of Spengler's *Decline of the West,* or Simpson's *Which Way Western Man?* which was 758 pages of indisputable verification that there was an ever-growing, desperate need for eugenics, racial segregation, and the deportation of Jews. The book was filled with footnotes, for the academically minded. Gayman had written God-only-knew how many books, articles, and pamphlets proving that the Jews were indeed the seed of Satan, and that the so-called Holocaust was a fabrication, invented to create worldwide sympathy for the most rightfully maligned group of people to ever roam the Lord's Earth. Edmund could hand them these, or more than a hundred other books that had been published over the course of the last century, from Jules Verne's time to the present. But sheeple wouldn't read these books; sheeple couldn't see past their own jobs, lies, and sexual organs. All they cared about was making sure they didn't eat meat, or that they didn't have to sit in restaurants or bars with people who smoked cigarettes. Sheeple felt honored to be on a first-name basis with maitre d's at fancy nightclubs; thought the high point of their lives was to get their names in the society columns.

Edmund sighed, consoling himself with the fact that—no matter how hard ZOG tried to keep it down—the movement was growing, and growing rapidly. The communists, and the Jews—who everybody with a brain knew were in collusion—would not win.

Groups such as the Aryan Christian Kinsmen were no longer referred to as "fringe" or "far right." There were more people who could tell you every word in the Constitution, quote not only the preamble and the Bill of Rights, but every article and every word of the later, illegal amendments. More and more states were allowing its citizens to not only arm themselves, but to carry concealed weapons. There were television preachers who had national platforms which they now used to carry the message.

Edmund and his brethren were well aware that television was the tool that had to be conquered; it was the key to the masses. These days, true patriots were no longer restricted to shortwave radio transmissions. They had phones, faxes, computer modems, and the World Wide Web. They had a handle on TV, and, since the Oklahoma City bombing, those newsmagazine and talk shows couldn't get enough of what was rapidly becoming a mainstream movement.

Edmund always got a kick out of it when he thought of the irony; the media, the beastly invention, created then wholly owned by the Jews, was now being used in the war against them. It didn't matter one bit to Edmund that Rivera or Springer always acted as if these patriotic groups were filled with mean, hateful people. Edmund and others like him would have blanched at the suggestion that the mainstream media were endorsing their goals; they did not *want* mud people like Rivera, or Jews like Springer, to sanction them. The fact was, every time one of those shows featured true Christian patriots, no matter which group was being represented—from the KKK to the White Aryan Resistance—telephone lines across the nation started ringing with eager recruits, wanting to know where they could sign up.

The true believers saw through the lies, and they were rushing to the movement in droves. Particularly the young, who could see through their parents' hypocrisies.

There were other ways to infiltrate the sheeple. Subtle techniques Edmund came up with during all-night thinking sessions, then taught to his men at meetings after he'd thought about them long enough to be certain they would work. For instance, most of the Kinsmen members held regular jobs, were blue-collar workers, with families. A lot of them had been married right here, in the basement of Edmund's house. Edmund had trained these men to approach other men they thought might be susceptible for Kinsmen membership, and get to know them, recruit them gently, let them see what good guys most of them were, let them get to know each other's families. Then, when the time was right, get the man alone and drop a tape in the VCR, let him see what had been documented, what the Jews—and their nigger lackeys—had done to America. The men had been taught to watch their beginners very carefully, to watch their expressions as they viewed the tape. If they were immediately appalled, then the man was to draw back, pretend to hate what he was seeing, act like he'd only shown it in order to get the man's opinion, see how he felt about such hateful, un-American trash. But if there was even a glimmer of interest in the man's eye as he watched the tape, well, then, that was another matter. The true recruitment could begin.

The recruitment process had to be slow, and steady. Edmund had learned not to inundate recruits with too much input, too quickly. You had to draw them in, like fish on the line, play them just right then reel them toward you when you were sure they were ready. Most of the Kinsmen's membership had been recruited from the scorched yet fertile pastures of the American justice system, but Edmund held pride in the fact that fully a fourth of his group were men who had no criminal background of any kind. Those were the men Edmund held the most respect for, those who had come to what they believed through their own, personal insights, men who had drawn their conclusions based on what they saw around them every day. Men who understood that there was no future for the working man. They had questioning minds, and wanted answers. They couldn't understand why the police officers who had defended themselves against Rodney King had wound up going to jail, while the niggers who had nearly beaten that poor truck driver to death had walked.

ZOG was everywhere, trying to destroy White America.

There was a light tap at the back door, and Edmund quickly stood, hand on the weapon at his hip, and walked through the kitchen and over to the door. He stood to the side of it, pulled the blind back a half-inch. He saw Trevor Ritchie standing on his back porch, looking down at his shoes. Edmund opened the door, and welcomed Trevor with a wide smile and a strong handshake. Edmund put his left hand on Trevor's shoulder, squeezed it in a manly gesture.

"Shh," Edmund said, "Daddy's sleeping. Come on in."

Trevor, still shy and tentative, entered the house, as if against his will. Edmund closed the door behind him, and took an envelope out of his pocket. He handed it to Trevor, who didn't seem to want to accept it. Edmund pushed it into Trevor's chest, held it there until Trevor finally reached up and covered it with his hand. Edmund squeezed Trevor's hand, embraced it, along with the envelope, then let his hand drop.

Close to Trevor, Edmund said, "Trevor, do me a favor, be a gracious receiver."

"I feel like less of a man."

"Because you want to feed your baby? Because you want to take care of your wife? Because you borrowed from your brother to do that? Listen, if I needed money to help my family, and you had it, wouldn't you want me to come to you?" Trevor looked up angrily, cheeks red. He stared hard into Edmund's eyes.

"I'll pay you back every dime, I swear it."

"When you can."

"With interest." Edmund's face hardened.

Edmund's voice was soft and gentle as he said, "I know you didn't mean to, but you just slapped me across my face." Trevor's eyes widened with the shock of his understanding.

"I didn't mean it that way, Edmund, I didn't. I wasn't calling you no Jew, honest to God."

"I know, Trev, it's all right. Now put the money in your pocket, and go on home." Edmund shook Trevor's hand again. Upstairs, Daddy screamed. Trevor looked toward the ceiling, frightened, then hurriedly looked back at Edmund.

"You need more, you come to me, you understand me, kinsman?"

"I don't know how to thank you, Edmund."

63

"You just did," Edmund said, and opened the door. He stopped, looked directly at Trevor, and said, "You're a Kinsmen. Your kids go hungry, mine get empty bellies. Your rent ain't paid, I get evicted."

Trevor's lower lip quivered. Edmund shook hands once more, knowing when it was time to shut up and let emotion take control.

"See you."

"Thank you . . ." Trevor's voice broke on the last word. Edmund closed the door behind him and hurried back to his computer. The printer was spitting out paper. Edmund sat down at the console, rubbed his throbbing temples with his fingers.

He thought that sometimes, keeping someone bonded to you was as important as recruiting them. Trevor was now Edmund's friend for life. And not because of a measly couple of hundred dollars, either, but because, when Trevor had been in want, Edmund had been there to help him out. It was the way he was; his daddy said he was too goddamn generous for his own good, but Edmund couldn't help the way he was, if a kinsman needed something, he had to hand it over. Whatever Edmund owned belonged to the entire White Race. If that wasn't the most simple, symbolic truth, then what was the point of everything else that he was doing? His daddy said his generosity would be Edmund's undoing. Edmund didn't think that was so; he wasn't any man's fool.

Take Gerald, for instance. Edmund's generosity toward him had ended some time back, when he'd figured out that Gerald was just a jailhouse Kinsmen. There were plenty like him, who looked out for each other in the joint, who were even willing to fight and die for one another inside, then conveniently forgot who'd help them get through their time once they got released. Edmund had decided that Gerald was like that; a user, not a giver. Edmund knew that he could go to Trevor Ritchie's house right now, hand the man a razor blade and ask him for some blood, and Trevor wouldn't even ask how much Edmund wanted until after he'd already rolled up his sleeve and slit his veins.

Gerald, on the other hand, never did anything unless there was a nice, tidy profit in it for Gerald. He didn't care about duty, commitment, honor, or obligation, he just mouthed the words when he thought someone would be impressed by his saying them, but he didn't mean them in his heart. In Kinsmen terms, Gerald wasn't worthy to be a pimple on Trevor's ass.

Edmund had plans for him, though. The boy could generate money. And now, after the other night, Gerald knew that Edmund was on to him, he would bring Edmund more money than he'd been doing as of late. Edmund bit his thumb as he thought of his disappointment in Podgourney; there'd been a time when he'd believed that Gerald could be his second in command.

A MATTER OF HONOR

Edmund had never had a brother. He had never known his mother. Daddy would not speak of the woman, unless he was roaring drunk, and even then all Edmund could ever drag out of Daddy was that his mother was the Whore of Babylon, a traitorous harlot of a slut who had betrayed not only her helpmate but her entire race in the process. Edmund didn't even want to think about what that might mean.

If the woman had given birth to two sons, though, and if Edmund had been able to pick him, he would have wanted the man to look just like Gerald. Tall, handsome, and muscular; a true Aryan warrior. With that gift for bullshit, the sly charm with the ladies. Daddy had sworn that he wouldn't marry Gerald again; he'd had enough of the boy. Daddy had told Edmund that he'd be better off killing Gerald, that he'd had a vision that had given him insight into Gerald's soul, a soul burned black from lies, and from the other sins Gerald had committed—not for the betterment of the White Race, but for his own self-interest.

Edmund had to bite off his disappointment in the boy, had to swallow it down and forget about it, or else it would drive him crazy. Edmund had done all that he could, or wanted, to do. Gerald knew where he stood with the Kinsmen now, was aware that if he didn't straighten out, his days would be as numbered as the hairs upon his head. Edmund was in no hurry to see that day arrive. In fact, he dreaded its coming.

Edmund been told that he was too good-hearted, had heard it a hundred times, from his daddy as well as from his fellow Kinsmen, and not just in Chicago, but around the nation as well. He'd allow one of his men to fuck up a hundred times if he thought there was a real chance that the man would someday straighten himself out and turn into a good, solid warrior. Perhaps Gerald would learn from his mistakes, would see the error of his ways, and would change them. Edmund surely hoped that he would; he liked the boy, and had no real desire to kill him.

The printer shut down, all the copies printed out. Edmund was getting ready to type in a command when the phone rang, startling him. In his experience, late-night calls never bore good news. This one was to prove no different. Edmund listened as a solemn voice that was filled with outrage informed him that a bunch of West Side niggers had set a white man afire.

CHAPTER

12

As he pulled to the curb in front of the police station in the unmarked police unit, Ellis Turner said to homicide detective Marshall Del Greco, "Can you believe that Africaan?"

"What'd he do now?"

Turner had been busy this morning, assisting the officers assigned to the burning death of the man last night, and being debriefed by his superiors on his report of last night's lecture. His answers to his inquisitors had been curt and sometimes angry; Turner hadn't liked their attitudes, they'd acted as if he'd gone to the mosque through choice, rather than order.

Del Greco had used the time alone to set up the interview that they were now on their way to conduct. It was just around lunchtime, and Turner had been lost in thought about the things he'd heard at Africaan's speech ever since he'd driven the car out of the lot down at Headquarters. Del Greco seemed lost in thought himself, and comfortable—as always—with Turner's silence.

Turner grimaced as he got out of the vehicle, as the heat slapped him hard, wrapped itself around him from the top of his head of close-cropped, receding hair to the soles of his highly polished shoes. He would have liked to have a talk with whoever had cut the order stating that homicide detectives had to wear jackets and ties whenever they were on duty, even in ungodly, sweltering weather.

Del Greco had waited on the sidewalk for Turner to come around, and now he said, "What was that about Africaan?"

"Man, you take a weekend off, you take a weekend *off.*" Del Greco shrugged, turned, and entered the building, and once they were inside, it was too noisy, crowded and hot to discuss the events that had occurred in the city over the weekend.

"You mind if we use interview room thirteen?" It was a small and unnecessary courtesy which Marshall Del Greco extended, and the desk sergeant recognized it as such, and appreciated the gesture. The reality was that homicide detectives could commandeer any unused interview room, in any district, in any police station throughout the city of Chicago, as long as they were in the course of an active murder investigation. Del Greco had in fact already staked one out for his appointment: an attorney-prisoner visiting room in the back of the building, just behind the prisoner lockup. He had come out front again to await the arrival of his interviewee, and to inform the desk sergeant in a kindly manner that the interview room was off-limits.

The desk sergeant, who had enough to worry about without having to sweat a couple of downtown homicide glamor boys on one of the hottest days in Chicago's history, which by itself had already caused the crime rate to go through the roof—on top of which he had to deal with the fact that every black criminal in the district was pretending to be up in arms over all that had happened over the weekend, and who were now claiming that their arrests were political, merely nodded his head, too busy behind his desk to pay them much attention; having checked Del Greco's identification, as well as that of his partner, Ellis Turner, he now returned to his work, putting them out of his mind.

Turner, uncomfortable in the heat of the non-air-conditioned room, looked over at Marshall, shaking his head in regard to his partner's decision to interview the kid in here, out of all the places they had at their disposal. Then again, it shouldn't have surprised him, as the inner workings of Del Greco's complex brain never ceased to give Ellis Turner a kick. Ellis had once told Claudette that this white man's mind was deeper than a whirlpool in the ocean, and just as active. The ocean analogy was pertinent, Ellis thought, because, being as close as he was to Del Greco, he was uniquely able to sense—and, on rare occasions, witness—the dangerous undercurrent that churned beneath that outer cool, under the seemingly unemotional exterior. Del Greco's mood seemed almost cheerful today. Turner hoped that Del Greco's weekend had gone better than his own.

Del Greco turned away from the desk and looked around the room, biting his lips, lost in thought, nodding in approval of his decision as Turner stood at his side.

Around them, more than two dozen people were congregated—willfully or otherwise—in the station. Some prisoners were staring sullenly, others were speaking in loud voices as they argued with their lawyers or with the arresting officers; some were shouting into each others' faces; a pimp yelled into the mouthpiece of a cellular phone; someone screamed at someone else in anger; there was a cry of inner pain. Three men were handcuffed to iron rings that had been drilled into the concrete wall, and they stood there almost casually, smoking with their free hands, glowering menacingly at anyone who was unfortunate enough to catch their eye. Other prisoners stood in place against the walls, out of the way, handcuffed behind their backs, unlucky enough to have been arrested later in the morning than the three who were chained to the wall; handcuffed as they were, they were not allowed to smoke, and just stood in place where the arresting officers had shouted for them to stay.

The heat magnified everything—even the prisoners' fear—and the noise never let up; the screaming, the shouting, the crying. Police officers, in uniform and street clothing, made their way through this maze as quickly as they could, trying to look off into the middle distance, their eyes scanning the crowd, meeting the eyes of no one else, hoping they could get through the sweaty crowd without being stopped, without having to be accountable to strangers who saw them all as being the same. Those officers interviewing witnesses or complainants would identify and then hurry over to the party they were in the lobby to collect, and they would get them away from the mass of humanity just as quickly as they could.

This was the first, precipitous step into the criminal justice system, and it wasn't a good thing for law-abiding civilians to observe for very long; those who do—who get to see it up close, as it really is—generally lose all faith in it.

The lobby of any urban police station is never a place of harmony, but even by general standards, this district was a madhouse. It was one of the oldest stations in the city, in the area that had the highest rate of violent crime, which was a short, logical step to its being the district with the highest murder rate. The lockup here was the most dangerous in Chicago.

Del Greco hadn't by any means chosen the place accidentally; he had given the matter much thought.

A bleeding woman was holding a handkerchief to her face as she sat on the single, long, wooden bench that was bolted to the floor, against the filthy wall, directly in front of the two detectives. The first time Ellis Turner had seen such a bench, his first thought had been of a church pew. He'd soon understood that if any supernatural force was at work in a police station, it was of the satanic variety, rather than that of any god. A female officer was trying to calm the woman, was trying to talk her into going to the emergency room over at Mercy. Turner heard the battered woman shout something loudly in Spanish. He turned his head and looked over at her, saw the open wound under the blackened eye, the heavy face covered with sweat and blood. She waved the handkerchief around in front of her face to emphasize her words. Their eyes met, and Turner caught a glimpse of her hatred and torment. Wishing to spare her, he looked away.

Turner leaned on the counter and observed his partner closely, sizing him up, as Del Greco pushed past two handcuffed drug dealers dressed in identical Michael Jordan jerseys, top and bottom, the clothing over-sized, the mesh hanging off of reed-thin, teenaged bodies. They wore three-hundred-dollar gym shoes on their sockless feet, the shoestrings tied and hung to the left. The jerseys were red, with black numbers. When the Bulls wore them, it meant they were playing an away game. When these kids wore them, it signified gang affiliation. The arresting officer had removed their baseball caps from their heads, and their hair was matted down and dirty. Turner could smell it in the heat, in the confined quarters. Turner looked hard at the two handcuffed children, and they glared right back at him, completely unafraid, and he had to fight to control a sudden urge to slap some sense into both of them.

This was not his district, and these were not his drug dealers. Still, he chafed at the sight of two fifteen-year-old kids who had more money hanging around their necks in gold than Turner would earn this month. Jail, to them, was a necessary part of doing business; the fact that they'd have to give up chunks of their lives to prison had long been understood as being further proof of the white man's oppression.

The events of the weekend just past hadn't done anything to change their minds.

Turner again looked over at Del Greco, who was now standing on the far side of the entry door, in front of a large standing fan, his wavy hair blowing in the false breeze, looking almost peacefully through the large, oblong double windows that had small, thin, round bars embedded within the glass. Steel bars, molded into glass, in a building where the doors were never locked. Now, why was that? Turner was puzzled. The doors were never propped open, either, by General Order; if they were, somebody could quite possibly toss a Molotov cocktail inside.

Turner smiled as he figured out the reason for the bars. They'd stop a bottle filled with gasoline, too.

Del Greco was a puzzle, too. A living puzzle with a million different solutions. Just when you thought you had him figured out, he threw a new angle at you, and kept you guessing. Bright, articulate, strong, hand-some and tall. With white teeth and all of his hair. Just the sort of white man that Turner generally resented. Turner might have done so, too, if he hadn't gotten to know him. It had taken most of a year before Turner had decided that the man wasn't racist, he just wasn't much of a talker.

Marshall Del Greco rarely wasted his words, particularly when in the presence of his fellow police officers, and when he did speak, his words were thoughtful, and his tone carried weight. He generally wasn't the sort of man to kid or to joke around; when he said or did something, he had reason. Watching Del Greco do his work was like watching a chess match when you didn't know the first thing about any of the rules of the game. Something about him was strange and fascinating, and made you want to learn more. But, unlike a chess game, that fascination never changed, not even when you got to know him. Knowledge of him only made Del Greco seem more confusing, and interesting. Made you respect him, too, seeing him do his thing, watching the enthusiasm he brought to figuring out who'd killed whom, and why.

Turner could kid Del Greco and get away with it; he'd never taken any shit from any white man on the department, and he never intended to, either. From almost the beginning of their relationship Turner had been cautiously disrespectful, but only after having done enough work with the man to have earned Del Greco's respect. After the first year or so, Del Greco had begun to sometimes even kid him back; he would say something witty in his laid-back manner, understated and smart, generally something that had to be thought about for a time before the entire point of what he had said could be clearly understood.

Turner and Del Greco took turns entertaining one another in their respective homes during the holiday season, their wives were friendly, and, two or three times a year, they would all get dolled up and go out and paint the town. Yet it still wasn't what Turner would call a close relationship. He was aware that he was as close to Del Greco as any man would ever be. Thoughtful, quiet, his mind always in overdrive, Del Greco was the sort who allowed his actions to speak for him. Not much of a party animal. Which was all right with Turner; neither was he.

Still, with all his flaws and quirks, Ellis had never seen anyone in the department work a homicide suspect the way Marshall Del Greco did; suddenly the thoughtful, charismatic silence disappeared, and he was schmoozing, coddling, *identifying* with suspects. Sometimes sympathizing with stone-cold killers until he extracted a confession, got it written up and signed. Other times he would glare at them coldly, speak in dangerous tones, scaring the shit out of them and having them literally begging to tell him all they knew. How to play a specific suspect was Del Greco's call, and his particular genius. Turner could never understand how he knew which approach to take with what suspect.

But more often than not he got the confession, and after he did, the cold mask of indifference went back on, and Del Greco was once more a sphinx, turning his back on his suspect until their paths met later on. The outgoing charm was gone, too, until the court date. Juries loved Del

Greco; he could turn his charm on and off with the same unthinking ease he'd use to turn the water on and off in the bathroom sink.

And he was doing it now, Turner watched it happen, saw Del Greco's deadpan gaze curve first into a shark's meaningless smile, then into a smile of warm welcome as the cocky white kid they'd arranged to meet here pushed the door open, stuck his head inside, and looked around. Graciously, Del Greco opened the door widely, and the kid swaggered inside.

The kid was wearing a tight, white T-shirt with a pocket. The top inch of a pack of Marlboros was sticking up out of the pocket. He was wearing designer blue jeans. His moussed hair was thick and long. For a tough guy, though, he didn't seem to have a lot of muscle tone, and he had already acquired the beginnings of a beer belly. Over the years, Turner and Del Greco had run across many kids like this one.

Turner watched Del Greco say something—probably thanking him for coming—still smiling warmly now at the young man, and then Turner watched the smile freeze stiff, then drop, replaced by a look of surprise as an attorney they both knew quite well walked in behind the white kid, smiling sardonically at Del Greco, telling him without saying a word that Del Greco wasn't kidding anybody by picking the most vicious police station in the city as the place to interview his client.

The kid strutted in and stood in front of Del Greco, then looked around, and lost some of his swagger. The attorney stopped, put his hand on the kid's shoulder protectively. The kid looked up at his lawyer, imploringly. Del Greco had composed himself. Turner pushed off the counter and walked toward them.

In a loud, booming voice, the lawyer pronounced, "You're making a big mistake, Del Greco."

In the seven years they'd been partners, Turner had yet to see that happen.

The kid said, "I don't want to do this anymore; let's go." The lawyer patted his arm in a gesture of paternal affection.

"As long as we're here, let's see what they think they have." Then, to Del Greco, the lawyer said, "I'm going to see that you regret this."

Watching all this, seeing the kid's fear, the lawyer's self-righteousness, and Del Greco's sudden, apologetic solicitousness, Turner thought to himself, One of you will, asshole.

CHAPTER

13

Mark Conroy, eighteen years of age, lost his composure and began to shake as he followed the big detective down the long corridor, past the rows of filthy, barred cells. Mr. Volpe's stubby hand on his shoulder was not having a calming influence. Mark was known far and wide throughout his predominantly white, East Side neighborhood as one of the toughest kids around, good with his hands and quick to anger, especially when he had a couple of Budweisers under his belt. All of a sudden, though, he wasn't feeling very tough. In fact, he was very afraid. He thought that he, Mr. Volpe, and the big cop in front of them might be the only white people in the entire building; everyone else was black or Hispanic. Mark had never known, and therefore had always feared—and hated—members of other races.

All the way over in the car, they'd talked. Mr. Volpe telling him in a calm voice what to say, how to act, told him to make sure that Mark always looked at Mr. Volpe before he answered any questions that might be posed to him by the detectives.

But Mr. Volpe hadn't told Mark that they'd be inside a place like *this*.

Maybe he'd never been here before. Maybe, to Mr. Volpe, this was just another police station. To Mark, who had been inside a police station or two in his eighteen years, this wasn't just another police station. This was hell, is what it was; Mark thought this and immediately began to feel the heat emanating from the white-hot flames, licking at the back of his legs as he followed the big copper down the hallway, past the cells.

Volpe said, "Is this really necessary, Detective," in an ironic voice directed at the big guy, Del Greco, who was slowly leading the way, and the detective seemed to welcome the chance to stop dead in his tracks and—still slowly—turn to face the lawyer. He raised his eyebrows in pleasant inquiry. Mark, who now had locked, overcrowded cells on either side of him in the filthy, narrow corridor, had no choice but to stop. It was that or step into the chest of the stone wall that was Del Greco.

"I beg your pardon, Counselor?" The detective stood there, calmly waiting, looking down at the short, fat, balding, middle-aged lawyer, who was wearing a cheap suit that had sweatstains under the armpits and around the beltline.

Mark looked back at his attorney, trying to appear unafraid as he did his best to avoid the appraising looks of the men who were locked inside the cells. The corridor stunk of stale sweat, blood, urine, feces, and fear. Some of that fear was Mark's, but even Mr. Volpe now seemed scared. The noise in here was even worse than it had been in the lobby. Mark thought that if this didn't go right, if Mr. Volpe had been wrong, Mark would be the one locked up in one of those cells, not Mr. Volpe.

How many clients did Mr. Volpe have? A lot, he'd bet. Mark wouldn't be the most important of them, his parents did not have a lot of money. Did Mr. Volpe even care about him? Jesus Christ, he hadn't killed anyone, he was really just a *witness!*

"PUT THAT BITCH IN *HE-AH!*" Mark jumped at the voice that seemed to shout directly into his ear. He looked past his lawyer, saw the shorter, more muscular, black detective—Turner—smiling at him and nodding encouragingly, as if he just couldn't *wait* to put Mark in the cell with that raging fucking maniac. Mark heard the derisive laughter of the other prisoners, felt himself blush. He saw the uncertainty on Mr. Volpe's face, and for the first time since this all had started, Mark began to panic. This was real life; life and death. He wasn't here for fighting, or on a charge of drunk and disorderly. Somebody had died, and these cops wanted to pin it on *him.*

Mr. Volpe must have been feeling some of Mark's panic, because he said, "This isn't necessary! This is duress, you're trying to intimidate my client!" Mark, watching and listening carefully, heard the suggestion of unease in Mr. Volpe's whining tone, and he stood staring at his lawyer, his mouth open wide.

"Let that bitch come on in here; *I'll* intimidate her ass!"

There was general laughter and shouts of encouragement and agreement among the men in the cells, but Del Greco didn't seem to have heard a word that had been spoken. He was similarly ignoring the hate-filled curses that were directed toward him and his partner; the hands reaching through bars, trying to get at them; the complaints as the prisoners shouted for food, for phone calls, for cigarettes; for their right to immediate visitation with their court-appointed attorneys. To Mark, it seemed like feeding time at the monkey cage at the zoo. But to the cop, to Del Greco, it didn't seem to be even happening. The guy just stood there, silently, a half-smile breaking the lower part of his face in half. Mark thought that the smile looked like a jagged crack in pottery; the mirthless grin of a jack o'lantern.

"Mark, don't you pay attention to a word those animals are saying. We're leaving here, right now."

"You try and leave," Turner said, "and I'll toss his ass into one of these cells with *those animals*. Charge him with accountability, for starters. For all we know, he was an accessory before, during, and *after* the murder." The men in the cells seemed to love this, chanting what they did to white bitches who were "accessories."

Mark could see that the cops' holsters were empty; they'd had to lock their guns up before coming back into this area. Del Greco's police star was hanging from the side of his belt, silver and shiny. A long way off down the hall, he could see an obese man in a blue uniform, sitting in a chair, reading a magazine. There was a little table next to the lockup screw's chair. His elbow rested next to an ashtray and a bottle of pop. Mr. Volpe impatiently waved his hand.

"Let's go. I want to hear what you have. And we'll see what a judge has to say about your techniques at a later time." Mr. Volpe's brusqueness didn't do anything for Mark's state of mind, as even Mark could tell that he was merely choosing the lesser of two evils—trying to get his client into an interview room, away from these screaming, bloodthirsty prisoners. Del Greco took his time, turning around slowly, continuing to ignore the shouting, cursing prisoners as if they weren't even there. Mark had seen Turner's look of impatience, had seen Mr. Volpe's look of distaste and fear—hell, he'd even heard the quiver of fear in his lawyer's voice— and he knew exactly how terrified he himself was inside. But this Del Greco guy seemed as calm as he'd be if he were walking into his church.

Silently, following the scary son of a bitch down the hall, Mark began to pray.

Mark felt a gob of spit splatter against his arm, and he leaped, emitting a small shriek of terror. He saw Volpe wince in surprise at the sound, felt Turner's hand on his back, steadying him and leading him on, as Mark wiped the spit off with his T-shirt. The men hooted and howled at the sight of his flesh, and Mark quickly lowered his shirt. The black cop said something to the prisoner, which was laughed off by the man in the cell.

But Del Greco didn't even flinch, just kept walking, slowly, still taking his time, strutting sluggishly down a red-concrete-floor corridor in hell, a corridor which, to Mark, seemed neverending.

A MATTER OF HONOR

*   *   *

The young man wearing the bright red warm-up outfit stood on the corner outside the restaurant, as if waiting for a bus. He was sweating profusely, but he wasn't worried; everyone else around him was sweating just as heavily. His name was Rashon Latribe, and he had recently turned eighteen. Rashon looked around the busy lunchtime street casually, then just as casually checked his watch. He looked behind him, lifting his hand to his head as he did so, as if inspecting the set of his baseball cap in the restaurant's plate glass window. He saw his prey inside the place, eating her lunch at the long, curved counter, laughing it up with one of her girlfriends.

She wouldn't be laughing for very long.

"Charge him or we're walking out of here, right now," Volpe said indignantly, and Turner looked over at Marshall Del Greco, wondering how he would play the string out. Del Greco was ignoring the lawyer, was staring with laserlike intensity at the kid, at Mark Conroy. They'd left the door to the interview room open wide so that the din of the caged prisoners could reach them in all its fury.

Volpe's own fury seemed to be lost on Del Greco. For that matter, it was lost on Turner, who said, "You want a cigarette, Mark? Go ahead, light one up. Once you're locked down in a cell, there's no smoking allowed. What with all those men crammed in there, it'd be like smoking in a coffin. Cramped as it is, somebody'd suffocate."

The lawyer said, "You're not putting him in any cell! Goddamnit, this is against procedure! You work downtown, and the murder you want to discuss occurred on the Southeast Side. There's no reason for us to be in some West Side station."

"Then why'd you agree to the interview?" Turner's voice was conversational; he knew that his partner needed some time to let his stare do its thing. Del Greco's eyes never left Mark's, and the kid seemed as mesmerized as a mongoose spellbound by the swaying of a fully hooded cobra.

"Where's the assistant state's attorney? Where's the court reporter?"

Turner decided to play with the man. In an accusatory, joking tone, he said, "Mr. Volpe, Mr. Volpe, Mr. Volpe." He shook his finger at the lawyer. "You been watching too many reruns of *Murder One,* haven't you?"

"Goddamnit, don't you take that tone—"

"You want an assistant state's attorney in here? Do you *really?*" Turner asked. He looked pointedly at Mark. "We got to call them in, by statute, *only* when we're charging someone with a felony." His tone was accusatory, and he looked back at Volpe with contempt. Turner sensed that Mark Conroy was doing much the same thing. He looked back at the kid,

75

and had to stifle a smile when he saw the look of betrayal on Mark's face. Ellis turned back to the attorney.

"As for the court reporter, sir, you want one in here, you know how it works: you have to provide for your own." Volpe looked at Conroy, as if sizing him up, wondering if his parents had the wherewithal to reimburse him for the expense.

Turner said, "We just want to talk to your client, ask him a few questions, that's all. This is an interview, not an interrogation." Turner once again looked over at his partner and the kid. Del Greco didn't seem to know or care that Turner and Volpe were in the room, he just sat there, looking at Conroy, as if feeling pity for him now because his lawyer was selling him out.

Del Greco shifted his gaze, ever so slightly, toward the door. Mark lighted a cigarette with a shaky hand and used the opportunity to peek quickly over toward the door himself—just a quick shot, checking it out. Conroy was already grossly aware of what was out there, he was constantly hearing it. Turner watched as the young kid shivered.

"Hey, hey! Del Greco!" Volpe put his hands on the table and leaned over as far as he could, between his client and the detective, purposely breaking their eye contact. Del Greco didn't seem at all upset at the interruption. Turner saw the relief that passed over Mark's face. He saw the redness of Mark's cheeks, the wetness in his eyes, saw the trembling in the kid's fingers, the quiver in his lower lip. Turner knew Del Greco had him. His kickass partner Del Greco, who was looking up at Volpe now, his expression changed, once again seeming eager to appease the lawyer.

"You mind if I ask him a few questions, Mr. Volpe?"

"Off the record?"

"My partner just explained to you, there *is* no record yet. I do have to read him his rights, though. Of course you understand that."

"No, I *don't* understand that." Staring at Del Greco, Volpe said, "Come on, Mark, we're leaving."

Del Greco immediately turned to the kid, and said, "Do you really want to do that, Mark? It's entirely up to you. Stay or leave, it's your decision; you can do whatever you please. But I feel the—responsibility—to ask you . . ." Del Greco looked pointedly at the lawyer. ". . . in light of all you've seen and heard today, do you really want to do that?"

"Mark, don't answer that."

"You see this place, Mark? You hear what's going on out there, what they said to you when we were coming in?" Del Greco's tone was benevolent, filled with understanding. He said, "The Cook County jail makes this place look like Mr. Roger's Neighborhood."

"That's a threat."

"It's a statement of fact."

A MATTER OF HONOR

"Don't pay any attention to him, Mark!"

Mark *was* paying attention, however, strict and undiluted attention, hanging on every word that came out of Del Greco's mouth. Turner saw the kid staring at Del Greco in the same way preachers stare at sculptured images of the crucified Jesus on the cross. Del Greco had barely spoken a hundred words, but Mark seemed aware that the detective was his single chance at salvation.

Volpe said, "I want an assistant state's attorney down here, right now! Charge him, or we're leaving."

"Is that right? Do you want us to charge you? Are you leaving, Mark?" Del Greco said, in his calm, soft, indulgent tone, and the kid didn't hesitate, he looked straight at Del Greco, spread his hands, and made an appeal to the father he'd more than likely never had.

"I never seen anything like it. I mean, I ain't never been involved in anything like *this* before," Mark said, in a quaking, little-boy's voice.

Del Greco held up a hand. "I know that; we've checked. It's why we wanted to talk to you. First, though, before we can talk, Mark, I have to tell you that you have the right to remain silent, that anything you say can and will be used against you in a court of law . . ."

CHAPTER

14

Rashon saw the work car turn the corner, saw the inquisitive looks on the faces of the two men in the back seat. He shook his head once, quickly and sharply, as if bothered by a fly he didn't want to trouble himself with swatting. The car would have to go around the block at least one more time. Maybe even more than that. The girls inside the restaurant didn't seem to be in any big hurry.

Which surprised Rashon: white girls always seemed to be in a hurry. Black chicks, now, they always seemed to have all the time in the world. At least the black chicks Rashon knew, and he knew more than a few of them. But he knew them in a neighborhood that was further removed from this one than any map could detail. Just about a mile west of here, but an entire planet away, when you thought about it. This was down-town, and downtown made Rashon extremely uncomfortable. So uncomfortable, in fact, that Rashon never even ventured into this area unless there was money to be made. And he didn't mean the kind of chump change that was pulled in by some of his homeboys who came down here and shined the white man's shoes, then intimidated the white man into paying more than he'd been told. Or the brothers who robbed boxes of candy out of stores, then tried to peddle it on the street, claiming the money went toward new baseball uniforms for their impoverished high school team. Rashon would never even have gotten out of bed if all he could have made was the kind of money picked up by beggars, wind-shield washers, *StreetWise* newspapers vendors, or even by the hustlers who snatched gold chains from around peoples' necks, then had the clasps repaired at one of the dozens of downtown stores that specialized in doing just that, then tried to sell the chains at "wholesale" prices on either side of the Michigan Avenue bridge.

No, Rashon had no truck for such people, nor for the small-time cash they were able to hustle on the downtown part of the city's broad and sometimes generous sidewalks. Today, there was real money to be made, and so Rashon suppressed his fear of the downtown area.

It was something Rashon was good at, hiding his fear. He had been doing it for as long as he could remember, and it came so naturally to him by now that the fear was nothing more than a slight tingle at the base of his spine, easily ignored, and never given in to. Rashon had first learned how to disengage his fear at home, with his mother, when she'd be yelling and screaming at him or one of his sisters; then later, with the bullies at school; always with the police; with the gangbangers who had first recruited him; and then with the killers he'd had to back down if he was going to earn respect. There was only one way to back a killer down, and doing what he'd had to do had put Rashon smack in their league . . .

A siren sounded at the curb right in front of him, and Rashon started, wishing he hadn't worn such obvious gang colors into this part of the city. He looked briefly at the squad car, then quickly looked away, relieved; the police weren't hassling him, he had used the siren so he wouldn't have to take his fat ass out of the squad car in this heat wave. He was just signaling to some white dickhead inside a silver Porsche parked at the bus stop in front of the restaurant that he had to move on. Rashon watched, surprised. The young white dickhead in the Porsche tapped at his rearview mirror, then tilted his head so he could get himself a better view of the squad car.

In Rashon's neighborhood, such behavior would get you your ass kicked, quick. He guessed that down here, everything was different, and that didn't come as a major surprise. Rashon had suspected for as long as he'd been alive that the white man got preferential treatment from the Man.

He angrily checked the restaurant again, relieved now that the girls at the counter were taking their sweet time. He heard the police's amplified and angry voice coming over the squad car's loud speaker; the man was still determined not to get out of the vehicle unless he had to.

"Are you promising my client that he won't have to testify in court?" Volpe was anxiously trying to save face; Turner was trying not to smile at the man's futile attempt.

"I'm saying if he's truthful with us, he might not have to be locked down, we can get the prosecutor in here, talk about the possibility of granting Mark immunity. And if we can't get them to go for that, we can do what we can, try and talk them into granting your client probation, if he pleads out. As long as Mark's completely honest with us, and we don't get any information that implicates him to a further degree." Turner spoke the words as if he believed them. He'd said "them" on purpose, trying to give Mark the impression that Turner and Del Greco were the only forces on earth that could protect him from all the lawyers and their legal, meaningless gamesmanship.

The room wasn't monitored, no court reporter was taking down his words. If it came down to whose word was to be believed by a sitting judge, Volpe's reputation would ensure that it would be Turner's. Volpe kept trying to speak to Del Greco, but it was Turner who answered the lawyer's questions.

Del Greco kept staring at Mark, appraisingly.

Volpe had lost control of his client, and he knew it. In an attempt to regain that control, he said, "Get an assistant state's attorney in here, right now. Get me a deal, in writing, and I'll speak with my client, see if he wants to talk with you."

"Sure," Turner said, then turned to Mark. "Let's go, son."

"Go where!" The kid's eyes widened, and he stared at Del Greco for guidance. Del Greco pursed his lips and looked away, shook his head; it was out of his hands.

"To the lockup while your attorney negotiates," Ellis said.

"NO!"

"You can't do this—!"

"Sure I can; it's the rules, check the manual, Counselor."

"Don't let them do this to me," Mark was begging Del Greco, not Volpe. The tension in the room was thick, the smell of terror in the air, filling their nostrils. The lawyer was glaring at Turner, who smiled calmly back.

"Come on," Turner's voice was deep and low, as he conveyed his sadness at being forced to do his duty.

"They can't do this!"

"I'm doing it," Turner said, and grabbed Mark's arm, lifted him half out of his chair before Del Greco softly asked him to let the boy go.

"Move the car; you're in a tow-zone!" The police's voice did not sound happy. Rashon felt the weight of the pistol in the waistband of his pants, felt the sweat that had formed around it. His frustration level was such that he considered waving it at the dickhead in the Porsche. Rashon watched as the police shook his head, opened the door of the squad car, and began to step out of the vehicle.

The Porsche started up with a loud, throaty rumble. The police stood glaring at it as Mr. Dickhead raced his engine. The engine's sound changed as the car was put into gear, and the Porsche began to pull away from the curb, and then it stopped, right in the middle of the street, teasing the fat police. The police stood with one foot out on the street, and the other still in the vehicle, holding onto the squad car's door, squinting at the vehicle, his expression growing livid.

The work car came around the corner again, and Rashon didn't even have to look at it this time; they'd have seen the police, and goddamnit it, the police had seen them . . .

Del Greco said, "It's not you we're after for the killing, Mark. We know you didn't kill anybody. You have a right to remain silent, and you did the right thing in bringing your lawyer in with you. Mr. Volpe's an excellent lawyer, he'll do right by you—"

"Don't try to blowjob me—"

Del Greco continued as if Volpe hadn't spoken.

"—but you have to remember, it's not *him* who witnessed a murder, it was you." Mark was nodding his head rapidly, seeing a way out for himself, a way that went completely against everything he'd ever believed in, for his entire life, right up until the last twenty minutes. The last twenty minutes had changed every aspect of Mark's belief system.

"We know you were there, we have a witness to the entire thing. What you have to understand is, we don't *need* you, Mark, we *know* who did it. All we need is corroboration from you, and if you tell us what you saw, even if you—say—just drove the car—" Mark started at this, and Del Greco nodded wisely as he continued.

"—we might be able to help you out. Depending on how cooperative you are, we can hopefully cut a deal with you before somebody else cuts one, in which case, you go to the County and spend two to three years awaiting trial."

Mark heard the vicious cries coming to him from out in the cells, from out in Mr. Roger's Neighborhood.

"Talk to me, Mark, in front of your lawyer. He knows what he's doing, and after you talk, he'll look out for your best interests. I'm just asking you to tell me what I already know, who the shooter was. I'm not trying to make any first-degree murder case against you."

"I didn't kill anyone."

"We know that already." Del Greco's voice was that of a priest absolving a penitent. "Tell me who did."

"It was Donny Helmner, he did it. Shot Bird down over a bad pitch in a fucking baseball game."

Volpe's voice was tight when he said, "One more word out of you, Mark, and I walk out of here."

Mark turned to him, stunned by the statement, his mouth open to pro-

81

test. Out in the corridor, as if on cue, someone started hollering—with great vigor—that the white man was the fucking devil, and every one of them had to be burned alive. Turner wondered if Mark Conroy was aware of Minister Africaan's statements of the night before. He wondered if Mark Conroy had any idea that Minister Africaan even existed.

Mark looked briefly toward the hallway, then back to his lawyer, and said, "I ain't going anywhere. Why don't you go ahead and leave, Mr. Volpe?" He had a coconspirator's look on his face as he turned to Del Greco and said, "I really think we can work everything out."

Ellis Turner slowly turned to face the lawyer, his broad smile conveying all that there was to say.

Rashon watched the police checking his boys out, looking at the driver in the front seat, then looking at Rashon's two boys in the back. The work car had to stop and wait as the Porsche idled in the street, Mr. Dickhead revving his engine, taunting the police just for the fun of it, rather than driving off the way he should have. Rashon saw the look on the police's face as he noticed that the work car's rear license plate was partially rolled up; as he noticed the mud that was smeared on what was visible of the license plate numbers, mud there even though it hadn't rained in weeks. Rashon saw the police mumble to himself as he tried to memorize the car's plate number, repeating it to himself over and over, as if the car wasn't right there in front of his dumb, ofay ass. Rashon cursed as the police sat his fat ass back inside his vehicle, and reached for the microphone of his radio.

Rashon was about to blow off the entire deal, was ready to turn and walk away, even though he knew that doing so would incur the wrath of King Youngy, when Mr. Dickhead in the Porsche revved the RPMs all the way up, and the police looked over at him, surprised at Mr. Dickhead's audacity. Rashon saw Mr. Dickhead's eyes in the still oddly tilted rearview mirror, saw the hand come up slowly, saw the middle finger shoot out, then saw the hand drop quickly—no doubt to the gear shift— as the Porsche pulled away down Dearborn with a squeal of tires and a burst of power.

The police, thank God, got all kinds of pissed off. He waved angrily at Rashon's boys to back up, and they did, giving the police plenty of room to clear the curb and give chase. As soon as the police was gone, Rashon waved for his boys to take the vacated curb space in front of the bus stop sign. He turned, looked into the restaurant, and the One Great Black Jesus was smiling down on Rashon once again; the two bitches at the lunch counter were just paying their bill, were getting ready to leave.

CHAPTER

15

"**Y**ou ought to be ashamed of yourself," Ellis Turner said, as he drove as quickly as the lunchtime traffic would allow up Jackson, heading back to police headquarters to inform their boss that their original information had been solid. Now all they had to do was to pick up the killer, and get an assistant state's attorney's approval for a charge of felony murder. An independent witness, along with the sworn statement of the driver, should be enough to get them that approval. It should also get them a warrant for a search of the suspect's premises. Considering the level of intellect they were dealing with here, it wasn't out of the realm of possibility that Helmner had hung onto the weapon.

Still, in Cook County, with elections eight months away, you never knew if you'd receive felony approval from the state's attorney; conviction rates had to remain very high, approval was never given on the cases that were thought to be marginal.

"What'd I do?" Del Greco said, looking out the windshield, as if deep in thought. The radio was turned down low; there wasn't much chance that their unit would get a call, but they weren't transporting a prisoner, and the rules were the rules. Turner sucked in on his cigarette. Del Greco didn't care about secondhand smoke; he had quit smoking five years ago, claiming that his wife, then a medical student, did not appreciate the habit. It was the only time in their seven years of working together that Turner had ever seen Del Greco bend to somebody else's will.

"Do? That poor white boy's sitting in the cell, crying like a baby over the way you betrayed him."

"Betrayed him? Did I say one word about cutting him loose? We had his lawyer there listening to everything we said." Del Greco paused, thinking, a slight smile playing on his lips.

"Surprised you, didn't it? Volpe showing up. I saw the look on your face when you spotted him."

Del Greco smiled at the windshield as Turner stopped at a red light. He turned to his partner, confused, and said, "You weren't expecting him, right?"

"Volpe? Not him, particularly. But I was sure Mark would bring a lawyer. You think about it, it's a good thing it was Volpe. A smarter lawyer, one with less of an ego, would have agreed with Mark and walked out of the place as soon as he figured out what was going on."

"But you acted surprised . . ."

"It made Volpe think he had the edge. Momentarily, anyway. And that was all we needed."

"You son of a bitch." Turner shook his head and smiled as a horn blared behind him. He had to sit waiting with the green light as six or seven cars ran through the red light. When the intersection was clear, he began to drive away, glancing briefly at his rearview mirror. "Definition of a nanosecond: the amount of time between a light turning green and some asshole blowing his horn at you."

"Watch it!"

A silver Porsche had come out of nowhere, was roaring toward them from the opposite direction, with a squad car in pursuit. It had switched into their lane to pass a cab, but now got back into its own lane and raced through the intersection that Turner had just passed through.

"He think he's gonna outrun the radio?" Turner shook his head at the driver's stupidity.

"Broad daylight—lunchtime—on a Monday afternoon." Del Greco seemed angry at the Porsche's driver, and Turner was glad to see it. He was always glad to have proof that Del Greco actually had feelings.

He said, "Wait a minute, let me get this straight; you knew the lawyer was coming, and you still set it up for—"

"Ellis, come on. Of course it was intimidation. I had to shake the kid up, and you did a better job of it than I did. I didn't miss all that fancy footwork you were using on Volpe, while Mark and I were—exchanging psychic energy. Once Volpe came through the door, though, I knew we had him."

"Why?"

"Because any lawyer with half a brain would have seen what I was doing, and would not have allowed his client to step foot in that place. Hell, even *Mark* was smart enough to want to get out of there, and Volpe talked him into staying—*after* he thought I was petrified with fear due to his presence. What's he going to do now, cry that his client didn't have a chance to consult with his attorney? He gave us a statement right in front of the man."

"Then was hanging on his pantleg, begging, when the assistant state's attorney charged him with obstruction of justice *and* accountability."

"You should have been a lawyer, Ellis. You predicted both charges before the state's attorney's office."

"What else was left? Couldn't charge him with the murder."

Del Greco said, "Volpe—no lawyer—would purposely disclose his own incompetence. He came in there thinking he was dealing with stupid, lowlife, incompetent homicide bulls. You heard him yourself, when Mark wanted to leave? 'No, let's see what they think they've got.' Even Mark had more legal sense."

"You saying Volpe's ego'll stop him from filing against us."

"Stop him from filing *what* against us? What's he going to claim? That he's incompetent counsel? Mark might use that argument down the road, to overturn his conviction . . ."

"And you walked him right into it."

"His superiority complex—and you—walked him right into it. I concentrated on Mark."

"The hell you did; you didn't miss a trick." There was more than a hint of concern in Turner's voice as he said, "What the hell is *this* now?"

A big, older, blue Buick was racing toward them, had just run the red light up the block. "Is this the Indianapolis Five Hundred today, or what?" Turner said.

Del Greco watched the Buick intently as the car raced toward them, then he turned in his seat to watch it pass by.

"Two male blacks in front, two in back."

"Front license plate was smudged."

"Rear one was half curled up, looked like it was smeared with mud, too."

Ellis said, "Bullshit, that's a work car. When was the last time it rained, three weeks ago? You get the number?"

Before Del Greco could answer, the dispatcher called all units to a report of shots fired, possible gang-related shooting, one white female down.

"All right, do me a favor, just wait over here until the other officers arrive, all right?" Judging by the sounds of the approaching sirens, it wouldn't take long for that to happen. Turner was trying to listen to the witnesses and at the same time keep the crowd away from the body until other units responded, and the crime scene could be secured. Then he and Del Greco could take off. They had been the first unit on the scene, but it would not be their case; other officers would investigate the shooting. And some of them would fight for the opportunity, as it looked as if it would be a hot media case. How often do you get a downtown, gang-related shooting? A young white girl, too, it looked like, one who was simply caught in the cross fire.

Turner knew what he looked like, the impression he made upon the public in his snazzy suit and his expensive tie, with his jacket open, the pistol hanging from his right side, his star clipped directly in front of the weapon. He held his arms out wide, his mere presence keeping people back.

This was downtown, and the crowd was for the most part made up of honest, hardworking business people. Turner's star would earn him respect in this part of the city. With the exception of the witnesses, whom Turner was keeping within his sight, the crowd had now mostly formed on the sidewalk across the street, pointing and staring, talking excitedly amongst themselves. Del Greco was trying to calm a hysterical woman who was having none of it; she was fighting him, yelling, screaming about her friend, how awful it all was.

Turner was already aware of how awful it all was. It got just this awful in Chicago three to five times a day when the weather was this hot.

"I heard him shout the gang name!" The overweight white guy who was giving Turner this information seemed surprised that it had happened the same way in real life as it had in movies he'd seen. That was one good thing about white people; they were far better witnesses than blacks, more willing to come forward and talk about everything they saw. In the neighborhoods that Turner generally worked, nobody ever saw anything. He understood it, he had behaved in precisely the same manner until he'd been accepted into the police academy, and discovered that life was never as simple as he'd once believed it to be.

Turner thought, with all these witnesses, that this case might turn out to be a slam-dunk, a career-booster for whatever team wound up catching it. Might not even be a homicide case, it would probably go to gang crimes, seeing as all these people were sharing stories with each other about hearing the gang's name shouted out before one punk started shooting at another, just as the girls were coming out of the restaurant.

Squad cars were screeching to a halt at the curb now, sirens dying down; flashers left on for effect; units left running so the insides of the cars would stay cool. A Hindu-looking guy who was probably the owner of the restaurant was staring with a frightened look on his face at a bullet hole in the restaurant's plate glass window. He was no doubt panic-stricken at the thought of losing all of his afternoon business. Turner thought the guy should relax, as he'd be the king of the city tomorrow, his restaurant filled with all the people who would want to hear the juicy details of an honest-to-God, gang-related killing in Chicago's safest neighborhood.

Uniformed officers were milling around now, one of them acting far more self-importantly than the situation demanded, telling the citizenry to get back, get *back*, goddamnit! Ellis wondered if this guy ever worked the South or West Sides. Shit, these white people were downright *courteous*, respectful, bending over backwards to be helpful, a policeman's dream . . .

Turner, surprise in his tone, said, "Del?" What the *hell* was the man doing now?

Del Greco looked as if he himself had been shot. Turner had a frame of reference for this; he'd seen Del Greco get shot before. White-faced, stricken, his mouth open, breathing heavily, Del Greco was sitting on the front seat of the police vehicle, half in, half out of the car, talking into the microphone of the vehicle's radio, staring off into space with a vacant, pained expression.

Turner watched him drop the mike, saw Del Greco open the glove compartment, put something inside, then take out the cellular phone, put it in his jacket pocket, then do the strangest thing Turner had ever seen this strange man do. Broiling hot as it was, he started running down the street, straight up Jackson, as if chasing the shooter himself, on foot, knowing where he was.

Turner walked over to the car, puzzled, leaned into the door that Del Greco hadn't bothered to close. He opened the glove compartment, and looked inside. Del Greco's beeper was in there, laying on top of a small pack of Kleenex.

"What the *fuck?!*" Ellis Turner said, and turned to look up Jackson, but Del Greco was nowhere in sight.

THE
HUNTING
BEGINS

CHAPTER

16

"**H**e left his beeper in the car?"

"He's not answering the cellular, either," Turner said. His sergeant looked up at him from her desk, as if she didn't believe what she was hearing.

"This is not like Del Greco." Cheryl Laney picked up her phone, dialed a number, waited, then said, "Hell." She glanced at her watch. "Rachel must still be at work." She hung up on the answering machine, and looked over at Turner with her eyebrows raised. "You remember the name of the hospital where Rachel works?" Turner did, but, not liking the sergeant's attitude, gave her a puzzled expression, as if he'd thought hard and drawn a blank. He shrugged, and shook his head.

"I *know* it, but it's slipped my mind."

"I know she's in the pediatric department . . . I think it's one of the Catholic hospitals."

It had been, but Rachel had changed her place of employment several months ago. Turner didn't share this information with Cheryl Laney, either. He merely said, "Want me to go down the list in the phone book, call around until I find her?"

"No." She paused. "I know Del Greco's tight with Rachel's family. What about the in-laws? You remember their last name?"

Laney's distrust was now apparent. Turner knew that Del Greco liked her, they were even rumored to have some sort of special, romantic thing going on between them, but Turner's personal jury was still deliberating, Turner wanting to look at all the evidence before coming to a conclusion about Laney. So once again, he pursed his lips, tried to look puzzled, and shook his head.

Laney said, "What do you think happened?"

"Pardon me?"

"What do you think made Marshall take off like that?"

"He called in sick, you said; maybe his tummy's upset."

Around them, several homicide officers were pretending they weren't listening, but the grunts at Turner's statement told both Turner and Laney they were. Turner wasn't surprised. Del Greco was a steady topic of conversation for them, of gossip at Tommy's Tap, following the change of shift. Del Greco rarely used the locker room, and he never went to the bars. To hear that Del Greco was acting in less than a robotic manner was something that most of these men were interested in knowing more about.

Laney said, "Look, Ellis, I know you want to protect your partner; I know that you're only giving me part of the story—"

"I told you what I know."

"Don't interrupt." Laney closed her eyes for a moment, trying to calm herself down. She opened them, and pinned Turner with a glare; a glare he answered with an expression of frank and explicit innocence. "I *hate* it when you guys interrupt me."

And Turner hated it when a superior officer—especially a superior officer who was younger than he was—treated him like a school kid. But he stood there innocently, like that school kid in the principal's office, pretending he didn't know what she was talking about.

"Let me ask you, do you think he recognized the corpse?"

"I wouldn't know. I told you, he didn't *say* anything to me, Sergeant." He knew that referring to her by her official rank irked Laney. Del Greco and most of the other detectives always referred to her by her first name; Ellis never did.

"Did he *look* sick? Did he *act* sick?"

"You know how such things come over you. One minute you're fine, the next, you're puking your guts out. He sure took off like he had to find an alley, quick. Or a bathroom."

Laney looked at him until she seemed to figure out that he wasn't going to be giving her anything that she couldn't get from any of the uniformed officers who'd been on the scene. Then she said, "Where are you with the killing down in Hegewisch, with"—she searched her memory—"that Jermolowicz murder?"

"Bird, they called him. Got killed over a beanball pitch in a baseball game in Mann Park. Looks like a winner, thanks to Del Greco. With all the people that generally hang out in that park, suddenly, after a shooting, no one was there. We got a list of the regular park punks; they told us it was too hot to go out. But Del Greco found a single witness willing to give up the shooter. He identified Donald Helmner, white male, twenty-six years old. Problem is, the witness's a stone junkie, with a record. And Helmner's one of the leaders of that bullshit white boy toy gang they got out there, which is why none of the other no-job-having, hanging-around-the-park-all-day-harassing-law-abiding-citizens punks from the hood is even admitting they were there when it happened. Helmner wouldn't say two words to us, except to go away, our witness was full of shit. He wouldn't let us in his house without a warrant, wouldn't even come in for an interview." Turner paused, then said, "Smart boy."

"And you couldn't get a warrant on the word of a junkie."

"We couldn't even come close. Del Greco figured this Helmner still might have the pistol, but he wasn't letting us in to look around. So Del Greco ran down the guy who drove Helmner away from the game. Kid named Mark Conroy. Trying to curry favor with the boss of the big, bad, gang, got him the hell out of there and took him home."

"You get statements from both?"

"Del Greco did." He saw Laney's look as she figured out what Turner was doing. He said, "He *also* wormed a signed confession out of Conroy—in the presence of his lawyer, Jackie Volpe—explaining the whole thing, saying that Helmner put the gun to his head, told him if he said a word to us, he was dead, the usual lies they tell you when they know you got them cold. I don't have to tell you the rest of it."

"You charge him?"

"Del Greco did; called the ASA, got her in there to listen to the statement. She nailed Conroy with two felony counts."

"And?"

"We—I—came back to find out if you think we should ask for first degree for Helmner. Both our witnesses claim he stewed and steamed for a while, after this Bird guy hit him with a pitch on purpose. Both said he had to go to his car to get the weapon, and then walk back about a block in the heat to shoot Bird."

Laney thought for a minute before she said, "Call and talk directly to Andy Bishop at the state's attorney's office. He's good about approving the tougher charges." Laney paused again. "You want to cut this Conroy kid some slack? For cooperating?"

"Fuck him. He didn't cooperate: Del Greco finessed his ass. Like I said, right in front of his lawyer."

"Del Greco, Del Greco. You've used his name ten times in two minutes. What are you saying, he does all the work while you stand around with your thumb up your ass, admiring him?"

Turner said, "You may remember—this was before you made sergeant and came over to homicide—Del Greco disappeared for a couple of days, after a seven-year-old little girl name of Kathy Reinhardt got murdered on the North Side. We found her naked in Lincoln Park, in the middle of February. Remember that one? I thought so. Del Greco called off sick that time, too, Sergeant Laney, but he wasn't sick—he was staking out the cemetery where little Kathy was buried. Eating there, sleeping there, videotaping landscape, didn't change clothes, nothing. For four days. Until he filmed this evil, perverted bastard, caught him on video jerking off on Kathy's headstone. Got a confession out of him, too, one that held up in court. After that, it all of a sudden became established procedure to put stakeouts at cemeteries where unsolved homicide victims were buried."

"He tell you how long he was planning on staying there?"

"I asked him that, Sergeant Laney." Turner saw Laney wince. He said, "He gave me a ration of his usual—how long would the spider, having spun his web, wait on the bug to fly into it? That sort of Zen shit he's always talking."

"You're trying to get me to think that Del Greco didn't just get sick. That he had some kind of brilliant reason for leaving duty, one that will become perfectly clear to all of us just as soon as he checks in."

"I'm trying to tell you that my partner's an excellent investigator."

"Nobody knows that better than I do."

"Which won't stop you from stomping his ass."

"I don't think we've got four days to wait and see what he's doing this time. Let's wait and see what he has to say for himself, first. Before we go any further. He broke procedure, but he's done that before and I've backed him up. Let's see what he's up to before we get all pissed off at each other over something that might not even happen."

Laney paused, looked away from Turner, then quickly looked back up. "He's got plenty of comp time coming. I'll give him the rest of the day, see if he checks in. Should you happen to suddenly remember what hospital his wife works at, or his in-laws' name, you give them a call, and see what you can find out."

"And report back to you."

"I'm not asking you"—she held up a hand—"Ellis, don't do it." Turner closed his mouth. He'd been about to interrupt.

Laney said, "Goddamnit, I can't cover for him forever. I'm not putting my neck on the chopping block, blind."

"Can I talk now, Sergeant Laney?" Laney glared at him, and Ellis raised his hands in a plea for understanding. "I know how you hate to be interrupted. So, I'm asking, are you through?"

Laney glared, and nodded tightly.

"He'd put his neck on the chopping block—blind—for *you*," Turner said, his voice dripping contempt.

He was going to his own desk when Laney shouted, *"Turner!"*

A MATTER OF HONOR

Ellis turned, stood looking at Laney, and watched as she calmed herself by the force of her will. His opinion of her rose. Not significantly, but higher than it had been.

"Don't try and pinch Helmner alone. Take someone with you." That wasn't at all what she'd intended to say when she'd shouted Turner's name, and he knew it.

With this in mind, Turner said, "It's getting on to two now; I'll try and grab him before the end of the shift, but if I can't make it, you want to authorize OT, or make it comp time?"

"Overtime's fine. It's your pinch, you have a right to be there. But if it's after three, Ellis, grab someone from afternoon's to take with you. The new lieutenant's not too happy about my authorizing a lot of overtime."

Turner nodded solemnly, and, knowing he had just been given all the time he needed, walked over to his desk to call Del Greco's wife at Northwestern Memorial Hospital, and, if he couldn't reach Rachel there, he'd try Del Greco's mother-in-law, Joanie Berstein, whose unlisted phone number was written down in small, perfect lettering inside of Ellis Turner's personal, wallet-size address book.

He quickly discovered that Rachel had left the hospital early after receiving an emergency phone call, and he soon thereafter learned that if she'd gone straight home, she was using the machine to screen her calls. Ellis tried Rachel's mother's number, and got the machine there, too. Neither woman picked up the phone when Ellis left his name. Which meant that if they were home, they were stiffing him. Ellis fumed.

He made another call, and found out that Del Greco still hadn't turned on the power on the cellular phone.

Turner looked around the squad room, saw Laney looking at him sharply, and he let his gaze wander past her without stopping to challenge her, Turner pretending to be searching for someone who could go with him to pick up this small-time punk Helmner, who'd recently stepped up to the major leagues. Turner had already made up his mind that he would effect the arrest alone; if he couldn't work with Del Greco, he didn't want to work with anyone.

Turner, growing angrier with each unanswered call, hung up the phone. He'd worry about Del Greco tonight, after Helmner had been pinched, booked, and delivered to the county jail. Turner knew that Del Greco was up to something, and was angry that, whatever it was, his partner was shutting him out of it. He decided that maybe he wouldn't waste his time worrying about Del Greco, even after he'd processed Helmner. He might even wait until morning to call again.

Then again, maybe he wouldn't.

CHAPTER

17

Gerald Podgourney saw the story in the morning paper and he smiled broadly because the niggers had done his work for him, and even if the coppers got lucky and the niggers got caught, there wasn't anything any of them could do to Gerald; none of them even knew his real name. Edmund might be a backwoods asshole, but he knew how to plan a crime, Gerald had to hand him that. Gerald read on, grinning, seeing that gang crimes investigators had been assigned to the case. Things just kept getting better.

Everybody knew that the gang crimes coppers were smart and plenty tough—a number of gangs had been run out of the city and now had to operate in the far less profitable suburbs; they had even been forced to move on to other states entirely—but it was also common knowledge that they weren't very imaginative, because they thought they were working with lowlife morons, which, when you got down to it, was the truth. The good thing about it was, the gang crimes guys wouldn't look beyond the obvious, would not look at the big picture.

Which was why he had not only gotten the niggers to do his work for him, he'd also been able to cheat them, had put half the money for the score into his own pocket, minus the five hundred dollars he'd had to pay Edmund up front. And on top of everything else, he was now owed a big one, too, was locked in even tighter with one of the most influential lawyers in Chicago, Mr. Arthur L. Horwitz, Esquire.

Gerald thought briefly about staying in today, because it was so hot outside. He thought about staying in his twenty-third-floor apartment, lying up in the large bedroom that had floor-to-ceiling bay windows, stay within the walls of the luxury high-rise joint that his recent good fortune had allowed him to rent. Suck up the air-conditioning and screw Amy all day long.

Amy was Gerald's fourth "wife."

He could get her into some of those positions she always said she didn't want to do when Gerald first suggested them, then went crazy over when he finally talked her into doing them. Pretty soon she'd be initiating it, begging for what she now called the "weird stuff." Amy wasn't very bright. She honestly believed that Adolph's wedding had been valid.

Gerald could hear her now, banging around in the bathroom early this Tuesday morning, Amy running late, as always, rushing around as she got ready for work, a young woman married to a dangerous player, and eating it up with a spoon. Gerald wondered if she had told her girlfriends what little she knew about him. Did she warn off the flirting of the junior partner lawyers at the firm she worked at by telling them she was married to a badass gangster? Gerald could see her doing it, Amy with her high, small titties, her tight ass, playing gun moll. They had met at their place of employment, at Horwitz's offices, where Amy typed up legal shit all day for Horwitz's army of lawyers.

Gerald knew he was the most exciting thing that had ever happened to Amy in her life.

He looked down at the paper, wondering if Horwitz would call and say something cryptic into the phone, pretending to be some sort of mob guy. Horwitz liked to do things like that, liked to make believe he was a tough guy. Horwitz could never see himself as Gerald saw him: as a man who could afford to hire tough guys. Horwitz would wave his cigar around in restaurants when Gerald was eating with him, daring anyone to say something about the smell. Gerald often wondered how the man acted when Gerald wasn't with him, wondered if Horwitz was a pussy when he was all alone, by himself. He suspected that Horwitz was.

Gerald might have been the best thing that had ever happened to Horwitz, too.

Horwitz thought he was a player, thought he was running Gerald. Gerald knew it was the other way around; he'd already scored big money from the lawyer, dragging the man into his schemes, as Horwitz brought Gerald into his own, performing what Horwitz called "unofficial assignments" for his well-paying friends and clients who weren't bound by petty nuisances, such as the laws of the land. Neither man pretended that Gerald was just Horwitz's driver-bodyguard anymore.

Gerald was big, and built. Young enough to be explosively violent, but wise enough to wait when the situation called for patience. He was twenty-five years old, and he'd made it; didn't have to punch a time clock like his old man had done for forty-three years, down in the mills on the South Side. Gerald always had money in his pocket, he had a nice car, and he always had a pretty girl staying with him, "married" to him, until he got too used to her and wound up throwing her out, and paying Adolph twenty dollars to declare him officially divorced.

Amy said, "Morning honey. You're up early." Gerald hadn't grown too used to his fourth wife just yet.

He looked at her as she came breezing into the kitchen, twenty-two-year-old Amy Francell, with her high school education and a framed certificate of graduation from secretarial school, living with a man for the first time in her life. She no doubt had fully deluded herself into believing that the two of them would enjoy a long, loving, and profitable marriage. Gerald was still smiling. Although Adolph had married them in the basement of his house, no one else had been present, as Gerald's marriages were no longer taken seriously. Fortunately for her, Amy hadn't been subjected to the other members of the Kinsmen, or to any of their wives. Though she spoke to Edmund regularly, as he was always calling the apartment and leaving mysterious messages for Gerald.

"You want some breakfast, hon?" her expression made it clear that she was hoping Gerald didn't. In case Gerald didn't get it, Amy frowned down at her watch, then made a face of fake surprise.

He said, "You, on toast."

"Don't I wish." Amy lowered her voice. "Mr. Horwitz *knows* about us, I told you. He told me it was none of his business as long as it didn't interfere with my work, but he wasn't happy."

"Listen to you. Standing up to the big, bad Jew."

"Well, he was right. It *is* none of his business." Amy sat down in a chair, propped her chin in her hands, and gazed at Gerald, thinking. He looked at her benignly, she was so easily manipulated, and Gerald did it so often that he would have felt guilty, if he'd been capable of the emotion.

"I could walk home for lunch. Meet you here, if you want."

"You know what I want?" Gerald said, and Amy gave him a somewhat troubled grin. He told her what he wanted, and he saw her grimace quickly before she covered it up with a tight smile.

"That always *hurts*." Listen to her whine. Gerald loved it.

He said, "You'll get used to it before you know it."

"Honest, Gerald, it really, really *hurts*."

"See?" Gerald said. "*That's* why guys go to whores."

"Don't do that! You can get diseases from them, God, don't you ever read the papers?"

"I read both of them every morning." Gerald smiled his secret smile. "Sometimes they make my day."

A MATTER OF HONOR

"The papers?" Amy was squinting down at a headline which announced that hundreds of people had died due to the intensive heat wave, with many more deaths expected. She looked up, puzzled, no doubt wondering what there was about that which could have made Gerald's day. Gerald didn't let her in on his secret.

He said, "Tell you what, I've got some work set up for this morning, then I'm running over to the gym. I'll get all pumped up nice and handsome for you, and meet you back here at noon."

"It'll take me a couple minutes to walk over here."

Gerald reached into his pocket, pulled out his roll, and peeled off a ten dollar bill. He said, "Take a cab."

"It's only four blocks."

"It's hot out."

Amy snapped up the bill. "All right." She stood, light hair still wet from the shower, dressed in one of the snazzy working woman power outfits Gerald had bought her at a fancy woman's shop up at Water Tower Place. She was more than likely the sharpest dresser in the typing pool.

"I'll run over to Walgreen's on my coffee break. If we're gonna keep doing *that,* I'm gonna buy some petroleum jelly."

Gerald was still smiling at her as she grabbed her purse and walked out the door.

Gerald wasn't smiling a half an hour later; he was grimacing. Gerald thought it had to be a pulled muscle; something was making him hurt. Every time he stepped down with his right heel, *bang,* the pain shot from his groin on up into his lower abdomen. He prided himself on never having taken a steroid in his life, on the fact that his powerful body was all natural, put together by lifting thousands and thousands of pounds thousands and thousands of times. He had hurt himself before, had pulled muscles in his arms, his legs, his shoulders, in his back, and now he'd pulled one in his groin. Maybe he should take a few days off, let the sensitive muscles down there relax. But he knew he wouldn't do that. Gerald was as addicted to pumping weights as he was to stealing, to conning, to lying. To The Life. He'd be back at the weights this morning, he knew, just as soon as he made this delivery. And got Edmund to go away.

The scrawny little son of a bitch was in the car he'd stolen, waiting. Gerald had convinced him that the tattoos sticking up out of the neck of the long-sleeve shirt he was wearing might raise suspicions in the mind of the old woman who owned the house. So now Edmund would want a piece of Gerald's action, for doing no work at all. Well, he *had* stolen the car, or had had it stolen. And it looked official. Gerald could hide most of the money before he came out of the house, tell Edmund whatever he wanted, how would the tattooed freak ever know? Even Ronzo hadn't known anything. It was the price Gerald had to pay for doing business; he was back in Edmund's good graces. Edmund was not a man Gerald could afford to alienate.

Gerald carefully mounted the cement steps, wearing an orange mesh vest over a tank top. The vest was marked with insignia and lettering announcing him as a worker for the Department of Streets and Sanitation. Gerald was carrying a heavy box, which he'd taken out of the trunk of the official-looking green Chevrolet. The box was marked PATTERSON COOLING SYSTEMS. Gerald lugged the box and sweated in the nearly unbearable morning heat, shook his head to toss off the sweat. His naturally curly hair had formed into ringlets from the humidity. He had refused to shave his head, no matter how hard some of the guys in the Kinsmen argued that he should. He walked up the porch of the bungalow, stepping lightly with his right foot, the excitement he was feeling overcoming the pain. Had it hurt when he'd come inside of Amy last night? He remembered a pinching . . .

"What do you want!" The nearly frantic voice screeched at him through the locked screen door. The heavy interior wooden entrance door was wide open, as were all the windows, in a pathetic attempt to rout the blazing heat. Gerald propped the heavy box on top of the iron railing, balanced it there with one hand as he wiped the sweat from his face with the other.

"Mrs. Jawocki?"

"Yes?" The old woman was tiny, skinny and frail. She reminded Gerald of a little bird, soft and yielding, vulnerable. Frightened, she stood looking out at the huge young man with trepidation, one hand on the heavy door, as if ready to slam it in his face. Behind her, a small, circular floor fan was having a little electronic heart attack as it tried to cool off the living room. Gerald smiled his winningest smile.

"My name's Tommy? I'm from the Department of Human Services, Department of Aging?" The old woman looked out at him, one hand still holding onto the door, the other clutching her light white robe to her throat, as if hiding a fine set of titties from Gerald's view. "Got an air conditioner here, Sister Mary Alice sent it over for you."

The woman craned her neck, tried to see past Gerald, to the street. She couldn't see the car. Edmund had no doubt taken off his long-sleeve shirt by now, and was sitting tall, stinking up the car with his cigarettes and unwashed body, with one decorated arm up across the backrest, in a display of Aryan pride.

The old lady said, "We can't afford no air conditioner." Gerald knew that wasn't true. He also knew there was no "we," but didn't allow his face to betray his knowledge of the woman's living arrangements. "I didn't order no air conditioner."

"I know that, ma'am. The Heat Hotline volunteers gave us your name, somebody called it in, said you weren't in the best of health, that you might be in danger in this weather."

"It's all that's been on TV, six hundred died already." Was there a quiver in her voice? The old lady was seeking pity. Gerald's informant had told him that she could be living in a suite in the Four Seasons Hotel if she wasn't such a cheapskate.

Gerald said, "Anyway, I got this eight-thousand BTU unit for you, if you want it. City'll help you out with the extra charge on your light bill, too."

"I didn't call the city."

"Well, *somebody* did." Gerald drummed his fingers on the box, drawing her attention to it. He smelled her sweat-stink through the screen, saw the sweat on her face. She had to be seventy-five years old; how could she pass up a deal like this?

Gerald took a less than calculated risk. "Look, I told you who I am. We're over at Ten South Kedzie. You don't trust me, call information, get the number yourself, call the office, and talk to Sister Mary Alice. If there was some mistake, she'll just tell you to send me to the next address on the list." He knew that the old woman was too cheap to have a telephone.

"Mistake?" Gerald had counted on the greed that came into the old woman's eyes. She hurriedly unlocked the screen door. "There wasn't no mistake. My grandson probably called them; he's always looking out for us."

Gerald had to hide his grin as he picked up the box with his gloved hands. Her grandson was looking out for her, all right. He wrestled the box through the doorway, took a few steps inside the house, and gently placed it on the threadbare carpet.

"You want to close the door, ma'am, and the windows, too. I'll have this baby up and running in about two minutes."

"You're working alone?" Was she afraid again? Gerald worked to calm her fears.

"Took my partner away, and got me working out of a car. So many seniors need our help, we're nearly out of equipment." There was a holy water finger-dipper mounted next to the front door, shaped in the figure of the Holy Virgin. Gerald looked away from the door. Ratty old drapes were hanging over the picture window. He walked to the side windows, closed one of them, inspected the other, as if looking to see if the air conditioner would fit there. He heard the wooden door close as he pushed the second window down.

"Aren't you going to put it in there?"

"This one ain't big enough, the kitchen might be better." The house stunk, filled with the stench of age, ancient cooking, and old, stale sweat. "All these BTUs, no matter where I put it, it'll cool off the entire house."

"Before you put it in, is there a form I sign for the city to pay my light bill?"

"Yes, ma'am, there is." Gerald followed her down a hallway, past bedrooms with closed doors. Past a small bathroom and into the tiny kitchen, where he closed the two windows, walked down two steps, and closed and locked the back door. He turned to the woman, saw that she was wringing her hands as she watched him.

"What city department did you say you were from?"

"Department of Aging."

There was a hint of fear in the woman's voice when she said, "Then why are you wearing a vest from the Department of Streets and Sanitation?"

Gerald sighed, grateful that he'd gotten the doors and windows closed in time. He turned to her, and said, "I understand you got every dime your husband ever made hidden inside this house. You want to tell me where it is, or do I got to fuck you up a little bit?"

The old woman, suspicions realized, opened her mouth to scream, and Gerald quickly went with option number two.

CHAPTER

18

"**L**isten to me," Arthur L. Horwitz said, rocking nervously back and forth in a plush leather judge's chair that was an exact replica of the one that Judge Ito had sat in during the Simpson trial. Horwitz curtly spoke the three words then paused, looking around his office, as if visibly seeking the presence of a listening device. The feds, a knowledgeable cop—or, for that matter, even some half-witted private eye—could have inserted covert eavesdropping equipment in this room, while pretending to be a janitor. They might even have compromised one of Horwitz's junior associates, or a secretary who had access to the room.

The phone, at least, was safe. Horwitz billed his clients for them, in order to save himself the trouble of a face-to-face visit every time one of them wanted to have a private conversation. They cost twenty-five hundred dollars per pair, ordered through the Sharp Company, with each additional, preprogrammed, single handset going for an extra fifteen hundred. They were boxy, heavy cellular phones, a pain in the ass to carry around wherever you went, but every word spoken into them was scrambled into gibberish before being decoded at the other end. Horwitz didn't represent any clients who couldn't afford one of these phones; he had underlings who were paid to look out for the interests of the smaller fish who came to the firm, looking to get themselves off of whatever legal hook they suddenly found themselves dangling from.

"What?" his client said impatiently into Horwitz's ear, and Horwitz took a deep breath, then let it out, feeling even more paranoid than usual.

Audio surveillance used to be complicated and expensive, used only by the government, or by well-financed, sophisticated corporate spies. With today's technology, sensitive eavesdropping devices could be purchased at any Radio Shack store for under twenty dollars.

Almost every call taken on this line was protected under attorney-client privilege, and even if the conversation was somehow unscrambled, the director of the FBI himself couldn't bring a transcript of what was said during those calls into a court of law. But this conversation wouldn't be covered by privilege, Horwitz knew.

Arthur L. Horwitz had conspired with this client to commit an act of murder. There were no convenient legal umbrellas that could cover him from the heavy downpour of justice if this fact were ever to become public knowledge.

"What!" his client said again, into his ear, and Horwitz grimaced. He was wondering, not for the first time, if he'd gotten in over his head.

Carefully, weighing every word, Horwitz said, "I'm going to have to fire the delivery boy who was supposed to have taken care of your package."

"What package? Why are you telling *me* this? I don't know what the hell you're talking about! What you do is none of my business."

"You don't understand. Something like this could cause—more potential problems—than we ever imagined." Horwitz had an ugly thought, and, trying to keep his voice calm, said, "Where are you right this minute?"

"I'm locked in the goddamn bathroom. And you should have asked that question before you went into your song and dance. Where are *you?*"

"In my office."

"I feel so much more secure, knowing that." There was a pause while Horwitz's client silently fumed.

Then the client said, "Why are we talking? Don't you know what just happened to me?" The client was smarter than Horwitz had thought, was being careful not to say anything which could be misinterpreted by anyone who might somehow be listening in. And the pleading of ignorance was a cute touch. It was the exact way Horwitz would have played it if he'd been in this client's shoes. Ignorant and angry. Horwitz admired the strategy.

He said, "Because you have to know about it, that's why! You're a part of this, you came to me!"

"I hired legal counsel to help me with a sophisticated judicial maneuver; that doesn't mean I have to hold your hand every time you're feeling insecure. It means you're supposed to hold mine, Artie—that's what I'm paying you for."

Horwitz managed to shout out, "*You paid me to*—" before the phone went dead in his ear. "Shit!" He slammed the phone down on the table, not caring what it cost. He stood up, hands on his hips, breathing very heavily, looking around the room this time as if solutions to his dilemma would be written on the walls.

"Mother*fuck* that goddamn Podgourney!" Horwitz held his open hand to his forehead, leaned down into it and rubbed his furrowed brow. He was worried about the room being bugged, and here he was, shouting the name of his future codefendant right out loud. What was wrong with him? He'd been under pressure before, and he hadn't cracked like this.

Then again, he'd never been under *this* sort of pressure.

"It'll blow over." He spoke this falsely reassuring phrase aloud, then he caught himself, clamped his mouth shut and gritted his teeth. He was losing it. Dear Christ, he was losing it. Horwitz made a distinct, conscious effort to calm himself. He took a long, slow, deep breath, let it out just as slowly, then ran slender, trembling fingers through his full head of elegantly graying hair. He ran both hands down the front of his expensive, striped shirt, patting his trim, toned body, as if verifying his own existence through the sense of touch. Horwitz sat down in his leather chair, folded his hands on the blotter atop his well-ordered desk, and once again looked around the room, at the trappings of his success, at the rewards of ten years of single-minded, strenuous effort.

Usually, in times of unease, looking at his possessions gave the lawyer a better sense of himself. Now, all he saw were the things that he had to lose. And not just the artwork, the expensive phone, the leather furniture, or the fancy office, either. Horwitz was seeing the fortune he'd amassed being taken away from him, saw civil suits flying at him from every conceivable angle as he sat impotently in jail, powerless, unable to deflect them. He gave no thought to his reputation, or to the damage any future arrest would cause to the three kids who lived with his ex-wife, in his ex-house in Winnetka. All he could think about was the Near South Side townhouse, the young girlfriends, the boat, the Ferrari, the T-bills, and his bank accounts. All of which would be gone because he'd gotten stupid, because he had to pretend he was some sort of an outfit player.

Things weren't going well enough. Being a millionaire wasn't good enough for him. No, not for old Artie. He had to pretend he was some sort of half-assed tough guy. A man of violence. He knew all about men of violence, had grown up in awe of them. From his teen years and on through the years of his education, Horwitz had envied them, had lived in awe of them. He had built his name, firm, and fortune by defending such men. He had made a habit of surrounding himself with them, being with them whenever he could, dressing like them, walking like them, talking like them, studying them constantly, in restaurants and bars, at fights and at other sporting events. He would bring them into his skybox at the United Center, use his connections to get autographs from the players for their children.

Horwitz was drawn to men of violence in much the same manner that roaches were drawn to sweets. Yet for all his pretensions, at a time such as this, with his stomach fluttering, tasting blood in his mouth, he could not lie to himself: Arthur L. Horwitz was acutely aware that he was not any kind of tough guy.

He had built his body into a tight, compact cord of muscle, but the mere thought of being punched in the face repelled him, filled him with dread. Being punched in the face, however, was far from his greatest fear.

He had stood in courtrooms with his tough guy clients and had observed them as they were sentenced to lengthy terms in various state or federal penitentiaries. He had seen them accept their fate stoically, viewing their sentences as just another enemy that had to be fought. He had shaken warm, dry, steady hands in manly gestures of farewell. Hands that would be folding jumpsuits in the prison laundry for decades to come, and the clients those hands belonged to had borne Horwitz no ill will, hadn't blamed him for their plight. He knew he himself could not behave in such a manner, he knew he could not handle that. He knew that if he were ever sentenced to prison, they'd have to drag him out of the courtroom, crying and shrieking, as he begged for mercy, begged for another chance. But the judges would grant him neither; they frowned on members of their own profession being caught in the perpetration of a brutal, ugly murder. Horwitz knew enough judges to understand that they wouldn't care about what he'd *done,* but would max him out for having been stupid enough to have gotten caught.

There was a bottle of Xanax in the middle desk drawer. Horwitz generally only took one half milligram pill to quell his frayed edges when he was meeting with a heavy, frightening client. He took three now, a full one-and-a-half-milligram dose. He dry swallowed the pills, staring vacantly out the window.

He had just humiliated himself in front of a client whom he'd gone to great lengths to impress with his insider's knowledge. He had shown his hand to the client, too, with that "having to fire the delivery boy" garbage. The client had never met Podgourney, would not know his name if told it, would not recognize his body if he stumbled across it dead in an alley.

Horwitz knew his voice had been strong, that even the client hadn't known how afraid Horwitz had really been, but at the moment, that was small consolation, nor was it a surprise. Horwitz was a coward who considered his greatest personal accomplishment to be the fact that nobody had ever discovered his cowardice. He covered it up through the application of various ploys: bullying men who were weaker than he; kowtowing to the strong and powerful; a combination of the two with others, whose strengths and weaknesses were not yet known. His voice had never quavered in public, and his gait was the walk of the arrogant, middle-aged rich.

But the client had known, had seen inside Horwitz's heart. Horwitz wondered who else this client might be speaking with; decided that the client had too much to lose to go around discussing his insights into Artie Horwitz's character.

In his heart of hearts, Horwitz knew exactly what he was. And he knew what he wanted to be. He'd been circling the law, circumventing it, for years; bending it. But what he'd now done hadn't been an act that had brought him large profits with little risk of being caught. His law license, disbarment, had been all he'd had to worry about before, and he'd made enough money and had stashed enough of it away to sit back and never work again, if he had to. Besides, everyone he knew was doing it, too; speculating, doing a little insider trading with a client who knew his business and would have a hundred layers of paper protecting them from any federal investigation.

This wasn't on that level.

This wasn't even on the level of sending his pet bulldog Gerald out to terrorize the boyfriend of a client's wife, or to break the arm of some deadbeat who wasn't paying his bills on time. This went a lot deeper than that. This was natural life in Pontiac, doing free legal work for uneducated, rage-filled gangbangers who in return would protect Horwitz from getting sodomized every night—if he got lucky.

Why had that asshole done it that way? Horwitz grabbed the edge of his desk and squeezed it, tightly. He'd said *accident.* He'd expected a vehicular homicide, or a fall down an elevator shaft, something simple and clean like that, a horrid tragedy, but the sort of thing that happened every day of the week in any major city. It was supposed to have been the sort of death that would have caused no inordinate police concern.

Podgourney might have thought he was being slick, but Horwitz, living in a different world, knew better, knew the truth. He knew what the racial climate was, and he knew the sort of damage that this sort of crime could do. The sort of damage it could do to him and his career. Fuck the city. Horwitz didn't care if the entire city went up in flames tomorrow.

He did care that the killing of a young, well-educated, hardworking white girl by a young, black, gangbanging male in the city's downtown area could bring as much heat down on the politicians of this city as the Rodney King beating had brought down on them in Los Angeles. Horwitz knew his way around politicians. He not only donated heavily to their election campaigns, he dined with them, he socialized with them. He attended formal balls with them, dressed up in his tailored tuxedo, smiling broadly for the newspapers' society columnists' cameramen. He knew—in a way that Podgourney could never fathom—what would happen if these politicians felt the hot breath of outraged voters heavy on their necks. They would call news conferences. They would stare solemnly into the cameras. They would vow that they wouldn't rest until the killer or killers of this poor young woman had been arrested, charged, convicted, and sentenced to death. Worst of all, as far as Horwitz was concerned, they would post a large reward for information leading to that conviction. That reward would grow, as terrified white people sent in checks, cash, and money orders, wanting to do their part to ensure that the sort of people who would kill an innocent white person—a person just like themselves—would be taken forever off the street.

Gerald Podgourney would never have considered how far this might go. His life was pussy and cash, he didn't think beyond paying his rent. He would now be thinking that he'd pulled off a dope move by having *shvartzers* kill the woman, but Horwitz knew what a foolish act it had really been; he knew the movers and the shakers, he had his finger on the city's pulse.

He had spent most of last night at his townhouse watching local TV footage about the killing of the bum by the off-duty cop, and he knew that Alderman Charge was involved, and was milking the situation for all it was worth. Horwitz knew the sort of power such a provocative man could wield. The murder had taken on a life of its own; Africaan was involved, and the gangs, and probably thousands of other, mostly black, people, who had taken it into their heads that the shooting was a wake-up call. Horwitz knew, too, that if Charge was involved, Crocodile Berkley was working behind the scenes, waiting and praying for an opportunity that would further transform his army of gangsters into a viable political force. Charge had set his sights on becoming the next federal congressman. If that happened, Berkley would be sitting to his right, would have his ear.

This woman's killing was exactly the sort of opportunity these men would have been waiting for, the chance for further, high-profile media exposure, as they advanced their political agenda behind the cover of fighting racism.

That stupid fucking Podgourney. It was supposed to have been an *accident!* They could be closing in on Podgourney right now. If they did, Podgourney might give Horwitz up, in an attempt to save himself. This was conspiracy to commit murder; this was a death penalty case.

Well, Podgourney wasn't the only violent man Horwitz had ever gotten close to. He'd simply been the only one that Horwitz had kept on the payroll. It was a power thing, a trend. Having a personal bodyguard on the payroll was as prestigious and necessary these days as having a personal trainer had been five or ten years ago. For the job he had in mind, however, Horwitz would need more than a personal, violent flunky. He needed a true man of violence, a man who lived by a certain code of conduct. The downside was that such a man, by his very nature, couldn't be owned or controlled, but would be a man who was used to doing the owning and controlling. Horwitz thought that he had a way to convince such a man to do his bidding.

Calm now, the Xanax kicking in, knowing what it was that he had to do, Horwitz unlocked his private Rolodex, pushed the blue, plastic lid back, and flipped through the cards until he got to the name he needed. He reached for the regular phone, shook his head, and picked up the cellular scrambler phone. He dialed in the number, waited while the phone rang. After a great many rings, a stranger answered, and Horwitz waited until the flunky got his boss on the line. Who opened the conversation with: "Artie! Am I in some trouble I don't know about?"

"You're in good shape, Benny."

"Yeah? Let me tell you, Jews *never* call with good news. At least not good news for *me*. It always costs me money."

"Not this time, Benny," Arthur L. Horwitz said. "You're going to come out way ahead on this one. I'll defend you, or any of your associates, gratis, next time you have a problem."

"In return for what?"

Hearing the excitement in Benny's voice, Horwitz smiled and said, "You happen to be free for lunch?"

CHAPTER

19

Angelo, middle-aged, weary, bearing the burden of overwhelming grief on his huge shoulders, looked down at his adult daughter, at Rita. He looked at her closed eyes, her peaceful expression, looked at her hair spread out on the expensive pillow, and he thought back, wondered how many times in his life he had watched her sleep without her knowledge. It had been almost a ritual with him, since she'd been just a baby until—when?—the time she was eleven or twelve? Angelo couldn't remember. He'd stopped at an age when he thought it had become inappropriate. Maybe she'd been thirteen, Angelo now wasn't sure.

Until that time, he'd performed his secret act with what was almost a sense of awe. *Could this really be* my *daughter?* How could any one man be so fortunate? Rita with the golden hair and the bright blue eyes, the happy expression, a child who was almost always smiling, that smile lingering on her face sometimes even as she slept. He'd watch her and he'd think of all the things he'd tell her the next day, and the things he'd tell her later, when she was older, at a time when she could understand the sentiments, when they wouldn't go to her head.

He'd told her those things, too. As she'd grown up and she'd needed her daddy.

Upset and confused? One of the girls at school said something cruel? Boyfriend dumped you? Angelo would hide his anger and his immediate desire to harm whoever had hurt her, and he'd talk to her, tell her how beautiful she was, how smart and how sweet and how kind. How there were millions of boys in this world who said their prayers every night

110

before they went to bed and prayed, begged God Himself to lead them to someone just—like—Rita.

His divorce from Rita's mother, though sometimes ugly and bitter, hadn't changed things between Angelo and Rita. If anything, the breakup had brought them even closer together. He'd moved into an apartment just a few blocks away from the family home, often picked her up during her last two years in high school, and they'd take the El away from their little isolated, white, Northwest Side neighborhood and right on into the heart of everything, into downtown Chicago, where they'd shop or go to the theater or to the movies, or just for a walk when the weather was nice. The two of them would stand on one of the bridges spanning the Chicago River and they'd look out at the sparkling jewel that was the city at night, and passersby would sometimes glare at them, and they'd ignore them, they were used to it.

He'd been a tall, massive, dark, obviously Italian male in his early middle years, and she'd been a tall, slender blond with piercing blue eyes, who was obviously not yet out of her teens. His pride in her was overwhelming and proprietary. Even the most desperate junkies would see the look on Angelo's face as they approached, and would back away, to seek their donations from other sources.

Angelo had never said a bad word about her mother in front of Rita. Though Rita had spoken plenty of such words to him. And he'd listened, patiently, and he'd always taken her side. Right or wrong, he'd told her, she was always in the right with him.

As she'd grown older Rita would try to match Angelo's mature, urbane sophistication, and sometimes she could even pull it off.

Now Angelo wiped a tear away, closed his eyes tightly and shook his head, teeth gritted, the man enraged at the world, filled with hatred but determined not to break down, not to make a sound.

Now the pain directly under his groin—chronic, always with him— grew suddenly sharp and intense, and Angelo drew in a sharp breath. He adjusted his footing, waited until it passed. He felt a shiver as Death brushed past him, then shook away his fear. Death would have to wait; it could not have him yet.

During the sordid divorce proceedings, the truth had been whispered to him by his sympathetic attorney, behind closed doors at the electronics shop that Angelo had spent his adult life making successful: Rita wasn't really Angelo's biological daughter. Did Angelo want the lawyer to play hardball in a custody battle? If he did, the lawyer told him, Rita would no doubt learn the truth.

The truth had shocked him, but he'd eaten it, held it inside, and he'd had his lawyer tell his ex-wife that Angelo would make it worth her while if the news never reached their daughter's ear.

111

If Rita ever found out about it, Angelo had later vowed to her, personally, with no lawyers within the sound of his voice, he would do everything in his power to destroy her. And his ex-wife, knowing him, believed it, and never told.

What did it matter? he had told himself. Did genetics make a parent? Or a daughter? Could he have loved her any more if his own sperm had caused the spark of her life? That wasn't possible. No man ever loved a daughter more than Angelo loved Rita. He told himself that now, but it was a very small consolation.

Trying to make himself feel better, Angelo thought briefly of his own childhood, compared it to Rita's upbringing, and nodded his head at his accomplishment. His childhood had been ugly, and, not surprisingly, Angelo had been a bad boy. Then he'd become a bad student. Then a reckless, foolhardy teenaged boy-man, tall and thick, the terror of the neighborhood. He'd gotten caught in the course of an armed robbery that had gotten out of hand, the victim had fought back, and Angelo, filled with youthful fear and pride, had beaten the man to death.

The judge had sent him away to the St. Charles reformatory.

Angelo had gotten his high school education there, and he'd learned something else, as well: He'd discovered that he wanted no part of a criminal career. He'd been arrested at fifteen and had been turned loose at twenty-one. Almost a third of his life had passed, and he'd had nothing to show for it but the scars of late-night battles behind locked steel doors.

So he'd set out to make something of himself. His juvenile record had been sealed upon his release; in the eyes of the world, Angelo's slate was clean. He set about the business of becoming a success. He got married at twenty-two and settled down, with a baby on the way.

Rita.

Rita had never known about that side of him, about his angry, violent past; even though the snakes still often slithered around inside his head, she'd never seen them, nor suspected their existence.

Angelo thought of every scraped knee he'd bandaged, every tear he'd dried. How he'd hold her hand as they crossed the street; how his heart had broken when she'd gone out on her first date. How he'd bitten his tongue and kept his mouth shut when she'd paraded the series of boyfriends over to meet him, seeking Angelo's approval.

When she'd gone off to college he'd moved into Marina City, right on the river, bought a small two-bedroom apartment so she could stay with him on her frequent trips home, semester breaks, and summer vacations. And she did, inevitably, having by then grown tired of her mother's ever changing and ever younger boyfriends. He'd walk home from his store in the summertime with a lightness in his step, hoping that she'd be there rather than out with one of her boyfriends, so he could take her out to dinner, and later, for a walk.

Movies on the VCR, the two of them sprawled out on the floor, eating buttered popcorn out of his large wooden spaghetti serving bowl. She approved of most of his girlfriends, and when she didn't, Angelo would drop them. Rita had an eye for people, a feeling for them. Her instincts about character were almost always right.

So why, Angelo wondered now, had she married such an imbecile?

Angelo, as in everything in Rita's life that didn't go as well as he'd wished, blamed himself, thought that her marrying a much older man was Rita's way of marrying *him*. He'd tried to talk her out of it and they'd had a tremendous argument, had wound up in each other's arms crying, he begging her to reconsider her decision, Rita agreeing to wait a year. In the end, though, she'd gotten married. And he'd never spoken a word against her husband, against Charles. Twenty years older than Rita, a successful broker with a downtown firm, a good man, Angelo thought, a winner, but still, that was a big difference in age . . .

Another sharp pain grabbed him, and this time Angelo softly cried out. He would have to sit down soon. The pain grew almost unbearable when he was on his feet too long. But it was even worse when he was sitting, he had to lean far forward, or sit way back, on his spine.

He remembered how Rita had responded when he'd told her, how she'd narrowed her eyes and tightened her lips; she hadn't gotten that from her mother, that was Angelo's brother's move. Maybe his own, too, now that he thought about it. He'd told her he had prostate cancer and she hadn't broken down or gone hysterical. Rita had, rather, gotten mad, and had grown even angrier when he'd immediately rejected her initial reaction, when he wouldn't let her quit her job and move in to care for him.

But she'd found out more about his cancer than he'd ever known, had presented him with her findings within three days, at his apartment. Twenty-four years old, married, working full time, and she'd somehow found time to go to the library and research Angelo's problem. Caught early enough, she'd announced, his type of cancer had a ninety percent recovery rate. Angelo was still relatively young—Rita had looked up at him, her eyes filled with hope—had they caught it soon enough?

Angelo had told her what his doctor had said to him just that morning—he thought perhaps they had.

Angelo now heard soft footsteps coming up behind him, quickly, and he spun around, expecting to see his brother, expecting to hear some news. But it was only Charles, red-eyed and stoop-shouldered, peering tiredly at Angelo through his little round, wire-framed glasses, as if he were afraid to intrude on Angelo's privacy.

The gray in Charles's sideburns contrasted with the blackness of the transplanted dyed black hair atop his head. Charles whispered, "You all right, Dad?"

When he was able to, Angelo said, "I'm fine."

"You moaned."

Angelo just looked at him. Charles lowered his eyes, looked down at his wife, at Angelo's daughter. He sighed.

"So young, so young. Caught in a fucking cross fire!" Charles lowered his voice even further and muttered, "Goddamned niggers!" Then said, "What are we going to do, Dad?"

Angelo walked away from his daughter's coffin without responding to his son-in-law's question. He sat in a chair in the front row, on the aisle opposite the ex-wife whom he didn't trust himself to even acknowledge, and he waited, fighting the urge to break down, to hold his head in his hands, and cry. No adult had seen him cry since he'd been thirteen years old, and only one more ever would.

Instead, Angelo sat patiently, awaiting his brother's arrival, thinking thoughts of justice, thinking thoughts of revenge.

CHAPTER

20

Sergeant Cheryl Laney walked purposely up to Ellis Turner's desk and stopped, stared at him with a look that told him he had better not try and bullshit her this time.

"Where is he."

"I don't know." He'd answered quickly enough to convince her that he was telling the truth. When she didn't seem upset with his response, Turner said, "I called the house a half a dozen times last night. Rachel's not real happy with him, either, Sergeant, but he's doing what he has to do, and she knows that, she accepts that."

"I'm not Rachel."

Turner didn't respond, as the only responses that came to mind would have insulted his superior officer.

"I know he's calling in, I know he's cashing in every favor and political marker he has in the department. There are plenty of cops who know what happened and who are happy to help him out. It's obvious he's working the case on his own.

"The lieutenant hasn't said anything yet, so maybe he doesn't know anything, but it's just a matter of time until one of his snitches tells him about the rumors that are swirling around. By now, everyone knows what happened, and what Del's probably doing. He could have taken compassionate leave, he could have done a hundred other things. He shouldn't have—"

Laney stopped herself. She'd been sounding far more concerned than a superior officer had a right to be sounding over the welfare of a subordinate.

She said, "I can't hold off much longer, Ellis, and I can't cover for him if I don't know what he's planning to do."

"He hasn't called me, Sergeant." Ellis was in fact quite angry that Del Greco hadn't called him. Del Greco would be thinking that he was watching out for Turner; Turner saw it more as a personal betrayal.

Laney watched him, seeking dishonesty in his expression. Turner kept his face as blank as slate, keeping his seething resentment hidden.

"If he does, goddamnit . . ."

"It's past time, I know. If he calls, I'll tell him he's got to talk to you."

"You don't think he'll call you though, do you?"

"If he hasn't by now, he's not likely to. He'll be thinking he's looking out for me, covering my ass." Turner regretted the bitter sound of his words.

But Laney wasn't paying attention to Turner's tone. She said, "Which means he's doing something stupid."

"Del Greco?"

"All right. Not stupid. Wrong."

"Alone's, more like it. He's always been a loner."

"If he doesn't check in, I'll have to have him picked up."

"Then you'll be responsible for whatever he does to whoever tries to pick him up."

Laney walked smartly over to her desk, picked up several sheets of paper that were stapled together, and frowned at them.

Turner raised his voice and said, "By the way, you see my report? I pinched that Helmner character last night. His lawyer and that Andy Bishop are hashing things out. Del Greco procured enough evidence so that Bishop says he's going for first degree, unless the guy agrees to his client serving twenty, minimum."

Laney came storming back to Turner, and thrust the papers out toward him. "Take this. You can do the initial investigation on your own, but I don't want you doing any interviews or making any arrests without backup." Her sharp look told him that she knew that Turner had taken Helmner down alone, against her implicit instructions. Reluctantly, Turner took the papers from Laney's hand, turned them around and began to read the top page. They had an old, reclusive, widowed, and now dead female, and a partial print on the side of an air conditioner box that had been stuffed with a broken TV set. The TV set had been clean, someone was running the serial number down, trying to find out who had sold it, and to whom.

Laney's voice was soft as she said, "We're not in an adversarial relationship when it comes to Del Greco, Ellis. I don't *want* to have to put a pickup order out on him."

Turner had forgotten she was there. "Then don't," he said, without looking up from the report. He heard the quick clicking of her heels as Laney walked away from his desk.

Cheryl Laney sat at her desk fuming, but keeping it inside. She could not allow anyone to know that they'd upset her; when people knew your buttons, they pushed them, it was a part of human nature. As it was, she was working on her anger, the way she'd act when somebody interrupted her. Men were like that, would cut in on her in a minute, thinking they had greater insight, that Cheryl Laney wasn't all that bright, even though she'd been promoted to sergeant. She looked down at the stack of papers on her desk, and thought about Marshall Del Greco.

She felt that he had deceived her, abandoned her. She had no real basis for this feeling, no logical frame of reference, it was the way it was, a feeling. She'd thought there was a special bond between them, that he knew that he could come to her if he needed to, that he knew she'd understand. She'd understood Daniel, or so she'd thought, until she'd been promoted. Then Daniel had copped an attitude. He didn't work for her, she was not even his boss, but still, Daniel resented her promotion, and his resentment had damaged their marriage.

She'd spoken of this to Del Greco, shortly after being assigned to his squad, and ho'd listened, calmly, intent eyes locked on hers until she'd had to lower her eyes, looked down at the top of the table they'd been sitting at, across from each other in a quiet lounge, Cheryl working on her second martini and still not sure why she'd invited him out for a drink, this man she'd barely known, but feeling that she'd had to, that he of all people would understand her problem.

Now and again he'd sip his ginger ale, but Cheryl had never felt his intensity waver for an instant. He'd told her that Daniel was an asshole, a good cop, but dumb. He'd told her that any man who resented his wife's achievements was insecure and weak. Even when those achievements surpassed his own—especially then, he had said.

Cheryl had listened, looking up at him, very aware of him in a physical sense, which made her feel uncomfortable.

He told her that the proudest day of his life had been the day that his wife, Rachel, had graduated from medical school. He spoke of his pride at her accomplishment, at the fact that she had done what he himself could never do. He'd told Cheryl these things, and she'd slowly become aware that he was telling her other things, as well. He was telling her that there was nothing he could do about the problems in her marriage, he was telling her that he himself was happy in his relationship.

117

He was telling her that he was unavailable.

Delicately, without ridicule, but nevertheless making the point. Cheryl was surprised to realize that Del Greco had been right; she *had* been hitting on him, coming on to him, and she hadn't even been aware of it until she'd figured out what he'd been doing. Had she been seeking marital advice, she would have gone to a counselor. She had wanted to be with him because of what he was, and she'd found out that what he mostly was was loyal, and he showed her that loyalty, showed her how an honorable man was supposed to behave toward his spouse.

Cheryl had been embarrassed, and had found a reason to end the evening early, but she'd never forgotten how well he'd handled the situation, how gently Del Greco had led her away from the temptation that could have led to an act that would have been destructive for them both. She smiled now, thinking of a cliché: the only men worth marrying were already married, or gay.

Del Greco was married, and happily so. Cheryl's choices were clear. But the way Del Greco had acted with her had bonded them together; he had treated her respectfully, as his boss, without being deferential or condescending in any way. In the time that had passed, she'd come to appreciate him even more. He was not only her best detective, he had become her closest colleague in the department. She could think of a lot of cops who would have taken her up on her offer, and would have made her think that it was their idea. And those same coppers would have been bragging about fucking the new sergeant before they'd even gotten out of their street clothes the next day, sharing all the juicy details in the locker room, to appreciative ears.

In the subsequent months, she'd watched how he'd conducted himself, and Del Greco had become her favorite, the detective she counted on the most. Turner ran a close second, but he had a black thing about him, he carried his race around like a chip on his shoulder, daring anyone to knock it off. She thought he had an obvious insecurity in needing to be the best-dressed member of the squad. Still, she thought that his sensitivity went deeper than he let on. She would have to watch him more closely, see how Turner acted. He'd directly countermanded her orders by arresting the punk last night on his own, and now Cheryl wondered if he was going to try to turn that into a habit. She'd quickly discovered that a lot of male detectives had their own, unbendable ideas about police work, and she'd come down hard on those who played the gender card with too much relish.

Del Greco never did that, and they'd become close friends. Come to think of it, Turner never did it either. Cheryl believed that their rare acts of insubordination would have occurred if their boss had been male.

Perhaps she had underestimated Turner. There might be more to him than there seemed.

She nodded her head and looked up, but he was gone. Cheryl looked back at her papers. She had a squad to supervise, and had to stop wasting time dwelling on two members of it. But she wished Del Greco would call. Goddamn him, why hadn't he called her?

CHAPTER

21

People were, on the whole, stupid. It didn't take most cops very long to figure this out, and it had taken Ellis Turner less time than most, as he'd suspected it to be the case since he'd been just a little boy. Growing up in the Robert Taylor Homes, the country's largest public housing project, he'd had firsthand knowledge of how stupid people could be.

Ellis had been a thirteen-year-old freshman in high school before he'd seen a white man who hadn't been wearing a police uniform. His mother's minister preached that television and radio were the devil's tools, so neither electronic device had ever been allowed in his mother's home. Men weren't allowed in that home either, after Ellis's father abandoned them. Ellis was the single most uncommon category of young black male in the entire project: he was an only child.

His entire world back then had revolved around his mother; school, which was just around the corner, part of the project complex; and the church three blocks away, to which his mother, holding his hand, would walk Ellis not only on Sundays but on Wednesday and Friday evenings. On the weeknights, church services lasted from six until nine P.M. On Sundays, they were at church all day, eating lunch and dinner there with the other worshipers (most of whom were adult females and their children; there were only seven adult males who were regular members of the congregation) who had spent all day Saturday cooking the meals they brought along, meals that were kept warm in a large, heavy, iron stove in the kitchen of the storefront church.

Back then, Ellis had thought that the entire *real* world was black, and that whites lived on the fringes of that world, and that everyone in it, both white and black, was desperately poor. He'd thought that cops had to be on the lower end of the food chain, and police work was the only job that the lowly white man could find.

Ellis, with the reverend's sermons ringing in his head, would watch in wonder, awed at some of the stupid things his own people would do, the way they would hurt each other. After the violence occurred, the white cops would come and—here was Ellis's proof of their stupidity—would actually expect the people in the high-rise project buildings to talk to them, tell them what they'd seen. They thought that black people were snitches.

Ellis knew what happened to snitches. The same thing that happened to a lot of the gangbangers sooner or later: they died. Got shot in the head with a Saturday Night Special, got stabbed, or beaten to death with baseball bats or fists, or got thrown out of the window of an upper-floor apartment. And still the police would come around, asking their fool questions, getting all angry and red in the face when nobody would tell them anything.

Didn't the cops know that the gangbangers ran the building? Didn't they know that you had to pay a tax to use the elevators to get up to your apartment? The gangbangers would sit in metal chairs, right in the hallways, with their hands out. There was a much smaller tax for using the stairways; the gangbangers weren't entirely heartless, and they were aware of the days of the month when the checks would arrive. Sometimes, when it was closing in on that date, they'd let the older women slide on paying the elevator tax. Younger women would have to go into debt. That, or they would have to trade elevator usage for sex.

Ellis would sit in the window of his mother's eleventh-floor apartment and look down at the street, watching, wincing when the gunshots came, thunderous and sharp, the sound echoing off the many buildings, making it impossible to tell where the shots had come from. The sound usually meant that another body would be lying in the street, on the sidewalk, on the grass or in the stairwell, and then the police would come, asking Ellis—and anyone else who hadn't ducked for cover when the squad car had pulled up—what he'd seen.

"I don't know nothin' about it," Ellis would say to them.

Which were the exact same words this stupid, weak, white, junkie son of a bitch was saying to Ellis now.

Ellis had woke him up. He had no doubt about that, having seen enough junkies to know what they looked like after a night of fitful tossing; it was a look that couldn't be faked.

121

There was also no doubt in Ellis's mind about two other points: the kid hadn't killed his grandmother; but he knew who had.

Ellis had seen the look on the boy's face as he'd broken the news to him, to Ronald Jawocki. Ronzo, to his friends. Couldn't be twenty yet, wouldn't make twenty-three. He was at least HIV positive, more likely had full-blown AIDS. Ronzo was all tight, veiny skin over fragile bone, with deep-sunken eyes that had even deeper circles beneath them. Hollow-cheeked, runny-nosed, pitiful Ronzo Jawocki, wearing a long, ratty robe, which he'd no doubt stolen from a cheap hotel, over an emaciated, naked body. He'd taken one look at Ellis through the glass window of the door and had pulled the sleeves down as low as they'd go, futilely trying to cover the track marks.

Ellis had told him his grandmother was dead, and he'd watched the vast array of expressions that passed across Ronzo's face: sadness; grief; awareness; fear; and then, finally, guilt. Ronzo had never learned to hide his nonverbal responses, and his expression of them was eloquent, easily read by Turner.

Now the kid was sitting in a wobbly chair at a small, plastic, cigarette-scarred dining room table, half-asleep, pretending to be surprised that his grandmother had been beaten to death. The apartment was tiny, but it had an ancient air conditioner built into the wall, working overtime as it tried to blow cool air into a room that smelled more like the medical examiner's office than a place where a living human being actually lived.

Ronzo was shaking and avoiding eye contact. Ellis could see the sheetless bed through the open bedroom door. The table was in the living room, which seemed to serve double duty as Ronzo's dining room. Ellis had not wanted to see Ronzo's kitchen, but he'd gone in there, dutifully, and was not surprised at the scurrying sound that was concurrent with his flicking on the light switch; panic-stricken cockroaches, with plenty to feed on, covered the grease-spattered walls, fought amongst each other to get into one of the many cracks in the walls, out of the glare of bare-bulb light.

Ellis was glad that Ronzo Jawocki was a junkie; was glad that he was ugly, too. Either one might be enough to handle, but the two combined would keep all but the most desperate women away. Which meant that Ellis had the boy all to himself, without anyone running around reminding Ronzo of his rights. It was an easy thing for someone to do when they themselves had no fear of arrest.

Not in the mood to play any games, Ellis said, "It'll take me most of the day to find out who you hang out with, who actually did the work. By then I'll be pretty pissed off at you, Ronzo. Keep in mind, the city of Chicago don't give a shit who goes down for the arrest, as long as it's cleared. County of Cook doesn't give a shit, either, as long as they get the conviction. State of Illinois is just as bad. As long as they got a body to lock up, they're happy." Ellis made a point of touching nothing. He didn't even want the hem of his jacket to brush up against the table. He pulled a chair out, inspected it before he lifted his foot to it, leaned his elbow on his knee, and moved in as close to Jawocki as Ronzo's smell allowed.

"What I'm saying is, Ronzo, you talk to me now, or whoever beat your granny to death will talk to me later. This is what we in homicide call a slam-dunk. You know what that is?" Ronzo looked up at him, puzzled, a dull, ignorant look in his eye. The frightened boy quickly looked away.

Ten years ago, in this exact situation, Turner might have slapped the truth out of Ronzo in about thirty seconds. But then his lawyer would have taken pictures of whatever marks Ellis had put on the lad, and, depending on the judge, would have had all the evidence thrown out, and a killer would have walked free.

Ellis hadn't spent seven years with Del Greco without having picked up a few tricks.

So now he said to Ronzo, "A slam-dunk is when we know without a doubt what happened. Usually, in such cases? We got the shooter standing there with a smoking gun, or somebody recognized him and gave him up." Ellis smiled down at Ronzo. Ronzo looked away.

"Or it's a case like this one here. All your granny's neighbors say you were always sniffing around her, trying to get some money. Granny tells them sometimes she gives it to you, sometimes she don't. Tells all those fine, upstanding, white taxpayers—how you think *they'll* look in court, telling a jury what your granny said to them about you—how you sometimes get mad and trash her house when she's not in the mood to feed your habit."

Ronzo was looking more and more frightened. Ellis would have preferred to have him at a station house, in an interview room, rather than here at the kid's apartment. Ronzo would feel more secure here. But so far, it seemed to be working out all right.

People were stupid, and Ronzo Jawocki was no exception.

"Now, there aren't any marks on your knuckles, and you *were* sleeping when I got here, anyone can see that, and I'll put that in my report." Ronzo looked at Ellis gratefully. Ellis broadened his grin, then said, "As long as you tell me the truth, tell me what really happened to Granny."

"I didn't kill my grandma." Ronzo was trying hard to make a tear come to his eye, but it wasn't working. He did manage to sniffle, though, and Turner thought this was due more to his need to put a match under his spoon and get his wakeup brewing than it was over grief about Grandma. Ronzo wiped at his nose with the back of his hand, looked down at what was there.

Turner said, "Give me a name, and I'll give you a minute alone so you can attend to your personal needs." Turner paused. He was about to find out just how stupid Ronzo was, and he didn't want to push it too far, just wanted to take it to the edge.

He said, "Before we go downtown and get your statement."

"I got to make a *statement?*"

"If you want probation, you have to. Otherwise, you go down with the killer. Case like this, the state'll usually grant probation to whoever talks to us first. You think the guy you told about your granny will stand up for *you*, after I catch him?"

Ronzo looked away, mouth open, tongue half out; what was left of his mind was working frantically, trying to find an out.

He looked back at Turner and said, "Maybe I should talk to a lawyer, huh?"

Was he looking for advice? Turner's expression was grave. "Fine, you do that." He turned toward the door. "Have a nice day. It'll be the last one you'll have for a long, long time."

"*Wait* a minute!" Turner had the door open, the heat was pounding him already. He stopped, turned back to Ronzo with an angry expression. "Come on back inside here for a minute!"

"Don't be wasting my time, son, the heat's fucking with my patience, and I got a homicide to solve."

"Please?" Turner came in and closed the door.

"What if—"

"Don't be fucking coming up into my chest with excuses. I don't want to be playing a lot of 'what-ifs' with you. Save that for the legal aid motherfucker."

"But I didn't know he was going to kill her!"

Turner leaned down into Ronzo's face and shouted, "Who!"

Ronzo leaned back in his chair, his eyes closed, and, stammering, said, "I only kind of mentioned once that my grandmother kept money around the house, that's all! I just maybe mentioned it one time, to one guy!"

"*WHO!*" Turner closed in for the kill, moving in so close that Ronzo couldn't lean back any further without falling off the chair. Turner breathed through his mouth. He shouted at Ronzo again. "Who, goddamnit!"

"Gerald Podgourney!" Turner backed away.

"You just 'sort of *told*' him that your granny kept money around the house. When did you share this information with him?"

"Couple days ago. It was over at the Tamburitza Inn." Ronzo had composed himself slightly, was nodding his head as he formed the lie in his mind, checking it for holes and finding none. "That's how I remember his name, it was just a couple days ago, and he kept asking me about

Grandma, if she kept cash around the house, I don't know, like, in conversation. I didn't know he was gonna go over there, I didn't know he was gonna *kill* her!"

Turner wondered how this Podgourney had known that Ronzo had a living grandmother; he wondered how Podgourney had known that the woman lived alone. He wondered how Podgourney had gotten the old lady's address. He wondered about these things, but he didn't ask Ronzo about them. He'd do that in a little while, down at the station, when he was worming a full confession out of this stupid, pitiful little white boy, in front of witnesses and an assistant state's attorney. A confession that would plant his junkie ass behind the wall at Stateville for a minimum of ten years, which would, in Ronzo's case, mean the rest of his life.

For now, Turner just said, "Go ahead and get dressed, Ronzo. And— take care of your other business. We got to go and write down a statement."

Ronzo got up, meek now, seeing his way out and leaping at it. Turner would let him think he was home free until the moment he was officially charged with murder. At the moment, however, he took out his weapon, held it in his hand, let it rest against his leg, then softly called Ronzo's name. Ronzo turned, and started at the sight of the pistol.

Turner said, "Leave the bedroom door open. I hear a window open, I'm coming in shooting. And you don't want to be coming out of that bedroom with anything but air in your hands, you understand what I'm saying?"

Turner waited until Ronzo was in the bedroom before he stepped into the kitchen, gave the phone an appraising look, shook his head and took a chance. He used his handkerchief to pick it up, and a knuckle to punch in the number at the squad.

Turner was in luck; the other detective working the case, Valencia, was in. Valencia told Turner that he had good news and bad news, which did he want to hear first? The bad news? Well, the TV had been a bust; the company that had made it had gone out of business twenty years ago. Turner said, "Wait, don't tell me the good news. Did the partial print come back to some squid named Gerald Podgourney?"

There was a pause on the other end of the line, and then Valencia told him it had.

CHAPTER

22

This Gerald Podgourney jagoff had a very interesting history. Ellis Turner looked at it as he sat at his desk, waiting for his phone to ring, waiting for Del Greco to finally check in. Goddamn that Del Greco. To Ellis, whose principles were deeply rooted in his Baptist upbringing, asking the Lord to damn somebody was the worst thing one man could do to another. Still, that didn't stop him from doing it again. God*damn* Del Greco. Why the *hell* hadn't he called?

Laney had made it clear that the lieutenant had ordered her to put the pickup directive out on Del Greco immediately, and Laney was countermanding those orders by not calling it in, by giving Del Greco a little more time. Turner had to give her credit for that. It wasn't exactly putting your neck on the chopping block, blind, but still, Turner had to hand it to her, she was trying to do *some*thing.

Ellis shook his head hard and looked back at the computer printout of Podgourney's rap sheet on his desk, trying to take his mind off Del Greco. Under the sheet were the handwritten notes and typed reports of the police officers who'd arrested Podgourney in the past. The rap sheet had been easy to bring up on the computer; the reports and notes more difficult, Ellis had had to go to each individual station house and talk to the arresting officers, ask for copies of what they had. The court files were a little easier, he'd gone down to the courthouse and gotten copies of the motions, and the motions to file.

Gerald Podgourney had started as a small-timer, but one who had quickly gotten involved with heavier and heavier crimes, and his sheet

A MATTER OF HONOR

reflected his progress: one count of inciting to riot; several counts of drunk & disorderly in his late teens, leading up to two vehicular and residential burglary arrests a couple of years later—Turner flipped back a page to check the guy's date of birth—when Podgourney had been twenty-two. The most interesting thing to Turner was that before and after those charges there'd been a couple of dozen misdemeanor theft arrests, most of them for shoplifting. He seemed to be a kleptomaniac; even as he'd moved on to larger criminal enterprises, the boy just couldn't stop boosting. As he'd gotten older, it seemed he'd turned to more violent forms of expression.

There were two felony arrests listed for the year that Podgourney turned twenty-three, both of them for assault. In both cases, the victims had been women, neither of whom had shown up in court, where the charges against him had been dropped.

Podgourney's last arrest was a doubleheader; he'd been arrested and charged with two armed robberies, had sat in the County for eight months, then had once again beaten both cases in court when the victims hadn't shown up to testify against him.

He'd given a different address for every arrest, and Ellis had neither the time nor the inclination to chase around town, running down taverns or empty lots. Something he'd noticed on one of the motions to file reports had caught his eye, and might make it easier for Turner to find Podgourney. He flipped back through the pages, until he found what he was looking for.

The lawyer of record for both armed robbery charges had been Arthur L. Horwitz.

Ellis Turner had something of a history with Horwitz. The fact was, over the last seven years, he and Del Greco had put three of Horwitz's clients on death row, down in the penitentiary in Menard. Horwitz had made his name defending what was left of the outfit guys, and had lowered his standards proportionately as the outfit had steadily been decimated by the FBI. He still liked to handle killers; death penalty and conspiracy cases were his personal specialty, his area of expertise.

Horwitz wore the wraparound shades, the three-thousand-dollar suits, the fancy, pointy-toed shoes. He leased a new Lexus every twenty-four months. Horwitz swaggered when he walked, ate in a different restaurant every night, usually with a different girl, who was generally half his age. Horwitz took boxing instruction at the East Bank Club. He ran a couple of half marathons every year.

But even with all that going for him, he wasn't fooling Ellis Turner.

For all his bluff and bluster, for all his strutting bravado, the guy was weak, and Ellis knew it. Ellis could smell fear on a man, and it came off

127

Horwitz in waves. Every time Turner ran into Horwitz, the lawyer's manner changed, his demeanor immediately became less aggressive.

The first time the two of them had ever met, Horwitz's client had walked on a murder charge. Turner and Del Greco had conducted the investigation which had led to the arrest and the subsequent trial, but Horwitz had worked the sort of magic he'd been able to pull off with regularity six or seven years ago; witnesses hadn't appeared in court, and those who had shown up had suffered convenient, severe mental lapses, memory losses on the witness stand. Somebody had gotten to them, Turner knew, money had changed hands. After the verdict, with his client a free man, Horwitz, swaggering and smiling, had approached the two detectives in the hallway, an arrogant look stamped on his face, but with his hand extended in a friendly manner.

"No hard feelings," Arthur Horwitz had said.

Turner and Del Greco had just looked at him for a moment, before Turner had said, "Don't believe it, motherfucker. There are all *kinds* of hard feelings," and he'd seen the emotion come into the man's eyes at the remark. Not the pain of rejection, not outrage, not anger, not grief.

Fear, was what Ellis had seen.

Horwitz, alone, without his killer of a client—or anyone else—around to back him up, had quickly withdrawn his hand and had lowered his eyes; a conspicuous gesture of submission. He had kept his eyes lowered as he'd turned and walked away. Del Greco, having seen the same thing Turner had, had whispered to Ellis, "Keep watching, he's gonna look back at us," and they'd both stood there, glaring at the lawyer's back. When he reached the elevators, Horwitz did look back at them, and he visibly started when he realized that both detectives were still watching him intently. He'd hurriedly looked away, and had literally leaped into the elevator when the door finally opened.

With the wide array of emotions that most criminals felt or pretended to feel while they were facing interrogation, Ellis would look for fear every time he was questioning a suspect. Fear was something he understood, something he was familiar with, an emotion he knew how to work, to take full advantage of.

He thought that Gerald Podgourney might not be all that hard to find, after all.

Still, it was awfully hot outside. Ellis looked at his phone. Could he intimidate the lawyer over the telephone? He wasn't sure. And an old woman by the name of Gladys Jawocki deserved more than a halfhearted gesture like a phone call; she wouldn't be worrying about going out in the heat anymore, because of what Podgourney had done to her. Ellis looked up, saw that Sergeant Laney wasn't at her desk. He grabbed his sweaty suit jacket off the back of the chair, threw it on quickly, and headed for the door before Laney could show up and start asking him a lot of questions, or ordered him to take somebody with him.

It was interesting what you could luck into seeing, when nobody knew you were looking. Turner thought about this as he sat in the air-conditioned city vehicle, a rented Crown Vic this time, without the green M license plates. The average Chicagoan could detect the Chevrolet Caprice unmarked police unit more quickly than a gangbanger could shout Five-0. Turner had gone up to Horwitz's lavish offices, and his personal secretary had told him that Mr. Horwitz was still at lunch, and she was certain that she had canceled all of Mr. Horwitz's afternoon appointments, and what was the gentleman's name again?

The gentleman hadn't given his name to her a first time, and Turner hadn't done so then, either. He'd left, had gone back to his car, and was now waiting in the parking lot across the street, back in the fourth row, with the engine running, the air conditioning blasting through the vents, looking at the building's entrance as he waited for Horwitz to return from lunch.

The woman hadn't said that Horwitz was gone for the day, she'd said he was still at lunch. Late lunch the man was having this afternoon. Still, his secretary had said she'd cancelled all his afternoon appointments. So the lunch wasn't only an extended one, it was an important one as well.

Turner waited, thinking about Africaan, a favorite topic of thought for him these past few days. A man must get a special, overblown sense of his own importance when he was surrounded by ass-kissers, by his own, handpicked sycophants. It must make a man look at things in a distorted manner. It wasn't just demagogues like Africaan who grated on Turner's nerves, it was even some of the people on the department, some of the brothers.

The police department was widely integrated today, but that hadn't always been the case. Even with the integration, only five percent of the detective division was comprised of African-Americans. Pretty low number. Turner didn't know what the white-black ratio was for homicide cops like himself. He knew it was very low, could think of only a handful of cops who were exclusively assigned to violent crimes, homicide.

Still, these new guys on the department today wanted to cry about oppression? They didn't know what oppression was. Turner could turn them onto Clete Mordell, down in Englewood, the very first black homicide detective ever on the CPD. What Mordell had had to go through would straighten out these youngbloods' hair. Even some of the things Turner'd had to put up with himself, dear Lord, a young officer in his twenties would shoot a white patrolman who tried to play the same game today.

Times had changed, and so had the people, and not all of the changes had been for the better. What had happened to the hope of the sixties? When Turner had been in high school, there had been hope for a better tomorrow.

He suspected that it all went back to something Turner had been intrigued with for most of his life: perceptions. He believed that an individual processed information the way he wanted to process it, took what he saw and viewed it through the smoky cataracts of his own personal beliefs. Turner knew very well that there were racists in the world, he didn't need spiritual leaders or politicians to pretend they were sharing some great insight by pointing that out to him. But he had decided a long time ago that he wouldn't let them get in his way, and he would *never* let them stop him.

Africaan had decided to capitalize on them, to suck the blood out of his own people, along with their money and their hope, as he gave them excuses and rationalizations for their personal failures. And the people ate it up. Some of them did, at least. Turner wasn't sure how many men showed up just to see what all the talk was about and how many were true believers.

Turner knew about oppression, and he had lived most of his life in poverty. But even in his worst days at the Robert Taylor Homes, he'd never seen the sort of remorseless killers that were being churned out today. But they never came from the midst of middle- or upper-class black families. The worst killers were always the poorest of the poor, those who had never learned not to imitate their oppressors.

Turner thought he understood it.

What chance can you have when your mother's a crack whore, and your father's gone, had abandoned you, was dead or else in jail? It was as if the kids were emotionally rather than mentally retarded, as if they'd never been taught to *care* about anything. Turner knew you weren't born with compassion; it had to be instilled. What could you expect from a child when he's been humiliated and beaten from birth, raised in abject poverty, subjected to the ugliness of the streets from the time he was old enough to go off to school, recruited into gangs and handed sophisticated weapons to hide, dope to deliver, had money put into his pockets, and taught that anyone who gets in the way of his business was to be shot down like a dog? The neighborhood role models were all money guys, sweet talkers who were sleeping with your mama, sometimes giving her dope in trade. Traditional religion was gone now, a joke, something to be disdained. These kids were continuously bombarded with negative input, were continuously told that nothing was their fault. The white man was to fault. The white man. What Africaan called the Snake.

It didn't surprise Turner that a third of all young black males were in some kind of trouble with the law. No more than Africaan's popularity shocked him. These people were screaming for help, and Africaan gave them the illusion of help, while he led them down the victimization path, filled their heads with hateful fantasies.

Turner personally believed that the ghetto would never make it, that it was indeed a contaminated landscape that had to be torn down—destroyed. But he was now beginning to see the same signs of hatred in the middle class that had once been confined to the ghetto, and that scared him. There were no Ellis Turners in the movies, or on rap videos; all blacks were the enemy of not only the whites, but of themselves, filled with self-hatred, and brutal to anyone who crossed their paths.

Turner believed that the culture these middle-class kids were now falling for—a culture created and perpetuated more by blacks than by whites—was as much to blame for the plight of the average black man today as anything white society had done to his people.

Turner had even gotten into arguments with some of the other black men within the department, when they'd blamed the whites above them, accused them of holding them back. You can*not* pass the sergeant's exam without a shitload of hard work and studying, he'd tell them, and they'd tell him that they were *owed* the position, that they had it coming to them. Turner was sickened by that sort of thinking; he'd never felt that anyone owed him a goddamn thing. In fact, to Turner's way of thinking, the truth was the exact opposite of what was these days being spewed.

He was the one who owed.

He owed himself success in his life and his career. He owed his people a good, hardworking role model for them to look up to. He owed his wife, and had devoted himself to playing his part in a loving, faithful, equal partner marriage. He owed his children a lot more than just a roof over their heads, food in their stomachs, and clothes on their backs; he owed them guidance, love, a safe harbor they could always turn to in times of fear and insecurity. And his Mama. He owed her something, too. He prayed for her soul every night. His church? He'd let that slip away, but he owed them, the congregation, the women who'd helped raise him. He felt guilty that he hadn't stepped foot inside that storefront church in more than twenty years.

Now Turner sighed, conflicted, understanding where some of these brothers were coming from, but in total disagreement with their views.

Everything Ellis Turner had, he'd earned, he'd worked hard to acquire. He'd busted his ass, and he'd been grateful for every opportunity that came his way, and he'd capitalized upon it, and what did he see all around him? Bumper stickers declaring that PROSPERITY IS MY BIRTH-RIGHT! He encountered kids like those two in the station house the other day, wearing two thousand dollars' worth of gold around their necks, with brand-new Mercedes Benzes parked in front of tenement apartments. Did they think that was all there was to life? How much you could score, and how quickly? They would tell him that they couldn't support themselves flipping burgers at McDonald's, and they were right about that. But on the positive side, you didn't go to *jail* for working an honest job, and what other career opportunities were there for young men who couldn't read?

None of them understood what it averaged out to, in the long run. They might make as much as a hundred thousand dollars over the course of a good, lucky, drug-dealing year, but that was offset by having to spend ten years in the penitentiary as a result of their criminal lifestyle, once that luck ran out. Average it out, and it was less money, all things considered, than they'd have made if they'd gone ahead and flipped those burgers in the first place. But these young ones today didn't seem to understand that there were many other options open to them, that it wasn't just money, sex, and drugs.

Ellis himself lived in a nearly all-black community, and the lawns on his block were green and mown, no matter how hot it got outside. The houses were well maintained. In the wintertime, he and his neighbors were out there shoveling snow, you could walk from one end of the street to the other in the middle of January and never get your shoes wet. Everyone pitched in and looked out for the two single mothers on the block, and the four elderly people who could no longer personally maintain their own properties. Almost everyone on Turner's block was a professional with a college degree, almost all of their kids went on to college. Some had been born to money; others, like Ellis and Claudette, had worked hard to get where they were, to get their financial act together. But there was a sense of community on Turner's block, a concern for each other that brought them together, made them want to help each other out.

Was Ellis supposed to feel guilty over what his hard work had brought him? Was he supposed to hate the Man? Or, in Turner's case, the Woman, as his own boss was a female, and his wife made three times the money he made? Turner could not bring himself to do it, wouldn't fall into that trap. If he suspected that someone was a bigot and—a lot more often than most white people might think—such people weren't shy about letting him know their views about racial issues, then Turner would shun that person, not even pretend to try to get along with him.

And he didn't project that asshole's views onto every white person he met.

Take Del Greco . . .

No, Ellis wasn't willing to think about Del Greco just yet.

He'd rather think about Minister Africaan, who lived in a million-dollar palace and told the people in the prisons and in the ghettos that the white man was their enemy. But the people in the ghetto weren't giving their money to the white man, they were giving it to Africaan. And to the Nation of Islam. And to the drug dealer, the liquor store owner, the guy with the lottery machine, salivating at his drugstore counter, and to the riverboat casino operators. They were looking to either escape or to strike it rich, while they blamed the white man—"society"—for their plight.

Ellis had a theory that there was some sort of mass neurosis involved in America, when it came to race. In today's society, everyone seemed supersensitive. Couple that supersensitivity with black skin, and add any sort of slight from a white man, and you had yourself a potential conflagration. Hell, just look at what had happened over the weekend. Or even before that, with the racial division over the O. J. Simpson verdict.

Where had these TV cameras and talk show pundits been when thousands of Italians had shown up outside the courtroom to cheer the not guilty verdict for John Gotti—three times? Where had they been when fireworks had been set off in the streets of Little Italy; why hadn't that been referred to as an example of the great *ethnic* divide between Italians and other Caucasians? Turner hadn't seen any such discussions, and suspected he never would. Italians weren't that easily identifiable; they fit *in* better than people with differing skin tones.

The world, in Turner's view, had changed, and it hadn't changed for the better.

Every white cop with an attitude was now being compared to Mark Fuhrman. Every black cop was a sellout, showing up for the white man, trying to impress his white peers and superiors. Rap songs celebrated that, told the brothers who were listening that working for a living was for hanky-headed fools. Videos depicted young brothers lounging around swimming pools, surrounded by women in skimpy bikinis whose sole goal in life was to fulfill their man's sexual desires.

And the kids watching and listening, black *and* white, fell for it, wanted that, yearned to emulate that lifestyle through the quick and easy sale of drugs, rather than working hard at a regular job, in the hope of someday saving enough money to purchase what they wanted legally. No, they needed to have everything right *now*. The need for instant gratification, on top of a lack of impulse control, added to insecurity, capped off with the sort of horrid self-image that could cause the wrong look at the wrong time, directed at the wrong guy, to get a man killed, was a formula for destruction, and one that was devastating his people.

Not his son.

Ellis thought that, then swore it to a God he had the greatest faith in, one he prayed to every night. It would not happen to his Quentin. Turner would die before he'd let Quentin fall prey to the seduction of the streets.

Ellis sighed, and wiped at his eyes with his handkerchief. He wished he didn't think so much. He wished he hadn't made such a big thing out of always showing up at work dressed as if he'd just stepped out of the pages of a man's magazine—this heat was wrecking his wardrobe . . .

He thought about these things so he wouldn't become overwhelmed by what he *had* been thinking.

Then he thought again that it was interesting what you could luck into seeing, when nobody knew you were looking, because a highly polished black Jaguar sedan was just pulling to the curb, directly in front of Arthur L. Horwitz's office building. The passenger door opened, and Horwitz stepped out. He was holding a hugely oversized cellular phone in his right hand. Turner shut his vehicle off, got out, and began to walk around the street as he saw Fat Benny Torelli get out of the driver's side of the Jaguar. Turner slowed his gait and waited, watched as Benny waited for Horwitz to get around the car, to come to him. Benny grabbed Horwitz in a bear hug, squeezed him hard. He pushed the lawyer away, but held onto his upper arms. Quickly, as if embarrassed, Benny pulled the lawyer to him and kissed Horwitz square and quickly and hard on the mouth.

That stopped Turner. Had he just personally witnessed Torelli give Horwitz the ancient, Sicilian kiss of death? No, the two men were now smiling at each other, patting each other on the back as they wished each other farewell.

Then Torelli noticed Turner, and his cordial expression changed. He glared at Turner, then turned to Horwitz, leveled him with the same look. He got into the car and slammed the door, roared from the curb with a squeal of rubber.

Horwitz, stunned, stood watching Turner's approach. Turner smiled at the lawyer, saw the man's mouth working without sound.

He said, smiling, "I interrupt a farewell kiss, Artie?" Horwitz did not respond. Turner shrugged, and raised his hands. "Hey," he said, "it's the nineties . . ."

Still nothing . . . or was there? The fear was there, lurking in Horwitz's eyes, making him have to bite his lips together so Turner wouldn't see them tremble.

What had Turner stumbled onto here?

Turner stopped fooling around and said, "I need to talk to you, Counselor," then waited. He intended to hear the man speak, wanted to see if the quiver of fear was in Artie Horwitz's voice.

And sure enough it was, as Horwitz said, "Concerning what?"

"A client of yours."

"I can't discuss my—"

A MATTER OF HONOR

"Gerald Podgourney."

Horwitz's knees actually buckled, and Turner thought that the man might faint. Turner put his hands on his hips and watched, puzzled, hoping the man would fall and bust his head on the hard, wide, city sidewalk.

But Horwitz didn't faint. He managed to straighten himself up, then reached into his back pocket and came out with a silk handkerchief that looked to be the same color as the one that Africaan had used to wipe the sweat from his brow Sunday night. Horwitz bought himself some time by mopping off his face, then he shook his head, as if surprised by his own reaction.

"I've been having fainting spells. The heat, I think."

"I need to speak to Gerald Podgourney immediately, Counselor. I'd appreciate it if you'd give me his home address."

Horwitz repeated himself. "Concerning what?" The color still wasn't back in his cheeks, and his eyes were radiating fear. Turner knew Horwitz was wishing that Torelli was standing beside him. The Italian gangster could hold the lawyer's hand.

Turner waited a beat before saying, "Concerning homicide."

Horwitz had to take a moment before he said, "I no longer represent Gerald Podgourney. And I can't give you his address. What I *can* do is try to reach him at the last number I had—" he paused, as if he'd known he'd made a mistake by trying to think on his feet, then said, "he used to work for me, until recently."

"Is that right?" Turner put as much accusation in his tone as he could.

"I'll try and reach him for you. I'll tell him you're looking for him. You're"—Horwitz snapped his fingers, acting confused—"Turner, right?" Turner nodded, knowing that Horwitz knew his name. He'd spoken it often enough during cross-examinations, while Turner had been on the witness stand.

Horwitz seemed composed now, almost back in control of himself. He turned and walked quickly toward his building's double glass doors. An extremely uncomfortable-looking man in a full uniform was already holding the door open for Horwitz, waiting, wilting in the heat.

Turner watched Horwitz walk into the building, curious, concerned, wondering what had happened, what he'd said or done that had caused the man to become so frightened. Was it seeing him with the gangster? Perhaps. Horwitz must still have remembered the lesson from their first meeting, because he didn't look back to see if Turner was watching him, although he did leap into the elevator.

Turner stood there a moment, looking through the doors. Could Horwitz have been so afraid because Turner had seen him with Torelli? No, it was no crime to spend time with a client; that couldn't be the answer.

Besides, he had almost taken his dive after Turner had mentioned Gerald Podgourney's name.

So what was there about a small-time kleptomaniac that could frighten a big-time lawyer?

Turner thought about that in the car, with the blessed air-conditioner back on. He was riding back to headquarters when the order came over the radio: all units were ordered to stop and detain Detective Marshall Del Greco on sight.

CHAPTER

23

It was the hottest night of a very hot summer, and violent crimes homicide detective Marshall Del Greco was well into his second night without sleep; and during that period he had spent almost as much time ducking his superiors as he'd spent working the murder. He'd turned off his cellular phone, only turning it back on when he had to make outgoing calls. The phone was charging now, plugged into the cigarette lighter of his personal car. He'd left his beeper in the glove compartment of the city's vehicle some fifty-some hours ago. Shut it down and had immediately gone off duty. He was working this one on his own, without the bosses, without his partner, without the department's backing, and without anybody's rules. He knew what he was giving up. Del Greco didn't care.

He hadn't fooled Sergeant Cheryl Laney for very long, or the new lieutenant, either. Del Greco kept turning up in places where a sick man shouldn't be, had spent too much time calling and talking to people, running plates, seeking favors from other coppers when he'd needed them, doing things that a man on sick leave would not do, drawing attention to himself as he did them.

Laney wanted to see him, yesterday.

The only way that Cheryl—or anyone else on the department—had of reaching him was through Del Greco's wife, Rachel, and Rachel had told him when he'd called in for messages that Cheryl had called the house at least a dozen times in the past two days. Which was a dozen times less than Del Greco's partner, Ellis Turner, who was frantic.

He'd find a way to make it up to Turner after this was all over.

It looked as if it would be all over in just a little while.

Del Greco rubbed at his scraggly, itchy beard, smelling himself and disgusted at the scent, squinting now to see clearly as he drove carefully down West Polk Street. He was close to his killer, he could smell *him*, too, but Del Greco didn't speed, for two reasons: First, this was not a neighborhood for a white man to be driving through at five o'clock in the morning; and an increasingly distraught Rachel had warned him four hours earlier that Laney had directed a pick-up-on-sight order on Del Greco.

Let some uniformed coppers try to pick him up when he was this close. Just let them try.

But Del Greco hadn't expressed that sentiment to Rachel, he'd calmly told her he was close to solving the case, trying to ease the fear she pretended she wasn't feeling. He'd told her that he loved her and that he would be home soon.

He'd have to find a way to make it up to Rachel, too.

Each set of oncoming headlights caused a firestorm behind Del Greco's eyeballs, and he had to nearly close them shut whenever the rare car passed him. Del Greco groaned aloud as a bus passed him; he swerved away, then quickly steadied the car. He'd breathed in too much air-conditioned air, hadn't had any sleep, he'd drunk too much coffee, and now he was nearly done in. That was all right, so was the case.

The weathermen were predicting today's temperature to be 107 degrees. Hottest day in Chicago in July, ever in recorded history. The city hadn't been prepared for this; over seven hundred people were dead already, and the number was climbing every hour.

There weren't a lot of air conditioners in the windows of the houses that Del Greco passed. The windows were all closed tight, and locked. You didn't do that around here, you had to worry about a lot more than the weather.

Around him, the ghetto was just beginning to stir to life. Women, mostly, were waiting at bus stops. A lot of them were wearing starched white uniforms that were already beginning to dampen from the high humidity. Oversensitive due to the lack of sleep, Del Greco imagined that he felt their eyes boring into the side of his head as he drove past them.

He cursed because he couldn't see the street numbers on the run-down, dilapidated, graffiti-covered houses. Most of the street numbers were hand-painted on the wood or on the siding next to the door, the effort taken only so the welfare checks and food stamps would be delivered to the proper houses. It wouldn't do to have your check sent to a different address, on different gang turf. Crossing gang turf this summer had cost 117 people their lives.

One hundred and eighteen, if you counted Rita, who seemed, at first glance, to have been an innocent caught in the cross fire. Del Greco still wasn't sure about that. He was about to find out if his suspicions were valid.

The tall building on the right—there—was that fifty-eight-eleven? Del Greco pushed in his lights and glided to the curb, left the car running so he wouldn't lose the air-conditioning. Across the street was an empty parcel of land that had been enlisted as a parking lot. A bunch of Cadillacs, Mitsu 3000s, and Mercedes Benzes were parked over there, in one of the most poverty-stricken neighborhoods in Chicago. The owners of those cars were greatly responsible for what had happened to the neighborhood, and in just a little while, Del Greco hoped, he would be getting some back for the hometown crowd.

He put the car in park and never looked down as he unhooked his cellular, then powered it on by feel, Del Greco's eyes now vacuum cleaners, sweeping the nearly empty streets. Someone would have seen him by now, would have sounded the warning. Del Greco didn't care. He hoped that someone had, was counting on it, in fact. He slowly ran his thumb across the keypad, punched in a number that he knew by heart, then let his finger run down the keypad until he found the *Send* button.

The phone rang two times before Cheryl picked it up.

"Laney." Her voice was thick with sleep and threat. Under other circumstances, Del Greco would have cringed. Or smiled. Now he just said, "This is Del Greco."

"Goddamnit, where the hell are you!" Cheryl was suddenly wide awake. Del Greco could hear her husband Daniel asking Cheryl who it was; he heard Cheryl tell him to shut the fuck up.

"I'm about to arrest Rita's killer. I will leave the car phone turned on. I suspect you're scanning for the number; you can find me on your own."

"Listen to me, Del. Don't throw your career away, don't you move. Tell me where you're at and I'll send units for support."

Del Greco saw movement out of the corner of his eye, and turned his head quickly enough to see a startled youngster attempt to pull his head around the corner of the tall building before Del Greco could spot him. Now, Del Greco did smile. "You know the regulations, Del, you know you can't do this."

"Rita's body wasn't cold and they were jockeying for position, saying it wasn't our case, not for homicide."

"All right, we can talk about it, we can straighten this out, Del, it's not too late."

The kid was at least a lookout, and, if he was in this gang, a killer. It was the initiation rite, one that guaranteed that the gang would never be infiltrated by an undercover police officer: you had to kill to get inside.

And the philosophy cut both ways; once you were in, death was the only way out.

"You know who works gang crimes downtown, Cheryl. Drunks and rookies."

Cheryl's voice was an urgent shout. "Think about your career; think about your partner, what this will do to Ellis!"

"I've got—"

"Think about Rachel!" Cheryl wouldn't know that he'd not only thought about her, he'd spoken to her. Rachel understood honor every bit as well as Del Greco.

To Cheryl, he only said, "I'm thinking about Rita."

Cheryl shouted, "There's no way this'll be righteous!"

"Don't believe it—"

"We've got you on tape calling off! Even if we didn't, it was your niece—you can't investigate her murder!"

Del Greco saw movement across the street, a head stuck out of a car window. Somebody from inside the building had called whoever it was in the car, and caught him sleeping. Del Greco saw the dome light come on inside the car across the street. He watched as it went out. He saw a figure shading his eyes, looking over slowly, tentatively, being careful, but checking Del Greco out. Del Greco reached over and opened the glove compartment, then depressed the button that popped the trunk.

"You want to, you can get those units over here, Cheryl."

"You can give what you know to Ellis, me, anybody else! Give it up, Del. Tell me where you are, then get out of there; we got to get a warrant, the investigation has to be approved—"

Del Greco didn't turn the phone off, just dropped it on the seat as he unfolded his large, muscular body from the car and squinted at the man who'd gotten out of the car across the street, the man who was now walking jerkily through the lot, as if his leg had fallen asleep. Del Greco saw that the man was holding a pistol down low at his side.

Del Greco walked quickly to the trunk of the car, reached in, and took out his short-barreled riot control shotgun. He stoked it, held it high in one hand. He had five shots in there, fifteen in his pistol, and three more clips for the pistol attached to his belt, in back. In spite of the heat, Del Greco was still wearing his tie and had on his suit jacket, the uniform of homicide; without them, he would have felt naked. He brushed back the hem of his jacket so that his adversary could see his badge. The man was halfway across the street; he stopped cold at the sight of the shotgun. Del Greco could see that he was young and thin; he saw that the boy's head was shaved.

"You want to stop right there, bro," Del Greco said, and the man did as he was told. Del Greco hadn't raised his voice, he'd kept it soft, low, conversational. "Now you want to put that weapon down, right there, that's right. Step away from it."

"Want me to lay down?"

"I want you to go into that building. I want you to tell King Youngy that Detective Del Greco wants to talk with him."

"Hunh?"

"Go on."

Del Greco took a step toward him, and the young man misunderstood Del Greco's intentions, gave a little shriek and turned and ran into the building. Del Greco looked down at the pistol in the street. A Sig Sauer. Imagine that. Seventeen year old with a Siggy. There was a time when Del Greco would have been surprised. He stooped, and used a pen to pick up the pistol, held it swinging in his free hand as he walked over and placed it in his trunk. He would remember the young man's face. He had his weapon, and the kid's prints would be all over the smooth barrel, probably even on the fat bullets.

So much for a warrant; Del Greco had his probable cause. He'd been counting on someone's stupidity to give him reason to confront King Youngy.

He turned back to the tall brown building. He looked at it for a moment, then began to walk toward it, very quickly, the shotgun at port arms.

CHAPTER

24

Cheryl Laney dialed the number from her bed, waving off her husband's angry words, his questions, angered at his demands. Couldn't he see that she had an emergency here? Daniel said, "Don't you *ever* tell me to shut the fuck up again!"

The phone rang in Cheryl's ear. She spun to face him and said, "Shut the fuck up," venomously, then said, into the phone, "This is Sergeant Laney. I need mobilization, immediately. Marshall Del Greco's affecting an arrest at"—she had to think to remember the number he'd given her—"fifty-eight-eleven West Polk Street. *Yes*, he needs backup. No. Don't call Turner. I'm on my way down." She listened for a moment, then said, "I want to keep this inside violent crimes; no uniforms if you can help it."

She hung up and got out of bed, excited, angry, wanting to fire Del Greco as badly as she wanted to comfort him. As she headed for the bathroom, Daniel shouted, "Who the hell do you think you are! I won't let you emasculate me!" When Cheryl still didn't answer, Daniel hollered, "You think you've been fooling me?"

Cheryl didn't even break stride. She had business to tend to, and no time for Daniel's ego. She didn't even know how much time she had for Daniel, period. But still, it bothered her, as she quickly showered away her sleep: what did Daniel think Cheryl was trying to fool him about?

King Youngy had been awakened by two of his bodyguards, and he'd leaped out of bed, reaching for the pistol under his pillow, had it in his hand and was ready to shoot before the frightened guards finally calmed

him down enough to convince him that he wasn't about to be assassinated. Now he sat on the edge of the bed, somewhat panicky, trying to
process too much information into a soggy, alcohol-addled, half-asleep
brain.

"Shit!"

"What you want us to do!"

"He *coming?*"

"On the stairs, man!"

"*Alone!*"

"Got a motherfuckin' shotgun for company."

"Shit!" King Youngy shouted again. He leaped from the bed, the pistol
still in his hand, and rubbed his cheek with it absently, not seeing his
woman flinch at the sight.

"I shoot him."

"You can't shoot a *cop,* Youngy!" Jason had spoken.

King Youngy looked over at him, honestly puzzled. "*What* did you
just say?"

Jason swallowed, held up both hands in fear and surrender. The other
guard, Renaldo, looked wide-eyed from man to man.

Renaldo swallowed his own fear and said, "He's right, Youngy, you
know he is. We shoot a cop, we get killed by them ourselves, and even
if we live, we don't *never* get out of the joint."

"Why is he *alone!*"

"Maybe he just wants to talk to you." His dope slave, Kirstin, said it
softly, from the bed.

"Anyone ask you your opinion, bitch? Shut the fuck up or I'll turn you
over to the rest of the boys."

"Youngy? She could be right."

King Youngy looked over at the young white girl, saw her pouting
expression, then looked away. He shook his head in frustration.

"I'm paying all of you hundreds of motherfuckers to guard me twenty-
four and seven supposed to keep this shit from happening to me!"

"We could shoot down a goddamn army, but we can't shoot a cop!"

"Where's Peeper?"

"Motherfucker was sleeping. Good thing Baby D was paying attention
out there. Peeper's out in the living room, you want to talk to him?"

"I ain't got time."

King Youngy was walking in tight little circles, naked, his weapon still
in his hand, as if it offered him some protection. He jumped a little when
the pounding began at the steel-reinforced front door. He stopped, stood,
heard his name called, looked at the wall, then back at his two men.
Steel door or not, it wouldn't take the police long to get in.

"You sure there ain't no other polices with him?"

"Ain't no others on the block."

Kirstin tried again. "He just wants to talk to you, Youngy." A male voice was shouting his name, demanding to be let in. Under the scrutiny of three people who lived or died at his whim, King Youngy made a snap decision.

"Go let the motherfucker in, have him wait while I get dressed."

King Youngy had decided to put on a suit, expecting to have a few minutes, while the police cooled off in the living room with three of Youngy's men watching over him, keeping him out of the bedroom. He smirked at Kirstin, angry because she'd seen him afraid. He walked over to his closet as the sound of scuffling broke out in the living room, then there was a deafening explosion, followed by the sound of a man's voice shouting. Youngy, half-deafened by the shotgun blast, couldn't hear what the cop was hollering.

If he was a cop at all.

King Youngy had this thought as he threw himself across the bed, tried to get under it, still naked, hearing Kirstin scream from somewhere above him. He was wriggling his ass desperately, trying to hide, when the big tall mean motherfucker with the shotgun placed both barrels right on Youngy's forehead.

"Grab some clothes, and get out here," Del Greco said to Kirstin. His tone was neither angry nor disgusted, was actually frighteningly calm; she was nothing more than a mannequin in the way of what he wanted, and he was moving her aside. He waited until the door slammed shut behind her before he pulled the shotgun a few inches away from King Youngy's head.

Youngy had dropped his pistol without having to be told, and now lay looking cross-eyed at the twin shotgun barrels, wondering if his men had been wrong, if this was indeed an assassination attempt.

Del Greco said, "I want you to grab that pistol by the barrel, and hand it over to me."

"You here to shoot me, then go ahead on, but I ain't gonna make it easy for you."

"I don't need you to make it easy. Now hand me the fucking gun."

"You ain't gonna shoot me?"

"Maybe later," Del Greco said, and waited as Youngy reached out a slow hand and grasped the pistol by the barrel, held it out to the police officer with his eyes wide, sweating. Without taking his eyes or the barrel of the shotgun off Youngy, Del Greco squatted down, and, very carefully, plucked King Youngy's pistol out of the young man's hand, grabbing it by the pebbled grips, then he stuck it in the waistband of his pants, around back. Del Greco straightened, and gestured with the shotgun for

A MATTER OF HONOR

Youngy to stand up, then he stepped back against the wall so he could cover the door, in case Youngy's men forgot their terror, got up off the floor and decided to charge the room to try and save him. Del Greco didn't think that would happen.

Youngy was looking at him, terror in his eyes, but, having no working knowledge of internal emotional functions, he set upon his face the only one he had down pat: his badass gangbanger attitude. He would literally rather die than beg, Del Greco knew that, and it was all right with him; he wasn't here to try and make King Youngy beg.

"You've come up in the world since I saw you last."

King Youngy frowned, trying to recognize Del Greco. He'd been arrested so many times in his life, any individual cop wouldn't matter to him, unless the cop was on the payroll.

"Yeah, you come to the house over on Monroe last year, a year ago ain't it? In May, I believe it was."

"May sixteenth," Del Greco said.

"Yeah, I remember that. You that crazy I-tal-ian-man, got hisself shot by the little boy right after that. I seen your picture on the news when it happen, I tell my boys I once got hassled by a television star."

Del Greco knew that Youngy was ignorant, illiterate, inarticulate, primitive and crude. He also knew that he was highly intelligent and vicious. The only two prerequisites to being a drug-gang leader. He would not know how to beg, but he would know how to bargain.

Del Greco said, "A woman was shot down in the street Monday night, right on South Dearborn. We both know that the heart of the Loop is no place to be having your badass gangster shoot-outs."

Del Greco could tell that Youngy was thinking hard, his forehead was deeply lined, a puzzled expression was on his face, along with something else: relief. He spat out his breath, as if disgusted.

"*That's* what you're here about?"

"That was no gang shooting, Youngy."

"Man," Youngy shook his head.

"The dead woman was my niece."

"Oh, man. You I-talians and your families."

"The killer was from your gang."

"I thought you was here to kill me."

"I might still be."

King Youngy waved a hand at him, shook his head impatiently.

"You want the boy shot your niece."

"For starters. You should know something, Youngy. There's about a hundred cops on their way over here—"

"Save it, man, I seen *that* on TV too—"

"They're not coming for you; they want *me*."

"I believe *that*."

"I want to know why you had my niece killed."

"The police, when they get here, what they gonna do?"

"Charge me with murder, I think."

"You kill my boys?"

Del Greco shook his head, raised the shotgun to his shoulder and watched King Youngy's pretense of coolness evaporate.

"No, no, don't do that shit. It ain't worth it, I'll tell you what happened." Del Greco lowered the weapon slightly, glad that he hadn't underestimated Youngy's intelligence. Both of them knew that whatever Youngy told him under the present circumstances couldn't be used against the gang leader in any court of the land.

"It was a work for hire."

"A work for hire." Del Greco's voice was flat, although his heart was racing. A work for hire. Perhaps Rita's murder wasn't as close to being solved as he'd originally thought.

King Youngy said, "Yeah, you know, what you people call a *contract*."

"My people."

"They an echo in this motherfucker? You know what I mean, you outfit people."

The outfit, Del Greco knew, loved guys like Youngy. The black gang-bangers were just as vicious but far more inexperienced than the outfit was, the gangs being disorganized because their upper-echelon members rarely lived long enough to gain much experience in corrupting politicians or the police—even though the money was there, they didn't know who to give it to. Guys like King Youngy got all the attention, while the outfit operated in anonymity, and were thought of with nostalgia by a citizenry that was saturated with violence.

"Explain this work for hire to me, Youngy."

"Rashon took it, I gave it to him. I don't deal with that small-time shit—hey, man, no offense . . . " Del Greco, involuntarily, had raised the shotgun again.

"Keep talking, Youngy." Far away, they heard the sound of many sirens.

"I give it to Rashon." King Youngy grunted a laugh. "A big old white boy come walking up the sidewalk, cool as could be, looking around, man, like he couldn't believe people lived like this."

"Was this guy in his late thirties, with glasses?"

"No, man, didn't look nothing like that. Young, mid-twenties, tops. Said his name was Franklin, but I think he was lying."

"Did this *Franklin* happen to pay you in hundred dollar bills?"

"In advance," Youngy said, proud of himself.

"Did he tell you what he wanted?"

146

"Funny guy, he was. Laughing, telling jokes. Even when he said he needed someone dead, he was joking around."

"Didn't tell you who."

"I look stupid to you?"

Del Greco looked at him, all skin and bones, naked, tight-muscled, with washboard abs. Hair cropped short so nobody could grab it in a street fight. Twenty years old and a millionaire, with more arrests than he'd had birthdays. Del Greco didn't bother to answer King Youngy's question.

"I wasn't about to talk about that with some white guy comes wandering in off the street."

"He had money, though."

"Big wad of it. Showed it to me right off, or he wouldn't have gotten through the downstairs door. Me, I thought he might be a fed, on account of I know *you* guys don't get a lot of money to flash around."

"How much did he have?"

"All told? Ten thousand dollars. Five then, five when the job was done."

"And you set him up with Rashon."

"Well, not exactly like that. I tell him I don't know what the fuck he talking about. I tell him he has got to be crazy, coming to this neighborhood all alone, with a big wad of money in his pockets. I tell him I is a businessman, I wouldn't kill another human being for ten *million* dollars."

"In case he was wired."

"They got shit now, goes up your ass. You strip a man naked and he can still record what you say. I ain't goin' down on no conspiracy beef."

"Smart thinking."

"So I have Rashon escort him out of the building, for his own safety."

"And act like it was his own idea to take on the contract."

"The work for hire, right."

"So you're saying you didn't know anything about it. Who it was, why she died."

"That's the honest to God's truth. All I know is, Rashon brings me twenty-five hundred dollars when the white man leaves, and he bringed me twenty-five more hundred up the night before last, when the job got taken care of. Rashon got to keep the rest of the cake for hisself."

"I'll be needing to speak with Rashon."

"You decided whether you going to fuck around and shoot me or not?"

"I'm not going to shoot you."

"Rashon, then. You're going to shoot him, aren't you?"

"I'm going to arrest him."

"You arrest him, he won't tell you shit."

"I'll convince him it would be in his best interest to speak to me."

147

The sirens had grown progressively louder, and now they were a wail. Del Greco was surprised to see the light of dawn breaking through the edges of the black mini-blinds that were hanging from the windows.

Del Greco said, "It'll stand up, if that's what you're thinking about. One of your boys flashed a pistol at me outside. I disarmed him, then chased him in here, right in through the door."

"You smarter than you look," King Youngy said. "Remember when I asked you, what your boys would do when they got here?" Del Greco nodded once. "I was wondering, was they going to arrest me?"

"Well, this *is* a crime scene. I had to smack two of your boys in the head out there, had to discharge my weapon . . . your living room wall's *all* fucked up."

"I like a good time as well as the next man, but I don't think we got a lot of time for much more of this negotiating."

"Is that what we're doing?"

Several of the sirens had now died. Youngy was right, they didn't have much time, just a few more minutes now.

"This apartment clean?"

"All I had was the gun."

"Then I don't see why you'd have to be inconvenienced."

"You tell them a good story, then, what you're saying to me?"

"And what do I get in return?"

"Rashon. And everything he knows." King Youngy paused. "And the man outside, Peeper. He flashed a gun at you, and you disarmed him. He'll have to do his year, I understand that." Del Greco still waited. They could hear shouting from out in the stairwell; the officers weren't taking any chances, the elevators all would have been commandeered and sealed off on the first floor.

"But he can't go to jail."

"Rashon."

King Youngy spoke quickly now, making his best deal.

"I take care of him for you, I give you my word."

"Are you a man of honor, King Youngy?" Del Greco was amused.

"I understands family. I understands that."

From the living room, a shouted order: "All right, stay right there, all of you." Then a different voice, "You! Baldy! What's going on? There a cop named Del Greco in trouble over here?"

Unhurried, Del Greco said to King Youngy, "I have to find out all that Rashon knows first, though."

"Everything he knows, no problem." King Youngy's pretense of unfazed cool was cracking; he was anxious now, sweating, his eyes darting to the door. Del Greco watched him nervously lick his lips.

Del Greco turned his head to the door and shouted, "This is Detective

Marshall Del Greco! I'm coming out with a prisoner." He lowered his voice to a whisper, said to Youngy, "You got a deal."

"What's this prisoner shit?"

"Don't worry," Del Greco told him, "you won't even have to go down to the station."

CHAPTER

25

Del Greco, on the other hand, had no choice but to go to the station, and there was a crowd awaiting his arrival. Now Sergeant Cheryl Laney, Lieutenant Foster, and Ellis Turner all stood close around Del Greco as he sat in the lieutenant's office with the door closed, waiting for internal affairs to show up; at the very least, at the bottom of the scale of his many potential problems, Del Greco had discharged his weapon, and he would have to explain the circumstances. He suspected that he would be forced to explain a lot more than that before he would be allowed to leave the station. He suspected as well that if his explanations weren't satisfactory to the investigating officers, then when he did leave, he'd be leaving his star and career behind him.

Del Greco's mind was racing furiously as it sifted through various truths and half-truths, subtle distortions, and outright lies: what he could get away with telling them—what would stand up in court.

"Are you trying to convince me that you just went there to talk with King Youngy about a partial *license plate* number?" Lieutenant Foster said. "You think I'm an asshole?"

Laney's look stopped Del Greco from expressing his personal opinion. He saw the expression of relief pass across Turner's face as Del Greco closed his mouth and shrugged his shoulders at his lieutenant. He wished that he weren't the only one sitting down. He knew that if he stood, it would be taken as a further indication of his disrespect for authority. Del Greco wasn't an equal in this room, he wasn't a colleague. Right now, at least as far as Foster was concerned, Del Greco was a suspect. Turner's

150

loyalty was a given—Del Greco didn't doubt for a second that Ellis was on his side. But Turner didn't carry any clout in the department, and Foster surely did. Del Greco would have to wait and see how Laney behaved before he would know if she was going to back him up or if he was on his own, was being hung out to dry to serve some greater political purpose.

"It was a personal vendetta, for God's sake, even Johnnie *Cochran* couldn't convince anyone it wasn't!" Foster was angry, and Del Greco let his mind wander, staring at the wall and thinking of his older brother as the lieutenant ranted and raved. Let him, Del Greco thought. It wouldn't change anything.

"We've got volumes filled with regulations, this isn't some unprecedented situation here, Del Greco. You're not fucking *unique*. There's an established code of conduct that you blatantly disregarded."

This stirred Del Greco to softly say, "Rita was my niece, Lieutenant." Del Greco had never called the man "sir."

Del Greco's voice was low and dangerous, but the lieutenant disregarded his tone. Foster said, "We've had coppers whose own *kids* have been shot down, we've had coppers whose *wives* and *daughters* have been raped, and they knew enough to let other coppers handle the investigations."

Del Greco kept his voice soft when he said, "They were giving it to gang crimes. My niece's homicide, Lieutenant."

Foster stood looking at Del Greco, shaking his head in disgust, breathing heavily, his hands on fleshy hips. Del Greco understood that the man was trying to be understanding. He also understood that the lieutenant was more worried about how Del Greco's actions would impact on the lieutenant's career than he was about how Del Greco would make out with IAD or OPS. He suspected that the lieutenant was also considering the racial aspects of the case.

"There are fourteen thousand coppers in this department. We can't have a single officer taking the law into his own hands."

"I was the first officer on the scene, and nobody ever officially took me off the case."

Foster held one hand up, a look of warning on his face. "Don't—just don't even start that backpedaling, self-serving bullshit with me. Save it for the Rat Patrol." He paused, pinned Del Greco with a look he probably thought was withering. "Or for a court of law."

Del Greco shrugged elaborately, holding his hands up, palms outward, in a universally understood, Italianate gesture of confusion.

"So what happens now? Am I suspended? Under arrest?"

"I supervise more than a hundred officers; I can't show anyone special privileges, not even you." Foster shook his head slowly, as he walked back around his desk. He sat down heavily in his wooden swivel chair, looked at Del Greco, and sighed.

Del Greco said, "If that's the case, Lieutenant, then I'd like a union representative," and he felt every head in the room turn toward him, but he didn't look at anyone but Foster.

Who glared. Del Greco glared back.

"That's the way it's going to be?"

"I'm not going to let you railroad me."

"*Rail*road—"

"Sir," Sergeant Laney's hand fell heavily on Del Greco's shoulder as she cut the lieutenant off before he could erupt. Del Greco craned his head to look up at her, feigning puzzlement. "Could I have a minute with Detective Del Greco, please?" It seemed to take a massive effort for the lieutenant to look from Del Greco to Cheryl. Del Greco looked from one to the other as if he were the game's spectator, rather than its football.

Slowly, carefully, quietly and deliberately, Foster said, "Do it in the squad room, Laney. Get him away from me."

Del Greco rose, nodded at the lieutenant, then looked at his partner, saw that Ellis was glaring at him nearly as malevolently as the lieutenant. Del Greco looked away, and followed Laney out of the lieutenant's office. He heard Lieutenant Foster punching numbers into the telephone before the door closed behind them.

Alderman Billy Charge sat in his great green leather chair behind a massive desk that dominated the room, the alderman holding a telephone to his ear and listening with rapt attention. His eyes passed unseeing over the African art that adorned the walls, the sculptures set on the tables, or standing on pedestals set in the corners. This was an *African* male's room—he'd always said that even a blind man could tell that much. This morning, however, Charge wasn't thinking about blind men, or about his Afrocentrically adorned den; this morning, Charge was listening intently to his caller, nodding his head as if the speaker was in the room with him, a serious expression set upon his aging, skinny face.

"One cop?" the alderman said at last, then listened again, nodding. He said, "No warrant? No backup?" He listened again, still nodding, running one hand up to absently pat his hair. He let the hand wander down to the side of his face, stroked the long scar on the left side.

"It would be better if he were German, but an I-talian will do." Alderman Charge sat forward, excited now, having processed the information and made his decision as to how to respond.

"Listen up. Forget about going through King Youngy, he ain't shit. That punk has never wanted any part of the Movement, he's never cared about anything else besides his own greed and desires. And besides, he can

A MATTER OF HONOR

hardly speak English." Charge was thinking furiously. After Sunday night, after Africaan's speech and the burning death of the white man, Charge had decided that he'd have to distance himself from the Minister. After Crocodile Berkley's well-publicized outburst of approval of the burning, Charge had decided he had to distance himself from Berkley, too.

So he said, "Here's what I need you to do for us, brother: Get ahold of Crocodile Berkley—in person, not over the phone—" Charge grimaced as the man on the other end began to argue, then cut him off with, "Listen to me very carefully: the Movement is more important than my ego—or yours. It doesn't matter how you feel about him personally, he's got the entire Gangster Apostle Nation behind that Year Two Thousand Voter's PAC he run.

"Tell him *I* asked you to call, said for him to call the troops—and I don't want a single *one* of them wearing gang colors—mobilize them, and get them down to Eleventh and State at"—Charge looked briefly at his watch—"twelve noon sharp. And I want them showing up in a whole lot more numbers than were at City Hall. Tell them to bring their girlfriends, we want black women in on this, too. Drag the bums out of the shelters, get their asses on a bus and haul them down there, too."

Charge paused, still furiously thinking. If he were going to become a federal congressman, he knew, he'd have to not only put some distance between himself, Berkley, and Africaan—while somehow still managing to appease them—but he'd have to curry favor with more traditional black role models.

He said, "Meantime, *I'll* call a press conference, and get some of the ward's Christian ministers to come down with me." He paused and listened patiently as the party on the other end again began to argue with him.

At last, Charge was able to say, "I need more than the Minister, this goes beyond just him or me! I *know* you're a member of the Nation. But I have to show solidarity, my brother, a united black front with more than just the Nation." He listened again, growing angry.

"They're Christians, and they care about their flock. They'll come down, and they'll bring anyone who isn't working. Now, you're a cop, and I understand your diffidence about working with Crocodile, but we need you, brother, the Movement needs you as much as the Nation does, maybe even more." Charge paused, waiting, but the caller had decided to stop arguing. Charge hoped that the man saw the wisdom of the alderman's argument.

Hoping this to be the case, Charge said, "Now, you know that hood, and the building. What I need you to do is find me one presentable, employed, young black man who lives within a couple blocks of Youngy's building. He'll need a reason to have been near the building. You want

153

a man who not only looks good, and has a job, but who can speak halfway decent English. Get hold of him, and tell him what we can do for him if he says he saw that policeman storming into that building shouting racial slurs."

Charge listened for another minute, accepting the caller's praise at the ingenuity of the plan, while debating his next move. Then, when he had it, he said, "Find me three more men—and none of them can have ties that can be traced back to Crocodile—who are willing to say they're scared to come forward. They can give interviews to some friendly media. Tell them we'll put them in profile, no names, and we'll distort their voices for radio and TV. Can you do that?" He wished he'd had these thoughts when Anthony Silver had been murdered. Charge heard and understood the hesitation in the officer's voice this time; the man could do what he'd been asked, but he wasn't certain if he wanted to go that far. He was a cop Charge had known for years, one who claimed to be a member of the Nation, but there were plenty of men just like him, who'd joined mostly for a sense of inclusion within an African-American group, but who didn't agree with Minister Africaan's more extremist views.

To calm him, and to get him back on the right side, Charge said, "Thank you, my brother, for calling me with this. The more corrupt police officers we can bring down, the more room at the top there will be for a man like you when I'm your congressman."

After accepting the startled officer's thanks, Charge hung up, sat looking for a minute at his artwork, still seeing none of it, then reached for the phone and began speed-dialing. He didn't have a lot of time, and there were a lot of preachers, priests, and reporters to call.

Just outside the lieutenant's office, in the squad room, at Cheryl Laney's desk, surrounded by a dozen busy violent crimes detectives who were trying to listen to every word the three of them were speaking while pretending that they weren't, Del Greco said, "If you let me run with this, I think I can bring down King Youngy's entire dope gang."

"He's not our issue right now—"

"Cheryl, I can—"

"Shut up, Del." She held her hand up as he opened his mouth. "Del, don't *say* it."

Phones were constantly ringing; voices intruded on their conversation as interviews were being conducted. A young boy stood waiting outside the squad room gate, reading the pro-police posters that were nailed to the concrete wall. His mother was being questioned by two violent crime homicide specialists, Del Greco could see them, trying their best to be gentle as they ham-handedly walked the trembling, terrified woman through the details of the brutal murder she'd been a witness to that morning.

Laney shook her head of short, thick hair, closed her eyes momentarily, then opened them and looked directly at Del Greco.

"I'm trying to understand why you did this. I'm really trying, Del, but it isn't easy. Don't make it any harder on me. And I'm telling you, quit interrupting, and just listen to me."

It was clear to Del Greco that Laney was doing her best to control her temper. The three of them sat in hard wooden chairs that had wheels on the bottom. The chairs were pulled close together, with Cheryl's in the middle. She was looking at Del Greco hard now, and he mentally predicted her next statement.

"If we're very careful, if the media doesn't go wild, we might be able to get you out of this."

"Cheryl—"

"Del, shut *up!*"

Del Greco fell silent, feeling the humorous stares of other hardened detectives, hearing a snicker directed toward him at Laney's embarrassing command. He wished she had her own office, that there was somewhere they could talk in privacy. He wished that his boss wasn't younger than he was. He wished Rita was still alive. Laney got herself back under control before saying, "The lieutenant only cares about how he'll end up looking. It'll make no difference to him either way whether IAD cans you, or pins a medal on you. Knowing you, I'm sure you came up with some way to cover yourself by now; you've had enough time to think of something." She gave Del Greco a look that told him how much she wished this to be true, then softly said, "But it's going to have to be good if I'm going to back you up on it." Cheryl paused, making sure that Del Greco wouldn't speak without permission. When she was certain that he wasn't going to, she said, "All right. Let's hear it."

One of the other detectives stood and held a phone out toward the trio. "Turner—for you on three." Ellis Turner looked over at the detective, angrily. The detective shrugged indifferently, then added, "Guy said it's about someone named—Pod-goor-ny?" Ellis quickly grabbed the sergeant's phone, turned it toward him, thumbed down the lighted button, and curtly spoke his name.

Del Greco said, "You have breakfast?"

Cheryl said, "You have to wait for OPS and IAD."

"It's not good that they're taking this long. That means they're having meetings, deciding to fire me for propriety's sake. Let them wait," Del Greco said, and rose without waiting for an answer.

Ellis hung up, looked triumphantly up at his partner and his boss.

"We got a line on him. Gerald Podgourney checked into Northwestern Memorial Hospital a couple of hours ago."

Del Greco didn't seem to care. He was lost in thought, staring out the window. Cheryl said, "Even if it's really him, he wouldn't have given them his correct home address."

"It's emergency day surgery, for a hernia, and—get this, Sergeant—he goes home in a couple of hours. We can follow him to wherever he's staying."

"It's a stretch. Call Andy again, see what he says about the legalities of pinching somebody fresh out of surgery. Knowing Horwitz, he's researched it already, and he's just waiting for us to move on Podgourney." She paused, then said, "This idiot gave his real *name?*"

"Looks like he had to. He's got insurance. Full coverage." Ellis flashed a tired smile; exhausted, but too pleased with this good news to lose his sense of playfulness, while at the same time trying to get a rise out of Del Greco. Ellis was very worried about Del Greco. "Guess whose employ he's in?"

Cheryl raised her eyebrows. Del Greco was still staring off at nothing, appearing pale, drained.

"Arthur L. Horwitz."

The sergeant didn't seem surprised. "His lawyer."

"Same man who told me just yesterday afternoon that Podgourney *used* to work for him, and that he no longer represents him. After I saw him and that outfit punk Torelli kissing each other on the sidewalk. I put it all down in my report. Horwitz gave the boy some decent benefits, too: Blue Cross, Blue Shield, only a two-hundred-and-fifty-dollar deductible." Turner smiled. "Makes you wonder how much Horwitz pays him."

"Makes you wonder what Gerald does to earn it. With a high roller like Horwitz, God only knows what Gerald might know."

"Horwitz is the weaker link; Podgourney's tougher, I think. If we can, we want to go through the lawyer, he knows more than he's saying. But a small-time hustler like Podgourney, not afraid to break legs, could be a valuable asset to Horwitz."

"Valuable pit bull," Cheryl said, then added, "This doesn't make sense. Artie Horwitz *knows* we're looking for Podgourney. He's too smart to let him check into a local hospital . . ."

"My boy at security spent twenty-four years right here in detectives. It's a positive ID. He says the man pulled his right nut pumping iron yesterday, at the gym on the forty-second floor of the Swissotel. Boy likes to live the high life. My man says Podgourney's in the recovery room as we speak."

Laney sucked in her cheeks, thought a second, appearing calm in the sea of havoc around her, then nodded. She stared at Ellis, making her

156

point as she said, "Take Valencia with you. Will Podgourney recognize either one of you?"

"This is his first at bat in the majors. I don't think he'd recognize any of us in the squad on sight."

"He live in an apartment, or a house?"

"Apartment. High-rise on East Wacker. Got a killer view."

"Don't follow him; you don't know what he might have on him. Call the apartment building first, make sure he really lives there, then wait for him on the street. We've still got the informant's statements, and all the proper data. We have an address, we don't need to have the warrant amended, or to seek fresh approval. Call Bishop first, though, before you go. Make sure you're legally covered. And don't forget Valencia."

Ellis nodded, turned as if looking for Valencia, then stopped, looked back at his friend and partner, at Del Greco. Del Greco noticed the move, nodded at Turner. "Go ahead, Ellis, it's a homicide, for God's sake. Ratchet the cuffs one extra notch for me."

"You gonna be all right?" Ellis's concern was honest, and for the first time that morning, Del Greco responded to a question with honesty.

"I don't know," he said, then looked at Laney. "You ready to get out of here, Cheryl?"

CHAPTER

26

"**I** was just a junior in high school when that little girl was born," Del Greco said, sitting in one of the tall-backed booths in Lou Mitchell's, the breakfast crowd noisy around them. The noise was grating on Del Greco's nerves, although the smells were refreshing, almost energizing. And the relative darkness, and the coolness inside the restaurant, were refreshing, too, and relaxing.

Finished with his breakfast, the first real meal he'd eaten since early Monday morning, Del Greco now sipped at his tomato juice, thinking back, trying to project to Cheryl a sense of nostalgic sadness. Across from him, Cheryl was no longer a sergeant, now she was his friend. And an attractive one, too, tall and thin, with that short, thick hair of hers falling down over her cheeks as she leaned forward, interested, wanting to hear what Del Greco was saying. The ten-foot walk from the car to the restaurant's door had left both of them slightly sweaty. Cheryl did not seem angry with him anymore; she seemed to be concerned.

He offered Cheryl a nearly shy smile. Del Greco had been forced to spend some time explaining the relationship to Rachel after the two women had met for the first time. Rachel had sensed the depth of their friendship, but on a different, more primal level than what it truly was.

It wasn't like that between them; Del Greco didn't sexualize other-gender relationships—although at one point early on, Cheryl had tried to do so—and he suspected that was one of the reasons why the sergeant felt so close to him; there was never any flirting or cute double entendres that had to be watched out for, stepped around, or stomped flat when

158

she was with him; he hadn't taken advantage of her attraction to him, and she seemed to respect him more deeply for it than she otherwise might have.

Since childhood, Del Greco had always felt most comfortable while in the presence of strong, intelligent women.

Now, Cheryl said to him, "You all right?" and the concern in her voice brought him back to the restaurant, to the sights and sounds and smells; the crashing of a coffee cup, the stench of some bore's cigar. He checked himself out emotionally, was able to nod his head at Cheryl.

"I'm tired," Del Greco said.

When he'd first figured out what it was that he had to do, Del Greco had taken the massive pain of his loss and imagined himself putting it into a box. At first it was a huge box, one with gaping holes, holes that he mentally taped over many times, so no sentiment could seep through. In his mind's eye, he'd pounded and shoved and had forced that box to shrink, the going slow, but steady. It stopped being the size of a building, then eventually it was the size of a shoe box. When it was down to the size of a box that would hold a small ring, Del Greco had taken it and shoved it into the deepest recesses of his heart, and he had been able to forget about it, and go about his business, fueled by a more savage emotion, and one that he was far more familiar with: rage. He wouldn't bring the suffering out again until it was safe, until he was with somebody he loved. Cheryl and he had a special bond, but she wasn't in that league.

Knowing where the pain was, and aware that it wouldn't come out to betray him, Del Greco was able to say, "Rita was like a—I don't know— it wasn't like she was my own daughter, but more of a baby sister to me, rather than a niece. There were only the two of us you know, me and Angelo."

"Your parents split up early?"

"We didn't have parents; we had DNA donors." The bitterness in his voice pulled Cheryl up short. She looked at him almost longingly, seemed about to speak, and Del Greco suspected that there was something important that she wanted to say, but then she closed her mouth, changed her expression, and seemed to decide it would be wiser for her to change the subject as well.

"Daniel said that you'd go off hunting the killer on your own, you know. Before we got the first report that you were calling around, pulling in favors."

"I worked with Daniel in the Fourth District when I was just a rookie. He's known me longer than you have." Del Greco didn't allow himself to betray his feelings toward Daniel.

"Were you serious about having a rep at the hearing?"

"If I'm going to be suspended? Absolutely. The PBA'll take my case to the Supreme Court."

"Only if they think you're getting screwed over."

"I'll have to convince them that that's the case."

"If anyone can do it, you can." Cheryl blew out her breath. She said, "After LA, and our own riots three years ago, after the cop shooting of that homeless guy the other day—Silver, I think his name was—"

"What shooting?" Del Greco said, but Cheryl didn't explain.

She said, "We haven't been held in high esteem by the public for a while now, Del. They might come after you on this one."

"A cynic might say that what happened last year would work in my favor."

"Oh, no doubt about it, it'll put a better spin on things. But you'll still probably get charged with official misconduct, at least."

"It was family, Cheryl."

"You're not in the outfit, Del."

Del Greco had to wait a second before he could respond. When it was safe for him to do so, he said, "It's not just the outfit, it's a lot more than that fictional romantic movie stuff, it goes a lot deeper than that, Cheryl, and you know it." Del Greco was offended by her flippant skepticism, and was trying not to show it, covering it up with a display of anger. He leaned forward and spoke earnestly, attempting to make his point.

"It was my only brother's *daughter*, for Christ's sake, Cheryl. My niece. If I wanted to keep the love and respect of my family, of my brother, of my wife—hell, if I wanted to keep my *own* self-respect—then I had to do something, I had to bring it to an end. What was I supposed to do, go to the wake and hold my brother's hand and tell him about the regu*l*ations and *codes*? About my fear of being charged with official mis*con*duct?"

"You could have let the assigned detectives work their case."

"I didn't interfere with any official investigation. I just worked my own. From what I heard—on the radio—they were working it as a gang-related shooting right from the start. It wasn't officially even a homicide case." Del Greco shrugged. "You know what happens with so-called *gang-related* shootings."

"Would you have done what you did if you weren't a cop?"

"The star, the gun, the authority—the *regulations*—they had nothing to do with what I did. Being a cop made things easier, but I would've done the same thing if I was a bricklayer instead of a cop."

"Which you might be soon."

"That's all right; Rachel's father owns his own construction company, and I don't mind working for a living."

"So it's worth it."

"For Rita?" Del Greco didn't have to consider it. "Sure."

A MATTER OF HONOR

"Even going against your own personal moral beliefs, cutting deals with scum like King Youngy so he'd give you the shooter."

That got Del Greco's attention. He sat up, no longer feeling tired or drained, his concentration level very high.

"How'd you figure that out?"

"Don't worry, nobody else will."

"How did *you?*"

"I know you, that's all."

Del Greco waited a moment before saying, "Can I ask you one question? No tap dancing around, walking on eggs?" Cheryl raised her eyebrows, it was the way she had of answering such questions; affirmatively, yet without her commitment that there would be no retribution if the words she heard offended her.

"Did Daniel tell you that?"

Cheryl didn't seem offended. She even smiled at him as she shook her head at what she saw to be Del Greco's ignorance. She said, "He may have known you longer, but I know you better."

Del Greco allowed his relief to show as he thought, You think so? but only said, "And?"

"You went in looking for blood, and came out with a single unregistered handgun pinch, which probably won't stand up. I think if you *hadn't* cut a deal with Youngy, he'd be dead by now."

That stopped him again. Del Greco narrowed his eyes and studied her for a time, then pinned Cheryl with a look, and softly asked, "You think I'd shoot a man down in cold blood?"

"Can I say it straight out? No dancing around, walking on eggs?" Del Greco didn't answer, nor did he return her smile. Cheryl's smile faded as she said, "Yeah, I think you would."

Del Greco's beeper went off, and when he shut it off and unclipped it from his belt he found that he couldn't read the caller's number.

"The numbers are swimming around. Can you read them to me?"

Cheryl held the beeper out at an angle, away from the Formica tabletop, squinted at the digital readout, then said, "Nine-seven-seven, nine-one-three-seven."

"That's the call I've been waiting for."

The sergeant's voice lost its warmth. "The reason you got me out of the squad room. Why you didn't want to wait around for IAD. Why you were so concerned about whether I'd had breakfast." Cheryl's expression was no longer pleasant. Like most people Del Greco had known, she didn't appreciate being manipulated. He cursed himself for being overtired; if he wasn't, if he'd been thinking straight, Cheryl would never have known that he'd used her.

"Excuse me," Del Greco said, and tried to rise, but Cheryl suddenly had hold of his wrist, was holding his hand to the table with deceptive strength.

"You might have been able to schmooze them, if you'd waited around, if you'd acted humble. But you didn't. You risked the one shot you had at saving your ass, to wait for a call."

"It's important."

"Important enough to blow your career?"

"I have to return this, Cheryl."

"Who is it, Del?"

"King Youngy," Del Greco said, and Cheryl sighed heavily as she let go of his wrist.

When he came back five minutes later, his face was grim and pale. There was a trapped, frightened look in his eyes. Cheryl looked up at him in surprise. She had never seen him frightened.

He grabbed the check off the table and said, "Let's go see what the big shots have decided about my life."

CHAPTER

27

Bodies were crowded together, close, in overwhelming heat, chanting slogans on South State Street, their voices raised in outrage. Dozens of frightened, heavily sweating police officers wearing hastily assembled riot gear guarded the entire block leading to the front entrance of the police headquarters building. The officers were sweating from more than just the heat of the blazing noonday sun. The news cameras were everywhere; held up on shoulders in the jostling crowd, set up atop vans above the swarming horde, sending the signal out live, as well as recording the scene for the afternoon and late night news, as reporters whose makeup was literally melting off their faces stood in front of those cameras and tried to explain in breathless, excited voices why they all were there. As those explanations were totally based on what they'd been told by Alderman Billy Charge, they weren't interpretations that conveyed a liberal viewpoint toward the police.

Charge stood at the front of the crowd, blocking the building's large glass doors, shouting for peace through a bullhorn, the instigator of the demonstration now feeling very afraid as he looked out at the monster he had helped to create. Charge wondered if he'd gone too far, had stepped over the edge.

Berkley was somewhere inside that crowd, working it, exhorting his troops, his hate-rhetoric coming to the alderman above the chants, the shouts, the curses, from Berkley's own bullhorn. Good Black Radical, Bad Black Radical; it worked for the police, why shouldn't Charge and Berkley give it a try? Charge had wanted a larger crowd than the one that had shown up at City Hall on Saturday, and he'd gotten it. This crowd was a hundred, two hundred times larger. This was bigger than King Youngy, bigger than Alderman Charge, even bigger than Minister Africaan, and everyone there knew it.

Another brutal, senseless murder had been committed against a young black male, and this time the entire black community was up in arms.

Charge stood in his place at the entrance to the building, as close to the blue wooden barricades as he could get, with a complete understanding as to how frightened the police officers must be; Charge himself was terrified, and he was one of the leaders of the attack. This was not the Million Man March on Washington, this was not even the Congregation on Congress, where Africaan had drawn a quarter of a million people. At both of those events—even Africaan's—peace had reigned. The brothers had listened to the speakers, cheered them, had even picked up their garbage when the rallies had ended.

This was not like that. This rally was not peaceful. Charge knew what he was seeing here was a prelude to a race riot. He did not like that knowledge, did not want things to come to that. He had to find a way to keep this peaceful, as whenever riots occurred, black people always suffered the worst of them. Billy Charge had lived through them before, had witnessed and been involved in three major race riots in his fifty-two years. And each race riot had been preceded by a scene like this one. Charge had expected the gangbangers, he'd expected the bums from the shelters. Both groups were driven by anger and resentment, and had nothing better to do than to shout that anger out at a symbol of the white establishment, such as the CPD. He'd even expected the preachers, had called them personally and implored them to come. They, and the reporters covering the rally, were the only calls made from his phone. Later, if there was trouble, a record of the calls made from his phone might well be subpoenaed. It had happened to him before, when he'd still been with the Black Panthers, and a charge of conspiracy had eventually been brought against him because of the records of whom he had called. Charge had made certain that none of the calls he'd made had gone out to anyone who had a criminal record. He hadn't even called the Minister; he'd only called those preachers whom he'd considered to be legitimate men of the cloth.

Who had shown up in droves, along with their constituents. Charge hadn't expected anywhere near this sort of turnout. There was an ocean of black people here, on both sides of him, for as far as Charge could see, lined up on the sidewalks, blocking the streets from traffic. Even across the wide pavement of State Street there was a sea of black bodies, standing in front of the quarter-million-dollar town houses the wealthy white people had bought so they could feel safe in the big, bad city, living directly across from police headquarters, where no niggers could break in and rape their wives and children, steal their precious color TVs, their VCRs, their fucking compact disc players. Charge could see some of those white people right now—women mostly; he guessed that they were nannies—their white faces aghast, looking from their second-story windows, afraid to come out into the street and witness this for themselves.

Charge looked back at them, looked at them hard, nodding his head, with the suggestion of a smile now playing around his lips. How did it feel for them, he wondered, now that the shoe was on the other foot? If Charge had anything to say about it, that shoe would stay on the other foot for a long time to come.

He hadn't been prepared for this; no one could have been. The shouts were deafening, the curses and threats frightening and heated. Word of the second black man's murder had spread through the African-American community more quickly than cancer during exploratory surgery. By the time the story had reached a lot of the people, it was claimed that the young dead brother had been tortured and sodomized by racist white cops, his body defiled, his genitalia cut off and stuffed inside his mouth.

Charge knew better. Charge even suspected he knew who had killed the second brother, and he suspected that the killers weren't white. But he wasn't telling, would not give it up for the world. He wanted this mass of people to keep believing exactly as they did; he wanted to feel their outrage, taste it, smell it in the air.

But he did not want them to riot, he had to find a way to make sure that not a single black man or woman was hurt because of his statements.

Charge looked at the crowd, aware that if he could get all of them registered to vote, and get them to spread the word, he could make it, he could actually fulfill his lifelong ambition and become the congressman for his district, which included a large portion of Chicago's South Side. The primaries would be held next March. He had eight months to get there.

His supporters had just finished setting up a makeshift platform with a microphone on a stand, right down the street, on the corner. Charge lowered the now useless megaphone, and slowly made his way over to the stand, seeing the officers on horseback withdrawing as the crowd slapped and punched at their mounts. Charge kept his expression solemn and controlled, but inside, he was shaking. He heard Berkley off in the distance somewhere, working up the crowd, shouting loudly through his own megaphone, about how they weren't going to take it anymore. Charge understood that this was the moment of his greatest life opportunity, this was the moment to receive the validation he'd spent his life seeking. Torn between his political ambition and his irrefutable love for his people, Charge thought of what he would say to them as he walked toward the platform. He mounted the three portable steps, tested the plywood platform, making certain it would bear his weight. He stepped to the microphone, called several times for his brothers' and sisters' attention. He adjusted the microphone so he would be able to stand tall.

He looked out at the swarming crowd, which extended well beyond Roosevelt Road to the south, and all the way up to Congress Boulevard to the north. Across the street, beyond the high- and low-rise exclusive housing of Dearborn Park, the brothers and sisters were congregated. He heard glass breaking somewhere far up ahead of him, and he squinted, saw that some young brothers were throwing garbage cans through the window of the White Hen Pantry. Charge winced. An air raid siren was going off somewhere else, but it wasn't close enough to quiet his voice, it was background music for the cameras.

The crowd was quieting down now, and Billy Charge had the attention of his audience. He would call for peace; he would beg for calm. His would be the single voice of reason among the babble of voices demanding violence.

Billy Charge believed without doubt that there was going to be a riot, no matter what he might say into this microphone. He felt it in his heart, he saw it all around him; the air itself was charged with violence; this was a mass of human gunpowder waiting for the match that would light its fuse. But this afternoon and tonight, on all five local news channels, all along the lakefront, with its liberal core of Democratic voters, Charge's voice and image would be stirring the souls of the TV viewers, the white viewers, the ones he needed if he was going to be elected to Congress. He believed that he had to be careful in what he said, or most of the black people out here now would not see those news shows; they'd be otherwise engaged. Particularly if Minister Africaan appeared at this protest, as rumored. Crocodile Berkley was unrestrainable, he could still be heard, screaming stridently and angrily into his megaphone, the amplifier lifting his voice over and above the many other strident, angry voices.

At that moment, Berkley began shouting for silence, and his minions, the hundreds of gangbangers, were enforcing that call, slapping the decent, hardworking people who weren't paying attention to Berkley's yell for silence. Charge couldn't stop himself; he shouted into the microphone, "Stop that!" as he glared at the young men, who looked back at him, bewildered. "We will *not* lay hands upon one another!" There was a loud murmuring of ascent from the crowd. "Or upon anyone else!" There was a smattering of boos. His palms were sweating; his stomach fluttering. He waited while the crowd quieted itself.

When it was just quiet enough Alderman Billy Charge began to speak about the racist fascist killer, about the scourge of the Chicago Police Department: violent crimes homicide detective Marshall Del Greco.

A MATTER OF HONOR

Five flights above that electrically charged crowd, violent crimes homicide detective Marshall Del Greco was being interviewed by two IAD detectives who were castigating him with every bit as much vehemence as the citizens were laying on him down there on the street.

He took it stoically, refusing to answer any questions, accepting the obligatory suspension that went along with his silence. He stared off at the far wall, ignoring the two detectives from the internal affairs division. His weapon and his star were on the table in front of him, the pistol empty, the slide open, the clip beside it, filled with deadly projectiles. Del Greco was waiting for the union rep before asking the men if he was under arrest. He knew that if he asked them now, they would more than likely say that he was, just to vent their frustration at his silence; he thought that maybe they wouldn't behave so emotionally if there was a union rep there, or better yet, a lawyer. He didn't push their hand, didn't say anything that could goad these men into making precipitous decisions.

The screaming came up from the street, in the pauses between microphone-enhanced accusations against him, as the speaker waited for applause, for substantiation of his words; as he took in a breath before he spewed more venom. The wild cheers for the speaker's words mixed in with isolated shouts for Del Greco's head. These calls were greeted with roars of approval.

"You hear that down there, dickweed? That's *your* ass they're calling for! How you gonna walk out past them?"

Both IAD detectives were young, white, and afraid. They were the sort of officers who were attracted to such work; it led to bigger and better things for those who hadn't joined the department to work the streets in the first place. Del Greco could see the fear in their eyes, could smell it oozing from their pores. It wouldn't take much to send them over the edge, these young men whose sense of propriety had been violated.

He didn't try to send them over that edge, he stayed quiet, completely ignoring them, hands folded in his lap as he calmly waited, hiding inside his head in a manner he'd been practicing and attempting to perfect for as long as he could remember.

Inside that head, Del Greco was making connections, putting together what King Youngy had told him with what he'd known to begin with.

"Goddamn you! What's your name: Fuhrman? What the fuck's the matter with you, sitting there like that when the city's about to fucking vaporize?"

It would do no good to explain the reality of the situation to these men. Their minds were made up, they wouldn't understand him even if he tried to explain. Would they know what Del Greco was saying if he told them that on the street, ignorance and anger were mined for votes, power and money? That the underclass was being exploited by their own, by people with selfish agendas that had nothing to do with justice, peace, or equality?

"Reverend Africaan's gonna show up down there, asshole!" Del Greco wondered if he was supposed to start trembling at the thought. He didn't care about Africaan.

All he cared about at the moment was Rachel, and Rachel would have seen the crowd on one of the early newscasts, and she'd have immediately known what to do. She'd be out of the house by now, would be with her mother in the mansion in Lake Forest. Rachel would have known the second she'd heard her husband's name spoken that the media would soon be knocking at their door. The burglar alarm would be on, and Rachel would be gone, safe. They had no children to take out of school. Del Greco had had a vasectomy at eighteen, to ensure that he would never be responsible for bringing a child into this world.

Del Greco told himself that Rachel would be fine. He told himself that if the situation seemed to call for it, her father would have a dozen burly construction workers come over to the house for Rachel's protection.

Del Greco told himself these things, commanding himself to not worry, not to behave like a suspect. All was fine, he told himself. Seventeen years of his life were about to come to an end, and all was fine.

He forced himself into a state of calmness, looking at a small speck of dirt on the wall, losing himself inside the speck, imagining it growing larger and larger, until it completely engulfed him. Voices came at him from various directions, but he couldn't hear what was being said.

If he'd been hooked to a monitor, the machine would have reported Marshall Del Greco as being in the alpha stage of sleep.

If a psychiatrist had been viewing the interview, the word "disassociation" would have wound up in the subsequent report.

To Del Greco, it was just going away, hiding out inside his head. It was what he'd learned to do after Angelo had been sent to prison, when Del Greco had been with *them* without a confederate or a friend, enduring the consequences of their brutal, base self-hatred, all by himself.

Some time later there was a single knock on the door, then Cheryl Laney pushed the door open and stepped inside. Del Greco smelled her hairspray, and brought himself out of his trance.

"What do *you* want?" the senior IAD investigator asked her. Del Greco thought he might be thirty. He was tall and skinny, with a head of blonde, razor-cut hair. Cheryl looked askance at his red-faced moral outrage, and immediately dismissed him.

She didn't dismiss Del Greco, however. He looked back at her, patiently—she'd get around to what she'd come in here to tell him sooner or later—he suspected that he already knew why she'd come in. But for the moment she seemed to want to study him, to check him out as if she were looking at him for the very first time. He saw pain in her eyes, and betrayal. She seemed as stunned as he imagined she would be if he'd just reached out and slapped her. Her color was the same as it would be then, too; her cheeks were flushed, her neck was red, dark eyes flashing with indignation.

"I'd like a moment alone with my detective, please."

"He's not your detective anymore, Sergeant," the second IAD investigator said. "He's *no*body's detective anymore. He's just a civilian waiting for the review board to make it official."

"What evidence are you taking to the state's attorney?"

"They'll do their own investigation; our report will be a part of it. And we don't think it's wise to discuss it."

"Even if you trusted me."

The investigator sneered. "Even if we trusted you."

Laney hadn't taken her eyes off Del Greco as she'd spoken to the detectives, and he looked back at her, impassively, waiting for her to explain herself.

Cheryl said, "Let me give you boys something you can use to form a basis of trust. It will help explain the size of the crowd outside." Laney paused for emphasis, then said, "At ten-thirteen this morning, the body of seventeen-year-old Rashon Latribe was unceremoniously dumped on the street outside O'Donnell's Funeral Home."

"Rashon Latribe?" the first investigator said.

"O'Donnell's Funeral Home . . . ?" his partner asked.

Cheryl was still staring at Del Greco when she said, "The late Rashon Latribe was one of King Youngy's most trusted lieutenants. And O'Donnell's Funeral Home is the site of Rita Cunningham's wake."

Del Greco pulled Cheryl's own stunt on her; he raised his eyebrows, quizzically.

"But you couldn't have had anything to do with that, could you, Del Greco? At ten-thirteen this morning, you were buying me breakfast over at Lou Mitchell's."

Del Greco's silence was her answer. He broke eye contact with Laney, and looked at the detectives. The PBA rep was more than likely out in the street right now, hoping a riot didn't develop. Del Greco heard his name spoken out, seemingly shouted through an electronic megaphone. He couldn't make out anything beside his name, but the tone was less than kindly. When the rep did finally get there, he wouldn't be in a very good mood.

Del Greco made his decision and stood, squared his shoulders, and pulled down the hem of his sport coat. He felt the empty spot at his waist where his pistol usually hung.

He said, "Arrest me, right now, and detain me, because that's the only way you're going to stop me from walking out of this room."

The IAD officers looked at each other, each seeking the other's advice.

Laney said, "There's no room in the department for a man like you, Del Greco."

The lead detective said to his partner, "Fuck him, we can pick him up any time we want to."

The second IAD detective was speaking to Del Greco's back when he said, "You'll be in front of a grand jury by this time tomorrow, jagoff."

Del Greco had every reason to believe that all three statements were incorrect.

THE
RIOT

CHAPTER

28

The warrant was valid, though weak. It was for a person, as well as a search. Assistant State's Attorney Andy Bishop had readily agreed with Turner's plan. Podgourney was unpredictable, and his record had indicated that he had been growing increasingly more violent, and hernia surgery was not the same as losing a limb; they went in with cameras now, used scopes to put the mesh inside you, and the entire procedure only left two small, round scars on your abdomen. Podgourney might not feel much like fist-fighting this afternoon, but he still had to be considered a dangerous subject, and it was best to scoop him up before he heard that homicide was looking for him, concerning the death of Gladys Jawocki. Podgourney would be ambulatory, and Turner wasn't discounting the possibility that he might be armed. Therefore, Turner had decided not to approach him on the street.

Nor would he approach him with Valencia. He hadn't bothered to inform the man that the sergeant wanted him in on Turner's pinch; he'd told Valencia to meet him at this apartment building at four—Turner wanted another officer with him when he tossed Podgourney's apartment, which he planned to do as soon as Podgourney had been safely transferred into the custody of the County jailers. Turner would square things with Sergeant Laney later, if the matter came up. With all that was happening in the city these days, it probably *wouldn't* come up, as Laney had more important things on her mind. As did they all.

Ellis was now standing across the street from Podgourney's apartment building, with a clear sight line into the fancy lobby. Podgourney hadn't taken his car; Turner's connection at Northwestern Memorial had told him that Podgourney's girlfriend had told the doctor that they'd be taking a cab home from the hospital, just as soon as Podgourney was cleared for release.

The river was directly behind him; Ellis could smell it as he casually leaned on the railing, smoking, just a well-dressed guy taking a midafternoon break from one of the nearby smoke-free office buildings. Fifty feet below him, tourist boats cruised by, their passengers not having a care in the world, on vacation in one of the world's most beautiful and safest cities, being driven out into the middle of Lake Michigan, where they'd be favored with a stunning view of a magnificent, world-class skyline. To Turner's left was the Swissotel, the site of Podgourney's injury. The building was all glass and reflective metal; Turner had to shield his eyes with his hand and squint to see the forty-second floor, where the gym supposedly was. Turner himself lifted weights, punched the bags, and rode the stationary bike three times a week after work, in the second-floor gym at the University of Illinois at Chicago's Circle Campus.

Less than a half-mile away from this spot were the law offices of Arthur L. Horwitz, who'd sworn that he wasn't Podgourney's lawyer, and that the man didn't work for him anymore. Turner believed neither statement. His experience with Horwitz convinced him that if Horwitz was talking, he was lying. Turner didn't take it personally; it came with the legal turf. Turner was standing on Upper East Wacker Drive, on a section of the drive that ended a block ahead, in a turnaround cul-de-sac type of deal that was comprised of a wide street, curved cement barriers, and protective steel railings. At the moment, three cabs were parked on the far shoulder, right at the spot where the Upper Drive ended. The drivers were up close to the railing, kneeling on carpets, facing toward the lake, their heads bent down low to touch the sidewalk as they prayed.

Even in a neighborhood like this one, you couldn't avoid big-city headaches. There was dog shit on the sidewalk; graffiti was there, too, mostly indecipherable tagging rather than gang-related scribbles. There was glinting glass from broken beer bottles littering the gutters. Across the street, a young man mounted the iron steps that led from Lower Wacker, holding onto the railing for all he was worth, bent over as if he were hurt. The man was wearing several layers of clothing, and he was wearing several woolen, winter caps on his head. He made it to the sidewalk, then took several staggering steps, then fell face first down onto the concrete. A businesswoman passing by first hesitated, then crouched down, but not too close beside him, keeping a safe distance between them, then she said something to him. Ellis saw the man swipe at her halfheartedly, saw her shake her head and get gracefully to her feet, a look of suffering on her face, rather than one of disgust. Turner looked away from the man.

A MATTER OF HONOR

If he stayed there, the police wouldn't have to worry about him, either; he'd be needing the meat wagon after he baked inside those clothes on the broiling sidewalk.

Very little traffic came from the east; only cars, cabs, and limos from the Swissotel. There was far more traffic heading in from the west, vehicles coming in to service not only the Swissotel, but the Hyatt Regency Hotel, as well. In the center of the drive were several lanes that would take you down to Lake Shore Drive. The trendy, expensive gym where Michael Jordan played pickup games was just two blocks away. This was not the part of town in which Turner felt most comfortable.

He had not bothered to talk things over with the doorman, nor had he informed the building management that he'd be arresting one of their tenants. He had called to ensure that Podgourney actually resided within the building. The friendly rental agent he'd spoken to had grown decidedly cool when Turner had mentioned Podgourney's name. Turner had Podgourney's picture in his pocket, would recognize him on sight. Even if he didn't make him right away from the photograph, he would just watch out for a great big white guy who was walking hunched over, holding the bandages to his gut, and favoring his right side.

Turner had discussed his plan at length with Andy Bishop: In the interest of public safety, he would allow Podgourney to enter the building, follow him in, breeze past the doorman, and present the killer with the warrant in the lobby, or, if it looked as if Podgourney was in good enough shape to argue, in the elevator. He would then cuff Podgourney, read him his rights, and take him down to the County, where he'd deliver him to the locked-down infirmary. Bishop had told him not to question Podgourney while he was still under the influence of anesthesia, and not to try speaking with him tomorrow, when he would still be taking painkillers. After he'd signed off on Podgourney, Ellis would return and, along with Valencia, give the apartment a thorough search. Turner thought this to be a good plan; not only would it cover them legally, down the road later on, in court, but it would give Podgourney, during a vulnerable time, a chance to think over his options, hopefully to have a face-to-face meeting with his conscience. Surgery did that to a man, made him take a long, hard look at his life, where he'd been, where he was heading. Turner was hoping this would be the case with Podgourney. The warrant in Ellis's pocket was an order of arrest for murder, but it had been gained on the word of a single informant, a coconspirator, and the only physical evidence that had been linked to their man was a single, partial print. Not a strong case, if Horwitz handled the defense. Ellis had distorted the truth enough to get a judge to issue the warrant, but there were no guarantees that it was worth more than the paper it was typed on.

In other words, it was enough to bring Podgourney in, read him his rights, and diligently ask him questions concerning the murder. But without a corroborating witness, Turner didn't think the print—on its own—would stand up at trial. None of the neighbors had seen Podgourney outside of Mrs. Jawocki's home; unless some of the other physical evidence found at the scene nailed Podgourney conclusively through DNA testing, then—if he was smart enough to keep his mouth shut—he was more than likely going to walk. Or they might get lucky and find some evidence—some of Mrs. Jawocki's belongings—in Podgourney's apartment.

Ellis was hoping this would be the case. He'd have a decent shot, even if all they found was some of the old woman's cash. Then Turner could get the boy alone and lie to him, tell him the old lady had recorded the serial numbers off of all the bills she'd stashed in her home. Turner would tell Podgourney that they had him dead to rights, and that a confession would save them all a lot of time and trouble and expense. Bishop might even offer the kid voluntary manslaughter, and he'd walk in ten. He'd be thirty-five years old when he got out of prison, still a young man. Younger than Ellis Turner was right now.

Ellis thought that he might not get any older, that if this asshole didn't get home soon, he might die of heat exhaustion right here in the street. He stood in the withering heat, fighting his resentment at the thought that a twenty-five-year-old punk like Podgourney was able to live in such a fashionable, luxury, high-rise apartment, in this neighborhood, with, on top of everything else, a killer river view. Man like that should be on the corner hawking *StreetWise,* or trying to sell gold chains. Or working behind the counter at the fucking 7-Eleven.

Turner forgot his resentment as he noticed a short, dark man standing across the street, right in front of the ramp that led to the underground parking garage, fidgeting and watching the door to Podgourney's building just as intently as Ellis was, only being more obvious about it. The man was wearing a heavy suit on one of the hottest days in Chicago's history. Ellis recognized the bulge under the jacket on the left as the type that could only be made by a concealed, large-caliber pistol. Turner pushed off the railing, stood straight and studied the man.

What in the *hell* was going on here? Had Sergeant Laney sent someone else, another detective, to back him up? Ellis didn't recognize the man—in fact, he'd never seen him before. He looked to have a bad complexion, looked to be about Podgourney's age, far too young to be a homicide detective . . .

Ellis Turner walked to the corner, waited for the light, then began to cross the street. Perhaps he'd moved too fast, for the man seemed to sense his presence, turned to face him, and made him as a copper right away. Turner picked up his pace as the guy turned first left, then right, as if seeking help, or backup. Or maybe he just couldn't decide in which direction he should run, because no cars whisked to the curb to pick him up; nobody came to his aid.

None came to Turner's, either, as the man began to run toward Ellis, reaching for the pistol that was stuck inside the waistband of his pants.

Ellis ran to meet him before the man could clear his weapon, charged into him hard, Turner's heart racing, his eyes wide with fear at this unexpected turn of events. He slammed into the man and wrestled with him, reaching for the weapon, and the kid seemed weak, out of shape, was breathing shallowly and screaming for help as the two of them fell to the street. Ellis felt a pain in his knee, disregarded it as he fumbled for the weapon. He thought he was suffocating, he could not breathe. The heat, the excitement, the fear, the adrenaline rush were constricting him, draining him of energy. He heard the squeal of tires, thought they were about to be run over, then he felt hands pulling at him, felt a forearm around his neck dragging him back. He heard orders shouted into his ear in a loud, commanding voice.

"Freeze you motherfucker, drop the fucking gun!"

"Please help me!" the younger man shouted. Ellis, struggling with unseen hands, being choked from behind, heard the young man shout, "This son of a bitch tried to mug me! Help!"

Ellis felt the powerful hands behind him twist him around, then he was thrown facedown on the pavement. He felt his cheek rip, felt it begin to swell.

"He tried to shoot me—there's his gun, in the street!" The man was screaming hysterically. Turner felt a knee slam into his back, heard a cop shout; "GUN!" as he pulled Turner's pistol free of its holster. Somebody was shoving the back of Turner's head into the blacktop. His nose was being smashed in, his lips; he could barely breath, let alone speak. Hyperventilating, humiliated, Turner struggled, trying to break free.

There were at least three of them. One was holding his head, one was kneeling on his back, one was holding his arms down—the only man now in front of Turner—and had pulled Turner's arms out in front, making it impossible for Ellis to pull away. Turner had a panicked thought: Where was the punk with the gun? Had he picked it up? Was he going to shoot them all?

Turner felt one arm being pulled behind his back, felt the cuff ratcheted tightly onto the wrist, then the other arm was forced back, and his hands were cuffed securely behind his back. He felt hands searching him, starting low on his legs, then grabbing at his inner thighs, working their way to his balls, around to his waist in back, and finally around to the front, where they touched, then hesitated, felt around on Turner's star.

Turner felt his police star torn from his belt, heard someone say, "Shit, he's a cop!'' felt the cuffs being manipulated, then his hands were free, nobody was holding him down anymore, and he was being helped to his feet.

Ellis stood waiting, rubbing his wrists, looking around for the man who'd had the gun while the patrol sergeant checked his identification. He was nowhere in sight. Fifteen feet away, Podgourney was being helped into his building by an attractive young woman. He wasn't paying them any attention. The cab driver who had dropped them off was glaring at Turner, as if Ellis was the cause of all the problems in the Middle East.

Ellis couldn't seem to control his breathing. He was gasping air in through his mouth, exhaling hard through his nose. He did not want his pistol in his hand just yet. He did not look at the small crowd that had gathered to watch. He particularly did not want to look at the officers who had done this to him.

"Jesus Christ, man, we're sorry . . . " Turner looked over at the patrol sergeant, who handed him back his ID. Another cop was holding out Turner's star and gun. Turner snatched them back, shoved the ID into his pocket, took the weapon and badge, put them back where they belonged. The crowd was dispersing now, the fun, the free entertainment, over with for the afternoon.

"You should have seen how it looked to us, Detective."

"Shut up," Turner said. "Shut the fuck up. Don't you say another god-damn word to me." Ellis was livid. There was a tear in the leg of his thousand-dollar suit. Blood from his damaged knee had ruined what a tailor might have been able to repair.

After a shamed pause, one of the cops said, "We pull up, here's this huge guy with a gun in his hand, with this little chubby guy under him." Turner spun on the officer angrily. Turner's lips were bleeding. He felt blood dripping from his nose. He was glad that he couldn't see his cheek. He was fighting the urge to strike out at these men, to attack them.

"We saw—"

"What you saw was a nigger wrestling with a white man, and you right away knew the nigger was wrong!" The man stepped back, startled, mouth open. Turner glared at him, then at the other officers. "In the meantime, the maniac with the gun got away!"

The patrol sergeant said, "Detective, you had to see it, it was a judgment call, you'd have done the same thing."

"Like hell I would."

Calming down now, standing on the sidewalk, his dignity returning in degrees as his breathing slowed, Turner looked at the officers, then purposely spat on the ground. The officers seemed more intimidated by the thought of what might happen to their careers than they were by Turner's anger. With Chicago's racial climate, Turner's filing a beef could land them a walking patrol in Hegewisch, and all three of the officers knew it. Turner was feeling better. He lowered his head and shook it from side to side, watching small drops of blood drip from his nose onto the sidewalk. He closed his eyes for a moment, rubbed at the bridge of his nose. When he was done, he opened his eyes and looked at his fingers, saw the blood. Turner sighed, heavily.

A handkerchief was held out to him. Turner took it, wiped at his face, then spat on it, reached down, swiped at the rip in his knee. He stood and attempted to hand the handkerchief back. The officer who'd given it to him told Turner he could keep it.

"You boys want to make yourself useful, I know a way we can all forget about this."

"What's that?" the patrol sergeant asked.

"A killer just walked into that apartment building. I was waiting for him when that punk with the gun almost blew a hole in me." Turner glared at them individually, then said, "I have a warrant in my pocket for his arrest. I go in looking like this, the doorman'll dial nine-one-one, and he won't take the time to look at my star. Come on with me, let's get this guy, and we'll all go back about our business."

"Detective?"

"Yeah?"

"Do you got *any* idea who the guy was with the pistol?"

"Never saw him before. You pick the weapon up properly?"

"Handgrips are pebbled. I bagged it. We'll do a report, request that the lab check the barrel and bullets for prints."

"You do that," Ellis Turner said, then turned toward the apartment building. "Let's go," he said, knowing in his heart that the worst of the day was over. With four cops knocking on his door, Gerald Podgourney would have to come along peacefully. The most humiliating afternoon of his entire police career was over; it would be all downhill from here.

Or so he thought. As Ellis Turner entered Gerald Podgourney's apartment building, he had no idea that things were about to get a lot worse.

CHAPTER

29

Rachel welcomed her husband into her parents' home with a frantic hug that made him feel ashamed.

"I stink."

"I don't care." She held him tightly as he walked through and closed the entry door, telling him how worried she'd been, wanting to know what had happened, why he hadn't checked in. Rachel questioned Marshall, clinging to him, as she led him through an entrance hallway that had more square footage than the entire Del Greco home, down four steps and into the living room, where his mother-in-law was seated in a wingback chair. The feel of Rachel's arm around his waist lifted him. They'd been married fifteen years, and her touch still turned the back of Del Greco's knees to water. She turned him to face the older woman, as if showing him off to her mother for the first time.

If it was true that you looked to your mother-in-law to see what your wife would look like in twenty-five years, then Del Greco had a lot to look forward to. Rachel had gotten some of her height from Joanie Berstein, and all of her good looks, the full head of wavy, shiny hair, the slim build. Her father, Paul, was a fleshy-faced, broad-shouldered, jowly, ex-street-brawler from the Northwest Side, whose parents had emigrated from Poland in the mid-1930s, while his mother had been pregnant with her first child, Paul. Joanie came from different genetic stock, her family had been in America for over a hundred years. Joanie's hair was still blonde (though Del Greco suspected that she had it dyed), and she had the height and bearing of aristocracy, which often came to women who had helped their husbands amass millions of dollars.

Paul was the iron fist, Joanie the velvet glove. It was a consortium that had worked quite well; doubters need only look at their children, at Rachel and their four grown sons. For all his physical strength, endurance, ambition, and his propensity to put in twelve-hour days, Paul still had the intelligence to realize where the real strength in the family lay.

Del Greco had been most pleased to have been welcomed into this family.

Joanie lifted herself out of the chair and hurried over to him, concerned. The two women held him close, and Del Greco felt the box inside his heart begin, ever so slightly, to tear. He let his weariness out, slumped into their arms, feeling as safe as a man such as he was capable of feeling; aware that he was loved more powerfully than he'd ever believed possible. It was not a one-way street; Del Greco loved them with all his heart.

"I'm so sorry about Rita." It was so much like Joanie not to meddle, not to ask about the speculation of the TV pundits.

Del Greco just said, "Thank you."

"You have to eat, and then sleep." Joanie was not making a request. Del Greco knew he had to be careful with his response.

He said, "I missed the first day of the wake. I should have been there, Ma. Angelo needed me. The funeral's tomorrow, I *have* to get to the wake today. I don't have any choice."

Joanie gently pushed herself away, and Del Greco felt slightly diminished. Rachel was crying softly into his shoulder, suspecting what the past two days had cost the man she loved, suspecting, too, the price they might both have to pay in the days, weeks, months, and maybe even years to come. Joanie's hand was still on Del Greco's forearm, and he felt the connection, strongly. He wished her silently to not let go, to not break the bond. Joanie's touch was healing.

"Paul's called his lawyer, he'll help you if it comes to that." Del Greco nodded.

"I don't think it's going to come to that."

"If it does, don't worry about—money." Joanie would have known that he was worried—for Rachel's sake, more than his own. Which was why she had said it. It needed to go no further.

Del Greco said, "Thank you, Ma."

"Did you do the right thing?"

"It's begun," Del Greco said.

Rachel sat on the toilet with the lid down and listened to Marshall as he talked to her while trying to shower away his exhaustion. She heard the details of the personal investigation he'd undertaken, how simple

181

police work combined with intuition, street knowledge, and keen intelligence had unofficially gotten the job done before the detectives who had officially been assigned to the case had gotten their own investigation started.

Rachel was already prepared for the wake, dressed in black on a hot afternoon. She rose as Marshall turned the water off, then she stepped into the bedroom and sat down on the edge of the bed. One of the servants had silently entered the room and had set up a silver coffee server on the nightstand beside the bed. Rachel poured Marshall a cup, stirred in the sugar, the cream.

He came out of the bathroom with a towel around his waist, cutting through the steam like a vision, and she looked at him, admired the strong, hard body, Rachel unable to look at the scar that a gangmember's bullet had put in her husband's chest. She'd spent three days sleeping on a molded plastic chair in the intensive care waiting room, praying that Marshall would live. She didn't need reminders of that time, though she had never told Marshall that the sight of the scar quickened her heartbeat. She could never do that; it was a part of him, what he was. Marshall didn't seem to ever give the scar a second thought.

Instead of looking at the scar, Rachel admired his defined abdominal muscles, then turned her eyes to the cut of his arms, the curve of the long, ropy muscles, the single, distended veins that extended from the top of both arms down to his wrists. Although he had the sculpted body an artist would love, he had never worn a sleeveless undershirt out in public. He hated the sort of men who would do that; hated braggarts, show-offs, and arrogant displays of strength or power. He'd wear baggy shirts in the summer, tail out, and never roll up the sleeves. He was a man who believed in hiding his strengths; a man who had learned many years ago that if you showed them, someone would do their best to find a way to turn them into weaknesses. He hid his intelligence in much the same manner that he hid his body; strangers only discovered the extent of his intellect when he used it to betray them for what they were.

He sat down beside her now and sipped at the coffee, taking short breaths, trying to delay the inevitable. Rachel patiently waited. At last, he put the empty cup down, put his elbows on his knees and rubbed harshly at his eyes. Rachel rubbed his shoulders, having a million questions, giving voice to none, knowing he would tell her what was on his mind when he was ready.

"We have two choices: I can quit; or I can get fired."

"Quit. Don't let them use you as a scapegoat."

Marshall nodded, defeatedly. "Seventeen years . . ."

"I didn't marry a cop, I married a man."

"A man without any other job skills."

"You can work with the boys, with Papa."

"You know I can't do that."

"Why not?" Rachel took a breath; he was tired, and he'd suffered a loss. It was no time to question his pride.

"Cheryl thinks I'm a psychopath. Said as much right in front of two guys from internal affairs. She thinks I orchestrated Rashon's killing, set it up so it would happen while I was with her for my alibi."

"Did you?"

"I didn't think of it. I knew what would probably happen to Rashon, but I wanted to question him first. Youngy would think he was saving me some time; doing me a favor. He's a real—"

"Psychopath."

"They're growing them younger and younger these days." He was a man who truly could make such a statement; the gangbanger who had shot Marshall had been twelve years old.

"What Cheryl said hurts you more than losing the job, doesn't it?" Rachel played his deltoids like a piano, rolling them, feeling them relax under her fingers; tension draining.

"It was different with her, she was my favorite boss."

"You suspect she had—problems in her childhood—right?"

"I'd bet she had a few."

"And how are you dealing with yours today?"

"None of it ever haunts me when I'm with you. It's only out there I . . ." His voice trailed off, he leaned his head further into his hands. Rachel allowed him to take his time, patting his back gently. He sat up a bit, but still didn't turn to face her.

"I thought I could make it through to the pension. There were the OPS beefs from disgruntled arrestees, and I cut a few corners over the years. But every cop does that. If you don't, you don't solve cases. I've got a couple hundred commendations. I never planted evidence. I never stepped on anyone's Constitutional rights. I never once told a lie under oath, even when it cost me the case."

"Cost you enemies, too. Inside the department."

"It did. Now it's over, and no matter what else I've done, I'll always be seen as the racist pig who went charging into the poor black kid's apartment, blasting away with the shotgun."

"How bad is it legally, Marshall?" Marshall shook his head.

"I didn't think it would be *noticed*." There was a touch of awe in his tone, then the steel came back when he said, "The arrest I made will stand up. I had probable cause to enter."

"I don't mean him, I mean you."

"They can rant and rave, but I didn't break any laws. Grand jury'll indict a ham sandwich if the state's attorney wants them to, but the PBA

183

lawyer'll make mincemeat out of their case if it goes to court. It may not even get to a grand jury, even with all the community outrage. I broke some procedures, some regulations, tore up the general rules of order. And if worse comes to worse, King Youngy'll stand up for me."

"You believe that?"

"He made a deal; I believe he'll live up to his end. He's insane, but he'll keep his word. Especially after he figures out what a mistake it was to kill Rashon."

"So the worst is . . . ?"

"The worst is what will happen at the hospital—"

"That's enough—don't say another word about *me*. I didn't go through medical school to be judged by journalists. To hell with the hospital. What's the worst that can happen to *you*?"

"They can fire me. If they really want to push it, they can charge me with a few low-end felonies. That's about it."

"And we've already decided you'll quit."

Marshall turned to her, and finally did what she'd been waiting for him to do all along: he hugged her to him, closely. She melted into him, into her lover, and squeezed him tightly, trying to get inside him so she could take away his suffering, bring it into her own soul. She thought that she could handle it. He knew that it wasn't possible.

He initiated the break, gently, held her at arm's length and looked carefully, forebodingly into her dark eyes, giving her his cop's look. Rachel didn't balk, though under different circumstances she might have. She looked back at him, trying to express how much she loved him through the intensity of her gaze.

"You know me, Rachel, better than anyone. Even better than Angelo. And you love me." His mouth twisted into a sad smile that put weight on Rachel's heart. "I never doubt your love. By now, though, our house's been all over the TV, they'll have interviewed our neighbors, they'll be picking through our trash." Marshall paused, lightly squeezed her upper arms. "And it's going to get worse, with all the racial animosity already in this city; what happened Sunday night; now Rashon . . ."

"And?" There was a shrillness in her voice that Rachel didn't care for. She forced herself to relax, she was safe, she was with her husband.

Who let her go, turned around again, and resumed his previous position, his back to her, his elbows on his knees, holding his head in his hands as he spoke.

"None of the good things I've done will matter now. The bad things will. Every case I ever had will probably be reopened. Killers might even walk because their lawyers will convince the appellate judges that I'm a bigoted cop. Everything negative that ever happened in my life, every

A MATTER OF HONOR

OPS complaint filed against me, every problem I've ever had, it's going to all get blown out of proportion, taken to the worst possible conclusion."

"You haven't done that much." He didn't seem to hear her.

"They'll make me look like I'm a stone killer who slipped through all the screening. This is every cop's worst nightmare, getting caught up in a high-profile, racially charged, media case." Marshall grunted. "The media's going to tear me apart.

"And the department's going to go on a tear, too. You know how they do you, we've seen it happen before. The superintendent'll go on television, talking about how I'm a rogue, and they're glad they caught me before I wound up killing someone. They'll point out that they *did* catch me, and that they relieved me from duty, forced me to resign."

"Marshall . . ."

"I was just saying, Sunday . . ." Marshall paused. "This is all I've ever wanted, my entire life." Rachel knew, but didn't answer. "A woman like you to love me, a family like yours."

"They're your family, too, Marshall."

Marshall nodded, then paused, gathering his thoughts. "What I'm saying is . . . " Rachel didn't rub his deltoids now, didn't rub his back. He said, "If you want, I mean, if you think I should take off for a little while, if you think you should stay here with your family, away from it all . . ."

There was a moment, just a flash in her mind, when Rachel thought she would slap at the back of his head. Then she caught herself. The white-hot anger receded, and she was able to think rationally. She knew that Marshall was the way he was today due to people slapping his head, and that such treatment only occurred on the days when his parents had been feeling especially magnanimous. So she controlled herself, and did not strike out, and she buried the sting because she understood him.

Then Rachel grabbed him by the shoulders, spun him around, and held his arms tightly as she spoke directly into his face.

"I know you're not a psychopath, because you have feelings. Sometimes, those feelings can be just a little too sensitive, Marshall. This is one of those times. You've been through a lot in the last few days, and you're coming down from two of the most emotionally painful losses anyone can experience: the death of a loved one, and your job. I understand that.

"But you have to understand *this*. I didn't run interference for you for the past two days to get shut out of the action now. My father's closing down the company for the funeral, and anyone who doesn't show up at the church won't have a job waiting for them Monday. My mother's out there watching shots of our house on TV, and she hasn't asked you any questions, didn't pry into what you did. All she did was offer you solace, a job, and money if you needed it. I've got four brothers who are pissed off at you because you didn't call them for help." Rachel saw the tears spring into his eyes, watched him try and bat them away. She felt something tearing deep within her at the sight, but she didn't allow any emotion into her voice as she said, "What I'm trying to tell you is I love you, I support you, and you're as much a part of this family as if you'd been born into it. Do you understand that? Do you understand what I just said? None of that happened because you're married to me. I've got a brother married to a woman who's barely tolerated around here, and *another* brother whose first wife divorced him because of the way we shut her out. If you get the royal treatment from this family, it's because you've earned it."

Marshall nodded. Now his eyes showed desperation, pain . . . Was there guilt shining out of them? Rachel couldn't tell. "And don't you ever question my loyalty. *I've* earned *that.*"

"You have."

Rachel softened. "You're not taking it very well."

"I'll handle it."

"*We*'ll handle it."

"Yeah," Marshall said, leaning into her, holding Rachel tightly, at last safe in the arms of a loved one, where he could let his box of grief explode.

CHAPTER

30

The media horde descended upon Ellis Turner as he and Claudette walked from the funeral parlor parking lot around to the front entrance of the building. There was a white butterfly bandage on the bridge of Turner's nose, and a small, colorless Band-Aid covered the cut on his cheek. The right side of his face was puffy, and he was walking with a pronounced limp. Still, when he saw the reporters racing toward him, Turner stopped, dropped his cigarette and stepped on it, motioned for Claudette to go inside without him, then folded his hands in front of his groin in a gesture that would later be analyzed on three different TV talk shows as an example of the average policeman's great, underlying fear of emasculation, and waited. The voices came at him all at once, cameras in his face, microphones thrust toward his bruised lips. Still, he said nothing, waited as the swarm of reporters and their support personnel set up, waited as the reporters began to shout at him.

Turner looked at the crowd across the street, beyond the blue police barricades, hearing their shouts, their insults. He read their handwritten cardboard signs, which had been stapled to thin sticks. The people holding the signs were waving them at Turner, as the crowd waves the "BRICK" signs at a basketball game when a player from the opposing team is standing at the free-throw line. Turner ignored the shouted insults and jeers, and at last squinted into the lights of the cameras, and began to speak in the most reasonable tone of voice he was capable of, considering the circumstances.

"I can't answer six questions at once . . ."

A young white man with big hair outshouted the others: "Do you believe your partner had Rashon Latribe killed?"

The crowd of reporters fell silent; this was the money question. Ellis knew how careful he would have to be in answering it; the highly critical, judgmental public would be watching tapes of what he said, and they would be seeing only Turner, would know nothing else besides the fact that a single policeman had answered a question. They would not know that he was standing in front of a funeral parlor in an almost exclusively white neighborhood, looking out at over forty people, most of whom were also white; they would not know about the support people, the camera crews, the sound technicians, the lighting people, as well as the reporters . . .

The public would not see that; they would only see Ellis Turner. And they would judge Del Greco as well as Ellis Turner—and the entire police department—not only based on what Turner would say, but by the way he looked when he said it; his stance, his attitude, everything about him would be dissected, torn apart and analyzed by an outraged public that had already been conditioned to believe that whatever a copper said was a lie.

Their beliefs would only be backed up by the constant catcalls in the background; the cries of Uncle Tom, of traitor, of white man's nigger; the calls for Turner's death. The TV and radio station managers would not excise these background shouts; they would consider the cutting of it to be censorship. Or they'd leave all of it in to give their reports a sense of balance, a slice of gritty street reality that would only serve to further exacerbate the already strained racial relations in Chicago. The curses, however, would be bleeped out; they could never allow swearing on the ten o'clock news.

Turner was fully aware of this. He was fully aware, also, that he himself had earlier had a humiliating racial confrontation with three of his fellow officers. He wasn't feeling particularly hospitable toward white cops at the moment. He had just come back from a briefing with the Rats, where he'd had to explain what had occurred after he'd recruited the three white policemen to help him serve the warrant on Podgourney . . .

Turner couldn't think about that now. He wasn't sure he even wanted to think about it later.

He took a deep breath and said, "Last summer, in June, a year ago, I watched as Detective Marshall Del Greco got shot in the chest by a twelve-year-old gangbanger. I was about a block away, knocking on the boy's grandmother's door, when the shooting occurred. Detective Del Greco saw the weapon in the boy's hand, and did *not* reach for his *own* weapon, not even after the boy had shot him. Detective Del Greco—with a bullet in his chest that damn near killed him—grabbed the youth in a bear hug and fell on top of him, effectively disarming the shooter until I could arrive and jerk the weapon from the boy's hand.

"Detective Del Greco had every *right* to kill that boy, and would have been justified in doing so. But he didn't; as I stated, he didn't even go for his weapon. He later told me that he wasn't looking at a black kid who had shot at him, or at a gangbanger. He told me all he could see was a little kid with a gun in his hand. The grandmother wailed in front of all y'all's cameras that we attacked her grandson for no reason, and you reported it. She also demanded that Del Greco be tested for AIDS, for having the audacity to bleed on her poor little grandson. The shooter was too young to be locked up under Illinois law, and is currently receiving 'counseling.' He is once again in the custody of his grandmother, and was recently arrested again, this time for dealing drugs.

"Del Greco spent three days in intensive care, two more weeks in the hospital, and two more months recovering at home before he was cleared for duty at the end of August."

"We aren't looking for speeches, Detective!" The derision in the reporter's voice was clear; Ellis turned to confront her.

"No you're not," he said, his voice rising in anger. The crowd was shouting more loudly now. He suspected that someone—probably an Africaan plant—was exhorting them, riling them, telling them that they had to make the plantation nigger—Turner—lose his temper, so he'd say or do something dumb in front of the reporters. "You're looking for a ten-second sound bite that will convict Del Greco of murder in the court of public opinion." Turner held up his arm, pinched the skin of his forearm.

"See this? What color do you see? We've been partners for seven years, and in all that time, my skin tone has never been an issue between Detective Del Greco and me. It's never been a problem for him." Turner pointed his chin at the crowd. "And I'm as black as anyone standing over there, and just as proud."

"So who killed Rashon, or had him killed? Why was Rashon's body dumped in the street in front of this funeral parlor?" Another reporter shouted, "Del Greco's rumored to have ties to the outfit; was killing Rashon their way of showing him *respect?*"

"Outfit?" Turner shook his head. "The only 'ties' Detective Del Greco ever had with the outfit was the two or three times we pinched one of their killers."

The crowd of reporters seemed surprised that Turner was still there. The anxious cries, the fighting for attention, had calmed down some; the impromptu interview had nearly taken on the manner of an arranged news conference. Turner stood, holding his hands together in front of him again, politely waiting for the next question, doing everything he could to help his partner. He heard the word *nigger* again, coming from the crowd, and didn't flinch. Could whoever it was cursing him actually believe this was the first time anyone had called him that?

A reporter said, "My station has recorded statements from three separate, unconnected sources who claim—on camera—that Del Greco was shouting racial slurs when he stormed into the Polk Street building this morning. Why are *you,* a black man, standing up for a white officer in light of such allegations?"

"You claim to have sources, so that makes whatever they say the truth? Bring them to me, show them to me! Let *me* question them! Not in the back room of some station house, but right in front of your cameras. Let's see how their stories hold up then. I'll bet my star against your cheapest hairbrush that I could prove all three of them to be liars in about ten seconds flat."

There was general laughter, and the reporter Turner had insulted sneered. "How? You weren't there, either, you can't be certain of what happened this morning any more than they are."

"I know Detective Del Greco," Turner said. "And I know how he conducts himself—on duty and off."

The reporters must have sensed that Turner had just reached his limit, because they began to shout questions at him again, loudly. Turner spun and walked right into some poor little fat man who wasn't bearing up very well to the heat and excitement; he was sweating mightily, had been holding a portable tape recorder out in front of Turner's face. As Turner spun, the recorder hit his injured lip. He reached up quickly, grabbed at it, as the short fat man tripped over the reporter beside him and went sprawling into the street. Turner tasted blood. He reached down, tried to help the man up, but the man's withering glare stopped him. Turner stepped back, then excused himself, walking rapidly through the crowd. They were shouting about Del Greco again, how could he stand there and say that he didn't think Del Greco had had anything to do with Rashon Latribe's murder?

Hadn't they paid *any* attention? Hadn't they heard a word he'd said? Or did they just not care? Did they assume he was automatically a liar because he was a member of the police department? Turner wondered how things had ever gotten to this point. He wondered if the public would ever trust the police again. Then, thinking of the little fat man, he wondered how long it would be before the lawsuit against him was filed.

CHAPTER

31

The Del Grecos and the Bersteins had to enter the funeral parlor through the rear entrance; they'd arranged their entry in advance, using the cellular phone in Paul's car. Fortunately for Del Greco, his father-in-law had driven, and the crowd of activists, politicians, rabble-rousers, gangbangers, concerned citizens, and newspersons hadn't expected the oppressor to roll up to the funeral parlor in a brand-new black Infiniti with tinted windows. The police had set up blue wooden barricades, and dozens of uniformed officers kept the crowd across the street, congregated in the lot of a Standard station that had been forced to close due to the size of the angry gathering. Officers on horseback pranced up and down the closed-off street.

Paul, stunned at the size of the crowd, said, "What do we do tomorrow? How do we get the—Rita—out of here, past them?"

Del Greco did not answer as he quickly followed Paul into the funeral parlor, holding tightly onto Rachel's arm. Joanie was leading the charge, hurrying past the anxious funeral director, who was holding the steel back door open for them, in a hurry to slam it shut and throw the deadbolt.

Almost to himself, Del Greco said, "This is King Youngy's fault; if he hadn't dumped Rashon's body here, nobody would have known where this place was until after the funeral."

"He's making a television appearance," the funeral director's assistant said, flustered and frightened, as the director shut the door, locked it, and leaned against it, breathing heavily, as if he were defending the Alamo. The director glared hard at Del Greco, who stared back without emotion as he tried to hide his disgust; the man was being paid for his services, and Del Greco had no patience with cowards. The assistant, seeming surprised that they had paid no attention to his revelation, tried again. "I just heard it on the news, that King Youngy person is giving a press conference at eight."

In an icy tone, Del Greco said, "Could you take me to Rita Cunningham's visitation room, please?" and the entire family stood staring stonily at the man who'd dared to pretend an intimacy with them that he'd done nothing to deserve.

Walking down the hallway, Paul Berstein said, "The boys're already here; Leslie's car was in the lot. He said he'd be driving." They were walking down a narrow paneled hallway, in twos, led by the assistant director, with the director taking up the rear. "I told them not to bring the wives, I hope you understand." Rachel's arm tightened under Del Greco's grip, and he saw Joanie's back stiffen, but neither woman said anything. Del Greco was appreciative of their graciousness. Joanie would let her husband know her feelings later on, and Rachel would probably not say a word, out of respect for Del Greco's grief. Del Greco could hear the older funeral director wheezing behind them, as he hurried to try and catch up. He was hoping that none of the Berstein boys had come to the wake armed. He was hoping that Ellis Turner would have the good sense not to show up at all. A time like this, with all those cameras out front . . .

"I want to talk to you," the director said, finally catching up to Del Greco, who ignored him, having no time for self-important old men with warnings in their voices. "Hey," the man grabbed Del Greco's arm, and Del Greco angrily pulled away without breaking stride.

"You put your hand on me one more time and we'll see how well you trained your assistant." The director, stunned, stopped short and stood in the hallway, staring at the four of them as the family turned a corner and entered the large parlor hallway.

Del Greco stopped at the entranceway to the visitation room, listening to the murmur of many people who were speaking all at once while still trying to keep their voices hushed. The large crowd had spilled out into the hallway, forming around Del Greco without paying attention to him, surrounding him. Del Greco's grip tightened again, ever so slightly on Rachel's arm, and she reached up and patted his hand, let her hand linger on his, caressing it. Taller than most in the hallway, Del Greco could see past the crowd, over their heads, on into the viewing room itself. Del Greco looked around at the people in the viewing room before they noticed he was there, and while he therefor was still afforded the luxury to do so, smelling the cloying scent of many flowers that were already beginning to decay.

He saw Charles, the spouse, standing in a corner, in quiet conversation with a group of people who looked a lot like he did; too-long hair wet and slicked back, round glasses without frames, well-dressed and whip-thin. There was a group of briefcases on the floor behind them, against the wall. From time to time, Charles would wipe at his eyes, as if distracted by the tears, or ashamed of them. He saw Rita's mother sitting in the first seat in the front row of folding chairs, holding onto the arm of her current boyfriend, who was looking around as if wondering what he had gotten himself into. He saw the back of Ellis Turner's head; he was standing with his wife Claudette—they were two of the surprisingly large number of black people in the room. At least a fifth of the crowd was not Caucasian, but were from the Berstein Construction crews, friends of the Cunningham, Del Greco, or Berstein families, or police officers who knew what Marshall Del Greco had done and understood why, and were there to show their support. Del Greco sighed in relief, for Turner's sake more than his own.

Ellis seemed to be the first in the room to spot him, and he left his wife talking with a group and hurried toward him, and Del Greco let go of Rachel's arm, looked quizzically at his partner's battered face. Ellis shook his head: Don't ask. Del Greco wouldn't think of doing so in front of other people. The two of them, for the first time in all the years they'd known each other, embraced. Ellis whispered into Del Greco's ear, "Fuck 'em, Del." Del Greco wasn't sure if Turner meant the crowd outside, the department, the press, or the world, but he agreed with the sentiment; it had been his lifelong philosophy.

Ellis said, "I've got to talk to you alone, as soon as you get a chance." Del Greco disengaged himself and nodded absently, still looking into the room.

The casket was there, in its place up front, but from where he stood, Del Greco couldn't see anything but the close-lidded lower half. Del Greco couldn't help himself; he began to breathe heavily, wondering how Angelo had made it, how he'd managed to sit there for the better part of the last two days, looking at the earthly remains of his only daughter, of Rita. Del Greco had seen death often in his life. He'd killed two men in the line of duty. On more than one occasion—although he would never admit it—he had felt gladness at the sight of a dead criminal. Surprisingly, for a man of thirty-nine, this was the first time in his life that anyone Del Greco loved had died.

Then again, there had been few people in his life whom Del Greco had loved. Everyone who qualified was in the building with him.

The crowd began to grow quiet as the people in the room caught sight of him; then it fell completely silent as suddenly all eyes were on Del Greco. They all knew what he'd done; there were no secrets in this room, and no matter what their opinions might be of his behavior, those who disagreed with what he'd done respected him enough to not voice their opinions. He didn't see their looks, didn't care who agreed with him, or who might think him a fascist. He felt Rachel's fingers pluck at his arm, but he kept walking, eyes searching, until he saw his brother, Angelo, who, surprised at the sudden quiet, looked around, startled, as if wondering what else could have gone wrong in his life.

Angelo saw his younger brother, nodded his head, and rose to his feet. Around them, the crowd parted as the two big, strong men—one well into middle age, the other just arriving—walked toward each other from opposite ends of the room. Del Greco felt his lips begin to tremble, pained almost as much by the sight of his brother as over the reason they were there.

Angelo seemed, to Marshall, slight, as if Rita's death had halved him. He walked bent over, shuffling, favoring his left leg. Marshall opened his arms and accepted his brother in a mournful embrace, the two men collapsing into each other, Marshall's lips tight as he squeezed his eyes shut and tilted his head toward the ceiling, Angelo's head buried in his chest, Angelo doing his best not to break down and cry in his brother's arms. Marshall lowered his head, kissed his brother's thinning hair, rested his cheek against the top of Angelo's head. At last, Angelo lifted his face, and kissed his brother on the cheek, right below his ear.

The crowd was all eyes, watching the tragedy as it played itself out. Several of the mourners began to cry loudly; a plaintive voice began to shout out a prayer. Only Del Greco heard the words his brother spoke into his ear.

"The boy outside, he was the one."

"He was one of them."

Angelo stiffened. Del Greco felt his brother's arms grow tight around his chest.

"Who else." It was a hoarse, barked demand.

"After the funeral, we'll talk," Del Greco said, and Angelo, a patient man with many secrets, nodded again, understanding even in his grief the wisdom of his brother's statement.

Ignored by almost everyone else in the room, Rita's mother had thrown herself into Del Greco's arms as he and Rachel had risen from the kneeler in front of Rita's casket. In a moment of weakness, Del Greco hugged her. He'd pulled away as soon as he could, and he hadn't spoken a word to the woman. Rachel's face betrayed her disapproval of his callousness at the same time that Angelo's glare exposed his feeling of betrayal; two sides of a tightening vice, with Del Greco caught in the middle. Del Greco took a quick inventory and decided that he felt slimy, as if having to acknowledge his ex-sister-in-law in front of Angelo had somehow tarnished him, made him smaller in his brother's eyes. Knowing this, he walked away, strode quickly over to Charles, interrupted the man's quiet discussion with one of his colleagues, took Charles into his arms and offered his deepest sympathies. Charles accepted Del Greco's embrace, and in a breaking voice thanked Del Greco for what he'd done. He asked if there was anything he could do to help Del Greco, told him that he was just a phone call away, if needed. Del Greco told Charles that he had enough troubles of his own right now, but thanked him for the offer.

Charles wouldn't have listened to the news on the radio, or seen it on TV. But he surely knew about the dead boy whose body had been deposited outside the funeral parlor earlier. He couldn't have missed the crowd of demonstrators, or the large group of police officers. Still, Charles didn't mention any of these problems, these disruptions of his grief, to Del Greco, and for that, Del Greco was glad; Charles might have been the only man in the room whom Del Greco would have accepted an insult from today.

Del Greco felt Angelo's eyes boring into the back of his head; he wondered if his brother would ever forgive him for hugging Angelo's ex-wife.

As soon as he could, Del Greco left Charles, and Charles moved on to speak to another man, a much younger man than himself, who had just entered the room. The sweat was still dampening the younger man's brow. Del Greco walked over and stood in one corner of the room, Rachel at his side. The Bersteins were comforting Angelo, whom they loved as if he were a cousin, consoling him with empty words that were appreciated far less for what they said than for the fact that they were spoken to him by people who cared. Del Greco spoke in low, respectful tones to the crowd that soon gathered around him, supporters from the department who would take their leave from him just as quickly as propriety allowed. Del Greco, although grateful to see them, would be just as grateful to see them leave.

A soft voice near his ear said, "Can't even step outside to have a smoke, with all the demonstrators out there." Ellis. Del Greco smiled for the first time since entering the building. He watched as Rachel and Ellis's wife, Claudette, hugged. The Turners hadn't brought the children. Another gratifying event.

"Excuse me," Del Greco said to the crowd, and led Ellis out of the room, walking quickly and looking straight ahead, so that no one would try and stop them. In the narrow outer hallway that led to the back of the building, Del Greco tried doors, burst in on the outraged funeral director talking on the phone in his office, and closed the door without apology. Finally he lucked into the door that led down into the basement, and he and Ellis descended the stairs without turning on a light. They stood there unaware that they were surrounded by caskets, as Ellis lit a cigarette and took a deep, welcome drag.

As he blew the smoke out, he said to Del Greco, "What'd you say to Youngy?"

Del Greco shrugged unseen in the darkness. "Enough, I guess. We'll find out soon enough."

"Boy must have known that you'd come back and blow him away if he goes back on whatever deal it was the two of you made."

It was the second time today that a colleague had figured out that Del Greco had made a deal with the devil. Were they that bright, or was he losing a step as he got older, becoming more predictable? They couldn't see each other's faces in the blackness of the room. Ellis's face glowed as he dragged on his cigarette.

"I gave an interview on the way in."

"How many times you get called Uncle Tom?"

"We were away from the crowd, but we could hear them. I told them how you didn't shoot the kid last year, after he shot you. How you disarmed him, fell on top of him, held him down when you thought you were dying and had the right to blow his head off."

The two men fell silent, thinking of what might have happened if Del Greco had done just that.

"I tried to make them understand that all you see is right and wrong. About how we've been partners now for seven years, and I never saw any signs of racism." Turner paused, then said, "They weren't paying a lot of attention."

"I'm sorry for what this—might do to you—Ellis."

Del Greco felt a sudden change in the air around him, sensed Turner's hot, angry attitude, and he flinched, half expecting to be hollered at, but when Ellis's voice broke the darkness, it was soft. "Don't you *ever* say something like that to me again," he said, in a tight, barely controlled voice.

"Everybody I'm close to is getting pissing off at me today."

"You're my partner; I don't know from white or black with you. You never showed me anything but respect."

Both men knew that Ellis had earned it before Del Greco had shown it; neither man had to say it; Del Greco had been forced to earn his respect from Turner, as well.

Del Greco reached up, touched Turner's shoulder, reached inside his partner's suit jacket, then felt his way down until he found the cigarettes in Turner's monogrammed shirt pocket. He took one out, chewed off the filter, spat it on the floor, lit the cigarette, and put the pack and the lighter back into Turner's shirt. Del Greco took in a deep drag, felt the dizziness, the light-headedness, let the smoke out through his nose as he took another deep drag. Even without the filter, he could taste the tartness of menthol. Del Greco closed his eyes in the darkness, and stood there, slightly swaying.

Ellis said, "I should have told them Charge would do anything to get his face in front of a camera, and that he wasn't much more than Minister Africaan's lapdog."

"Thank God you didn't." Del Greco didn't agree with the statement; he knew that Charge was more than that, but he didn't say any more, he'd already accidentally offended Turner once. He was somewhat surprised that Ellis was even speaking to him. Del Greco wasn't at all certain how he'd be feeling now if their situations had been reversed, if someone Turner loved had been killed and Del Greco had been shut out of the investigation.

Ellis said, "I'm down with you. That's all there is to say."

Del Greco wondered how Ellis felt, a black man in a white man's world, in a department where less than ten percent of the detectives had his skin tone. Ellis had never let Del Greco's race stand in the way of their friendship, but this was beyond one-on-one now; the whole city was watching, drawing assumptions, listening to people who represented themselves as being spokesmen for some vast, unnamed "community" that wasn't intelligent enough to survive without their help and guidance, some enormous group of semi-retardates who had to be spoken for and to, and who perhaps even had to be told what they were allowed to think.

What Ellis had said to the reporters would alienate him from a lot of his fellow black officers, and it could come back to haunt his wife, could cause his children insults at school. Del Greco was as aware as any white man could be as to how much racism there actually was within the Chicago Police Department. Some of the bigoted white officers—and there were far more than the bosses and politicians wanted to admit or believe—would now consider Turner to be nothing more than Del Greco's lackey.

In the darkness, Del Greco reached up a hand, gripped Ellis's shoulder again, but this time left his hand there, and he squeezed, hoping his gesture wouldn't further alienate the man.

Del Greco said, "What happened to your face?"

"The Podgourney pinch didn't work out as planned."

"He do this to you?"

Ellis blew out his breath. "Shit . . ."

"What?"

"It went bad. I went by the book, didn't have to get a new warrant, nothing, but the second we got in the apartment door, man, everything went to hell."

Ellis didn't seem willing to discuss it any further, and Del Greco, more interested than he would let Ellis know, decided it would be wiser, for the moment, not to take it any further.

Ellis quickly changed the subject. "Cheryl Laney wants to come to the funeral; asked me to see if you'd mind."

"No." Del Greco barked it; a single, bitter syllable. Ellis's silence spoke more eloquently than the facial gesture that Del Greco could not see. Owing Turner more than he'd given him, Del Greco quietly explained. "She gave the Rats more than they already had to hang me with, and she did it on purpose; keep that in mind in the future."

"If I got one."

"What?"

"Forget about it."

Del Greco kept quiet about it, but he did not forget about it. He filed it away in the back of a mind that forgot very little.

Ellis said, "You two were pretty tight."

"Nobody should ever get two chances to fuck you. I'm resigning, so Cheryl's had the only shot she'll ever get. I won't have her here, acting like she cares about me. If she did, she'd have backed me up today."

"Did you do it, Del? I got a right to ask."

"Do *what?*" Del Greco asked impatiently, knowing very well what Ellis was asking him. He saw Ellis's face light up again, the ember of the cigarette glowing red. He saw that Ellis's eyes were squinted, that he was concentrating on Del Greco's face.

"Did you set it up that way? You can't blame Cheryl for thinking that; everybody knows you got a perverse enough mind."

It seemed to be the question of the day. Cheryl suspected he had set her up as his alibi, and even Rachel had wanted to know if Del Greco had planned the murder. Del Greco couldn't blame Ellis for thinking that way. He would not have blamed Cheryl, either, if she hadn't made a point of voicing her suspicions in front of two investigators from IAD.

"We better get back upstairs before O'Donnell calls out SWAT."

"Wait a minute." Del Greco watched the hot red ember hit the floor, watched it disappear as Ellis stepped on the butt. He smelled the smoke strongly in the darkness, wondered if the room was filled with dead bodies, waiting for O'Donnell to come down and do whatever he did to make them presentable for viewing. He finished his own cigarette, and stomped it out. He didn't care who else might be down here, living or dead.

Turner said, "Take a few days compassionate leave; they got to pay you. Don't quit, Del."

"I was suspended without pay as soon as I refused to speak to the Rats."

"Then wait for the air to clear. The media's a bitch, but they're sometimes fair, and they love a backlash, one reporter against another. They'll

198

look into what I told them, some of them will, anyway. They'll check it out, you know how they are once they sink their teeth into something. This entire thing could spin around to your benefit."

"I won't live or die by the media." Del Greco's thoughts came out of his mouth more harshly than he'd planned.

"Then what're you going to do?"

"I'm quitting," Del Greco said, in the darkness of a basement room that was filled with empty caskets. "It's over."

CHAPTER

32

Amy, at last, was home. She wouldn't be for long. She was getting out of this apartment just as quickly as she could.

It had taken Arthur L. Horwitz's outraged, shouting presence at police headquarters before the cops would finally cut Amy loose. She had collapsed into Mr. Horwitz's arms when he had entered the tiny, cell-like room where they'd been keeping her, and Mr. Horwitz had held Amy tightly, hugged her to him even as he'd been yelling at the matron who had attempted to inform him that the touching of female prisoners by males was not allowed in *her* detention area. Within half an hour, he'd had everything straightened out—or so Mr. Horwitz had informed Amy in the car, as he'd reproached her during the drive from the seedy old building on State Street to the far more grand environs of her East Wacker Drive building. Lay down with dogs, get up with fleas, Mr. Horwitz had said, more than once. What did she think she'd been doing messing around with a scumbag like Gerald? Amy had felt Mr. Horwitz's strong, thin arms shaking when he'd hugged her, and she'd heard his voice breaking as he'd driven her home, with Mr. Horwitz half-hollering at her all the way, but acting as if he were really trying to understand; as if he were her father and Amy had been arrested for a curfew violation. She hadn't told Mr. Horwitz that she and Gerald were married. She wasn't really sure if they were, in fact, legally joined. She and Gerald had both been drunk that night, and she didn't remember all that much about it, except for a few things: the sleaziness of the house they'd gone to; the rank smell of the half-drunken preacher; the ring on her finger the next morning, and the gifts and clothes that Gerald had been showering on her ever since. Of course, she'd had to pay for it all, in her own way. Gerald was the most perverted man she'd ever met, or was likely ever to meet. But she couldn't think about that now, she had to keep her mind on her goal: getting out. Now. Before things got worse.

Amy had looked over at Mr. Horwitz then, as he paused in his quiet harangue, driving his zillion-dollar car and acting as if he truly cared about her, and she'd felt shame. She had believed that his trembling and the shaking in his voice were due to his concern for her, to Mr. Horwitz's distress over the horrid treatment of a loyal, hardworking employee at the hands of a brutal, neo-Nazi police department.

Amy had been crying on and off since the police had broken into their apartment, and she'd cried again during the drive home, shaking her head and agreeing with her boss—Amy had never expected that Gerald's business would ever touch her, she'd told Mr. Horwitz. She had never suspected that the cops would come and kick down the door of their *apartment*. Amy assured Mr. Horwitz that she would be moving out that night, that she'd call her mother just as soon as she got home.

Amy had seen herself as this young, hip, city chick with a fuck-you attitude—and had learned in a matter of minutes that she was another thing altogether. Her self-respect was shattered. The names the cops had called her, the things they'd said, the implications, were more than her fragile, still-forming ego had been equipped to cope with.

Now, quickly packing, in the relative safety of the high-rise apartment, Amy was at last getting her emotions under control. She was getting some of her attitude back, as well, although she'd jump a little bit every time a door closed outside, and she would sometimes cry out, thinking it was the police coming to get her again. The police had told her that the women's wing of the Cook County Jail was overflowing with hard-core dykes who would eat Amy alive, who would draw straws to see who got to shove the broom handle up Amy's . . .

Amy couldn't think about that anymore.

Amy's makeup was smeared, the outfit she was wearing destroyed, covered not only with dirt and grease from the bench down at the station, but also covered with Gerald's blood. The apartment manager had left three messages on the answering machine, but he'd at least had the door frame repaired, so the neighbors hadn't been able to steal their belongings, or come inside to gawk. Amy had listened to the apartment manager's messages after she'd picked up an overturned chair and sat herself down in the dining area. The morning newspapers Gerald loved to read so much had been torn apart, were strewn across the table and all over the floor. Trembling Amy had sat there drinking a strong drink, scotch, without water, without even ice cubes to curb the liquor's bite. The police had dumped the ice cubes into the sink, looking for God only knew what. Amy was amazed that the cops hadn't stolen the scotch—it was twelve years old, and bonded. She'd had to close her eyes so she wouldn't have to look at what the police had done to the place. She wondered why the doors in apartments were so flimsy. She shivered as she remembered a time—just that morning—when she'd believed that a one-inch deadbolt lock, built into a wood-core door, afforded her safety, some sense of extra protection.

The drink had calmed her down enough to enable her to call her mother: "I'm on my way," Mom had said, the most welcome words that Amy had ever heard. Amy's mother had hated Gerald from the moment the two had met. Her mother had shrieked, then cried into the phone, when Amy had told her that they'd eloped. Her mother would be calling Amy from the cellular phone in the Taurus wagon just as soon as she got off of the expressway, and she wanted Amy packed and ready, as she had houses to show that evening. She would not come up, would be waiting outside, under the building's canopy. Amy did not want to keep her mother waiting.

Still sniffling often, Amy now hurriedly threw her clothes into the suitcases that lay open on the floor, thousands of dollars' worth of clothes that Gerald had bought for her, which she had to pick up off the floor, where the cops had thrown them after searching through them for evidence of some crime. It had gotten dark outside, it was getting late; where was Mom? For the first time since she'd moved into the apartment, Amy could not appreciate the view. She would look out the floor-to-ceiling bedroom window and not even notice the river, she would not see the Tribune Tower or the Wrigley Building, brightly lighted. Amy expected to see helicopters hovering, spotlights crashing in on her as the police ordered her to come out with her hands up.

Mr. Horwitz had wanted to know what the cops had taken from the apartment, had made Amy promise him that she would make up a detailed list. Amy could have studied before-and-after Polaroids and would not have been able to fulfill his request. She had never paid much attention to what was laying around the apartment; she had never known Gerald's hiding places, if he had any. She had asked no questions. She should have, she knew now.

The way the cops had left the place . . . Mr. Horwitz would have to ask Gerald himself, if the bastard lived. Amy didn't intend to ever speak to Gerald again after the way he had cursed her—worse than the police had later done, and she'd only been trying to help him!

The police had questioned Amy about some money they'd claimed they'd found, but Amy hadn't been able to tell them anything about it; didn't they know that Gerald never told her anything? She couldn't make them understand. She'd ask them what this was all about, and get the standard television reply: "*We're* asking the questions, here." Thinking this, remembering their insensitivity, made Amy begin to sob again. Her mother would understand. Her mother would sympathize with her.

Which was why Amy hadn't changed her clothes, nor taken a shower. She wanted Mom's sympathy, wanted Mom to see her, see the blood, so she would know what Amy had been through, so she could comprehend how greatly her daughter had suffered that day.

The police had destroyed more than Amy's fragile self-esteem; they'd literally, absolutely demolished the apartment. Amy had to struggle to turn the large, wooden dresser upright, so that she could get at her underwear. She let it slam into the wall. What did she care about marks on the wall now, or, for that matter, about the next-door neighbor? The cops had even cut holes in the furniture, had ripped apart the bed and chopped the pillows into handkerchiefs. They had tossed pots and pans and plates and dishes and bowls out of the cabinets, had left them lying on the floor. They'd copped a few feels, too, as they'd handcuffed Amy and left her lying on the bedroom floor for what had seemed like *hours*. They'd even torn the paintings and prints off the walls, had ripped apart the frames.

Gerald could worry about all of that if he ever got out of the hospital. He could worry about cleaning up, too, could worry about the manager of the building, and the neighbors who probably right this minute were talking about what a whore she was. Amy never wanted to hear Gerald's name mentioned again.

She was breathing heavily from exertion as she closed the third and final suitcase. She did not concern herself with what was in the bathroom; she could replace her toiletries at any Walgreen's, and God only knew what the police might have done with her toothbrush, she'd heard stories . . .

Amy glanced into the bathroom briefly as she lugged the first suitcase out of the bedroom, then stopped, looking at the large bottle of petroleum jelly she had just bought—it couldn't have been only yesterday. Amy put the suitcase down, stepped into the bathroom, and lifted the jar. The lid was off, the police had looked inside, but none of them had relished the idea of sticking their fingers into the sticky goo. Amy thought about the way Gerald had treated her earlier that afternoon. She thought about how she'd taken care of him since he'd hurt himself yesterday, how she'd spent nearly twenty-four hours lavishing attention on him, waiting on him hand and foot as he awaited this morning's surgical appointment. She had rubbed his distended lower abdomen, she had brought him food and Pepsi, she'd treated him like a fucking king, and look at the price she'd paid, from both Gerald, and the police. Amy thought about the sexual things Gerald had talked her into doing, the perverted stuff . . .

Amy carried the jar of petroleum jelly a few feet out into the bedroom, wound up, then tossed it as hard as she could at the triple-door bathroom mirror. As it left her hand, Amy covered her face and turned away, hearing the satisfying crash of glass as the jar smashed the mirror into a million pieces. Amy opened her eyes, saw the damage she'd done, and smiled.

At that moment the phone rang, and Amy leaped, terrified, then turned to face the enemy, certain that it was the building manager, that he'd somehow known what she'd just done. Then she calmed herself. That was ridiculous. Unless the manager, in cahoots with the police, had put a hidden camera in the bedroom.

This thought humiliated Amy more than anything Gerald or the police had said. If they'd seen her, if anybody ever found out what she and Gerald had *done* on that bed!

Amy forced herself to relax; it was her mother calling, that's all. She walked over to the phone, surprised that the cops hadn't torn it apart, grateful to finally be getting out of this place. Amy snatched up the phone and said, "Mom?"

"No, but I could be your daddy, sweetums; I got around a little bit in my younger days."

"Who is this!"

"Calm down, sugartit, you're replaceable. Where's Gerald?"

"Edmund?"

"Woman, what did I just tell you to do?"

Amy took in a deep breath. All she knew about Edmund was that he was the leader of that moronic religious group Gerald belonged to—the one that thought white people were superior to everybody else. Gerald was always using racial slurs, and calling Mr. Horwitz Jew-boy. Edmund had more than likely planted those ideas in Gerald's head.

What else did she know about this group? Amy didn't have to think too hard. It was the group that believed women had only been put on earth to breed. They even had their own church; it had a dirt floor. Amy and Gerald had been married there. Gerald said he only did business with them, as he did business with a lot of cops; same difference. Gerald had told her not to worry about Edmund, he could handle him. Just don't talk to him for long on the phone; the guy had a problem with women. As if Gerald didn't have some serious problems with women himself.

Now, breathing through her mouth, Amy was frightened but energized, excited, seeing an opportunity to get back some of her pride. Her voice was nearly a whisper as she said, "Gerald's in the hospital. A great, big *nigger* cop kicked in the door, beat the shit out of him, then took him away, crying and bleeding. Gerald was telling him everything he knew about you before the ambulance guys even got him out the door."

A MATTER OF HONOR

There was a stunned silence on the other end of the line, as if Edmund could not believe what he was hearing. Amy rushed into the void before the idiot could collect whatever thoughts he might be capable of having.

"He said your name over and over again, blamed *you* for some money the cops found in the apartment, said *you* stole it, and he was just holding it for you. If I were you, Edmund, I'd start running." Amy put the phone down, waited a second, then removed the receiver and put it on the carpet. She would go down and wait for her mother on the street. Amy carried her suitcases out of the room, noticing that the luggage felt somehow lighter.

CHAPTER

33

No matter what Del Greco might have said, it wasn't over and Turner knew it. Turner thought about what Del Greco might be planning as he stood as unobtrusively as he could against the wall in the funeral parlor visitation room, watching him, Del Greco's face a gaunt blank slate as he circled the room, occasionally leaning down and lowering his ear to a set of whispering lips that spoke words of consolation, then he'd nod, make eye contact, pat the speaker on the arm or the shoulder as he strongly shook a hand, then he'd continue his circuit of the room, not spending too much time with any single person.

It seemed almost as if Del Greco was ashamed to look into the casket.

Rachel and her parents seemed to have Angelo under control, were consoling him as he struggled hard, tried to carry an unbearable burden. Rita's mother and her boyfriend had left some time ago. From the looks of them, from Turner's assessment, they were probably in the bar across the street. Rachel's brothers were all gathered close to their mother and father, were watching them closely, as if they were bodyguards instead of mourners. Claudette was out in the lobby, surrounded by armed, off-duty police officers and therefore safe, deep in conversation with the president of the African-American Female Police Officers Association.

Turner looked around the room and thought, This is what it's *really* like. Movies and TV could play games with it, glamorize it as they trivialized its impact, make it seem attractive and less important than it is. Rap singers could raise it to a level of spiritual importance, as a rite of passage that all black men were expected to accomplish. But Turner knew that murder wasn't something that should ever be taken lightly.

This, right here, in this room tonight, was the harsh reality of the aftermath of a murder.

People crying and silently suffering; Angelo up there nearly shaking apart in his grief over his loss. Del Greco's job gone because he wanted to make sure that his niece got justice, and he'd stepped over the line in his zeal to see that happen. Most importantly and most tragically of all, a vital, happy, beautiful young woman had been shot down in the street, and, as this wasn't a movie set, she wouldn't be getting up and moving on to another job after this one; Rita Cunningham wasn't ever, ever coming back. The tears were real, the pain gripped the heart and the mind and squeezed them tightly and would not let go.

Everyone who knew the woman had thought that Rita's life had still been ahead of her, and now here they were, grieving because they'd all been wrong. This is what it was like, this was what no movie or song could capture. The many lives that had been deeply, painfully touched, lives that would never be the same again; many hearts that would forever be missing a critical, vital piece.

Nobody in this room knew what to say or what to do, but they had all come nevertheless, with their grieving expressions that said more than mere words could ever convey; the fact that they'd shown up in the first place was more of an act of compassion than any of the family members could have expected.

Nobody felt at place at a wake, no human being could feel at home.

When Ellis had been a little boy, funerals had been high drama; screaming, sobbing, flailing women had done the 47th Street Wail, bouncing off the walls as they shouted the name of the deceased, sometimes dragging the deceased from their caskets. People sought attention at these places, and they received it, but nobody but a psychopath could feel untroubled in such a setting. Turner's mother's death had been merciful. Down to seventy pounds and feeling flames licking inside her womb, spreading upward, death had blessed his mother, had been a sweet, long-awaited kiss; she'd been begging for death to come and visit, to kiss her, at the end. But death did not ever bring comfort to those who were left behind.

Who did get anything out of ceremonies like this? Ellis wondered.

The undertaker, and that was it, nobody else. From a business point of view, it was a no lose situation that wasn't influenced by outside economic indicators: people died during depressions and upswings, during times of feast and famine. And their loved ones grieved, and held services such as this, where they banded together and looked at rotting flesh that had been dressed out in its finest clothing—a guest of honor who always showed up at the party, but was never in attendance.

Turner had filled out a form, his driver's license was stamped and signed, and Claudette was aware of his wishes: when he died, his entire corpse would be donated to the medical school at the University of Chicago. No wake, no funeral, no kneeling, no praying, no 47th Street Wail for Turner. No memorial service, either, where people who wouldn't give him the time of day when he'd been alive would hop up on their soapboxes and go on with tearful reminiscence as to what a fine fellow he'd been. One day Turner would be there, the next day he'd be gone. The people who loved him would have their memories of him until they themselves died; there would be no celebration, no party, not of Turner's death.

Turner shivered, brought himself out of his thoughts. He looked over at Del Greco again, trying to figure out what he was doing.

Del Greco would not have made a deal with Youngy without good cause. So no matter what he'd said downstairs, there was more to it than he was telling. And he'd take care of it himself when he could, at his own pace, and without the protection, authority, or weight of a policeman's badge. He'd be flying solo, with no help from anyone. It was the way a man like Del Greco would operate, with deliberate aforethought, making his move when the time was proper. Nobody else in the room would be aware of it to look at him—Del Greco was too good to let anyone see what he was doing—but Turner knew his ways, had closely observed him at his work for seven years. Del Greco's mind was racing; he was already working the angles. Planning something that could plant him behind a thirty-foot wall in a state penitentiary.

Perhaps, after the funeral, it might not be a bad idea for Turner to check up on him, keep tabs on his ex-partner, and maybe save him from himself. Men with brilliant minds could often outsmart themselves; thinking themselves superior, they fashioned their own nooses. Turner was not about to let that happen to Del Greco. He was too good, too smart, and he had too much to lose. Turner watched Rachel, as Rachel watched her husband. He saw the worry on her face, the look of knowing in her eye. She was aware that he was up to something, too. He hoped that Del Greco wouldn't allow his hot Italian blood to cause him to lose that woman; a man such as Del Greco would not be lucky in love two times.

Turner wondered where King Youngy fit into the equation. What would Youngy want for killing an innocent white girl—was he sophisticated enough to ask for five thousand dollars? A dope millionaire killing a white woman for a lark. A man like King Youngy would see it as pocket change, but fun.

And that's right where it took him, the answer to the question he would never ask Del Greco: Somebody had paid King Youngy to kill Rita. Who? Turner didn't think it was the grieving husband. Charles was barely able to stand. He wondered if Del Greco had already figured it out and hadn't told anyone, least of all his brother, who would kill whoever it was on the spot if he suspected that the man had something to do with Rita's death.

Which all led to the fact that that Rashon kid who'd been dumped outside the funeral parlor earlier today had been the shooter, King Youngy's hired executioner. Turner frowned, puzzled. Grasping at something in the back of his mind, something that wouldn't shake loose. Was that all there was to it? Had Rita actually been caught in a cross fire, and Del Greco had promised King Youngy his freedom in return for the shooter's death?

The crowd was thinning out now, it was getting late, and Turner watched as Claudette came back into the room, watched as she said good-bye to a number of their friends. Although Turner would never tell Del Greco this, he knew that these people had not shown up tonight for Del Greco's sake, but rather as a show of support for Ellis and Claudette Turner. Ellis walked over and joined Claudette, nodding and thanking people for coming as he shook their hands, saying his good-byes with the solemnity the occasion called for. He'd never met Del Greco's brother, so they didn't have too much to say to each other. With most of the crowd gone, Del Greco's movements were easier to watch.

He was definitely plotting something, the look was on his face. Turner had never seen his partner grieve before, though he'd seen him shot, and thought that Del Greco would die from the wound. But he'd seen him plotting, plenty of times.

The question was: What? And against whom?

Turner did not know; with Del Greco you *never* knew, until he told you. He did what he felt was best for the occasion. Del Greco knew the facts better than Turner did—Ellis hadn't been a part of his investigation.

So what had actually happened? Ellis, with his lip throbbing, his nose sore, his cheek burning, and his leg hurting, tried to figure out what his bones were telling him was the truth.

All right. Take it as a given that Del Greco believed that there was more to what had happened than an innocent young woman shot down in gang cross fire. What would any of that have to do with an insane, wildass gangbanger like Youngy? Ellis felt a hand on his shoulder and turned, expecting to see someone he knew from the department. Instead he found himself looking into the eyes of the assistant funeral director, a young man with an attitude, Ellis had noticed earlier.

The man's tone was distinctly chilly as he said, "You may want to tell Mr. Del Greco that Ellihue Blandane is about to go live on channel nine. I've got it on in my office."

"Who's Ellihue Blandane?"

"King Youngy."

Ellis looked at him as if he'd known that all along. This close, he could smell a familiar scent on the young man's clothes and breath. "You smoke marijuana in there, you won't get all assed up about us lighting up Kools in your office, right?"

The young man seemed panic-stricken for just a moment, as if he'd somehow forgotten that the room was half-filled with cops. Then he steadied himself and said, "It's for glaucoma. And you may certainly smoke in my office."

"Thank you," Turner moved quickly toward Del Greco.

"I don't want Angelo finding out about this." Del Greco hadn't thanked the young assistant director for informing him about the news conference, but was now instead giving him orders. Del Greco would have smelled the smoke, too, known right away who was in charge, and was now taking advantage of it. In his grief, he would not take the time to be polite to a stranger, to work him as he would work a suspect in a homicide. Del Greco had his hand planted in the small of the young man's back, was rapidly ushering him out of the office, the man with a look of disbelief on his face, Del Greco's jaw firm; lips tight; there would be no argument. Del Greco closed and locked the door behind him, walked to the desk, grabbed the phone, and disconnected it. A freshly wiped, clear glass ashtray was in the middle of the desk; the small TV was on a stand in one corner, with a VCR attached to it, placed on top of the set. Turner didn't even want to think about what the young man might film and watch in here, late at night, when he was all by himself.

Del Greco walked over to a second door, opened it, saw it was a bathroom, then pulled the door closed. He went over and sat on the desk, accepted Turner's cigarettes, shook one out, went through his ritual of tearing off the filter before he lit it, then put the pack and the lighter on the desk beside him, where both of them could have easy access.

On the screen, a half a dozen tall, muscular, young black men dressed out in black military fatigues were leading a smaller figure toward a podium. There was a lectern on the stage, and a group of microphones, taped together, was attached to the front of the lectern. Youngy was going for effect. His bodyguards all wore matching black baseball caps, and their expressions were grim and tough, their hard glares bouncing around the room as if the assembled reporters somehow posed a threat to Youngy's life.

"Fucking kid, look at him," Turner said, to no response. Del Greco's expression was as grim as that of any of the bodyguards, but his eyes didn't waver, they glared at the screen, focused with intensity on Youngy. Turner thought he understood. An anxious public, both black and white, would be watching this scene with interest; what Youngy said tonight could either calm the differing factions of the city, or incite them to violence. And if Youngy chose the latter course, the riot would be forever linked with the name of Marshall Del Greco.

Youngy walked quickly up the three steps that led to the stage, strode to the lectern and stood there, surrounded by his guards. He was wearing sharply creased, black dress pants and a long, flowing, African shirt. He wasn't wearing any jewelry. He had on a round, multicolored hat that matched his shirt, and black-framed sunglasses, which he now adjusted in the blinding light that was glaring at him from the cameras.

Contracts and deals made under duress were not legally binding to the parties involved. Would Youngy hold up to his end of some deal he'd made as Del Greco held a gun to his head? Or would he—now that he'd had time to think things over—further attack Del Greco, use this forum as a platform for character assassination? With someone like Youngy, it could go either way, depending upon his mood, depending on what he might think would work to his best advantage in the future.

Del Greco was taking a drag on the cigarette as Youngy said, "I am here to make a *state*ment." He bounced on the balls of his feet as he spoke, like the Baptist preachers of Turner's youth. If Youngy were making a statement, he would be making it off the top of his head, or from memory. Ellis was absolutely certain that he would not be reading from any prepared text. King Youngy was a total illiterate; he could neither read nor write.

King Youngy said, "This morning, July nineteenth, at five A.M., Detective Marshall Del Greco came over to my apartment, looking to aks me some questions." Youngy spoke slowly and uncertainly, as if this were hard work. He must have memorized his statement, practiced it in front of his own image in the mirror, over and over again until he thought he had it down. Now he took the time to adjust his shirt, to smooth it down, as if just now suddenly realizing that his image was being recorded.

"One of the boys in the 'hood had a pistol in his hand, and he ran away from the police. Knowing me to be a prominent neighborhood *busi*ness*man, he came to my apartment for help."

He paused for emphasis, then said, "Detective Del Greco was allowed into my apartment, at which time he arrested the man with the weapon, after accidentally firing a shotgun round off into my living room wall. He didn't kick in the front door, and he didn't beat no one up. Anyone that says otherwise is a godda—is a liar. I don't know no Rashon Latribe, whoever he is. I'm sorry for his family. And that's the end of that. Everything else is bullshit." Youngy flashed a boyish, apologetic smile, as his attentive audience tittered. He shrugged. "Sorry."

Youngy, having reached the end of his statement, obviously decided to improvise. His tone changed, became less formal as he said, "I don't know where y'all claim to have found all these people who said the man came into my building, going all insane and yelling nigger and everything like that. It didn't happen. I was *there*. I could make a lot of money by suing the department if I stood up here and lied to y'all tonight, and told you that all that bull—all that *garbage* happened. But I ain't gonna do that. The city say they gonna pay for the damage done to my apartment, and that's enough for me."

Youngy put a serious, shame-on-you look on his face, and said, "As for certain aldermens, and ministers, and criminoid types who run around claiming to be reformed—and wanting to be elected aldermens, along with all the rest of them out there screaming and yelling—we got enough trouble with racism against our community, 'specially amongst the police, without havin' to pretend it is where it ain't." King Youngy took a quick step away from the microphones, and the reporters went berserk.

"Mr. Blandane, Mr. Blandane!"

Youngy stepped back in front of the microphones, shaking his head as if speaking to a group of foreigners who did not understand what he had said. In a voice dripping with disdain, he said, "I ain't got nothing else to say to none of you." And with that he was gone, hurried away by muscular camouflage.

Turner, relieved, looked over at Del Greco, noticed that he had visibly relaxed. Del Greco closed his eyes and lowered his head, took several deep breaths, and let them out slowly.

"That boy ought to hire himself a public relations firm." Turner shook his head. "Most people like him, you see them on TV, they got their coats over their heads. Old Youngy stood there *proud*." When Del Greco still didn't respond, Turner said in a more serious tone, "You think someone got to him? Or he's smart enough to figure out that a race riot would be bad for business. That, or he was afraid that you'd come see him again."

Del Greco raised his head and opened his eyes. He crushed the cigarette out in the ashtray, then put the plug back into the phone, turned it around, lined it up in the spot on the blotter where it had been before he'd touched it. He seemed to notice the cheap paintings on the wall for the first time, let his gaze pass over them before he turned back, looked at Ellis.

"I think," Marshall Del Greco said, "that King Youngy understands family."

CHAPTER

34

It was a hot night in the city; hotter for some than for others.

Marshall Del Greco tossed and turned and sweated in his sleep in the air-conditioned comfort of one of many bedrooms in a mansion where his wife had spent her childhood. Rachel lay beside him, wide awake, listening to his groans, his grunts. She wanted to wake him and comfort him, but he hadn't slept in days, she didn't know how an abrupt, sudden interruption of sleep would affect him. She was not a psychiatrist, and would not—as a great many members of her profession have no such qualms about doing—pretend that she was, that she knew what was best for her husband's mind. His body she could heal, but his mind, Rachel knew, had taken nearly forty years to become whatever it was; no magic pill or miracle elixir would cure what was wrong with his mind. Though time might. Rachel prayed that it would. She knew that the best she could ever hope to offer him was the temporary absence of suffering. For Rachel, it wasn't enough. Marshall, however, believed that small, passing moments of alleviated pain were enough to sustain him, were sufficient.

Rachel was secure in Marshall's love for her, and she returned it with a devotion that surprised even her tightly knit family, who knew a thing or two about love themselves. He had the hungriest heart she had ever seen, yet he had high walls around it, protecting him from further hurt. That wall had been hard to penetrate, but Rachel had kicked her way through. Now, after knowing him since his days as a rookie in uniform, she thought it well worth the effort. She had told him the other night that she had spent her childhood dreaming of a man like him; what she hadn't said was that she'd known that he'd done the same himself. The difference between them being that Rachel had known she would find the man she was seeking, while Marshall had held no hope at all of ever attaining his dream. She'd proven him wrong on that point. And she had every intention of seeing to it that he never had cause to think he'd chosen poorly.

Marshall's great and quiet strength had been what had initially drawn her to him; his unwillingness to compromise in matters of principle had been one of the driving forces that had led her to fall in love with him. Rachel had had her pick of physically strong, good-looking men, but had found them to be superficial and often vain, and nearly always intellectually vacuous. Marshall's good looks and his well-sculpted body had not been decisive factors in Rachel's emotional decisions concerning him. What he had inside, his character—and the manner in which character is always proven, through behavior—had been what had done it for Rachel. She'd made her decision while still a teenager, while in her junior year of college, to marry the strong, quiet police officer, and she had rarely had the motivation to regret her decision. His thoughtfulness, his romanticism, his gentility toward her, Rachel knew, were rare qualities for a man to possess, even today, in the so-called gender-neutral decade of the nineties. His lack of jealousy and petty possessiveness, his understanding and support of her goals, his willingness to see her attain them, and his help and support as she struggled through the grueling years of her medical training were not things he had ever taken for granted. She'd known that he'd had struggles with what she'd been doing, and she appreciated the fact that he'd kept them to himself. They'd had their share of arguments through the years, but there'd never been so much as a cross word about her schedule, the restrictions on her time, or her desire—Rachel's demand—to be totally self-sufficient. Rachel would allow neither Marshall nor her parents to subsidize her schooling; the debt was hers alone, acquired through student loans, and she intended to pay off every cent herself, with no help from anyone.

And now, at the point in their lives where she could finally begin to pay back her debt, at a time when they should be planning for Marshall's retirement, as they looked forward to a life together with less stress and obstacles in their paths than they'd ever had before, this had to happen. Marshall's career was being taken away.

Rachel had been supportive earlier, in this very bedroom, as they'd discussed what Marshall should do, but she'd known how important his work was to him, how much he *needed* to be a police officer, driven by his desire to right the wrongs that had been done to him throughout his formative years. She wondered now how he would handle these events; wondered what Marshall might do.

A MATTER OF HONOR

He'd given seventeen years of his life to the police department, and now those years—in the eyes of the department—had never existed, were worthless. The scar on his chest—which her husband would carry around as a reminder for the rest of his life—didn't matter to them, either. They would more than likely be wishing that he *had* died on that day last June, when he'd been shot by the twelve-year-old boy, when he'd spent three days in intensive care, stubbornly clinging to life. If he had been gracious enough to have died back then, he would have saved the department from this current, public embarrassment.

Rachel watched him, saw the muscles in his jaws tighten as he clenched his teeth, ground them. A pained moan escaped him, and he turned over onto his side, facing her. Rachel was very careful when she put her arm around him, afraid that he might, in panic, strike out. She leaned in close, formed her body into his. "Shh," she whispered into his ear. "Shh, Marshall, everything's going to be all right," Rachel whispered, even though she suspected that nothing would ever be all right again.

In a large, well-appointed guest room down the hall, Angelo Del Greco slept with a broad smile on his face. He was dreaming of his daughter. In his dream, Rita was a little girl again, and it was the middle of the wintertime, and they were happy, standing in front of a cage at the Lincoln Park Zoo. The animals kept changing shape on them though, converting into different animals right in front of their eyes, and Angelo was troubled by this, but Rita wasn't, it amused her. She laughed unashamedly, with her mouth wide, both her hands covering lips that were cracked from the cold.

In a few short hours, the happy dream would be replaced by a stark and brutal reality. Angelo would awaken from his pleasant dreams, and the grim truth would descend, and he would be plunged into the despair that had gripped him since the moment that his brother Marshall had come running into his electronics store, early Monday afternoon. Carrying that, Angelo would shower and dress, would join his brother and the family that his brother had made, ride in their car with them to the funeral. He'd asked them to ride with him in the limousine, to and from the service.

But all of that was in the future. For the moment, Angelo was at peace in a world without suffering, where young people didn't get murdered, where cancer didn't lurk, waiting to bite at his testicles with sharp and vicious teeth. Angelo allowed his trepidation to evaporate and he smiled in his dream, now holding Rita's hand as a monkey transformed itself into a giraffe, Angelo indulgently smiling in his dream, as his precious Rita covered her mouth with her free hand and laughed and laughed and laughed.

*   *   *

King Youngy was laughing too, the life of the party at his fifth floor "penthouse" apartment on the far West Side. Youngy was surrounded by two dozen men he trusted, who'd brought their girlfriends with them to help him celebrate their leader's masterful manipulation of the entire Chicago media. Even Kirstin had become part of the peripheral, journalistic circus.

As Youngy had been making his live statement, Kirstin had been on the phone giving an exclusive interview—which would be printed in tomorrow morning's paper—wherein, upon Youngy's instruction, she had scolded the media, the police department, Charge, and Berkley for the way they had all conspired to turn a simple arrest into a racial incident. At the conclusion of the interview, Kirstin had sent a GlamourShots photo of herself over to the paper, via messenger. The picture showed Kirstin in something of a provocative pose, reclining on a black velvet couch. It was a copy of Youngy's favorite picture of her.

When the reporter had questioned Kirstin about the connection between the relatively minor arrest for possession of a handgun and the murder of Del Greco's niece, Kirstin had pleaded innocence and ignorance, explaining that her "husband Ellihue was a real estate speculator, and a gambler, and he ain't mixed up with no drugs, like you people always be saying." She had also stated that neither she nor her "husband" had ever heard of anyone by the name of Rashon Latribe. The reporter, herself a black female, had been surprised to discover, when the photo had been delivered, that Kirstin was a blonde-haired, blue-eyed, white girl. The reporter had never asked, and the information had not been volunteered, as to how Kirstin and King Youngy had gotten together in the first place, so the public would never know that two years ago, at the age of fifteen, Kirstin had been given to Youngy by her father, as payment for her father's dope debt. Youngy had used her daily as his sex slave, and he'd used her hard, and there had been the ever-present threat that—as she was his property, with no more emotional ties to him than a car or a suit or a telephone—Youngy might turn her over to his boys, which was something that he often threatened, but for some reason had never done. Now, two years after having been deeded away as if she were property, Kirstin had deluded herself into believing that she was with King Youngy through "choice"; never understanding that she was a willing participant in her own debasement, a trophy of Youngy's who had assumed an attachment that did not exist, as Youngy was totally incapable of effecting emotional connections.

Now King Youngy (who never touched the poison he had grown rich from pedaling to his community, nor allowed anyone around him to indulge in its usage, either) was drinking Courvoisier on the rocks and smoking Kools, as a videotape of his statement was repeatedly played on a Sony VCR that was attached to a fifty-inch, rear projection television set. Several of his closest homies were gathered around the set, grinning, pointing their bottles and glasses at the screen, hooting at Youngy's genius.

Youngy reveled in their toadying, saw it as his due.

Ellihue Blandane had been arrested as an adult for the first time just one month after turning eighteen. He'd been picked up by a joint task force of agents who had stormed his grandmother's apartment, seeking to put an end to his criminal reign before it got the chance to transform into a dynasty. He had faced a forty-two-count indictment, seventy pages in length, that his lawyer had taken one look at, then told Youngy to make a deal.

Youngy had fired the lawyer.

Locked up without bail in the MCC, Youngy had spent his entire—and even then considerable—cash fortune on a new cadre of attorneys and investigators, a group who knew what this case was really all about: plain and simple racism. A higher street tax had been imposed on every drug criminal then active, a tax that had lasted until the conclusion of the trial, and further income had been supplied by Youngy's backers, the older, more established gangbangers, who didn't want to see one of their most vicious and hardworking moneymakers go away to the penitentiary.

After a seven-month trial, a jury of twelve of his peers had acquitted Ellihue Blandane, after less than one full day of deliberations. Later, one of the jurors had stated during a press conference that the sight of Mr. Blandane's elderly, sickly grandmother on the witness stand had been one of the key factors in her decision to acquit. Youngy had watched the woman on TV, and he'd smiled a satisfied smile; it had been his idea to have his poor old granny make certain that she wore her oldest dress and her cheapest wig during her court appearance, and that, while testifying, she sat with her legs open wide, so that the jurors could see for them- selves that granny wore Depends, and would then take pity on Ellihue, her only source of income.

There had been a double-stretch limousine idling on Van Buren, awaiting Youngy as he'd walked out of the MCC. He'd had a glass of liqueur in his hand, a Kool fired up, and a young woman unzipping his trousers before the limo had pulled from the curb.

Now, over the noise of the party, one of his homies hollered across the room, shouted to Youngy that an emissary from Crocodile Berkley was on the phone, and Youngy told him to tell the man that he didn't waste his time talking to bitches. The man relayed the message, laughing into the phone, then hung up, smiling and shaking his head, repeating Youn- gy's words aloud.

That's why they called him King, the young man thought, as he turned his attention back to the party.

Across town, on the South Side, Crocodile Berkley was not having any party. He sat in a comfortable stuffed chair in the reception room that led into the Minister's mansion, surrounded by and glaring at four members of the Seeds of Africa, who were doing their best to glare right back, and falling short in the attempt. The Seeds stood at attention, as Crocodile was sitting in the only chair. They had not allowed Crocodile into the presence of the Minister because Crocodile hadn't allowed them to search him for weapons. Saturday morning, he'd told them, they hadn't insisted upon any such search. He was told that the rules had changed, that it was no longer Saturday morning. Crocodile was not carrying a weapon, but he wouldn't allow them to search him, he viewed it as a matter of respect.

Now Crocodile took his time, staring hard at each of the young Seeds, giving them a full fifteen-second glimpse of his fabled inner ferocity before directing it toward another. Most of these men had been in the penitentiary, and they had been fearless since the days of their births. In order to be admitted as members of the small and prestigious cadre of Seeds of Africa, they had taken a pledge to die for their leader if the need to do so should arise.

But they had also come up on the South Side, and therefore knew who the Crocodile was. Two of them looked away whenever Crocodile turned his attention toward them, as if they were ashamed of themselves. That was good; he thought that they ought to be ashamed.

Crocodile could hear the Minister's shouted voice, coming from within the next room, that unmistakable, powerful voice now raised in anger, ego, and outrage. There was no sermon being delivered now, no followers or sycophants shouting agreement at every statement. This was the venting of hostility, and Billy Charge was its recipient.

Crocodile twisted his face into a sneer which displayed his sense of disgust. He grunted, rested one elbow on his knee, and was glad that he wasn't in the room with Charge. If he had been—in spite of Crocodile's nearly mythical awe of the man—the Minister might at this moment be meeting his match.

Crocodile had been born and raised in the Englewood area, among the second generation to be born after the Great Conversion, during which thousands of white people had fled the neighborhood in terror, that terror fueled by the scathing rhetoric of greedy, overzealous real estate brokers, who had assured the simple, hardworking, but nevertheless ignorant white folks of the area in no uncertain terms that their property rates were going to plummet after the first black family bought a house in their community. Crocodile had never known his father, and there were times throughout his early, developmental years when he'd wished the same were true of his mother.

By the time Crocodile had turned thirteen, he'd been running with the gang. He had also already become thoroughly convinced that the posturing of the politicians was half responsible for his plight. The color of his skin was responsible for the other half. He hadn't come to these realizations through thoughtful contemplation, but rather through practical examples.

In Englewood, such examples abounded.

He—along with dozens of other young gang members—had been ordered by the gang higher-ups to attend the trial of a white police officer who had admitted to shooting two black teenagers while off duty, out of uniform, behind the wheel of his own, personal vehicle as he'd been heading home after working the afternoon shift on a balmy September evening. Gang members weren't the only people in the courtroom, intently listening, on the day of the officer's testimony. The reporters had shown up, too, as had more than a hundred working-class black people, many of whom had taken the day off from work without pay in order to be able to come to court and listen to the excuses of the man who had shot down two of their own in cold blood. They had all sat cramped together in a high-ceilinged courtroom at Twenty-sixth and California, directly in front of the county jail (where the accused double-murderer had never spent a single night) in the dead of winter, and Crocodile had listened as closely and as intensely as anyone to the officer's testimony, glaring the glare that had later come to strike terror into the hearts of those who knew the weight of the man behind it.

Why had the officer shot the youths?

Because one of them had spat upon his windshield, as they'd been crossing Sixty-third Street.

The officer had sworn that he'd been in fear for his life. The officer had sworn that both boys had been known to him, and that they both had extensive juvenile records. The officer had sworn that he'd seen one of them reach rapidly beneath his shirt, as if he'd been going for a gun.

There had been no witnesses to the shooting, and what it had come down to was this: the officer's sworn testimony versus the silence of two black corpses.

When the judge who'd been hearing the case without a jury had found the officer not guilty, the young Crocodile Berkley had played a pivotal role in the ensuing riot, and he himself had done the swearing, afterward, when the very same police officer who had gunned down two of his friends had gone onto the local news, offering commentary on the uprising.

"See? See how *they* act? Like animals, they act," the white officer had said. "You people out there got no damn i*dea* what we have to put up with every single day of our lives." He'd said this into the camera, speaking to the rest of white Chicago.

Crocodile Berkley could have spoken the exact same words, with far greater authority.

Crocodile had wondered many times in the years that had followed the policeman's acquittal, How many black men were serving life sentences for doing the exact same thing that the white cop had done? He'd known from the start that it had never been about spit on a windshield, no more than today's drive-by shootings were about somebody looking crazy at somebody else.

It was about respect; nothing more, nothing less.

The pig had believed himself to have been disrespected, and two young, unarmed black males had died because of that pig's perception, and the pig had not only gone free, and become a spokesman on the TV news, but he'd also gone back to his job as a bona fide Chicago hero. Fundraisers had been held by his fraternal brothers, to help him through the financial hard times that had been caused by his suspension. His lawyers had been hired through the PBA, which meant that his defense hadn't cost him a dime. If the man had been convicted, he would have remained free on bond while his lawyers appealed his conviction. In the unlikely event that the appeals would have withstood judicial scrutiny, the officer would have then been sent to one of the minimum security joints in Southern Illinois, and he would have done his time standing on his head, a role model and hero to the country assholes that the state hired as hacks.

But the officer hadn't been convicted; he had been reinstated to his job, with full back pay, and he'd retired as a captain, was even now living very comfortably down in Florida, as the head of his own security firm, and he was often called for quotes as an "expert" on the distorted attitudes concerning race relations by his white friends in the media.

When a brother did what the white cop had done—and did it with the exact same rationale—he was held in the Cook County Jail without bond, would have some twenty-six-year-old lawyer appointed to him out of the public defenders' office, and, upon conviction—and there always *was* a conviction—the brother was sent to one of the max-out joints, Stateville, Pontiac, or Menard, where he would live under the heavy thumb of those very same white, racist, hate-filled, country asshole hacks, and he would stay there until his youth was long gone, eating garbage that wasn't fit for human consumption, under conditions that had been outlawed for prisoners of war. The Geneva convention didn't carry any weight with the Illinois Department of Corrections.

Crocodile had never forgotten the distinctions between black and white;

had had it forced down his throat every minute of every day during the forty-one years of his life.

Crocodile was torn from his reverie by the sound of Charge in the room with the Minister, the alderman now groveling. Explaining to the great man in a whiny voice that he couldn't control King Youngy, that *nobody* could control King Youngy. The Holy Minister couldn't expect Charge to personally control every outlaw gangbanger in the city, could he?

Crocodile frowned as the intent of the words sunk in. What was Charge saying? There was an implication there that wriggled around inside his head. Did the man—Charge—think that he controlled the Crocodile? He couldn't. He just couldn't *be* that stupid. Crocodile Berkley leaned forward in his chair, trying to hear more clearly, but the alderman had already lowered his voice. Crocodile could hear him talking, but he couldn't make out the man's words. He felt suddenly embarrassed, and hid it, would not show it in front of these men.

A dozen years ago, after being released from the state penitentiary, having served eleven years for a murder that he had not committed, and with the full knowledge all along that he'd been nothing more than a political prisoner, Crocodile had stood on the broad driveway that led into the Stateville penitentiary, and he had looked hard at the reporters and politicians, and all the other supporters whose hard work, dedication, and ceaseless investigation had earned him not only his freedom, but a simultaneous pardon from the governor of Illinois. He had stood there and, in a low, but hard voice, had spoken a single sentence—he had stated the philosophy by which he intended to live the rest of his life.

"I will never again suffer an indignity at any man's hands," Crocodile had said, and from that day to this one, he hadn't.

With that in mind, Crocodile wondered again, What was Charge really saying? What meaning was really behind those whimpering, cowardly words? Crocodile had learned many years ago that every statement had several meanings, could be taken in various ways.

He began, within, to seethe.

Had the alderman only introduced him to the Minister in a blatant attempt to control him? Didn't the man appreciate or understand that it had been Crocodile who had brought the news of Silver's death to him, and not the other way around? The man had *thanked* him, had repeatedly referred to Crocodile as "my brother" in the days that had passed since the killing. He had put his arm around Crocodile's shoulders Saturday afternoon, at the rally in front of City Hall, in front of all those reporters, in front of all those TV cameras. Crocodile had thought that Charge had done it as a gesture of respect, love, and brotherhood, but now the gang leader had a sudden, repugnant thought: Had Charge put his arm around Crocodile's shoulders because the man viewed him as his *pet?*

Crocodile had to physically prevent himself from leaping out of the chair.

The boy who had grown up to be identified with the world's most vicious reptile had dropped out of high school after his third term as a sophomore; he'd received his G.E.D. in the Illinois State Youth Center, the juvenile prison, not far from the men's penitentiary, down in Joliet. Not all that many years later, Pell grants had enabled Crocodile to take college courses while he had been locked down in Stateville, and he'd been the first prisoner in Illinois history to receive a master's degree in political science from behind the walls of that loathsome prison. Berkley had read Mike Royko's book about Mayor Richard J. Daley, *Boss,* so many times, had studied it so hard and so well that he could recite entire passages from the book with the same ease with which he could quote from the speeches of Malcolm X, or those of Minister Africaan. Crocodile had in fact patterned his own political action party—Year Two Thousand—after the first Mayor Daley's political sponsoring organization, the Hamburg's, which—there was no way around it—had started out as a violent street gang. Back then, a gang called Regan's Colts had been the Hamburg's main opposition, sort of like Youngy's Vice Kings were Crocodile's today. Crocodile had risen from drug runner to enforcer, and was now one of the leaders—second in command—of the Gangster Apostle Nation, behind Terry Glover, who would be locked down in the pen for the rest of his life for the murder of two policemen who'd been attempting to serve him with a warrant.

Crocodile Berkley wasn't any man's pet.

Nor could he be controlled. He had vowed that he would never again suffer an indignity. So he would ask the man about it, as soon as they were alone. He'd confront Charge in the car, alone, see what the man had to say for himself.

Crocodile's cellular phone went off, and two members of the Minister's elite security detail quickly reached for their weapons. Crocodile shook his head, still sneering, and he added a contemptuous smile. He took his phone out of his pocket, making no attempt to do it slowly, refusing to pander to the paranoia of these sentinels—refusing to show them even the slightest form of respect.

It took every ounce of self-control Crocodile possessed to keep the emotion off his face when he was given Youngy's message.

In another house, one far more humble than those belonging to the Minister or the Bersteins, and far less expensively appointed than the apartment of King Youngy, Ellis Turner had finally finished explaining to Claudette the circumstances surrounding the arrest of Gerald Podgourney, a story his anger had not allowed him to tell her before the wake.

Her face had betrayed her increasing horror as he'd spoken—until now she seemed almost dazed, appalled by what she had heard. Claudette asked him if he intended to turn the names of the three white officers over to internal affairs; surely he was going to file a complaint, at least put it in his report? Ellis explained to Claudette that that just wasn't a possibility, and for two distinct, separate, but equally important reasons: there'd been three white cops, and sure, they'd fucked up, but they'd had time to get together and come up with a likely story. If it came down to it, if they had to face an official inquiry, whose word would be believed, that of the black Ellis Turner, or that of the three white cops? Considering what had happened when they'd taken down Podgourney's door, Ellis told Claudette that he would consider himself lucky if he got nothing more than a letter of censure, and a couple of days off without pay. He tried to ignore the anger on her face, the disappointment in him that was clearly stamped there. Claudette could hate, deeply. Ellis suspected that some of that hate was directed toward whatever power had caused her to be born black.

He hurriedly told her the second reason, the one that was more important to him, due to grounds that were plainly clear: in cases like this, cops didn't rat out other cops. And even if he did, how much good would it do? Would it make anything better for any other black cops? No, he'd explained to a still uncomprehending and enraged Claudette, an already ugly situation would not be improved by Ellis's complaints.

Claudette did not seem to accept this, either, and Ellis could tell that it wasn't easy for her to stay quiet. He had one last thing to say to her, a favor to ask her, before they went to bed.

Would she make love to him tonight? Would she take it all away? He wanted her holding him, kissing and licking and sighing—not some passionate, heated, wild tryst that would end in muffled screams, leaving him burnt out, gasping for breath, and ready to pass out for the night. Ellis wanted it to be gentle, tonight of all nights, he sought tenderness.

Claudette looked into wide, wet, imploring eyes, and he watched, almost in awe, as her anger drained away. She took her husband's hand, lowered her forehead down to it, and stayed that way for a very long time, before sniffing, wiping at her face, then getting up and leading Ellis by the hand, down the hall and into their bedroom.

CHAPTER

35

"The Minister sleepin'. Besides, he don't never speak over the telephone. You ought to know better than that, *Alderman*." The voice in Charge's ear was condescending, superior, and the sound of it made him furious. The man on the other end of the line was more than likely an ex-con, in his mid- to late twenties, who'd found the One Great Black Jesus while serving time, and had come to the conclusion that He bore an uncanny resemblance to Minister Africaan. Charge pictured the Seed member in his mind—they all were cut from the same mold—tall, muscular, never had an original thought in his life, knew nothing of true struggle, or of suffering, though he would believe that he had the market cornered on both of those two commodities—commodities that were abundantly available within the black community. This man wouldn't care about his people, only about himself. He'd have been sent to the pen for pushing drugs to his own brothers, or for committing a senseless act of violence, and he would have discovered inside that certain strong religious beliefs could keep you from getting fucked up the ass. Once someone had read all the hate-whitey literature to him, he'd have become convinced that he'd found his calling.

Charge sighed into the phone, then wearily shook his head. He couldn't do this, he had to stop himself. This sort of thinking led to turmoil, jealousies, and bloodshed. He leaned back in the chair in his den, held the ice pack to his swollen cheek, and in as calm a voice as he could summon, said, "What's your name, young man."

A MATTER OF HONOR

"Don't matter what my name is; the Minister say he don't want to be disturbed, especially by you."

Do you know who—" There was a soft click in his ear; the son of a bitch, he'd had the nerve to hang up on him.

Charge half-stood and threw the ice pack across the room, but the unwieldy rubber lost its velocity in flight, barely made it to the far wall. He watched it flop over on the zebra carpet, saw the splattered condensation marks that it left on the wallpaper. Alderman Billy Charge cursed aloud, took several deep breaths, then, almost against his better judgment, he reached for the phone again, and rapidly dialed the number of Crocodile Berkley's cellular phone. His mind raced as he waited for the connection to be made from a satellite hovering hundreds of miles up in space, Charge frenziedly trying to think of something he could say to the man that would make things right between them.

There never was a ring, just a click as the call was transferred, then he heard Berkley's recorded voice, and hung up on Crocodile's voice mail.

Charge slammed the phone down, hard. "Out of control *maniac*," he shouted. He touched the side of his face, winced, pulled his head away as his fingers touched the tender spot where Berkley had slapped him with the back of one large, rock-hard hand. That side of Charge's face was grossly discolored; there were red slashes in the white of his eye. He squinted, focused on a pen on his desk, and was relieved that it didn't swim around in his vision; he probably didn't have a concussion.

No brother had ever done this to Charge before; the beatings he had taken throughout his life had always been given by the white man, by the pigs. He had been a figure of authority and respect for twenty years, a member of the city council, a leader within his community. He'd been attempting, fighting, to be a force for good since he'd been just a teenager, since he'd joined up with the Black Panthers and had gone through their rigorous training program, then through virtue of his superior intellect, his ambition, and his effort, had quickly ascended through their ranks to become one of the leaders of the Chicago organization.

The white populace—which got its information from the white-controlled media—had been woefully misinformed as to what the Panthers were about, but Charge had been there, he'd been the Minister of Information, he *knew* the Panthers mission. Angry rhetoric concerning law enforcement, shouted by rifle-waving young blacks, was what got the public's attention, was what drew the media to them, and what got them money from the liberal whites, who accepted them into their homes, and held fund-raisers for their cause. The insiders were aware that such fiery rhetoric had been calculated and shallow. There had never been any plan to shoot the pigs, or to kill whitey. The Black Panthers had not been a street gang; it had been an empowering entity, a precursor to Africaan, and an alternative to the Nation of Islam. Filled with strong young black brothers and sisters who'd been solely dedicated to the uplifting of their people.

And they *had* helped the community. Charge knew how many meals had been served to poor schoolchildren, knew how many frightened old women had been escorted to doctor's appointments, hospitals, supermarkets, or just down to the currency exchange to cash their welfare checks. Having been there, he knew that even though physical violence in response to a direct police assault was always a possibility, it would, if it happened, be a reflexive, defensive gesture. The Black Panthers had in fact been trained to *not* engage any agents of any government—federal or local—in armed struggle, unless it was absolutely necessary, unless there was no other way to avoid it happening. They were trained to fight, and capable of fighting, and fighting hard, but they would always be fighting *back*—the Panthers would never initiate such a battle.

That philosophy had been instilled into their training regimen for a very clear and simple reason: to do otherwise would be to ensure the Black Panthers' instantaneous extinction. If one of them were to ever shoot a cop, two events would immediately ensue: their credibility would be destroyed in the eyes of the white majority, and the white police establishment would have all the excuse it needed to kick in their doors and come in, guns blazing, wiping out the movement before it came close to achieving its goals.

Which, in the end, was exactly what had happened anyway.

Charge rubbed at his temples now, grimacing, fighting a growing sense of unease, and a sense of self-loathing over what he'd become, as he remembered how important those days had been, how much promise there'd been in the wind.

They had demanded respect, the Panthers had, and had wound up destroyed, their leaders murdered in their beds as they slept by pigs who had come in with that sole agenda. Lies had been told to the press, which had reported them as facts. Even after the initial flurry of headlines had died down, and the truth began to slowly emerge, editorials had been written, chastising the remaining few, preaching that if they wanted change, they had to accomplish it through the system. Charge had done exactly that, and what had he gotten in return?

A backhanded slap across his face by one of the men who could have helped him accomplish his goals, and another slap in the face—metaphorical, but just as painful—by a demagogue Charge had enlisted in his zeal to aid the Movement.

Both men were angry over what King Youngy had said to the press, speaking from a podium in a rented hotel conference room, dressed as a son of Africa, with three-hundred-dollar shades protecting his eyes from the glare of the cameras. Crocodile was incensed because he had figured out that Charge had not been judging him as an equal, and had been trying to control him from the outset. Africaan had been equally incensed because Charge could not control King Youngy. Both Berkley's and Youngy's gangs sold drugs to ensure the economic growth of their undercover empires. The difference between the two men was that Berkley truly cared about the future of his people, and was not above taking money from junkies who had no future in order to try to make the next century a better place for the rest of his people.

While King Youngy, on the other hand, cared about nothing but bitches and money.

Charge knew that gang summits that led to public truces were worthless, as long as the killing and the drug dealing continued. Africaan understood that, as well, but his ego and his messianic complex—coupled with his pathological hatred of the white man—prevented him from ever being able to join together with others with the betterment of the black man's tomorrows as their single-minded goal.

Too many egos, too many volatile personalities. Too many people starving for respect, who were willing to accept fear as an alternative. Charge knew that he himself was not above such behavior. Earlier this week, even earlier today, all he could think about was how he could use what was happening in the city to his personal benefit, to win himself a congressional seat.

From there, he could have really made things happen. Once he'd gotten tho prize, he could have effected real change, not only in Chicago, but on a national scale. But he'd gone after the winning of that prize with a tunnel vision that had blinded him to the significance of anything else, and he'd overlooked the sort of things that had once been of the utmost importance to him. Even the thought of a riot hadn't quelled Charge's fiery ambition; he hadn't thought of the lives that would have been lost, hadn't thought of the suffering that would come to his people, he'd only thought about how the riot could have been used to his own best and greatest good.

Where had it all gone wrong? He'd been an idealistic youth, who had transformed into a fervent, firebrand believer in what the Black Panthers could do for its brethren. He'd moved on to political office, with his peoples' best interest as his main concern. He'd battled street thugs as a child, the police as a young man, aldermen and their constituents throughout his years in political office, and what had he learned in all that time?

He was still demanding respect, and still wasn't getting it.

Charge now suspected that he would never get it at all if he continued to seek it in so many wrong and ruthless places. Deals with the devil, with the Berkleys and the Africaans of the city, could have short-term gains, but in the long term, they'd be disastrous, would stop him from doing what he'd set out to do all those many years ago. His own Daddy had advised him, when he'd been just a little boy, "Dance with the devil if you has to, but don't you never get in the bed with that evil motherfucker." His father had been referring to the white man at the time, but the same principle held true for his fellow blacks as well. Charge had learned that lesson the hard way.

He had thought that he had been dancing, but the truth was that he'd been getting fucked.

Charge nodded his head now, his anger fully gone, a feeling of righteousness filling him. The slap had been a good thing, he thought. He was grateful to Crocodile Berkley. It had knocked some sense into his head. If he were ever going to be a congressman, he would have to represent *all* the people of his district. As Harold had done, when he'd been mayor. As Lucille had done, as well, before she'd been shot down in the street.

And a man couldn't expect to receive the respect of all the people if he didn't first respect himself. A man who fucks the devil all night never feels good about it when dawn arrives.

Charge decided that he would rethink his priorities, first thing in the morning, after he got a little rest. He wondered if his wife kept her door locked at night; he wondered if she would accept him into her bed, if he crept into her room right now. He wondered if she kept a lover; he couldn't blame her if she did.

He wondered at last about Crocodile Berkley, hoped that the man, in his anger, wouldn't do anything stupid, something that would screw things up even worse than they already were.

CHAPTER

36

Crocodile Berkley sat at the head of a long, rosewood table in the paneled basement of a safe house; his lawyer's newly rehabbed city home on Sixty-third Street. The lawyer—who did not want to know any part of Berkley's plans until they got him into trouble—was upstairs in the master bedroom, pretending to be asleep, none too pleased that his most important and dangerous client had called an emergency, late-night summit meeting of his gang's leadership, and having it at his house. The lawyer wasn't in a position to complain, however, as he was with his lady, who had been given to him as a present by the Crocodile. A present the Crocodile wasn't above discussing with the lawyer's suburban wife, should the lawyer step out of line.

Downstairs in the basement, Berkley was surrounded by a group of men he trusted, ten of them, leaders of their own factions of the gang. All of them were men who had killed before in the service of the gang; all of them were men who understood that Crocodile spoke for and in their best interests.

All of them seemed to know, too, that at the moment, the Crocodile was highly pissed off.

Though he hadn't said a word to make anyone aware of the state of his mind. His glare did that for him; Berkley's silent, smoldering rage. The last of the ten members of the factional leaders, Fushay Grant, had just come down to the basement two or three minutes ago, and had gone over to the bar and poured himself a drink. He was just now settling down in one of the plush, red velvet chairs that surrounded the conference table, Fushay looking furtively at Berkley, then quickly looking away. In the hour since he'd come to this house and beeped them all with a nine-one-one page, Berkley had hardly spoken a word, except to tell them where to meet him when they'd returned his beeps. He had sat there glowering as he'd waited, thinking the sort of dark thoughts that led to the performing of dark deeds, Crocodile scowling at the men who'd gotten there before he was ready to talk to them, and had asked him what was up. The men were speaking to each other, though, warily, talking softly, waiting for their leader to call the meeting to order. Crocodile looked briefly over at Fushay Grant, at his disheveled hair, at his hastily thrown-on, dirty-looking clothes, and he grunted.

Berkley was a tonal chameleon; he could speak in the precise and educated tones of the college graduate he was, or he could rap a version of ghettoese that even the most sub-literate could comprehend. For tonight's meeting, Berkley decided, he would be moderate. He would not come off like a ne-gro trying to show the white man how assimilated he was, nor would he get too down and dirty. With these men, he could be himself; he'd known most of them all of their lives. This was Englewood, and along with English, there were four other languages that were spoken in this part of town: The most clearly understood could be folded in half, and a lot of that language was always in Crocodile's pocket; the second was stuck in the leather holster under his arm. The third was nearly incomprehensible, but Berkley had it in abundance; the ability for others to know—just by looking at him, without having any other knowledge about him—that he was a true heavyweight; that his was no act. The man they were looking at was not playing around or pretending. The fourth language was juice. In the Englewood neighborhood, Crocodile owned just about all the juice there was to have.

"Brothers." Crocodile spoke the word softly, but every man at the table sat up, stopped speaking, and looked up at him respectfully. Berkley was wearing his shoulder holster, had his silver-plated Nine sticking out of soft leather, the Velcro strap undone. He looked around at each man as he spoke, trying to see what was in their heads. "The time has come for a sor-tay." A surprised murmur went around the room, then just as quickly as it started, it stopped.

"When we go, we'll go in strength. But I only want brothers who've been 'blessed' in, served their probation, and been down with you for at least five years. I *only* want men you trust. Not any of those young sissies you *think* about trusting; I only want men who been tested by fire. I want each of you to call in five men, get them on the phone right now."

"Fifty motherfuckers . . . " Big Gangsta Rap was shaking his head at the thought. Berkley jumped all over him.

"You got a problem with that?" Big was one of the brothers who could always be counted on to speak his mind, and he did so now, after opening his hands to make sure that Berkley understood that he wasn't arguing, but merely explaining his position.

"Croc, I thought this call-out had to do with another protest. I thought all you wanted was to mobilize pickets. A sortie, without planning . . ." The look on Crocodile's face made Big try another tack. "You know what time it is? It's the middle of the night. We called out our boys two times this week, already. A lot of 'em ain't happy about that."

Berkley pulled his Nine from his holster. Sounds of warning and fear came from the men, but not a word of argument.

Berkley said, "Tell me who ain't happy, Big. Give me the names of the brothers who think they don't owe their leaders their propers." Berkley was holding the gun pointed toward the ceiling—he wasn't here to start a gunfight, he was trying to make a point. He put both elbows on the table, leaned toward Big Gangsta Rap, and said, "Tell me who it is who don't *like* all that we've given them, who ain't *happy* with what we've done for them. Come on, Big. Please. Tell me who don't like the living they make, the respect and backup they get just from being part of the Nation." Berkley shook his head, as if he truly didn't understand, then said, "Are you honestly telling me they's boys who ain't happy with all they're making out on the street—not to mention the safety they have in the jails? Tell me who these ingrates are, Big." Berkley paused, then slammed his free hand down on the table and shouted, "Give me their *names*!"

"I—"

"You *nothin'*," Crocodile said. The pistol barrel had lowered, fractionally, and nine set of eyes were closely watching it; only Big Gangsta Rap was looking into Crocodile Berkley's eyes. He twisted his face into a look of incomprehension, opened his mouth, then shut it, afraid to speak.

Crocodile said, "I just had a private audience with Minister Africaan." He waited a moment, while the men on either side of him processed what they'd heard. "I just bitch-slapped Alderman Charge across his face, as well; he ain't down with us no more." Another pause; Crocodile looked around the expensive table in the lawyer's basement, looked at each of his men with as serious an expression as they'd ever seen on his face.

Crocodile said, "I set this thing up twenty years ago, after the punks who started it went off to jail, died, or stopped giving a fuck about anything but their own damn selves. They were losing it, they didn't care about what was going on, or who was getting hurt. It was *me* who trained boys—some of the boys who are in this room right now—to enlist the neutrons to go down to the Office of Professional Standards at one time and beef out the cops who were getting too close to us. Guess what

231

happened—the cops got transferred out of the district! That was *my* idea, and it been working now for more than fifteen years.

"It was *me* who organized forty different, wildass groups of men into one tight, cohesive unit, and it was me who established truces, so we could all get our piece of the pie without a whole bunch more of us dying. It was *me* who elevated every man in this room into a position of authority inside those groups." Crocodile paused for emphasis, waiting, but nobody was in the mood to argue. He said, "And it was *me* who gave every single one of *you* the goddamn power you have today." Crocodile could have gone on all night, but he'd made his point. Ten of the toughest gangbangers in the city of Chicago were remembering back to what they'd been, remembering how little they'd had before taking up with Crocodile Berkley.

Crocodile said, "The Old Gangsters, they didn't care about you, or your women, or your kids. They never had a plan of action. All they ever changed was their *own* damn standard of living. 'Racism' was a word they only shouted out long and loud when they got their asses arrested. *I* changed all that, me and my boy Terry. We made damn sure everybody ate, everybody made their money, we didn't keep it all for ourselves, we were generous, we shared the wealth. We overthrew the old regime. We *earned* our respect, and we didn't cry and moan if we had to lose sleep to go out and help our brothers, we saw it as the privilege it was. And once we got that kind of respect, my man, we never let anyone take it away from us."

Big said, "I'm sorry, Croc; it's late, I wasn't thinking."

"It's all right. But get it out of your head right now, Big. We all have to think clearly from here on out, tonight.

"We been disrespected. Not just me, not just Charge, not just the Minister, *all* of us, the entire Gangster Apostle Nation. Been disrespected by a pussy-ass West Side punk don't come to no summits, don't care about nothing but fuckin' white girls and wearing a load of gold 'round his neck like some kind of seventies TV actor. We got brothers dyin' in the street every day, killed by cops, each other, and by plain damn indifference, and this punk goes on TV and tells the whole *world* nothin' happened, then he insults me, along with the Minister, and some of us in this room don't want to do nothin' about that? Gonna worry about wakin' people *up?*"

He had them all now, Crocodile could tell. Big was blinking rapidly, having thought his apology was understood and accepted. His tough glare softened into a look of fear and respect.

"I said I was sorry, man, I didn't mean—"

"I know you didn't." Crocodile nodded his head and looked around the room as he put the weapon back under his arm. He saw the looks of relief, nodded his head again. Charge or not, he still had respect where it counted. "Anyone has some boys working for them don't want to do what they're told, think they're bigger than the group itself, bring it to me, and do it quick. We got where we are today by disciplining ourselves, and by not letting up on that discipline." Crocodile smiled.

"I ain't killed nobody myself since nineteen-ninety-four; I think I might be getting a little rusty. It was supposed to have been explained to these boys when they were brought in what was expected of them, and discipline has always been left up to the individual faction leaders."

"But it leads back to you, Croc," Fushay said, trying to make up for being late. Berkley looked over at him.

"Me and brother Glover. Boys out here don't like the way I do things, they can go inside and see how Terry treats them. See who they like better as their leader." There were grunts of assent from the men; Terry Glover's disciplinary tactics were widely known, and always feared.

Crocodile knew a little something about spraying fear.

He held power over these men, although he rarely flaunted it in their faces. Life and death, rich or poor, power; the ability to make or break a man, a block, or an entire neighborhood, if he so chose, with a snap of his fingers. As a younger man, coming up as an enforcer, he'd humiliated the men who'd served under him when they displeased him, would make them run around the block backward, while Crocodile timed them with a stopwatch. Never knowing what time would be acceptable to him, they'd gone as fast as they could, often falling down and being laughed at by the men who hadn't invoked the Crocodile's wrath. He had made other men who had angered him bark like dogs or bray like mules while he held them at gunpoint, while he extracted solemn promises from them that they would obey any and all of the Crocodile's future commands without thought or hesitation.

Glover disciplined the men in his own hard-core prison manner, honed by his having served more than twenty years in various Illinois state penitentiaries: He sodomized them.

It was widely understood within the Gangster Apostle Nation that you were not to get on the wrong side of either of these two leaders.

Civilian liberals would never understand the rigid code of discipline that was enforced by the gangs, inside the prisons as well as out on the street. Conservatives would smile in wonder, would want to know how it was done. Glover would sentence full-grown men to serve determinate terms as prison sissies; Berkley would verbally humiliate them, terrorize them, beat them, or—if their breach was serious enough—he would order them to die.

The gang understood that without strict, harsh, swift, and certain punishment for even the slightest infractions of the rules, there could be no control; they also knew that without control, there could be no power. And power was all, everything; in the world that these men lived in, having juice on the street was more important than having millions of dollars in the bank.

"The Minister and I are in agreement on two things: First, Charge is out. We don't lift a finger to help him, ever again, none of us. Pass that down to everyone, there ain't one brother in the Nation allowed to work to get him any more votes.

"Secondly, we come to a mind that we been going about things in the wrong way. Killing each other doesn't serve any purpose, hell, it's become so common, it barely gets in the papers anymore. White people don't care if we kill each other all day long, as long as we stay out of *their* neighborhoods." For the last time that night, Berkley looked around at each of his men, individually, pinning them with his glare, one by one, the intensity of his stare giving them the impression that he was looking *through* them.

As he looked around at them, he said, "But if we were to go into *their* neighborhoods, bring it to 'em, we'd get their full and undivided attention, wouldn't we?"

Crocodile Berkley, in full control again, the most powerful member of the Gangster Apostle Nation, told his astonished apostles to start working the cellular phones, as it was time to start waking up the Nation, and with it, the world. The Nation's wake-up calls were being made this very minute; the world would have to wait until precisely twelve; high noon.

CHAPTER

37

A highly agitated Edmund had called an emergency session of the entire ACK Chicago chapter, and he now stood looking out at what had shown up, patting the Mauser that was strapped to his side, and doing what little he could to hide his bitterness, resentment, and disappointment. There were 112 men in Edmund's Chicago cell, all of them oath-sworn to him, as well as to the Aryan Christian Kinsmen. One hundred and twelve men who were under Edmund's direct authority.

Seventy-two armed and highly dangerous men were packed into the stifling, rank basement. By Edmund's calculations, that meant that nearly a full third hadn't bothered to answer the call to arms. Kindhearted or not, as far as Edmund was concerned, the men who hadn't shown up this morning were nothing more than the lowest form of race traitors, and he had already written down the names of those who hadn't heeded the call. He would take care of them before he dispatched his troops to the street—send the list via fax to his own superiors, in code. They in turn would post the names on the Internet, as well, so that when Edmund and all the other men in this room were martyred, all of the right-thinking White Men in the world would know whom to blame, and upon whom they should seek retribution. The men who hadn't bothered to show up today would swing from their necks when the moment was right, and, after today, that moment would be soon in coming.

But Edmund couldn't waste a lot of time worrying about the traitors right now; he had something else, something far more important, on his mind: Gerald. Gerald fucking Pod-gore-ney. You want to talk about a race traitor? He was as bad as it got.

He'd manipulated Edmund, lied to him, used him, and cheated him. He had used Edmund, along with the rest of the Kinsmen, as he used toilet paper—Gerald had wiped his ass with the obligation of his duty-sworn, loyal allies. And, in so doing, he had committed the most unforgivable of all possible sins.

And he was more than likely getting ready right now to commit another one that was nearly as bad, by bringing a swarm of cops down on Edmund's ass. Edmund now had no doubt in his mind that Gerald would sell him out in a second if the opportunity to do so was presented before him, if Gerald thought he could make a deal with ZOG, to save his own self at Edmund's expense.

Edmund had called around to the hospitals last night, after talking to Gerald's woman. He'd gotten lucky on the fourth call; had discovered that Gerald was not only in the hospital, but was in an intensive care unit. Edmund didn't know if ZOG could mess with you when you were still in ICU, but he suspected that they could. Weren't all doctors Jews? That, or Indians who got their degrees at some veterinarian school in the Dominican Republic, then came over here at ZOG's beckoning, and injected the liberal white men—the sort who thought it cute to go to nigger doctors—with the AIDS virus. ZOG was more than likely debriefing Gerald at this very moment. Amy had told him that Gerald had been ratting Edmund out, had been blaming all sorts of things on him before the paramedics had even gotten him out the door.

He had no choice but to operate under the assumption that ZOG had a willing Gerald in their unholy clutches.

There were only a few criminal acts Gerald knew about that could cause Edmund grief should Gerald share them with agents of ZOG. And the fact was, Gerald had instigated all of the crimes in which Edmund was even tangentially involved.

But the boy could lie his ass off, could talk the panties off a nun. The thought of what he might be saying to the FBI was enough to make Edmund crazy.

Edmund had spent a sleepless, paranoid night, surrounded by weapons and protected by four of his most loyal and trusted men, men he had called in the night to come and help him, as he awaited ZOG's arrival, Edmund and his lesser cell leaders as prepared as they could be, ready for the commencement of Armageddon. He'd lain open-eyed on his cot and had looked at an image of Gerald on the ceiling, watching it almost like a movie, images in full color, Edmund seeing the tape recorders and videotape machines, the filing cabinets in the office. He heard Gerald's nervous laughter as the boy attempted to ingratiate himself, tried to make points with his new masters. ZOG's men all wore suits and trench coats, with the collars pulled up on the coats, hiding their treacherous faces. To Edmund, they all looked like Dick Tracy. Edmund had wondered if this was just his imagination, or if he too, like Daddy, had the gift of vision.

Edmund had watched Gerald telling his lies to the agents of ZOG, telling them that Edmund had killed the old woman, that Edmund had paid the niggers to kill that young girl the other day. Edmund had read about both cases in the Jewspapers; he knew that the Jews media had an interest in both killings. He knew just as well that if Gerald was under arrest, Edmund himself would be their next target. And they'd grab him for two murders; one a contract killing, the other a murder that had been committed during the commission of another felony. Which meant that both of them were capital cases. If the federal government didn't lock him in their hole-in-the-ground, super-max prison in Colorado, the state of Illinois would give Edmund the needle. Either way, Gerald—Edmund's Judas—would walk.

Why, oh *why* hadn't he paid stricter attention to Daddy's visions? Daddy had never been wrong before. He had the wisdom, the Vision, granted by Jesus Christ Himself, bestowed upon Daddy so he could help lead the true Israelites out of the darkness. Edmund, in his ignorance, hadn't heeded his daddy's warnings.

And now ZOG would be coming for Edmund, would lock him up and then would kill him.

What they wouldn't be counting on was the fact that there was no fucking way on God's green earth that Edmund was going to let that happen; he wasn't even willing to allow himself to be taken in for questioning, let alone placed under arrest. Even forgetting the death penalty altogether, Edmund couldn't see himself going anywhere with the police, let alone letting himself be arrested, tried, and sentenced to some Illinois penitentiary. Such places were filled with niggers, the scum of the earth. The Jews' mindless servants, an entire race of slaves who were too stupid to know how badly they were being used by the fraudulent bootlickers, the pretenders to the true Israel, who were in fact descendants of Satan. It could be proven in the Bible.

ZOG and Gerald, Edmund thought. A match made in hell. Gerald would know how to play them, with his slick manners and his fancy charm. They'd know how to play Gerald, too, ZOG being fully aware that Gerald was just a tiny fish in a sea that was ruled by Edmund the way the heavens were ruled by the Lord Jesus Christ. They would pander to his ego, flatter him and tell him that he was a hero to his nation, a patriot—when the truth was Gerald would be nothing but a traitor.

Edmund had been preparing for this moment since he'd been just a little boy, since his Daddy had taken him to an Aryan Christian Kinsmen conference in Washington state, where he'd heard about ZOG for the first time. He'd been preparing, and training his cell; the problem was, they weren't ready yet; there was much preparation that still needed to be done. But there was nothing Edmund could do about that; he'd chosen the war, and knew how he'd fight it, but, this time around, at least, ZOG had been able to pick the battlefield.

Edmund knew that he had to be careful about what he said. Some of the men in this room had warned him about Gerald Podgourney, taken Edmund on the side and complained about the man, wanting to know why it was that Gerald hadn't shown up for training sessions, why he was allowed to hardly ever attend supposedly mandatory ACK meetings. Some men had wanted to give him a chastisement—wanted to kick his ass. Other, more radical members of the Kinsmen had suggested to Edmund, in whispers—two men who trusted each other, alone and talking business—that maybe it was time to put Podgourney down like a sick dog.

And Edmund had hushed them all, had consistently taken Gerald's side. Edmund would not appear to be much of a leader if he told these men the truth. If he told them that he thought Gerald would be able to turn himself around.

But he could not lie to these men, he could not mislead them. They had to be told why they were heading out to their possible deaths. Edmund had to tell them in a manner that would not cause them to lose their confidence in him.

He could tell them an honest reason why he had always backed Gerald up, and could do it with a clear conscience. Because Podgourney's scores, as few as they were—and as much as he had lied about the amount of money they brought in—still handed more money over to the Kinsmen than any five other members' criminal activities combined. As Christian-based as the Kinsmen were, they'd been trained to believe that it was all right to steal from thieves, performing acts that Edmund's daddy referred to as "plundering the Egyptians." This plundering included not only violent criminal acts, but more subtle activities as well, criminal enterprises that were designed to bring about the downfall of ZOG's economy: the counterfeiting of ZOG's money, the passing of bad checks, the issuing of phony money orders, these were all the tools of the Kinsmen. The money was passed onto the leaders of the movement, who used it as they saw fit, and Edmund never kept more than he needed to eat, pay the usurious taxes that were leveled on his daddy's home, and pay the utility bills that both men worked hard to keep at their lowest amounts. The fax line and the Internet bill, were, to Edmund, staggering, but necessary, and in the long run worth every penny. It put them in touch with like-minded Aryan warriors on a national scale and allowed them to dispatch information and disinformation, depending on what the occasion called for. It also allowed Edmund and his group to download and print out files that told the Truth about Waco, Ruby Ridge, and hundreds of other examples of a government grown out of control; a power no longer of, for, and run by the people, but rather a diabolic bureaucracy that was operated exclusively in the interest of the Jew.

Judgment day was not supposed to begin until everything was in order, until the ten-percent solution seemed not only viable but absolute: Five states would be handed over to the white man, where they could live in a free and independent nation, under the colors of the Aryan flag. Edmund—along with the other chapter leaders, who'd been planted in every major city in the country—would get a call when the time was right, and a password would be whispered into his ear, and he would have the mandate to begin what was called The Chicago Siege. The day was to begin with the blowing up of a federal building, and was to end with a show of firepower in the streets; Kinsmen shooting down Jews and niggers, and anyone else foolish enough to stand in their way.

As a chapter leader, Edmund had the authority to move that day forward, if he thought that his chapter was in imminent danger from ZOG. And now, he was about to do just that. That was all right with Edmund. He had been prepared to die for his beliefs for a long, long time; he had in fact never expected to live long enough to see the realization of the ten-percent solution. But he had always hoped that the seven children he'd fathered would have lived to see it, he'd sorely hoped they would have been someday allowed to live as free men, in a state that was devoid of the racial, ethnic, and religious taint of the mud people, a taint that was destroying what little was left of what had once been the greatest, most prideful country in the world.

Edmund looked around the basement, looked sadly out at his group of men.

Edmund's chapter had been cut up into ten smaller cells, each with its own leader, whose word carried the same weight among the cells as that of the Lord Jesus Christ Himself. It had been the cell leaders whom Edmund had called, and they, at least, were all present this morning; some of them were hanging their heads in shame at the woeful turnout of manpower they had been able to produce. Edmund nodded his head, eyes shining, no longer angry or resentful, but, rather, filled with pride, as he looked out at his valiant warriors, at his Kinsmen.

This wasn't like the nigger gangs, or the ZOG-owned politicians, or even the Mafia the dagos used to run; there were no egos out of control here, no small men reaching beyond their grasps, wanting to unseat Edmund and take his place within the Kinsmen. The cell leaders—who had life-and-death power over the men they commanded—were as humble as everyone else in the room, waiting for Edmund to begin the meeting.

Great sacrifices were about to be made by some of these men—the ultimate sacrifice; they would be giving their lives for their beliefs. Edmund felt honored to command them. He cleared his throat, and the quiet mumbling in the basement ceased. Edmund nodded again, then put his hands behind his back. Some of the men were standing at attention, while others leaned against the walls, or sat on the basement's dirt floor, cleaning their weapons, silently awaiting Edmund's words. They were excited, their insides churning, probably wondering if the day they'd long prepared for had finally arrived.

Some of these men had taken off from work to be here; others held no job. Some had left wondering wives with questions unanswered; others were intentionally single, wanted no woman to come between them and their duty to their race. There was a predominance of dark-haired men in the crowd, but that didn't bother Edmund; their own messiah, in Heaven with Jesus now, had had dark hair himself. There were fat men here, and skinny men like himself, but all were pure white, all were pure of heart, all were devoted to their country and their people. Edmund loved the men in this room with the same passion with which he hated Gerald Podgourney.

Podgourney. The name was now burned onto Edmund's soul. He swore that if he survived this day, if he somehow came through it alive, he would hunt down everyone and everything Gerald Podgourney had ever loved. Hunt it down and kill it, and make Gerald watch as the beginning of his punishment. Podgourney was the sweet-talker, the asskisser. The smooth, muscular weight lifter, whose only commitment in life was to himself.

Edmund might not be able to talk as sweet as Gerald, but his impassioned speeches to the masses of the ACK had brought him more than one standing ovation since he'd been chapter leader.

Edmund closed his eyes and lowered his head, began the meeting with a prayer, speaking slowly and carefully, so the men could hear him clearly, then repeat the words he'd spoken. He asked The Lord Jesus Christ to cripple, blind, and, if need be, strike their enemies dead, asked Him to lead them righteously this day. The response from his men was loud and rumbling; their shouted "Amen" nearly brought him to tears.

Edmund looked up, tried to make eye contact with every man in the room. Edmund had never felt as proud as he did right now, standing in stifling heat, in a dirt-floor basement, on what he truly believed would be the last day of his earthly existence. He lifted his arms, held them out before him, up high, as if blessing his men; anointing them.

Edmund said, "Kinsmen! We have taken a blood oath to defend our country, our Constitution, our women, our children, and each other. We have sworn that if one of us was ever harmed, the rest of us would hunt down whoever had hurt our fallen brother, we would run the perpetrator to ground, and we would kill him. We have vowed to let our very life's blood run red into the gutters, as patriots, as warriors, as guardians of the green grass that flourishes over the graves of our sires!

"The streets are on fire, my kinsmen. The mud people are taking over, and it's now worse than it's ever been before in the history of our nation. A white cop shoots one of *them,* and there're TV cameras, and protests, with thousands of unemployed gangbanging mud people getting interviewed by the blow-dried, trained lapdogs of ZOG's electronic media. A *white* man gets burned alive on the streets of the West Side, and what happens? Nary a *word* is made mentioned—they reported the death, all right, but not the race of the *killers!*"

There were murmurs of assent from the gathered, which gave Edmund strength, which encouraged him. He was hitting home with most of them, but he could sense that others weren't enthralled. He had to win them all over before he could ask them to go out and kill—and probably die—for his mistakes.

"Thomas Jefferson said that rebellion to Tyrants is obedience to God! Do you believe in God?" The resulting roar almost bowled Edmund over. He smiled, and when he spoke now he used his hands, emphasizing points with them, jabbing with his index finger, Edmund's eyes crinkled with the righteousness he was feeling, his limbs strong with the power that God Almighty had instilled within him.

"My Daddy warned me, long ago, that a certain day was coming. A day when all honest white men would rise up from under the boot of tyranny, and take the country back by force! The Bible predicted it—read Ezekiel if you don't believe me—Gog would invade Israel from the North! *We* are the true Israelites! Gog is invading—as—I—speak! Do you hear the rumble, do your eyes bear witness to the evidence? Can you see that the nigger is taking over our women, our blocks, our neighborhoods, our cities, our entire *coun*try? What did our fathers fight and die for? So our country could come to *this?*!" Edmund waited as his warriors shouted out their disapproval.

"The End Times are coming, Kinsmen!" Edmund lowered his voice. "Today is the day we've been preparing for." He waited while that sank in. With the exception of breathing, there wasn't a single sound in the room. When Edmund spoke now, his voice was low and sad.

"Gerald Podgourney has betrayed us. He is right now telling ZOG's agents all that he knows. They'll be coming for us soon, brothers, and when they do, they'll come in droves. I was the one who stood by Gerald. I was the one who allowed him to infiltrate our chapter. It was me and me alone who stood with him, when other, more reasonable, voices saw the problem Podgourney posed, and spoke against him. I'll be the one to go down fighting, trying to get to him, to slit his throat as he lay in ZOG's hospital bed. And if need be, I'll save the last bullet in my gun for myself.

"Too many fine Aryans whose only crime was loving their nation are right now behind bars, growing old in ZOG's penitentiaries. I will not ask a one of you to go down with me. I'll leave your choices up to you.

"First, let me see a show of hands of those who have not fathered sons." More than twenty hands were raised, some quickly, some slowly, as if the men were embarrassed by their inadequate fertility. Edmund had his hand close to his weapon when he said, "Y'all're excused, right now." Several of them seemed relieved, while others seemed bitter and angry.

In an effort to appease them, Edmund said, "Kinsmen! The most fundamental rule of our Nation is this: You can*not* bring armed aggression against the enemy without first having sired a son. Who will fight on in your name, should you die? I ask you as men, leave now, and further our work after we're gone."

Edmund had warned his cell leaders that there might be some dissenters in the crowd. He'd warned them as well not to raise their hands or weapons against those who might not take well to what Edmund had to say. He watched now, as the Kinsmen who stayed applauded those who were reluctantly leaving. The applause drowned out some of the cursing that was being spat out by a few of those who were being expelled.

Edmund waited until the basement door was bolted behind them before saying, "I need your help to get to Podgourney. We have to take it to the streets, create a massive diversion. I won't blame a one of you who doesn't want to do this, who walks out the door right now. You should have raised your hands when I asked who didn't have sons, but still, if you don't think I'm doing the right thing, I won't hold it against you. Go in peace."

The forty or so men who were still in the room did not stir. Edmund saw that some of them were crying, and he wondered if they were emotional over their fates, or if his own words, his magnanimity, had moved them to tears. It didn't matter either way; the men in the room were on his side.

"Your leaders have your instructions. We start downtown, and then y'all work your way west and south, while I go east."

"What's to the east besides the lake, Edmund?" one of the men asked. Edmund knew his face, but couldn't place his name.

"The hospital, where the traitor Podgourney lays."

CHAPTER

38

The protesters hadn't shown up for the funeral.

It was the first thing Ellis Turner noticed as he drove up to the funeral parlor. He could not believe that someone of King Youngy's lowly stature could convince an agitated, worked-up populace that the situation had been defused, but he obviously had, Youngy evidently had that kind of clout. For the first time in his life Ellis Turner felt pleasure at a reminder of the sort of power that underworld kingpins held in his city. Turner drove around back to the parking lot, where the young assistant funeral director—who was dressed in a heavy, dark suit, in spite of the terrible heat—waited for Ellis to power down his window, then handed him a purple sticker that had the word FUNERAL written out on it in large white letters. Claudette peeled the protective papering from the back and placed the sticker on the windshield as Ellis pulled into a parking space.

Claudette was dressed in a simple, sleeveless, black frock; Ellis was wearing his best black suit, a longsleeve white shirt with his monogram on the pocket, and a black silk tie that would not be loosened until after the funeral.

Today, the parking lot was only half full; the police officers who had shown up last night for the wake would be working now, would not take the day off in order to attend the official ceremony. Ellis got out of the car and stopped, staring. A new, dark brown Buick Riviera—Cheryl Laney's personal vehicle—was parked a couple of slots over. It already had the purple sticker attached to its windshield.

The police had come, expecting crowds, and they'd used their energy to corral the media, had them behind barricades half a block away, in an empty lot. Turner was happy to see it. He hadn't seen any TV newscasts, but both papers had misquoted him and had only used a small portion of his statement; the part where he'd challenged the media's alleged witnesses. Turner was quoted as having said, "Let me at them, give me five minutes alone with them." He didn't expect he'd be talking to the media anytime in the immediate future.

The Standard station was busy; Turner had heard on the radio driving in that the station's owner was considering filing a lawsuit against everyone involved, trying to win back the money he'd lost due to yesterday's emergency shutdown. The way things were shaping up, the man would have to get in line. Turner ignored the shouts from the reporters, looked away from the cameras. He'd said what he'd had to say to them; from his point of view, it was over.

They entered the dark coolness of Parlor A in time to see Del Greco warmly greeting Laney—the man who last night had forbidden Laney to attend the funeral was now hugging the sergeant, his head buried in her shoulder. When Del Greco looked up, his eyes seemed shiny. Ellis noticed that Rachel was watching her husband very closely, as she stood next to Laney's husband, Daniel, whose face was dark and solemn, appearing almost ashen in the dull light of the room.

"What the hell is *this* all about," Turner said, and Claudette squeezed his arm.

"Maybe he's the forgiving type." Claudette's tone told Ellis that she didn't believe her own statement.

Angelo was slumped in a chair, his forehead bridged by one open hand. His elbow was on his knee; he seemed to not want to take the last look at his daughter. An extremely attractive, well-dressed woman in her middle forties had her hand on his arm, and a stricken look on her face. She was crying. A girlfriend? If she was, the relationship was obviously more important to her than it was to Angelo, who was basically ignoring her. The cloying smell of decaying flowers began to give Ellis a headache. Where was Charles? Ellis wondered. He looked around and spotted him, in the corner, to the far side of his wife's casket, standing in half shadow, beside a flowing rose curtain. He was staring into the casket with grief and surprise, as if he still could not believe that it was his wife lying dead in that box, and this would be his final sight of her. Ellis looked away.

He had to avert his eyes again later, too, when Charles took a dive on the coffin at the gravesite, shrieking with grief.

CHAPTER

39

Finally, it was over, and the two brothers were at last alone in one of the smaller back rooms of the Bersteins' many-roomed North Shore mansion. Angelo suspected things, Marshall was certain of that, and he blamed himself for having planted the seeds that had bloomed into his brother's suspicions—he'd been the one who'd told Angelo that Rashon had only been one of the men who were responsible for Rita's death. Marshall wondered, not for the first time, if he was slipping, giving away too much, and blaming it on his being overly tired, or on his grief over Rita's death. He had never been the sort of man who allowed his emotions to interfere with the process of his thinking.

Outside the room, on the other side of the house, most of Del Greco's family was eating a light luncheon, leaving the two of them some time alone for themselves. Rachel was the only family member not present in the house; Del Greco had asked her to go to the hospital, there was an errand that needed tending.

Angelo's ex-wife was entertaining the rest of the mourners at a more traditional post-funeral luncheon, one that was being held in the back room of a tavern on the Northwest Side. Angelo had refused to attend the function, had come back to this house with his brother and his family. He did not know how he would ever walk into the Marina City apartment again. He did not know how he had been able to spend two nights there, all alone, while Marshall had been doing his work. He never wanted to let Marshall out of his sight again, and when he told this to his brother, Del Greco's expression did not waver; he was acutely aware of the fact that suddenly, once again, for the first time in twenty-three years, he was all that Angelo had. It was a reality that Marshall would use to his full advantage, one of the particulars he would use to manipulate his brother.

Which didn't mean that he would not be there for Angelo, in the exact same manner in which Angelo had always been there for him, when the two of them had been children, and beyond. Even when Angelo had been in St. Charles, he'd written to Marshall, telling him about the place, warning him away from the life of violence that he had led. He'd written that he'd been insane to do what he'd done, and Marshall could believe it.

Marshall could remember the first time he realized that his brother Angelo was indeed insane, and his life would be one of crime. Marshall had only been six or seven, which would have put Angelo in his teens, and on that day Angelo had been wearing their father's self-hatred all over his face. He had been standing by the window, while their father had still been at work; Angelo had been fat then, overweight, withdrawn, and shy. Their mother had been out at the Laundromat, and Angelo had been baby-sitting Marshall, playing the radio and trying to escape, to go to that place in his mind where he could be safe. A Beatles tune had been playing, Marshall remembered, as he remembered Angelo trying to dance, the radio up loud, Angelo's body jiggling as he shook it in time to the beat, waving his arms around, his eyes wide open, staring off into space with a panicky look, thick blood blisters under both eyes, swelling them. Angelo had moved, swayed, singing unintelligibly, his voice high-pitched, girlish, Angelo gyrating and pretending to fit in in a world that had already abandoned him, Angelo's nose smashed over to the right, one ear already cauliflowered, Angelo so young and yet already filled with the knowledge that he would never, ever fit in, while fitting in was all he wanted. He looked out over the swelling, not seeing much more than red, as the realization dawned upon him that he would never dance with a young girl at the high school homecoming ball, would never fumble with a bra in the backseat of a car, parked behind the IGA, late at night. Would never be touched, talked about in whispers, admired the next day at school. He would never run a touchdown pass through the goalposts, or catch the final out in a baseball game, working center field. Marshall saw all that in Angelo's eyes, as his brother desperately pretended he could dance, and he saw Angelo's shoulders droop, and the defeat came into Angelo's face, the knowledge that it was over for him before it had ever had a chance to begin, and then he watched his brother as Angelo tried to fight it, as he began to dance more wildly, more excitably, with more abandon, moving his feet, waving his arms, thrusting out his torso like Tom Jones on the TV show. And then it was over, Angelo was out of breath, looking over at his younger brother, exhausted and destroyed, and Marshall looked into those beaten, crying, puppy-dog eyes,

246

and he knew, he knew that his brother was insane, and that there was no hope for him; Marshall had believed that he was to suffer the same fate himself.

Throughout his life, though, Angelo had always put what little family he had above all else in his world. No girlfriend had ever had a key to his apartment, and he had never even considered remarrying. One woman friend had once stated, over dinner, that she believed Rita to be "indulged," and Angelo had glared at her until he was certain that he had regained enough self-control to be able to get up and leave the restaurant without saying or doing something that he might later woefully regret. None of his girlfriends had ever been very important to Angelo, and they'd known up front how he'd felt; he was sometimes fun to be with, and he had—and could meet—certain needs, but there could be no deep emotional attachment, it was all explained to them, explicitly, up front. Rita's marriage hadn't changed anything for Angelo, he hadn't believed that it would last. Rita would implore him to get serious about one of his girlfriends, to find somebody to share the rest of his life with, someone with whom he could grow old. But Angelo was adamant, for reasons that Rita could never fathom. Reasons that did not stray all that far from his brother's statement to Ellis, last night, in the funeral parlor basement: Never give anyone more than one chance to fuck you. Angelo had believed his first marriage would last forever; once he'd been proved wrong, his sentiments had done a one-hundred-and-eighty-degree turn.

Sometimes, though, the women in his life didn't understand how he was, they thought that they could get through Angelo's walls, tear them down through the sheer force of their wills.

Like today, at the funeral parlor. Denise had been devastated by Angelo's treatment of her. Denise would have to learn to live without him. There were only two things that Angelo cared about now: his brother's welfare—and his personal revenge.

"I told you I'd hold off until after the funeral," Angelo said now, in a nearly formal, grave tone. "When you first told me, I said I would wait. You asked for that much time, for Rita's sake, you said, so her father wouldn't be in jail when she was laid into the ground." Angelo was sitting in a chair that had been upholstered with a bright, floral design. The chair was too small for a man of his size. Del Greco sat close to him, on the matching hassock, his legs turned to the side, but still, just inches away from his brother. Bright sunshine streamed in from the bay windows on the other side of the small reading room. Books lined the walls, stored on thick, hand-built shelving that reached all the way up to the high, beamed ceiling. Beyond the window was a long, wide, well-maintained backyard, with a large swimming pool as its centerpiece. Beneath-ground sprinklers had popped up, were now spraying. Beyond the lawn there

247

was a vast wooded area, acres and acres of trees and brush, thorny thatches that would destroy panty hose and rip through trousers.

If the media did find out about this house, they would be stymied by the closed front gate, and they'd never be able to find the back of this house from the woods. This thought relieved Marshall Del Greco. He thought that none of what had happened could hurt his family any more than it had already been hurt. He would look back at that feeling and his sense of relief later, would think of it ruefully, as he reflected upon the foolishness presumed in an expectation of lasting security.

Del Greco washed his face with one hand, slapped at Angelo's leg with the other. It was a gesture of love, grief, and companionship; it could have been seen as a gesture of surrender.

"You remember when we were kids, how you'd take the beatings? He'd put us in a room alone, come up with one of his lame, bullshit breach-of-discipline things, tell us one of us was gonna cop to it, or we were both gonna catch a beating. You'd tell me, 'Marshall, let me, it's all right, I'm used to it.' You'd wait a while, then go out and take the blame for things neither one of us had done, just so he wouldn't hit me."

"Her, too. She was just as bad."

In Marshall's case, she'd been worse. But he didn't tell this to Angelo now, in the flowery room in the back of a house that looked out onto a pleasant forest.

Instead, he said, "That's what I was trying to do the other day. I was trying to tell you that I'm used to it, to hunting; it's all right; it's what I do. And I needed you to let me."

"She was my daughter."

"I know that; I respect that."

"She was my only child."

Marshall paused for a moment before saying, "The family outside there, the Berstein boys? You want to hear something weird? In their entire fucking *lives,* their parents never raised a hand to them, never hit them. Can you believe it? None of them ever cried themselves to sleep, or went to bed hungry. None of them ever had to hide under their beds, or run over to the neighbors' houses, bleeding. They never wound up in the hospital from a beating, never had to lie, tell the doctors they fell down, knowing if they told the truth, they might wind up dead for snitching. The state never put any of them in foster homes. None of them has ever seen the inside of a jail cell. As for Rachel, forget about it; she was raised better—and with a better sense of protectiveness—than your average queen of England." Marshall shook his head, blew out his breath. "Can you imagine being raised like that? I can't."

Angelo's eyes were wide, cautioning Marshall, not sure where Marshall was going, but warning him not to go too far.

Marshall tapped his brother's leg again, and said, "Rita could imagine it, she knew all about that, Ange."

"That doesn't make me feel any better, Marshall. None of that did her any good."

"I wasn't trying to make you feel better, I was trying to make a point. And besides, you're wrong, it did her a world of good. You know what her mother was—"

"And I saw you hug that—"

"Let it go!" Marshall paused, surprised that he'd raised his voice. Angelo seemed surprised, too, was looking at Marshall oddly. When Marshall spoke now, his voice was low and calm.

"In spite of her mother, Ange, you raised a first-class girl. I never saw a daughter who loved her father the way Rita loved you. And no man ever loved a daughter as you loved Rita."

"She always came first . . . " Angelo's voice cracked, and now he put his elbow on the arm of the chair, lowered his head into his open hand, as he'd done the day before, while sitting in a padded chair at O'Donnell's. Marshall had been counting on that, on being able to make his brother cry. If he couldn't throw Angelo off base and keep him there, then Angelo might be able to see through the lies that Marshall was preparing to tell him.

"Think Rita'd rest in peace if her father was in jail?"

The hand came away from angry eyes. "I don't care about—"

"I'm not *asking* what you care about—I'm asking what Rita would think." Angelo did not respond. Marshall's hand was on Angelo's knee now, rubbing it in a calming manner. "I'm asking you if you want to do this to her memory."

"Rita's *dead!*" Angelo covered his face with his hands now, was leaning forward, was sobbing silently in a locked room, alone with the only man still alive who had ever seen him cry, or ever would. Marshall reached up and hugged him, held him closely, his own eyes tightly shut, feeling something ripping, a searing pain, deep in his chest, a pain that had as much to do with the deception he was about to enter into as it did with his grief over Rita, or his compassion for Angelo's suffering.

Marshall said, "You're the only human being on earth who has always been there for me, every time I've needed you. I'm scared to think what I might be if it hadn't been for you." Marshall pushed off a few feet, held his brother by the shoulders.

Angelo tried to smile; he sniffed, and rubbed at his eyes; his nose. His pride in what he'd helped his brother become momentarily overwhelmed his suffering. "For a while there, it was touch and go. You had a lot of hate inside."

"And you still took me in, you got me *away* from them. I know how your wife felt, I knew she didn't want me around."

"*I* wanted you around."

"I know, I know, I know you did." Marshall was gently squeezing Angelo's shoulders, kneading hard muscle with powerful fingers while his brother sat with eyes now tightly closed. "You got me through high school, you supported me financially."

Marshall had to pause as he remembered his first summer job, working for Angelo in the electronics store, proudly handing his paycheck over to his brother every week, to help with his support. On the day Marshall had left Angelo's home to strike out on his own, Angelo had handed him a bankbook. He'd saved what Marshall had given him, gave it to him as a cushion, a nest egg for Marshall to fall back on, should he need it.

But he couldn't think about that now. Couldn't think about the love he'd received, the caring, the understanding, the sometimes harsh hand that had guided him through his turbulent and troubled late-teen years. If he thought about those things, he wouldn't be able to lie to his brother.

He said, "I had Rashon Latribe killed." Angelo's eyes popped open, and he stared at Marshall.

"I figured that."

"So did everybody else. I found out who did it, and I made a deal with his gang boss: give me Latribe, dead, and I wouldn't make a project out of the boss, wouldn't devote the rest of my life to putting his sorry ass in prison."

"What about the driver? Somebody was driving the car."

"There was one other guy. He'll be taken care of, too."

"And the gang leader?"

Marshall shook his head. "He didn't know anything about it. It was a spur of the moment thing, that's all. Two rival gang members saw each other, started woofing, and Rita got in the way."

"The guy in the car, that was who you were talking about last night, when you said Rashon was 'one of them.' "

Marshall looked directly into Angelo's eyes and said, "Yes."

Angelo sighed heavily, leaned back in the chair. Marshall watched as he seemed to deflate, as the rage that had been stored up within him slowly seeped away. Angelo's baggy eyes now lost their look of grief.

"So it's over then."

Marshall nodded solemnly. "It's over. Now what?"

Angelo shrugged. "What do you mean?"

"What are you going to do? I'm scared you're going to kill yourself, and leave me all alone."

"You're not alone. You've got Rachel." He waved an arm around him. "And all *this*. They love you, Marshall, they're the family we never had."

Angelo said this, then his eyes narrowed, and he stared hard at Marshall. Slowly, thoughtfully, Angelo said, "You're telling me this as a fact, aren't you? I mean, you found it all out, there can't be any other way?"

"What do you mean?"

"There's no way around this, I have to ask you straight out: are you telling me the truth? Or just handing me a line you think I'll fall for, so I won't do something you'd see as wrong."

"Look me in the eye." Marshall pointed his fingers at his eyes, stared directly into Angelo's wet, wishing eyes. He held his brother's shoulders tightly with both hands, and he squeezed them slightly, almost with every word, to emphasize the truthfulness of his words.

Marshall Del Greco said, "Rashon Latribe killed Rita. Nobody else had anything to do with it. I held a shotgun to King Youngy's—the gang leader's—head, and I had the legal authority to use it, and he knew I wouldn't hesitate. He would have told me if there were any more."

Angelo looked at Marshall for a long time, seeking dishonesty. Marshall's gaze did not waver. Angelo nodded.

He said, "Marshall, oh dear Jesus God in heaven, what am I going to do without her? What am I going to *do*?" His voice was a wail, his eyes half-closed, as if trying to see into a future so bleak and desperate that a merciful God would not allow him to even glimpse the horrors that awaited him there.

Marshall, greatly relieved that Angelo believed him, and without any answers to give him, turned on the hassock and gazed out the window so he wouldn't have to think about his brother's question. A family of deer had made their way out of the woods, and stood at the edges of the lawn, lapping at the puddled water. The animals all seemed very thin. The heat and the dry spell had overridden their normal caution, conspired to drive them out into view, in full daylight, seeking nourishment. Marshall thought that he would have to find out what it was that deer ate, find out and take some out there, put it into the woods for them. He'd seen too much hunger, too much need. Too much fucking *want*.

He felt Angelo's hand on his shoulder, turned to his brother, Marshall fighting his impotence and his rage, fighting the fear that he might not be able to control them.

"I'm dying and I don't have anything left!"

"You've got me."

Angelo moved closer to Marshall, put both hands on his brother's shoulders. "I know," he said, "I'm sorry . . ."

"You'll always have me, Angelo."

"Hang onto me, would you?" Angelo said, as he pulled Marshall into a bear hug, and Marshall did so, clinging to Angelo for his own sake as

251

much as for his brother's, and they held each other tightly, Angelo's head buried in Marshall's shoulder, until the loud pounding came on the locked door, and Paul Berstein's frantic voice shouted that they had to open up, right away, the city was on fire, and the rioters were blaming it on Marshall.

CHAPTER

40

Ellis Turner got paged as he was driving home from the post-funeral reception. He groped for his beeper, taking his eyes off the street as he fumbled with it, trying to see who had called.

"Ellis . . . " Claudette generally had a world of patience where it concerned her husband, but she had none at all when it came to ego-driven anger that could result in physical harm. She knew that Ellis was upset because Marshall Del Greco hadn't invited the Turners to join them at—wherever they'd gone after the funeral. The Del Grecos hadn't shared their plans with the Turners, and that was eating at Ellis, Claudette knew.

But that was no reason for him to kill them. "Watch it!"

"I've got it." Ellis looked over at her sheepishly, still fumbling with his beeper.

"You were in the wrong lane."

"Shit."

"What is it?"

"Call-out signal from the division."

"*I'll* dial them, you keep your eyes on the road."

Both of them were aware on some level that their touchiness was caused by a mix of geography and the color of their skin.

At stoplights, the people in the expensive foreign cars on either side of them were white. White people—dressed for the heat in their bright summer shorts and halter tops—walked the streets, waited on the corners for buses, hailed cabs, or Rollerbladed swiftly down the sidewalk. One shirtless idiot on Rollerblades was pushing some sort of weird-looking, three-wheeled, needle-nose baby carriage, swerving wildly, in and out, weaving through pedestrian and vehicle traffic, with a small child out in front of him, involuntarily taking the point. Other parents or nannies pushed small children down the sidewalk in expensive, elaborate baby buggies. Yuppies navigated fancy bicycles down both the street and the sidewalks, naked or sports-bra-wearing backs bent low over the handlebars, wearing funny Styrofoam hats on their heads, their well-muscled backsides packed into Spandex shorts.

The only black people in this neighborhood seemed to be mental cases wearing heavy coats over layers of other clothing in the heat, or panhandlers standing on the corners, shaking wax soft drink cups, or trying to sell *StreetWise* to passersby.

Ellis and Claudette were both well dressed, were an obviously semi-prosperous couple in their thirties, and they were driving a one-year-old, unpretentious Chevrolet Impala. But still, they felt marked, out of place in such a neighborhood, and that knowledge infuriated them, made them short with each other.

Claudette, more rage-filled on a calm day than Ellis was on his worst, and therefore more aware of what was happening than Ellis, calmed herself down as she hit the Send button on the car phone, then placed the handset next to Ellis's ear. He took it from her, his eyes now again on the road, apologizing through his actions rather than through words.

"This is Detective Ellis Turner; what's going on?" Claudette watched the shock come upon him, saw Ellis first slump, then snap fully alert. He wasn't black anymore; he was blue. Her husband was now a cop.

Ellis squinted through the windshield in the bright sunlight, caught a break and pulled across two lanes, swiftly maneuvered the Chevy into a tight parking space. He said, "We're on our way home from Rita Cunningham's funeral, we're less than two blocks from the Dan Ryan. I'll be there as soon as I drop my wife off at home, and grab my uniform."

Claudette watched as Ellis listened, then grunted something more, then her usually fastidious husband absently dropped the phone. Claudette watched it bounce off his leg, saw it fall and land face-up on the interior burgundy carpet.

"What's wrong?"

"King Youngy's dead—"

"Oh My God—"

"—and they found his head on a fencepost in front of Del Greco's front lawn."

"Is Marshall there! Are they in danger?"

"Nobody knows where he is; they're looking." Ellis put the car in gear, checked the mirror, waited, and, when he had his chance, tore away from the curb. "The department learned from its mistakes last time; now they're better prepared. They're cancelling all furloughs, vacations, and days off; *everyone* below lieutenant is being ordered into uniform and hitting the streets." Ellis took a sharp turn at the corner, headed for the expressway, raced down the ramp, hit the blacktop and floored it, heading south.

"They're calling you in because some *drug* lord was killed?"

Ellis didn't look at Claudette as he said, "The riot's already started; they're battling it out downtown."

CHAPTER

41

The fifty trusted members of the Gangster Apostle Nation had been called upon to perform one essential task: an assault on Youngy's head-quarters. As violent as it became, the assignment hadn't been difficult. They'd crept up on the watchers, as they'd rested safe in their cars with the air-conditioning running, and they'd taken them out swiftly and silently.

They'd found a set of keys to the building in one of the guardians' pocket.

The house had been easy to take; the walls made of heavy brick, muf-fling the sound of gunshots. Surprised but complacent bodyguards had been messily but quickly dispatched.

Youngy had been dragged from his bed naked; Kirstin had been killed. They'd kept Youngy's body in the trunk of a stolen car until it was time to make their move; ten heavily armed men in three cars had been dis-patched to Marshall Del Greco's house, with explicit instructions as to what to do and when to do it. As soon as the mission had been accom-plished, five of the faction leaders had been sent back to the neighbor-hoods they controlled, given orders as to what to do, where to meet, and when. They were to pound on doors, drag the bodies out and get them ready for war, make sure the people were ready and willing to follow orders. There would be no reliance on telephones this time, no chance for somebody to say they didn't get the call. Strict discipline was to be maintained this time, also; there could be no shooting until Crocodile Berkley himself gave the order.

A MATTER OF HONOR

By noon, if everything went according to Crocodile's design, there were to be five hundred armed men lingering downtown, awaiting further instructions.

The five hundred men showed up—in fact, almost double that number showed up, looking for, expecting, and prepared for war—but that was the only thing that day that went according to Crocodile's design.

The other men who had taken part in the assault on Youngy's building were, at eleven-thirty on this sizzling, summer morning, on their way to meet their comrades, in a dozen cars, driven convoy style, the drivers obeying all traffic laws as they made their way carefully from the West Side to downtown. Each car was equipped with a cellular phone; any last-minute changes of directions and plans could be easily passed along, in case any of the cars got lost during a last-minute move.

Crocodile Berkley was in the lead vehicle, riding shotgun in a brand-new red Mitsubishi 3000. A police scanner blared from the back seat, turned up loud, set to hop back and forth between the routine First District calls, and the City Wide 1 band, which monitored gang crimes.

So far, everything seemed calm.

Crocodile had a short, single-barreled, Streetsweeper riot shotgun between his legs, barrel down, the twenty-shot ammo drum resting on his knee. The weapon had a striking similarity to a 1920s machine gun. Crocodile's legs were wide apart, to accommodate the drum, the pistol-grip stock held loosely in one hand, with his cellular phone held just as loosely in the other. Berkley was wearing a fifteen-shot semiautomatic pistol, the weapon riding in a holster beneath his flowing shortsleeve shirt. There were five extra clips of ammunition, fully loaded and ready, in various zippered pockets of his silk parachute pants, ready to be slapped in just as soon as a clip was empty.

As they drew closer to the heart of the city, Crocodile sat up stiffly. His jaw muscles began to jump around in his cheeks. His heavy muscles were pumped; he was ready for this.

Crocodile Berkley had been preparing for this moment since the day he'd been born.

They were almost there now, were on the edge of the West Loop, closing in on downtown, and Crocodile had to physically force himself to relax. He sat still, closed his eyes, laid his head back against the rest. He was picturing it in his mind, what would happen, his masterpiece. He was fully prepared to die before its completion. Crocodile wanted this to happen, he wanted this so bad. . . . Let *them* see what it was like, let *them* lose something for once. Let *them* know what real fear was, as they felt the waves of terror crashing down on their heads, rolling over them, drowning them. He prayed that God would allow this city's oppressive, white motherfuckers to live just one goddamn full *day* of their lives feeling the sort of terror, experiencing the kind of suffering, that Crocodile and his people felt every single day of their lives, what they'd been feeling for hundreds and hundreds of years.

Berkley heard the police call come over the radio, on the routine, Area 1 frequency, an almost bored voice dispatching a unit to a disturbance at Rudolpho's Clothing; he heard the address spoken in that unique Chicago police accent, the one that every white male officer in the city affected. It made them sound as if they had all grown up on the same block.

Crocodile raised his head; opened his eyes, wondering.

He heard a response, another bored voice identifying its police unit by letter and number, informing the dispatcher that they were en route.

Rudolpho's was a large, Michigan Avenue clothing store that catered to African-American males. Crocodile hadn't given any specific instructions to the faction leaders, hadn't told any of them to make Rudolpho's one of the places for the men to congregate, but he suspected that it was only natural for some of the boys to gravitate to such a place.

Now there was another, more cautious voice on the radio, requesting more units, advising the dispatcher in police lingo that there seemed to be over a hundred YBMs—Young Black Males—creating a disturbance at Rudolpho's, and that the disturbance was spilling onto the sidewalk, and out into the street.

Crocodile whipped his head around and glared through the back window, as if by doing so he could identify which faction leader had told his men to meet him at Rudolpho's—the stupid motherfucker. Look at what he had caused.

There was no doubt it was Apostles, the cops were screaming at each other over the airwaves now: young black males this, young black males that, talking about their colors, the way they had tilted their hats, the police voices growing more frantic with every second they were on the air, fear now entering their tones for the first time as they seemed to understand that they were facing a lot more than just a couple of geechie shoplifters in a downtown clothing store.

Over all the hollering, Crocodile could hear the unmistakable sound of gunshots.

The phone rang under his hand, and Berkley clenched the shotgun between his knees, stabbed at the Send button as if it were an eye he was trying to enucleate.

"What!"

"Crocodile, it's Billy Charge."

"Man, mother*fucks* you!" Crocodile had been expecting a progress report from somebody on the scene—he was in no mood to be entering into discussions with hypocritical politicians. Those days, as far as the Crocodile was concerned, were over.

Charge said, "Channel Five just interrupted the soap operas with a special report about King Youngy—"

Crocodile exploded. "He wasn't the king of nothing! He was never king of shit!"

"Oh, my God, then you *did* do it!"

"You gonna try and lay this bullshit on me over the *phone,* you lyin' motherfucker? Tryin' to set me up! Didn't you learn *nothin'* from the slap I gived you?"

Charge's voice was nearly calm, almost resigned, as he said, "Crocodile, where are you."

"Turn your TV on, bitch. You'll see me soon enough." Berkley punched the button off, then threw the phone against the dashboard.

"Goddamnit, move it! Can't you hear what's happening?" The driver speeded up, disciplined enough, frightened enough, to do as he was told without question. The men in the backseat sat silently. Berkley felt his pulse pounding, shook his head in anger at the outright disobedience of his explicit instructions.

There was a traffic backup, right at Wabash, the street before Michigan Avenue. What the fuck was going on? There seemed to be hundreds of people running down the street, coming toward them, heading west. Disregarding the traffic lights and the sidewalks, as well as the withering heat, they ran through the sea of honking cars, terror stamped on their faces, some of them looking over their shoulders, as if checking to see if anything was after them. Up at the intersection, a taxi had run head-on into a minivan. There appeared to be several casualties. The driver's side of the van's windshield was totally shattered, thousands of shards of glass lay in the street. The rest of the windshield was cracked in a spiderweb pattern; there was blood all over the vehicle's short, sloping hood. Other cars tried to drive around the wreck. Even with the windows closed, Crocodile could hear the sounds of fender benders and squealing tires.

Berkley's driver tried to pull around the wreck, tried to get into the second lane. The pedestrians wouldn't let him change lanes, the flood of them stopped all traffic. Behind and all around them, horns honked and tires shrieked as the other cars in the convoy attempted to follow suit. The streetlight turned red. Berkley heard the wail of sirens, saw the bright flashing lights of an ambulance trying to navigate through the dense late-morning traffic under the El tracks, heading toward them. Surprisingly the ambulance turned east, away from the wreck, toward Michigan. This far north, Wabash was a one-way street, heading south. There were a half-dozen cars still in the intersection, blocking the convoy's way as the light now turned green. There were vague, distant popping sounds. They had to be gunshots.

Berkley shouted, "God*damnit*!" and punched at the dashboard, leaving a deep impression on the black leather. The Mitsu's driver tried another tack, lowering his window and pointing his pistol and screaming at all the white pedestrians who were running around them in panic. His actions didn't inspire an atmosphere of calm.

"Motherfucker, put that goddamn gun way!" Berkley screamed.

He told himself that discipline was all, discipline was everything. Even the chaos surrounding him could not stop him from being who he was. Crocodile had seen worse, experienced worse, and had always managed to come out on the other side in one piece. There was nothing going to happen on Michigan Avenue—or anywhere else in the world, for that matter—that could match the horrors Crocodile Berkley had survived within the confines of Stateville prison.

Premature acts of violence could cost them the battle. The element of surprise was gone. Everybody was supposed to be in place, to begin shooting at one time, when he told them to . . .

He would find out, later, whose group it was, and he'd see the man's head on a stick, as the world no doubt had already seen Youngy's. Charge knew about it, said it had been on the news. It wasn't twelve yet, was still a few minutes till. Somebody had fucked up—*everybody* had fucked up. He'd get them later, Crocodile swore. If he lived through this, he'd make them pay.

For the moment, however, he had to stay in control. There were five hundred armed men in the downtown area now, whose lives depended on Berkley's leadership. He had to focus himself, had to keep the convoy away from the disturbance. Those men who had been engaged in battle early could be written off, they'd brought it on themselves. They'd have to stay the fuck away from Rudolpho's—

"You hear that, Croc?" It was a frightened voice from the backseat. Crocodile had to work to bring himself out of his thoughts.

"Hunh?"

"*Listen!*"

A frantic white voice was shouting over the radio now; the sound of gunshots could be heard, loud and often, in the background. What was he screaming about?

Armed *white* males?

There was a moment of confusion, several officers shouting over each other as portable lapel mikes were simultaneously keyed. Crocodile managed to pick up fragments of coherent, heated conversation through the jumble of screams, shouts, and gunshots.

He heard about random drive-by shootings on Michigan Avenue; large, heavily armed, well-organized gangs of white and black males, racing through the streets, joined in combat, shooting each other down.

A terrified scream of 10-1 crossed the airwaves; this would take precedence over all other calls.

Crocodile knew 10-1 to be the police department code that meant that an officer needed help.

As he realized this, the shouts came over the radio: "POLICEMAN SHOT!" Then a different, highly agitated voice: "*POLICE OFFICER SHOT!*" The officer screaming it was hysterical, was clearly scared out of his wits.

Crocodile said, "Fuck it." Almost casually. He turned to his driver. "Let's get it on," he said. He opened the car door and stepped out, bringing the shotgun to bear in one smooth motion. He leaped catlike onto the Mitsubishi's hood, fired a round into the air, turned, holding the weapon above his head, and waved it back and forth toward his troops, signaling them to follow. Crocodile ignored the loud screams of terror around him; these were civilians, punk-ass scared white bitches, not the real, armed enemy. The enemy was up ahead a block, awaiting Crocodile's arrival.

As Africaan had always predicted he would be. The white man, seeing his power threatened, had come hunting; the day had arrived. The radio had said armed whites. And Crocodile and his men were in the unique position to stop him, to fight back. God had put them here, today, right here and now, a group of proud black men, a force that could do battle. Berkley looked briefly to the heavens.

It was black against white now, the way Minister Africaan had always envisioned it. Any Caucasian with a weapon in his hand was to be mown down like the dog he was. And it didn't seem to be the white man's day, armed or otherwise. Although he himself didn't plan on wasting any bullets, Crocodile's boys didn't seem to have any compunctions about doing so.

He could hear them behind him, opening up on the crowd. He hoped they knew enough to shoot to the side, and behind, their own men.

Crocodile jumped lightly to the pavement and began the fast, block-long march, exhilarated, excited, eyes half-closed as he strode, sweeping the weapon from side to side, finger on the trigger, enjoying the panic he caused, feeling his boys catch up, form into a protective squadron around him. He turned left onto Michigan Avenue and saw what was happening, right there in broad daylight, in the middle of the city's showcase street.

The sight before him caused Crocodile to race forward, the shotgun down and ready.

CHAPTER

42

Ellis Turner sat on a wooden bench that was attached to the metal wall of the long, wide, Chicago Police Department SWAT van, breathing heavily, trying to tell himself that he had to stay in control, that he could handle this. There were perhaps two dozen other officers crammed inside the van with him, sitting on the benches or on the floor, or standing and holding onto whatever they could for balance as the van raced around corners, throwing them around. All the officers were wearing riot gear, the shields of their helmets were down, their weapons locked and loaded, ready. Their objective was not a show of force; they were there to quell a riot by any means they deemed to be necessary.

Even if he had been allowed to, Turner wouldn't have been able to smoke; he couldn't even get at the cigarettes that were buried in the uniform shirt under the huge, bulky, bulletproof vest that covered him from his neck to his groin. His back itched, fiercely. It was too tight in the van, close, he was feeling claustrophobic. Along with the stale smell of sweat, Turner could smell the fear coming off the other officers, suspected that they could smell his fear, as well. He wondered how many of them had had fights with their wives after the callout.

Turner's greatest fear as a police officer had always been slamming out the door after a fight with Claudette, going on-duty, and getting killed before the end of his shift.

He had made it a rule throughout his career to never leave for work angry, to always resolve whatever problems he and Claudette might be having before he left for the job; the thought of the guilt Claudette would feel for the rest of her life, should he die on duty without their making amends was, to Turner, as devastating as what he himself would go through if he should be unlucky enough to see death coming, with the knowledge that his last words to Claudette had been words of anger rather than love.

Yet that was exactly what had happened today; Claudette had actually *demanded* that Ellis not respond to the citywide officer's callout. They'd had a running argument while Ellis had been searching through the closets, trying to find his uniform, Claudette frightened and anxious because Quentin wasn't home, Ellis shouting at her that their son would be fine, goddamnit, the problem was downtown. The entire thing was planned, a setup, couldn't she see that? Turner had raced out of their house with Claudette's words ringing in his ears: "Don't you dare go! Don't you *dare!*"

Don't you dare? Ellis could not remember Claudette ever challenging him in such a manner.

And she had to do it on a day like this one, when a riot was going down.

Turner was a homicide detective, which meant, by definition, that he arrived on the scene only *after* the crime had been committed. The odds against his dying during the course of any single investigation were staggering; in fact, he could not remember the last time a detective had been shot in Chicago, let alone killed in the line of duty.

But now he'd be doing a patrolman's job, not sure what was out there, what was going on. He'd be racing blindly into the proverbial dark alley, not knowing if he was outgunned, and if he was, how badly. Now there was a riot, and—if the radio reports were accurate—three police officers had already been shot. Three that they were aware of; there might well be more, a lot more, shootings that had been missed in the initial, frightened reports.

The van suddenly rocked to a jarring halt, and Turner sat up, and forgot about his fight with his wife. He forgot about everything except the sudden surge of fear that overtook him as one of the officers threw the doors open wide, and he took his place along with the other coppers in the van, marched out quickly to face the enemy.

Turner hit the street, felt the heat assault him, and nearly stopped dead in his tracks at the sight of the downtown area. Where were they? The Unit Eight sergeant had said their van was going to Michigan and Wacker Place. Until the sergeant had spoken the words, Turner hadn't even known that there *was* a street named Wacker Place. He got his bearings, saw that the train station was just a few blocks away, at Randolph.

The usually busy area was a war zone now, dead and wounded bodies seeming to be everywhere. Screaming, moaning victims were lying on the sidewalk, in the storefronts, in the middle of the street, while their more ambulatory counterparts were shouting, whooping, making coyote sounds and Indian war whoops. Through the helmet, over the sound of the rioters, Turner could hear the gunshots: the single, loud reports of revolvers and semiautomatics; the sharp bursts of multi-shot automatic weapons; the loud booms of shotguns. The heavy-duty Plexiglas face cover was fucking with his view; his peripheral vision was cut in half, he felt as if he were wearing blinders. His paranoia and fear increased, there was no way he could see someone sneaking up on him; he wouldn't be able to hear them.

The other coppers were fanning out, weapons down, ready for and anticipating engagement, some of them eagerly, others with trepidation. Turner stopped, stood frozen for a moment as some officers raced past him, bumped into him.

All of the bridges across the river had been opened, to help them with containment. Turner could see the risen, thick-looking slabs of concrete, dividing, as well as limiting, the battleground. Unit Eight's mission was to secure the few blocks between where the van had stopped on up to the Michigan Avenue bridge.

Turner joined the other officers now, double-timing down the street, shotgun held at port arms, prepared to use it only if he had no other option, not about to fire upon anyone who wasn't shooting at him or another officer. Turner felt dizzy, felt the sting of sweat in his eyes. His hands were shaking, there was a weakness in his knees and in the back of his legs, a pain in his chest that had nothing to do with possible physical ailments. He couldn't seem to catch his breath.

There were no windows left in any of the stores that lined both sides of the avenue. Hordes of people were racing in and out of the glassless windows, their arms filled with merchandise, oblivious of the battles that were occurring all around them. *HawkQuarters* and the athletic store right next to it seemed to have attracted the largest crowds. Turner and his fellow officers waded into the fray, trying to break up fistfights and pistol-whippings, not being gentle about it, the whir of news helicopters overhead having no bearing on their behavior. It seemed as if a lot of the armed combatants had run out of ammunition; they had reversed their weapons and were using them against one another as clubs.

A young, thin, white man ran directly toward Turner, shouting curses Turner couldn't hear above the cacophony of screams, shots, and sirens. Turner butt-stroked him, dropped him in his tracks, kicked a useless weapon away from the youth's reach. Turner dropped quickly to his knees, dropped his weapon directly in front of him, pulled a plastic flex-cuff restraint from the dozens that were hanging from the webbing around his waist, and flipped the kid over quickly and cuffed his hands behind

A MATTER OF HONOR

his back. Another youth, this one black, kicked at Turner and tried to grab Turner's riot gun. The youth's foot met Turner's well-padded chest with little impact. Turner grabbed at his weapon with one hand, used it to sweep the kid off his feet. He stood quickly and pointed the shotgun at the youth's face, and the kid shut his eyes, flipped over without having to be told, and put his hands behind his back. Turner secured his wrists and left him there, stood and tried to get his bearings.

Fuck the stores; they were insured. They were there to restore the peace, not to protect the property of merchants. The rioters were running now, heading west, away from Michigan. That was fine with Turner, Wabash was closed off by hundreds of police officers, who would detain anyone who came their way, while only allowing emergency vehicles to come east, toward the action.

Turner grabbed a guy coming out of one of the stores, a well-dressed son of a bitch in a suit, holding thousands of dollars of Black Hawks jerseys close to his chest. White male, mid-twenties, caught up in the frenzy, eyes blazing. He seemed angry that a copper had dared to detain him, halfheartedly tried to pull away. Ellis Turner looked into a pair of annoyed, pale blue eyes, and lost it.

He acted without thinking, before he could stop himself. Turner struck out with a gloved hand, slapping the man hard, a stinging blow, causing him to drop his loot. Turner held onto the shotgun with one hand, used the other to punch the looter in the face, again and again, until he fell bloody to the sidewalk. Turner lifted a foot, ready to stomp the man, then somehow managed to stop himself, stepped back and looked at what he'd done, thought about the helicopters overhead, wondered if one of their cameras had caught him in the act.

He realized that with all the riot gear, the hat, the face shield, no one would be able to recognize him.

No matter what he did.

Turner shook himself, disgusted. His right glove was bloody. Something small and hard zinged harmlessly off his helmet. A dozen yards up the street, three skinheads were stomping an officer. The officer was on his back, hanging onto his shotgun, but the skinheads had no doubt been practicing, one of them was swinging the officer's own club at the officer's knees and his unprotected shins. Turner wiped his bloody hand on his vest, then began to run toward them, the shotgun held in both hands now, either end ready for action. He butt-stroked the first skinhead in the face, spun, and used the butt again, this time jabbing it hard into the second man's stomach. The third skinhead had the club, and had been swinging it at the back of Turner's legs. Turner, screaming in pain, swung the shotgun around and aimed it directly at the youth's face. The youth spat at Turner; the saliva dotted his face shield. Turner began to squeeze the trigger, an involuntary act that he was able to control. The youth slapped at Turner's head with the nightstick, and Turner saw his face register shock and pain before he heard the blast of the gunshot. Blood exploded through the youth's chest, splattering Turner, and Ellis looked wildly around him as the youth fell dead at his feet.

An officer with a short-barreled riot shotgun waved to him in a comradely fashion, and it was all Turner could do to stop himself from shooting the officer down. He turned, his head swimming at the sight of the surreal world he'd been plunged into, and realized, suddenly and with shock, that he was crying. He raised an arm to wipe the saliva off his face shield, smeared it around, but was able to see more clearly. The entire front of his bulletproof riot suit was covered with blood, and probably with shotgun pellets, too, though he hadn't felt the shock of them hitting. A well-trained hostage barricade team began to fire their shotguns in the air, screaming, "DOWN, DOWN, DOWN," between volleys, and Turner saw rioters all around him dropping their weapons and throwing up their hands and dropping to their knees; saw others running in every direction, firing indiscriminately at whatever caught their fancy. He saw officers opening up on these renegades; they'd been warned, they deserved whatever happened. A terrified preteen-ager stood in the middle of the street, a large handgun hanging loosely from his right hand, eyes wide as he faced a police officer whose shotgun was pointed directly at the child's chest.

Turner ran toward the boy, got himself between the youth and the officer before the officer could fire, and, using the barrel of his own weapon, slapped the pistol from the boy's hand. He kicked at it as the boy began to scream in fear and pain, and Turner looked behind him, saw that the officer was glaring at him, but he'd lowered his shotgun. Turner knelt down and grabbed the kid by his upper arms. He was, at the most, ten years old. His right arm had been firebranded with the symbol of his gang, the flesh sticking up and out, marking the boy forever. Turner shook him, hard, seeing the wet stain on the front of the boy's pants; a line of spittle that dribbled from his mouth, connecting to his T-shirt. Turner stopped shaking the boy, pulled him close and hugged him.

"It's okay, little man," Turner said to him. The boy struggled, tried to fight the much larger man, screaming about his hand, about how he was going to sue the motherfucking city. Turner let him go and spun him around, and, with sadness in his heart, flex-cuffed him and moved on.

It was getting dark, and Ellis Turner had had enough. He sat on the sidewalk, with his back against the concrete of the Cultural Center, helmet and gear off, the riot contained, at least in the downtown area. Turner was smoking his last cigarette. Were there any drugstores around? Turner chuckled tiredly at the thought.

He was not alone. Scores of other officers were sitting on the sidewalk, or standing around, looking sad and tired and confused and weary, the more intelligent among them probably wondering whether their lives would ever be the same again. Light blue summer blouses were soaked through with sweat. Sweaty, bloody riot uniforms were stacked all over the sidewalk, empty shotguns on the bottom, barrels pointed toward the street. The helmets were on top. Some of the helmets had fallen off the piles, had rolled onto Michigan Avenue. Nobody had bothered to pick them up. Turner had been too young to fight in Vietnam—he had spent two years in Germany—but he thought he knew now how soldiers felt after battle. How did the Vietnam veterans live through an entire year of this and come out on the other end with their sanity intact? Turner did not know. He did know that he would rather be dead than to be forced to live through another day like this one.

Turner was hanging on by his fingernails, and he was smart enough to know it. He looked around him, seeking and gaining relief from the sight of the many other officers who were denying feelings similar to his own.

A temporary command post had been set up inside the building, the brass was inside, plotting strategy and reporting to the politicians. Every now and then, a report would come out to the troops, a sympathetic sergeant or lieutenant would come out and clue the officers in on what was happening.

A lot was happening.

The West and South Side ghettoes were uncontainable, both sections of the city were burning down, the Arab- and Jewish-owned stores had been looted before being set aflame.

But it was safe here. The downtown area was secure. Turner wondered how many black people owned the high-rises down here, or the businesses that thrived inside them. He had never thought much about such things before, even when Claudette had been calmly stating her case that the city was owned and run by and for Caucasians. He'd been arresting black people—and white people—since he'd been a rookie, but he'd never had to fight his own kind before, one on one, in pitched battle, with the lines so clearly drawn. He felt, momentarily, like a traitor. He worked hard to fight off the feeling, looked around him again, saw plenty of black faces in the crowd of weary officers. He told himself that he wasn't the only one.

Then he noticed that the black officers were mostly grouped together, away from the whites. Turner had just plopped himself down where there had been room, in the first available space he'd come to. The officers on either side of him were white. He wondered now if he should go over and join one of the black groups.

Turner drew in a deep breath. Maybe none of their lives ever would be the same again. After today, everything might change.

Large troop trucks filled with National Guard soldiers were rolling off Randolph Street and onto Michigan Avenue, in order, one turning north, the next turning south, Turner watched them: one-two, one-two. They were filled with armed men and women whose duty it was to protect the throng of medics from the very people to whom they'd be tending. Fresh police officers, in crisp uniforms rather than riot gear, would be patrolling the sidewalks, ready to arrest any stragglers, or anyone who had only been playing possum. Ellis looked at the Guard units, and did not envy them their jobs. They would be collecting the dead bodies and practicing triage on the live ones. Those who could be helped would be aided by portable field medical units, others would be quickly transported to area hospitals. The worst of the bunch would be left alone, and most of them would likely die before a doctor could safely reach them.

"They're using Soldier Field for a temporary lockup." The lieutenant was speaking to the crowd in general, passing along information he'd received inside. It was reliable information, which was quickly passed along and discussed, judgment passed by foot soldiers. Turner did not want to go home and see the other kind of information, the kind he knew was right this minute being spewed over airwaves rife with media speculation, educated guesses, and downright lies. Which of the three was heard would be dependent on the channel, a flick of the clicker would be all that divided them.

Turner wondered about the wisdom of putting white and black prisoners together in a mostly unsecured area the size of Soldier Field. He decided that it wasn't his problem. He had done his job.

"Why didn't they just put fucking targets on our backs?" Some white officer was letting off steam, standing on the curb and shouting at the darkening sky. Turner felt sorry for the man, but didn't understand his problem. What should the brass have done, sent them in armed, wearing street clothes? The last he'd heard, eight cops were dead. Thirty-some others had been taken to area emergency rooms. At last report, there had been seventy dead civilians. Nobody was even venturing a guess at how high the body count would get once they were able to get into the West and South Side ghettoes.

"Who's here from Unit Twelve! Anyone here from Twelve?" Ellis believed he was with Unit Eight, but at the moment he wasn't certain. He didn't even know where his unit leader was. He wasn't sure what the guy's name was, didn't know if he'd recognize the man if he walked up and shook Turner's hand. He could not remember the last time he'd felt this weary, this bone tired.

Not just physically tired, either, although he was exhausted, every single one of his muscles ached. Turner was trying desperately not to think, doing his best to deny not only what he'd seen that day but also what he'd done. He told himself that he hadn't fired a single shot, he hadn't had to kill anybody. Thank God for that. Though he'd come close, more than once, as they'd cleaned up the few hard-core gangbanging stragglers. He had leveled his weapon and been ready to pull the trigger. Every time, the party he'd been about to shoot had chosen to surrender. Which was a good thing, as far as Turner was concerned. He would be having enough nightmares without having to relive shotgun deaths over and over in his dreams.

There was one dead guy, he had more hateful tattoos scrawled on his skinny ass than Ellis would have thought possible. Lying shirtless in the street, FUCK NIGGERS tattooed on either shoulder, writ large. Ellis had seen a black officer spit upon the corpse; saw another kick at it. Turner had thought about defiling it himself, but he'd controlled the urge. He would not imitate the oppressor.

Crocodile Berkley, too, he was dead. Dead a dozen times over, in fact, shot in the chest and stomach repeatedly by someone who had no doubt seen his face on TV or in the papers, and taken it upon himself to ensure that the Crocodile was not only dead, but would never be coming back. For some reason that he couldn't understand, Ellis felt saddened at the thought of Berkley's death.

Turner closed his eyes, but the images behind his lids were too vivid, too brutal. He opened them again, angrily jabbed his cigarette out on the sidewalk beside him. He could hear people crying, and trying hard not to, muffled sobs like those of a child who was determined not to let his father know that the whipping was getting to him. He thought about Soldier Field, filled with prisoners. Thought about the hospitals, too, filled with gunshot, knife, and beating victims. He wondered about the men he'd beaten, wondered why there had been so many *men*. Didn't women riot? Was there some genetic principle at work that prevented females from experiencing joy in the acts of looting and killing?

The man sitting next to Turner said, "This wasn't any spontaneous action. This fucking thing was *planned*." He said it as if he had just figured out what Ellis had known from the moment he'd gotten the callout, as if he were sharing this huge conspiracy he'd uncovered with Turner. Turner nodded his head at the man. The officer tapped Turner's arm, as if the two of them were in on a secret. "Gonna cost the city *millions*. Maybe even billions."

"You got a cigarette?"

"I don't—"

"There an Ellis Turner here?" Turner was on his feet before the sergeant finished the sentence.

"Yeah!"

The sergeant came over to him quickly, walking around the shell-shocked men and women who loitered on the sidewalk, too tired to step out of a superior officer's way. The sergeant was sweating through his uniform, the night hot and sticky, his job distasteful. He took Turner's arm and led him toward the building's entrance.

"You all right, man?" the sergeant asked, looking at him quizzically as the two of them strode quickly through a crowd of soaking wet, tired officers who had the exact same looks on their faces as Ellis.

"I'm fine. What's wrong." Turner was in no mood for pleasantries, for this chubby white man's pretense of concern. The sergeant hadn't let go of him, was leading Ellis toward the broad set of stairs that led into the Cultural Center. Turner pulled his arm away. The sergeant stopped, opened his mouth as if to say something, then shut it, and shifted his gaze away from Turner.

When he looked back, he said, "Up the stairs, there's a bank of phones in the hallway. You got an emergency call, on three. White chick behind the desk."

Inside the hallway, at table three, Claudette's barely recognizable voice shouted into Turner's ear.

"You didn't answer your beeper! I kept calling your beeper!"

His beeper? He'd left it at home, had forgotten about it during the heat of their argument, in his haste to perform his duty. "Claudette, honey, what's the matter!" Turner couldn't conceal his panic. The female uniformed dispatcher was pretending not to listen. Ellis turned his back on her, as if doing so would offer him privacy.

He knew terror when he heard it; shock, too, for that matter. Turner was hearing both now, and he fought himself for control, wanting to scream but keeping his voice level and calm as he said, "Claudette, tell me what's wrong."

"They shot Quentin, they shot him in the back!"

"Where are you right this minute."

"I'm at the University of Chicago Hospital. Quentin's in surgery. I've been trying to beep you for *hours* . . . "

"You wait right there," Turner said, then spun, slammed the phone down, and ran out of the building, looking for the first vehicle that had the keys in the ignition.

WINTER
VENGEANCE

CHAPTER

43

It was the coldest day of what would be the city's coldest winter, one of those vicious, freak seasons that used to only come along once every decade or so, but which now seemed to descend upon Chicago one out of every three or four years. As usual, there hadn't been much of an autumn; the hottest summer on record had simply ended sometime in mid-September; there had been a few weeks of mild but increasingly cooler weather, then the temperature had plummeted, and along with it, the city's spirit.

It was even colder in a small town in Minnesota, where a newly unemployed construction laborer by the name of Marshall Del Greco sipped cheap bourbon on a Sunday afternoon while he patiently listened to a Chicago lawyer complain about the weather. The lawyer told him that Del Greco wasn't in a position to be generous; that he was now out of a job because he'd taken too many days off from work. Del Greco replied that it was too hard to work when it was so cold outside. He told the lawyer that he knew damn well that Del Greco had business in Chicago that could only be transacted during the work week. He told him that other guys took days off when they had hangovers, it wasn't just him. The lawyer sighed, and got back to the point of his call.

He did not want Del Greco to pretend that he didn't need money; in fact, he wanted Del Greco to sue his ex-wife, Rachel, for a financial settlement. Now that he was out of work, he might be able to pull it off. Del Greco listened, draining his drink, looking out the window at the bleak, white landscape, his heart heavy, his face grim. Squinting, he could see his reflection in the glass. It wasn't a mirror image; he couldn't see the gray in the stubble of his beard. A hearty bird was picking at something, outside in the snow. Del Greco watched it, wondering how it survived, until it flew away. The lawyer told Del Greco that if the case was reopened, Rachel might even be forced to pay him alimony. He told Del Greco that if *he* had handled the divorce for him in the first place, Del Greco would have walked away with a comfortable settlement, instead of with nothing. He explained to Del Greco that more and more judges were giving settlements to the husbands, didn't he want what he could get? After all, Del Greco was now unemployed, and Rachel was a doctor. The lawyer told him that he might even have a lawsuit against Paul Berstein; he'd gotten Del Greco a job, but had conveniently gotten him fired within two months of Del Greco's agreeing to all the stipulations in the divorce that Rachel's lawyer had wanted. Del Greco leaned forward and poured himself another drink. He lifted it, held it to the light. He'd had to walk two miles to the liquor store; he wanted to make this bottle last. He put the glass down, lighted a cigarette, and waited for the lawyer to finally run out of breath. Then he told the lawyer that he did *not* want to sue Rachel—told him that he did not want any lawsuits filed at all, that he did not want any money from Rachel, and that he did not want any more handouts from his ex-in-laws. He told him that he was leaving Minnesota for good in just a couple of hours; his rent was due, and he was out of work, and the lawyer knew as well as he did that Del Greco had pressing business elsewhere. He was grateful to the lawyer for all he'd done for him, and for what he would do in the future, but he did not want to even hear the Berstein name again. That was all behind him. The lawyer asked him if he was drinking; Del Greco told him he'd had a few. The lawyer said he might have a job lined up for him, was he interested? Del Greco told him that he didn't want to think about that right now. He finally got off the line, leaned forward, stared at the wall for a minute, then grabbed the phone and dialed his brother's number. He hung up on Angelo's answering machine. His bags were packed, and were stacked close to the door. He was surprised at how little clothing he had; then again, he'd never been one to carry a lot of baggage.

Ten days later, in Chicago, the city at last reported that the official heat death toll for the summer had been confirmed and entered into the record books at 892—not counting the 112 people who had died during the three days of rioting.

It was a sad ending to a sad chapter in the proud city's history, and there were more than a few citizens who were afraid that the worst was yet to come.

Although winter still had not even officially begun, the bitter cold was already being blamed for the deaths of close to three hundred people. Frozen bodies of the homeless were turning up every day, in the parks and in the vestibules of buildings; on the wide, downtown sidewalks; in alleys and under railroad viaducts; in Dumpsters and under porches, wherever they had crawled seeking warmth, attempting to find shelter from a biting wind that never seemed to let up in its attack, its icy teeth constantly gnawing, chewing, until it had eaten its way through clothing, beyond flesh, and on into the vital internal organs, continuing its malignant feasting until it consumed the last, warm spark of mortality from bodies that no longer had the ability to fight. The deaths of the disenchanted had become such a common occurrence that the local TV stations and the newspapers no longer bothered to inform the public about them.

For the past two weeks, the news had focused on the deaths of people who had places to live, but who were nevertheless far from immune from the cold weather's deadly impact.

Most of these dead had been very young or very old, and almost all of them had been poor; their electricity or gas services had been cut off months before, prior to the date when it became illegal for the utility companies to interrupt such essential—though expensive—services. The local TV news stations ran nightly footage of little children, some of them in body bags, others wearing nothing but diapers under the blankets of their rescuers, being carried out of homes that—the police reported—had neither heat nor a competent parent. Arrests had been made, the Department of Children and Families Services had taken over custody of the surviving children, and they were farmed out to foster families, turned over to total strangers who, as their compensation for taking the children in, received a token check each month from the state of Illinois, checks that were lower than the welfare payments the mothers of such children had been collecting before they lost custody, therefore guaranteeing that the cycle of poverty did not get broken.

Many of the dead had succumbed to hypothermia; others hadn't been so fortunate—fire had burned the life out of many of them; the worst form of death imaginable. Overloaded gas pipes had exploded as the poor who still had access to that service used their kitchen ovens as emergency heating devices. Cheap electric space heaters had been placed too close to curtains or clothing or bedding, and just a spark was all that was needed to consume an apartment, a home, the lives of everybody in an entire subsidized housing building. People were shooting each other over parking spaces that had been staked out, the curbs lined with chairs and tables and stolen, orange city cones.

The middle class was not entirely immune, either. Carbon monoxide poisoning had taken its toll on a couple of dozen of them; odorless and colorless, the gas snuck silently and inexorably through the homes of people who hadn't bothered to have their furnaces cleaned, or who hadn't thought they should spend the money to have them cleaned this year. In response, the city fathers had unanimously passed an ordinance making carbon monoxide detectors mandatory for every home in Chicago; a law had been put on the books that made it legal for teams of inspectors to enter private homes, in order to ensure that the occupants had complied with the law, and had in fact installed detectors that were up to the specs of the city's new code. Nobody questioned the supposedly altruistic motives of the politicians, and nobody ever found out that the largest contract to manufacture such detectors had gone to a company that did a lot of business with one of the city's most clout-heavy aldermen. There wasn't even much of an outcry about the inspectors' ability to enter the premises of private citizens without a duly sworn warrant. The Fourth Amendment didn't carry much weight when lives and health and media scrutiny and votes hung in the balance. The conventional reasoning among the public was, What did it matter . . . unless you had something to hide?

On every slow news night since the cold snap had begun—at five, six, and ten—some politician would appear on one of the three local TV news stations, holding more than press conferences; they were holding their opponents responsible for the weather, blaming the other guy for all these horrible deaths. In order to keep things interesting—as well as in the interest of fairness—those who had been challenged were allowed air time in rebuttal, simulating concern, and shouting that those who had no heat should call the hotline number which would put them in touch with city services, operating under the assumption that those who couldn't afford heat *could* afford electricity to run their televisions, and could afford an operating telephone, which they could use to call for help. A lead editorial had been run in the conservative newspaper, wondering why Alderman Billy Charge had been silent on the issue, speculating as to whether the good alderman had learned his lesson after last summer's riots, which his reckless actions had helped to cause. The TV stations had picked up on the speculation. There was no response from Charge's office; reporters' phone calls were not returned. Charge had spent the months since the riot in quiet reflection of his life and career, feeling partially responsible for the riot that had rocked the city. He had pulled in every political favor he had left, and had been able to duck a few housing codes, and he had opened three homeless shelters in his ward, and a soup kitchen. The complaints of his middle-class constituents, who did not want such places in their backyard, were ignored. Charge did more arm-twisting, and got the funds necessary to implement an after-school basketball program at a local park district gym. Since most of the young children served were black, many of the people who lived around the park complained, but Charge paid them no attention. The polls showed that, despite all his good works—and perhaps because of them—Charge could not win an aldermanic reelection, which was all right with him; he had no intention of running for public office again, though the irony of the situation was not lost on him; when he had been his most bombastic, doing the least for his constituents and the most for himself, his approval ratings had been higher than the mayor's. But Charge did not care about that now, as he did not care about his political career; as he did not care about the media.

There were plenty of elected officials, however, who were not so circumspect. Some of these other, more ambitious politicians arranged photo opportunities at the homeless shelters, where they pointed at the empty, three-inch mattresses that had been set up on the floor, and wondered aloud as to why there were empty "beds" in such places: Didn't these people want to help themselves? Would anyone in their right mind actually *prefer* to sleep on the street? Questions such as these could be answered in the most simplistic of terms by those who had never been subjected to the rigors of abject poverty, people who had never been forced to live—and survive—on the streets.

For the poorest of the poor, the weak, and the infirm, the street was a far safer place to be than any homeless shelter, and it did not take the newly homeless long to figure this out.

Predators roamed most of the shelters, stealing possessions, committing physical and sexual assaults, and threatening even more harsh retaliation if one should decide to affirm one's rights and complain to the people in charge. On the street, as in prison, a person was easy to find, there weren't many places to hide. Even the safest shelters stole things from human beings that should never be taken away: dignity and independence. They took personal belongings away from their clients, made them wear what they wanted them to wear, sing the songs they were told to sing, sleep when they were told to sleep, and pray before they could eat. They threw them out at six in the morning, and from there they were on their own, supposedly to walk from warming station to warming station, until the shelter doors opened again at eight. The doors were locked at ten.

Most eschewed the warming stations. Libraries and other public buildings were safer and far more accessible, and were a lot easier to get to, and the government could have a lawsuit on its hands if its agents tried to throw anyone out. It was simpler to beg for money to buy food, with the hope that there would be enough left over to rent a room in an Uptown flophouse for the night, where you would be assigned to a cubicle that was seven feet long by five feet wide, with the three-by-six-foot bedframe taking up over half of the space. The walls would be seven feet high. Above that point, chicken wire would be strung across the length and breadth of the room. The building's wooden ceilings would be several feet above the chicken wire, the wire having been put there for ventilation, as well as for security. There would be more chicken wire at floor-level, too, four inches of it all around—a see-through baseboard. Some of the walls would be made of corrugated metal that had been nailed to wooden two-by-fours. There would be hundreds of such cubicles in any given flophouse, and every one of them had tenants who had been there for years, unseen and unspoken for, living desperate lives, looking no further than day to day, sometimes tavern to tavern.

Such a place was more of a cage than it was a room, but it kept you out of the cold, it kept you alive for one more night. Gerald Podgourney had healed in just such a place, had stayed there until he felt strong enough to go out and put into practice a scheme he'd thought up while lying on his back in the flophouse, staring up at a cockroach that was making its way across the ceiling.

Gerald had begun his return to a life of hustling by becoming what the police soon began referring to as homeless pimps. After Gerald had organized the first bunch, such pimps had begun showing up with the frequency that carjackers had in the years just recently past, and the Gangster Apostles had taken over the scam, so Gerald had been forced to move on to another occupation. The pimps had stables of homeless people working for them, rather than hookers. They offered protection, safety, food, and the barest of warm lodgings at night for those who lived in terror or disdain of the legitimate homeless shelters; cigarettes, booze, and dope were provided for those who had other needs and desires. Once the Gangsters got involved, they began to rent entire floors of cheap loft space and put their disabled charges in them to sleep, in shifts, with an armed guard watching over them, and low-ranking recruits—usually the preteen-agers who had yet to earn respect—were assigned to feed, clothe, bathe, and delouse those who needed such assistance. Children and women were most at risk of such exploitation, but the occasional pitiful—but hard-hustling—male was acceptable. The pimps would drive the homeless around in their specially equipped vans, would drop them off at busy corners, making them work from early in the morning until very late at night. They worked hard themselves, as well, trying to watch their charges as much as they could, they would bring them sandwiches and cups of coffee or hot chocolate, would then kneel down beside them, giving the impression to passersby that their hearts were filled with compassion and caring, while they gathered all the bills out of paper cups, cans, or whatever else their dependents had put into service as collection buckets. And, like the pimps the police compared them to, they would beat or abandon those whom they caught withholding money from them, or those who could not generate enough income to be considered cost-effective.

The people with money, as was always the case, had it the best this winter. Layered in Gore-Tex and Lycra underclothing, with L.L. Bean outerwear, or discounted furs on their backs, their greatest fears were the windchill factor, animal rights activists, and hat-hair. The men wore newly fashionable ear-flap hats with fur linings, and the women, for some reason, took to wearing court jester hats.

The east-west downtown streets were the most treacherous for such people, where the bitter wind whipped around the buildings, tore hats from heads and umbrellas from hands, tore through layers of clothing with an arrogant ease, as if Mother Nature were putting the populace on notice, letting them know how unimportant they were.

Not that all of them paid attention.

There were fools about on this bitter, mid-December day. Young men in heavy, waist-long ski jackets or parkas—with gym shorts and basketball shoes—hurrying from place to place, Christmas shopping or heading to the gym, or merely out walking the dog; these hardy, urban pioneers passed their lesser brethren with hardly a glance. But that was downtown, that was in the white neighborhoods. Where pretense ruled, credit was as good as money, and you could ignore the poor who approached you, hands outstretched, eyes beseeching.

Another man who wasn't paying any attention to the poor was a prosperous lawyer named Arthur L. Horwitz, who hurried up the steps of the criminal courts building this afternoon, fighting his way through the swarms of media personnel who'd been sent to cover the trial. The lunch break was over, and he was about to give his closing statement to a jury of his client's peers. Horwitz had not spoken to the press since the trial had begun, even though the jury was not sequestered, and he assumed they were watching the news every night, and reading the papers every morning. Most of his defense played around the destructive force of the media; he did not want them going into the jury room believing him to be a hypocrite.

Horwitz stripped off his leather gloves and then his coat as he walked briskly down the hall, then stopped in front of the locked door of a room that was just down the hallway from the courtroom. He patted down his hair, shook his head in disgust at the reporters who surrounded him, and waited for the bailiff to tell them to move away before he knocked on the door and announced his presence to the man who was hiding inside. Once he was inside the room, with the door closed and locked behind him, Horwitz consulted with his client for just a minute, patted his arm and told him not to worry; he knew what he was doing, he'd done this a hundred times. Hadn't Horwitz gotten him this room to shield him from the media? There were a lot of other tricks up his sleeve, the client had to have faith in him.

Horwitz thought that his client would be filled with gratitude because a man such as himself was handling the client's case himself, rather than just assigning it to one of the junior attorneys in his firm.

Horwitz thought wrong.

The client resented Horwitz, actually hated him, and he seethed at the lawyer's arrogance as he vowed to bring the man down to his knees. But at the moment, the client had no choice in the matter, he could not afford to pay a lawyer of Horwitz's stature, so he had to sit there and quietly eat whatever Horwitz served up.

In the courtroom, the client stood up twice in rapid succession—first when the jury was brought into the courtroom, then right after them, the judge—then he took his seat at the defendant's table, dressed in a suit that no longer fit him very well, the ravages of the last several months apparent on the client's face and body. He no longer seemed big and strong. No longer appeared to be powerful and tough. He seemed, rather, afraid. The client winced when the judge smacked his gavel on the bench, and declared that his courtroom was now entering its post-lunch, afternoon session.

CHAPTER

44

"**H**ow's it feel?" Ellis Turner nearly whispered it, man to man, into his son's ear, as Quentin settled back in the wheelchair. Ellis was leaning down, holding onto the handles, and now he waited, only moderately surprised, as Quentin chuckled through his pain. Ellis had an idea as to where the kid had picked up his newfound sense of humor—right here in this hospital. Since July, Ellis had been learning, people with spinal cord injuries didn't look at things the same way the rest of the world did; their vision seemed somewhat skewed. They often laughed at things that weren't funny, and invented dark jokes, displaying the sort of gallows humor that would cause a veteran copper to either blush or turn green with envy.

They were in the swimming area of the SPIU—spinal cord injury unit— and Quentin had just finished the day's therapy. Ellis had fought a lump in his throat as he'd watched Quentin slicing through the water. The pain was distinctly written on Quentin's face—along with courage and determination. Quentin had concentrated, had squeezed out every move, going for maximum effect, wanting to heal as quickly as possible.

Quentin was breathing hard now, leaning back in his chair, dressed in tight swimming trunks, his strong young body exposed in the cavernous, long, temperature-controlled room that had a fake glass ceiling painted black, stars surrounding a large full moon. Around them, other victims, all male, mostly young and black, were swimming in the Olympic-sized pool, while still others were locked in the canvas-seated wheelchairs that were stamped as property of the swimming pool, watching the luckier of their brethren work with their therapists in the water. The patients' regular wheelchairs were kept away from the pool area, so they wouldn't have to be wiped free of water every time one of the patients came into or left the room.

Every one of the patients in the room was male; the genders were strictly separated in this building. It was a good idea to keep people who were suffering, whose emotions were still raw, away from members of the opposite sex; it kept the false love quotient down, kept the broken heart rate down too, as well as the suicide attempts—although there were women in the room, relatives or other loved ones, visitors of the patients.

The sound of mechanical breathing was so common in this unit that everyone took the portable respirators for granted, would have wondered what was wrong if they hadn't heard the electrical wheezing above the sounds of laughter, cursing, and playing. Under other circumstances, Turner would have enjoyed watching them swim. Every male in the pool would have learned to swim almost as soon as he'd learned to walk; the first Mayor Daley had been big on putting pools in the ghetto parks, and the parents from those ghettoes had been big on dropping the kids off there to swim, leaving them there from the time the pool opened in the morning until it closed at night.

"What's so funny?" Ellis said.

"I can't answer that." There was a pained humor in Quentin's tone, as if he were trying hard not to laugh. He turned his head to look at Ellis, showing his father an impish grin.

"Of course you can, son." Ellis spoke normally now. The sound of his voice echoed off the water; off the high ceiling of the room. "I asked you how it feels, you can tell me. I'm your father. You can tell me anything."

"First thing I thought was, it hurt like a *mother*fucker."

"*Quent*in . . . !"

Ellis disregarded the smiles, snickers, and outright laughter of the other patients, the disapproving looks of the older white people in the room. The quadraplegics bonded tightly with their own, as did the paraplegics; put two of them together, you had an instant family. But the biological families of these people were going through their own emotional upheavals. Experiencing anger, resentment, bitterness, hatred toward the world due to the unfairness of it all. Ellis certainly was. Quentin had told him that the cripples got it out of their systems right away: the doctors, nurses, orderlies—and their fellow patients—would not allow anyone on the unit to sink into self-pity, would yell, joke, or shout insults at you until you worked your way out of your depression.

But the families were something else; the families could be worse than any group of old gossips sitting on a porch stoop.

Quentin had been lucky; there had been some spinal damage, just a nick, but he would eventually heal. He had to do an hour's worth of stretching exercises every morning at home, and an hour again every night, and he had to come back to the hospital for therapy three times a week, but he was walking again, tentatively, under closely monitored conditions. Pretty soon, they'd told him, he would be able to lose the wheelchair altogether. Quentin would go from the chair to a walker, from the walker to a cane. Eventually he would come out of it with—the doctors hoped—just a slight, lifelong limp. Quentin would never play basketball again, would never slide into home plate, and he'd always have some pain, but other than that, he'd get by, he'd be almost normal.

There were plenty of mothers, fathers, wives, and friends of some other unit patients who held that against him, as if his luck—or the shooter's bad aim—was somehow Quentin's fault; they held petty little grudges, shot him mean looks, and talked about him behind his back. Quentin didn't much care, it was Ellis who got mad. The doctors had told him that if the bullet had entered the boy's back just a fraction of an inch to the left, it would have spelled doom for Quentin, would have sentenced him to the wheelchair for life, or might even have killed him. The bullet was still lodged in his son, was resting close to Quentin's spine.

Ellis thought about the changes that had been thrust into their lives over the course of the past five months, as he waited while the orderlies helped Quentin take a shower, helped him come down from the intensity of his workout. After carefully drying the water off him, after blow-drying his hair, after dressing him in his heavy winter clothes, they would set Quentin into his regular, collapsible wheelchair.

Since Quentin had been shot, Ellis had become much more of an angry man. He was aware of this, although he mistakenly believed that he kept most of his anger bottled up inside, didn't let anyone see his anger. He would glare right back at the men and women who were jealous of Quentin's progress, would snub them when they said hello, attempting a pretense at civilized friendship. Ellis did not have much patience for hypocrites. Not these days. Not after what had happened to his son.

His philosophy now was, fuck 'em. Let them talk. They could talk at Quentin's back pretty soon, when he walked out of their small-time lives forever.

Ellis heard the shower turn off. He shifted his winter coat to his other arm—dying for a cigarette—and leaned against the wall, thinking of his marriage.

Claudette had taken it further than Ellis; she'd turned from a woman who kept her rage bottled up, and only discussed it at an intellectual level, into an Afrocentric radical. Claudette had quit her job at the university, had taken a teaching position for far less money at Malcolm X College, a city school. Claudette did not go out of her way to alienate her few Caucasian students, but she did not go out of her way to win them over, either. Though she graded them by stricter guidelines, without the curve she allowed the blacks. When Ellis was working, one of Claudette's students with free afternoon periods would bring Quentin to his therapy. Quentin expressed a fondness for some of them, others he thought to be assholes. He would sometimes tell his father about them, would make fun of them, aping their speech and gestures when the two of them were alone. Quentin did not disrespect the students in front of his mother, ever.

In the aftermath of the riot and the shooting of her brother, Anne had begun having nightmares; she was seeing a psychotherapist every Wednesday, right after school. Claudette had arranged her schedule to ensure that Wednesday afternoons were always left open, enabling her to drive Anne back and forth from her sessions. Claudette waited while Anne talked with the doctor, then she brought her home when the session ended. There would be no walking home for Anne; no bike riding in the neighborhood this summer, either, or unsupervised playing. Claudette would lay her cool, superior look on the shrink when the woman would try and reason with Claudette, wondering aloud if Claudette might be behaving in an overprotective manner. The woman did not know that she was married to a homicide detective, who had told her that the new, hot, profitable crime among the drug dealers was the kidnapping of other drug dealers and their children. They would hold the hostage for ransom; sometimes they would get it, other times they wouldn't. Theirs was a world in which the FBI was the enemy—the thought would never enter the head of a victim's family to turn to the government for help.

Sometimes, though, they made mistakes, snatched up the wrong kid, grabbed the wrong person off the street. That would not happen to Anne. Not as long as Claudette drew breath.

Ellis wondered if Claudette had forgiven him for what she had thought to be his inexcusable absence on the day that their son had been shot. Working for the white man, she'd said to him, when your flesh and blood had needed you. It was the only time she had made the accusation, and it had been made in the heat of anger, in a hospital corridor, while their son had been under the knife. But the words, a full five months later, still had a harsh, shameful sting, and Ellis wondered if it would burn forever, or would eventually fade out, to be brought back into focus only during certain distinct instances, like the nagging memory of a humiliation suffered in early childhood.

Oddly enough, Quentin was the one who seemed to be handling what had happened better than anyone else in the family. At least he wasn't acting out; he didn't seem to be holding anything in, either. He had explained it to Ellis once—again, when the two of them had been alone—right after Quentin had come home from three months of inpatient treatment. He had told his father that he remembered the shooting, remembered the pain of the bullet, remembered the abject terror he had felt, and then everything had gone black. His return to consciousness had been slow, had occurred over a period of several long, torturous hours. Quentin had told his father that he had felt himself swimming up out of the blackness, searching for sunlight. He had had the impression that he was unable to breathe, had gasped for air as he'd struggled toward the light. Quentin's eyes had nearly closed as he'd described the scene for Ellis, his initial terror over not even knowing who he was settling into a state of near panic as his identity, along with his memories, came slowly back to him. Quentin had been unable to open his eyes, had been barely able to think, wasn't even sure if he was alive or dead, or how badly he'd been damaged.

Quentin told Ellis that he'd made a pact with God: Let me be alive, give me another chance, and I swear I'll never complain about my life, no matter how bad it is. No matter what happened.

Quentin had thought he'd been blind. When he'd finally acquired enough strength to open his eyes, and had then discovered that his head was screwed into a steel halo, and that there was doubt as to the extent of his spinal injury, Quentin had had second thoughts, had considered renegotiation. But a deal was a deal, and Quentin had kept his part of the bargain.

Ellis had never heard him complain, not even once. Although he did not know what was going on inside the boy's mind. He wished with all his heart that he could trade places with his son. Would have gladly made a deal with God in order to do so, if his faith in God had still been alive. As it was, these days, Ellis Turner believed only in himself.

And in Quentin, who was now pushing himself out of the locker room, fully dried and fully dressed, his hands encased in heavy gloves that had the fingers cut off at the knuckle. Quentin was wearing a shearling coat; he had a thick, wool cap on his head. Pneumonia was Quentin's worst enemy; it killed nearly as many spinal injury patients as the initial trauma did itself, pneumonia and shock were the enemies. And falling down. And car wrecks. God only knew what the bullet would do if Quentin's spine was to receive a harsh, sudden jolt.

"You ready?" Quentin asked, never knowing how ready his father was to get out of this place.

"Where to now?"

"What time you got to be in court?"

"It's not exactly court."

"Whatever."

Ellis walked slightly behind Quentin as the boy pushed himself up the long, gently sloping basement ramp. Ellis put on his coat, patted his pockets, pulled out his hat and gloves. "The Podgourney thing should be up around four. I want to be there."

"That leaves us a couple of hours together, am I right?" Quentin spoke over his shoulder as he picked up speed, heading toward the elevator, aware that his father would go to great lengths to appease any of Quentin's moods. There was a white man walking rapidly toward them from the other side of the basement. He had a confused, angry look on his face. He had obviously gotten turned around in the hospital's labyrinth of corridors. Ellis, having a nicotine fit, hoped that Quentin wouldn't offer the man assistance.

"You feel like hitting Water Tower Place?" Quentin asked. "I want to get Annie her Christmas present."

Ellis stepped into the wide, long patient elevator and stood beside his son, hit the button that would bring them up out of the basement and into the hospital's lobby. Quentin's arms were getting stronger, more powerful. He pushed himself everywhere, did hundreds of sit-ups and push-ups alone in his room at night, would step out of his wheelchair and walk carefully around the room, after his home tutoring sessions, after all his homework was done, after he was through playing around on his computer, which had become his link to the outside world. Ellis could hear him in there at night, Quentin in his bedroom, groaning.

"You want to hold that elevator?"

Slow ass goddamn doors. Ellis wasn't planning on holding anything. It had been a white man's voice, and now the befuddled-looking white man Ellis had noticed earlier stuck his hand between the doors as they began to close. When they reopened, the man stepped into the elevator with them. The white man was about Ellis's age, but was short and fat and mostly bald. He had an air of impatience, of arrogance. He reminded Ellis of the sort of man who would delight in being a suburban Little League coach. The little man made a point of not looking down at Quentin, or over at Ellis. Even though Ellis had made no effort to stop the doors from closing, he still felt a bite of resentment over the fact that the white man hadn't thanked him. The white man hit the button for the third floor, and the doors slid shut.

"You talk to your mother about that?" Ellis said. He looked down at Quentin, who seemed oblivious of the white man's ignorance. "Christmas, I mean."

"What about it?"

"I don't think she's planning on having Christmas this year. I think we're doing Kwanzaa." Ellis thought he heard the white man grunt. Ellis looked over at him quickly, saw the smirk on his face before the man was able to cover it up with his hand. Through great emotional effort, Ellis was able to keep himself from grabbing the man by his throat.

"You got something to say?" The white man did not respond. Ellis felt his son tugging at his coat, trying to get him to stop. Ellis tapped the man on the shoulder, felt the man shrink at his touch. "Hey, Shorty," Ellis said, "I'm talking to you. You got something to say?" This time, Ellis spoke the words more forcefully.

The man wasn't smirking now, was staring up at the digital numbers above the elevator door, as if appealing to a higher power to make the elevator ascend more quickly. The elevator came to a stop, and the doors slowly opened. Quentin pushed himself out into the lobby, stopped the chair on a dime, and quickly spun it around so he could face his father.

"Dad!"

Quentin's voice seemed to be coming at Ellis through a long, metal tunnel. Ellis was stepping out of the elevator backward, his hands open wide, held down low, away from his body. He said it one more time, before the elevator doors could close. "You got something to say?" then quickly added, "I didn't think so," as the doors closed, blocking off the sight of the frightened little white man's face.

"Why you got to act like that?"

Ellis turned to Quentin, angrily. "That didn't bother you?"

"*What* didn't bother me?"

"You didn't hear him grunt? You didn't see him smirk?"

"I couldn't see him. And all I heard was a cough."

Ellis was aware that people in the lobby were observing him, he was even more acutely aware of his son's disapproval. Hospital personnel that had grown quite friendly with Quentin were now stopped in their tracks, watching them, misreading the situation, and were ready to step in and help out if the need arose. They were used to breaking up physical confrontations in this ward; broken male bodies feeling the need to prove their manhood. Conversely, there was never any violence over in the women's wing.

Ellis shook himself, telling himself that the man really had only coughed, that he hadn't been making fun of them.

Feeling for his cigarettes, Ellis Turner said, "Wait here, I'll go get the car."

It was Quentin who kept them all together, who kept them strong. Ellis reflected on this as he followed Quentin, as the boy politely made his way through the Christmas shopping crowd in the Water Tower Place mall, and he wondered what would have happened to the family if Quentin had adopted a different, more hostile, attitude. He loved Claudette with all his heart, but there were times when she seemed to be an entirely different woman.

Thinking of his wife's pain caused Ellis to suffer as well.

Claudette made nightly phone calls to other women, her network, she called it. As soon as she put the phone down, it rang. Black women reaching out to each other; women, desperately seeking . . . what? Peace? Harmony? Some sort of basic understanding that they believed to be in- · comprehensible to males of their race? Ellis used to be able to fill all of Claudette's emotional needs. Until Quentin had been shot.

Sometimes in the middle of the night Claudette would grab Ellis and would tear him up, but she was reluctant when Ellis made the first move, though she did not rebuff him often.

Claudette attended black feminist consciousness-raising meetings, where no men were allowed.

Since the shooting, the family dynamics had changed, all their relation-ships had shifted. Ellis sometimes felt as if he were adrift, floating in a universe not of his making, rather than safe and comfortable in the world he had created for himself. That safe, comfortable world had been hit by a meteor last July. Ellis often asked himself if his world would ever recover.

Ellis and Quentin had to use the great glass elevator to go up to different floors, and Quentin seemed to want to make an appearance at every store in the place. The elevator was usually full, without much room for a wheelchair. People had to squeeze in next to each other, shoulder to shoulder. Little children had to give up their view of the glass elevator's dramatic rise. Once free of the elevator, Ellis followed Quentin through the mall itself, contrite, sorry that he'd made a scene back at the hospital, watching as his son worked his careful way past people who acted all put out because they had to step out of the way of a cripple. Some eyes were averted when Ellis glared into them; others glared right back. Ellis breathed in slow and easy; he was here to Christmas shop, he wasn't here to fight. He was embarrassed by the way he'd acted with the white man in the elevator. Quentin didn't pay these people any attention, so why should he?

Quentin was young, he was learning to adjust. Ellis was nearly three times Quentin's age. Things were different for him, he couldn't adapt to change quite as easily as his son. The people around them—mostly white—seemed to have adjusted all right. They seemed mostly carefree and happy, if a bit too self-satisfied for Ellis's tastes. None of them seemed sad, upset about the aftermath of last summer's riots. None of them would have lost anything more than a day or two at the job. Though they would have been angered by the National Guard—enforced curfew. How could one make dinner reservations when one got arrested for being out after dark?

Ellis caught himself, fought off his resentment. He put a benign look on his face as he followed Quentin through the crowd.

The fact of the matter was, Ellis wanted his other life back. A healthy son, a wife who loved him, who played with him, joking back and forth as they took their lives a day at a time. He wanted a daughter who didn't spend her nights thrashing around in the throes of nightmares.

He wanted Del Greco back, too. Quentin could probably tell him things about Del Greco. He would no doubt tell his father not to be so god-damn touchy.

Ellis glanced at his watch. He had to make the hearing. He would get through it, and hopefully catch himself a little of what Anne's shrink would call *closure*. One way or another, things were supposed to be resolved by four o'clock this afternoon. Ellis wondered if the anger he'd been feeling all day long was due to the hearing, was because of Gerald . . .

Ellis listened to the Latin American music being piped through the mall and once again forced himself to calm down. He was with Quentin, shopping. His son was alive. There were plenty of people who had things a lot rougher than they did. They had just left a basement swimming pool filled with them.

Quentin rolled into a store called Little Miss Piggy. The place was crowded, filled with merry shoppers. Ellis noticed, was acutely aware, that all of the other shoppers in the store were white. Some of them looked down at Quentin as he excused himself, then quickly looked away. Others stared at him in pity. Still others seemed angry. Those who were too self-important to move aside got a gentle bump from large, thin, rub-ber wheels, along with another, louder "Excuse me," as if Quentin had done it accidentally. Ellis resented them all. For the hundredth time that day, he told himself to calm down. He wondered what was wrong with him today, why he was feeling so hateful and angry.

Quentin was holding up a T-shirt, had scrunched up his face into an eye-closed grin and was rapidly waving at Ellis, telling him to come take a look. Ellis stood next to him, looking at his son instead of the shirt. Ellis couldn't help himself; he smiled. There the kid was, in his wheelchair, in his pain, making cute faces, trying to act normal.

"See this? Don't this look like Sparkles?" Ellis wouldn't think of cor-recting his son's language in a room filled with strangers, so he just looked down at the T-shirt. It had a four-color picture of a long-eared cocker spaniel on the front, and it did sort of look like Sparkles. Their Spaniel had died two summers ago, at the age of thirteen. Ellis had bought it for Claudette when they'd been dating. Anne had always acted as if the dog had been her twin. "You think it'd bother her?"

"Is he always so positive?" A middle-aged woman in a long fur coat had been listening in on their conversation. She was now speaking of Quentin as if he couldn't hear what she was saying. Ellis looked at her, at her patronizing smile, her lined face, her lacquered hair. Her up-raised eyebrows.

Her white face.

An ignorant, pampered woman, grown used to being promptly answered.

"You always so motherfucking nosy?"

Quentin laughed, shaking his head. "Excuse him, lady." He couldn't seem to stop laughing. When he could speak, he said, "Christmas is hard on some people . . ." and was off again, bursting out in a gale of laughter as the woman stiffened, threw her head back, and curtly walked away. Quentin took a moment to get himself under control, then, without look-ing back at the woman, said to his father, "Well?"

Ellis watched the woman's rapidly retreating back, then turned to face his son. He said, "I think Anne would love it."

"I didn't bring my wallet."

Ellis smiled. "I brought my checkbook."

He wondered, in the checkout line, if everyone who paid by check in this store was asked for picture identification. He showed his police ID to the woman, and she nodded her head, approving the transaction. She was punching Ellis's account number into a little machine when Ellis asked her, "Who do I make this out to?" and she told him "Little Miss Piggy."

Next to him, Quentin said, "Oh, don't be so hard on yourself," and he and his father shared a laugh, while the saleswoman looked at them in a state of incomprehension.

Ellis thought that it was hard to maintain an attitude of hatefulness when Quentin was around.

Quentin placed the bag on his lap. "Where to now?"

"The parking garage," Ellis told him, not looking at him, not wanting to see the disappointment that he knew would be on the boy's face. He stood behind Quentin, waiting for the elevator, surrounded by bustling shoppers who didn't seem to have a worry in the world.

"You got that Gerald Podgourney thing? Already?"

Ellis leaned forward so nobody else could hear him, holding onto the wheelchair's handles, whispering, but knowing better than to push. "I *have* the Gerald Podgourney thing. Not *got*."

"You don't think I *have* enough people around me all the time, telling me what to do, Pops?"

Ellis straightened up, moved to the side of the chair, looked down at his son's face, and was glad to see that Quentin was smiling up at him.

"One more won't do you no harm," Ellis smiled back.

CHAPTER

45

The client sat straight, with his hands folded, trying to appear as innocent as he could, as Arthur L. Horwitz began his spiel to the jury.

"Ladies and gentlemen of the jury," Horwitz said. "Over the last three days, you have listened to all the testimony. You have seen all the state's 'evidence.' You have heard from the state's 'witnesses'—all of whom stated under oath that they were telling nothing but the truth. And, at last, just this morning, you heard from the state itself. The powerful state of Illinois, who brought these so-called 'criminal charges' against my client." Horwitz turned to face his client, looked at him in appraisal. He motioned at him, pointed him out to the jury.

"Look at him, ladies and gentlemen. Take a good, long look.

"Before you sits a man who was once proud and strong—before the state set him up to take the fall for their own malfeasance. He's sure lost his pride now. He's lost his strength too, wouldn't you say? I want you to look at him, and I beg you to think about what else he's lost as you look."

Horwitz lifted his fist, raised his thumb to the jury.

"Let's begin with the most important loss. My client lost his wife. After that horrible afternoon—the afternoon you heard so much about from the state's witness's testimony—his wife left him. She did not leave him as a matter of conscience, as the state has led you to believe, but because *she couldn't take what* they *were doing to them anymore!*"

Horwitz began to pace back and forth in front of the jury box. He kept his thumb pointed out, shaking his fist back and forth for emphasis.

"The state had spread lies and vicious rumors, innuendoes that they promised to prove to you in sworn, open, testimony, but which they somehow, and conveniently, failed to do, even with all of their so-called evidence, and the testimony of their many so-called witnesses. Those rumors hounded his wife, the innuendoes became too much for her to bear, and a strong marriage was ended before this trial even began."

Horwitz stopped and lifted his hand and pointed his index finger, now holding up an L, his other three fingers closed tightly together.

"My client has lost his job. A job a lot of you might think wasn't important, but still, it was his, it afforded him—and the wife who has left him—a decent lifestyle. Dragged through the mud of the conspiracy, my client had to give up his job."

Horwitz thrust out his middle finger.

"Now let's talk about reputation. Does the man before you even have one anymore? I think you'll agree that he does not. In the public's eye, this man is a racist. In the media conspiracy that resulted from last summer's uprising, my client was arrested, then tried and convicted in the media before a grand jury was even convened. For nearly six months now he has had to live under the assumption that he is a racist, a hateful bigot." Horwitz paused, then stared meaningfully at the jury, making brief eye contact with all twelve before continuing.

"But not one of the state's clients was able to state under oath that they had ever heard this man utter a racial slur! On the other hand, you did hear witnesses—black *and* white—who testified, all of them under oath, that my client was as liberal as anyone else in this room. No matter what you might personally think about our witness' work, the jobs they held, or their admittedly favorable feelings for the defendant, the fact is, we've proven beyond any reasonable doubt that he is *not* a racist. In fact, we have indeed proven the exact opposite."

Horwitz waited a minute, let that statement sink in. He was speaking to seven black women, three black men, a Mexican male, and a lone white female. This point would be crucial in their subsequent deliberations. When he thought the time was right, he shot his ring finger out.

"As I've stated, you've heard from a few of his friends. But the truth is, my client has lost a number of those—friends, I mean. He's been abandoned by them, they jumped off the ship like rats just as soon as the first irresponsible charges were leveled at him, through our 'friends' in the media. Close relationships he held dear are now gone, including family members who rushed to judgment, without waiting for the criminal justice system to even begin to run its course."

Horwitz shot out his pinky; knowing the audience to whom he'd be playing, he hadn't worn his ring today.

"And, at last, my client has lost his self-respect." He closed his hand into a fist, took a risk, and shook it in their faces. He shot out his index finger, pointed it at his client.

"*Look at him.* He's worn the same suit to court all three days of the trial. You've heard testimony detailing how he's had to deal with the constant death threats, the phone ringing in the middle of the night, the hateful letters, the attacks on the street from people looking for simple answers to incredibly complex questions."

Horwitz closed his hand and pounded his fist on the railing that separated him from the jurors.

"The *state* brought that on, fed my client to the lions through their manipulation of a media swarm who care more about ratings than justice!"

He pounded the fist that represented his client down onto the railing once more.

"The *state* and the *media* don't care a whole lot about *evidence!* They don't care about such unimportant little details as the *facts.*"

He leaned forward and spoke in a stage whisper, his face pinched into a conspirator's frown, as if informing them of things they should have been aware of all along.

"All the politicians care about is getting reelected! All the state's lawyers care about is learning their trade, going into private practice, and making a financial killing by defending the same sort of scum they'd once pledged to put in prison!"

Horwitz had to wait a moment as the state's objection was sustained. He shook his head—it didn't matter, his message had gotten across—then continued.

"All the media cares about are ratings: who's watching which station at what time; how many radios are tuned in to what station; how many newspapers are sold on a given day."

Horwitz turned and pointed his finger at his client, and his client held his gaze.

"This man was set up to take the fall from the very beginning. The evidence has proven that he was never anything more than a scapegoat of the same sort of people that opinion poll after opinion poll declares to be the least trusted in the entire country: politicians, lawyers, and the media."

The state's objection was overruled. Horwitz nodded his head, as if the judge's ruling had given credibility to his statement.

"Thank God for the American jury system. If it wasn't for you—you twelve people sitting in those horrid wooden chairs, taking time away from your families, your jobs, your lives, while in the performance of your civic duty—my client would have been hung from a tree by now, lynched, set afire, and forgotten about.

"But we have remedies in this country, opportunities that no other nation on earth has. In America, we're allowed the opportunity to bring the accused before twelve people such as yourselves, lay out all the evidence, good and bad, and ask those twelve people what they think about what they've heard.

"I'm asking you to do that now, ladies and gentlemen. Please. Enter into your deliberations while thinking about what the state presented, and what *we* presented. If you do that fairly, if you do that impartially, then there is no other conclusion for you to reach than that of not guilty.

"I want to thank you for your time, trouble, sacrifice, and effort." Horwitz nodded his head at them, more of a little bow, then turned. "Thank you," he said, looking not at the jury, but at his client, who nodded toward the jurors.

Who voted to acquit on the first ballot, after less than ten minutes of deliberation.

Arthur L. Horwitz was prepared for the outcome.

His office had issued a press release that morning, informing the media that he would discuss the case with them in the conference room of his offices, exactly one hour after the verdict, good or bad. Had the verdict gone the other way, he would have used the opportunity to excoriate the jury, discuss the appeal, and, not incidentally, mend his broken media fences by telling the assembled reporters that he'd been too busy with the case to try it in front of them.

Now, he would applaud the jury's decision, state what a great day this was for the justice system, and, not incidentally, mend his broken media fences by telling the reporters he'd been too busy with the case to try it in front of them.

Those fences would be a little harder to mend, after his escape from the criminal courts building.

Four men had been hired to maintain a depression through the swarm, to get Horwitz and his client down the steps, across the sidewalk, and into the waiting car. The men were all off-duty police officers who were moonlighting for Horwitz, being paid by him, but prepared to swear that they'd done what they had out of a sense of responsibility, rather than for money, should the question arise from their superiors. The riots, in the minds of these four officers, had been caused not by Horwitz's client, but by the rampaging, hate-filled niggers.

Horwitz kept his head high, and he kept one hand tight on his client's arm as he guided him through the jostling crowd, the client's face set in stone, the man not about to break his months-long silence now. One of the guards opened the back door of Horwitz's car, and the client was shoved in, pulled the door closed behind him, locked it with his elbow and turned his head away from the cameras. Horwitz pulled open the front passenger side door and jumped in, and the car raced away from the curb before he even managed to shut the door, leaving the shouting reporters behind. He'd be seeing them in an hour.

Horwitz turned in his seat, looking at his client. His client shook his head, just slightly, and inclined it toward the driver, telling Horwitz that he was not about to say anything in front of a man who was unknown to him. Horwitz nodded, understanding his client's wishes. He turned to the driver, patted him on the arm.

"Jimmy? Pull over. Here's fine." The driver glanced over at him, surprised, but did as he was told. He stopped the car in the middle of the lane, causing a sudden, immediate backup behind them, cars whose drivers immediately began to impatiently blast their horns. Horwitz looked back at his client, giving him a shark's smile. "Now, get out," he said to Jimmy.

"Hunh?"

"You heard me, Jimmy. Get out."

"How'm I gonna get back?"

"I don't give a shit how you get back." Horwitz reached over, shut off the car, and took the keys from the ignition. He got out of the car, walked around to the driver's side, ignoring the honking horns that were blaring madly behind him. He pulled the driver's door open, his hair blowing in the icy wind, the hem of his knee-length mohair coat slapping against his legs.

"Come on, Jimmy, get out; it's fucking freezing out here." A car pulled around from behind him, whisked into the outer lane of the two-lane road, its driver narrowly missing Horwitz, the driver laying into the horn, cursing loudly enough to be heard through his tightly shut windows.

It was too close for Horwitz, who, tired of arguing, reached in and grabbed Jimmy by his coat collar, dragged him from the car, slid in, then slammed the door closed behind him and locked it. Jimmy ran around front, attempting to block Horwitz, who started the car, put it in gear, and began to drive away. Jimmy pounded on the hood, jumped to the side when it became obvious that Horwitz was not going to stop. Jimmy kicked at the passenger door as the car passed him by. Horwitz was breathing heavily, exhilarated by his actions, pumped.

He let out a little whoop of triumph before saying, "I'll take the damage to the door out of that asshole's final paycheck." He was laughing as he veered the car into the passing lane, glancing in his rearview mirror. "Where's your car?"

"There's an outdoor city lot just a few blocks down, on the other side of the street."

Horwitz waited, but his client remained silent, so he said, "You must be feeling pretty good, all things considered."

"Good? No. I don't feel good." There was a pause that Horwitz allowed to drag on. He waited, driving slowly. He saw the lot up at the corner, court parking, eight dollars, including city tax. He slowed, preparing to U-turn into the lot. He didn't bother to turn on his signal.

Horwitz said, "Look, the jury thing was good lawyering, but we weren't counting on it, the outcome was never in jeopardy. The judge would have thrown out their conviction. He's in my pocket." His client, goddamn him, did not respond.

Horwitz said, "Greylord just got the stupid ones, the greedy judges. There are still plenty of crooks left in Cook County . . . But you've got to know where to look, how to find them."

After a moment, his client said, "I . . . appreciate your taking the case." He paused, knowing he would eventually have to say more, then blurted out, "I don't know how to thank you."

Horwitz felt a thrill that was even greater than the one he'd felt when the jury had announced its verdict; even greater than the thrill he'd felt when he'd muscled Jimmy out of the car. In the courtroom, after the verdict, he had wanted to hug his client, give the media something to write about, but the man, playing the stoic, had stared straight ahead, as if the nightmare wasn't even half-over. The man had been like that since he'd first come into Horwitz's office, cold and silent, almost resentful, as if getting the best legal defense the city of Chicago had to offer was his due. Like he had it coming to him.

But now Horwitz had him. He had gotten him to admit that he was in Horwitz's debt. I don't know how to thank you, hell. Horwitz knew precisely how the man could cover the debt.

He made his illegal turn, raced into the lot, waved off the attendant who was standing at the lot's entrance—hillbilly-looking son of a bitch, wearing heavy, hunting coveralls, a plastic hat with earflaps, his breath clouding white, coming out of his mouth—glaring at Horwitz. Horwitz drove down the aisles of cars until his client told him to stop.

"That's mine, the blue one."

"I know how you'll thank me," Horwitz said, as he braked. "I didn't fire Jimmy for my health." Horwitz put the car in park, turned and looked back at his client.

"Remember that job I told you about last week on the phone? When you were being so fucking loyal to the precious memory of your marriage? Well, here's the deal. You're coming to work for me. I'll take a small cut out of your check every two weeks, until we're even on your fee. I'll give you five hundred a week, plus medical, full dental and eyecare." He flashed a scornful grin. "No HMO for my firm. We're talking Blue Cross, Blue Shield." Horwitz felt that thrill again, felt it even more strongly, as his client lowered his eyes. He wanted to ask him how it felt, how *he* liked being underneath someone's foot. It couldn't have hit the man as a big surprise. Horwitz had done the near impossible on his behalf, and the guy thought he was going to skate? Head back to Minnesota and—what?—send in twenty bucks every month until his legal bill was settled?

"Remember what I told you when you came to me, begging me to represent you? I told you not to worry about the bill, we'd work something out. Well, here's what I worked out. You're taking Jimmy's place. You get to drive me around, sit in on my conferences, act as an all-around chauffeur-bodyguard. Outside of health care, other benefits include eating in fine restaurants nearly every night of your life and never picking up a tab. More women than you ever thought you'd have in your life. Sitting courtside at Bulls games, a skybox at Comiskey Park—"

"What if I say no."

"Then I jump into the line of people waiting to sue the shit out of you, and I'll end up first in line. Legal fees take precedence over any debt except federal taxes. I'll brick your check, get a third of every dime you're paid. I'll get a lien against all your current or future earnings. You know what that means? You hit the lottery, it'll end up in my pocket. But it doesn't have to come to that, does it? I'm offering you good employment, better than you'd ever have in Minnesota. A shot at a lifestyle you've never had before." Horwitz reached back and lightly punched at his client's shoulder. His client didn't move; the shoulder was still hard and powerful.

He said, "Come on, Marshall, what choice do you have?"

Marshall Del Greco, gaunt and tired, with deep blue circles under eyes that hadn't seen sleep any time lately, looked up at Horwitz, made eye contact, then quickly looked away.

"When do I start?"

"That's the boy." Horwitz punched at the shoulder again. Del Greco did not look at him.

"Take the night off, go out and celebrate your good fortune." Horwitz turned back, reached into his pocket, took out a roll of bills, and peeled off ten hundreds. He turned again, held them out to Del Greco, who just looked at them. Horwitz shoved the bills into Del Greco's coat pocket.

"That's an advance. Go on, go out and have a good time. Where you staying?"

"My brother's place. At Marina Towers."

"That's a hopping spot now, with the House of Blues. Broads everywhere. Good address, good investment. Pop into the office tomorrow afternoon, say, around one or so. We'll have lunch together, discuss your new responsibilities. Leave that junkpile you call a car with whoever it belongs to, and take a cab over; your days of driving shitboxes are over." Horwitz watched him nod, watched Del Greco reach for the door handle.

"And you can call me Artie," Horwitz said. "Not Mr. Horwitz, or sir."

Del Greco paused, looked at him, nodded his head again, and pushed the door open.

"Unless I tell you to call me Mr. Horwitz. Or sir. Say, if I have a special client that I'm looking to impress."

Del Greco got out of the car and closed the door softly behind him.

Horwitz put his car in drive and pulled quickly from the lot, elated, but, nevertheless, angry. He cursed the press. He cursed Gerald Podgourney.

He could go get laid right now if he hadn't promised the press a meeting in his office, and if he didn't have to represent that musclebound sack of shit. Horwitz felt as if he could hump himself into heaven today; he could not remember the last time he'd felt this good, this *alive*. It would have been before the riots, before he'd gotten into trouble with the outfit, before that shit with Benny . . .

But it had all worked out all right. In fact, Benny had put him on the inside track for more than a couple of good deals, including one low-budget, non-union movie, which had been shot for peanuts and had gone on to make mid-six-figures on cassette and in overseas sales.

And getting laid could wait. He had the press conference first, but he could duck out of that early by citing the hearing at City Hall, a hearing he absolutely had to attend, because, as the lawyer of record, he had to sign the papers for Gerald's settlement. Barring any city council interference, that should be wrapped up by five, at the latest. He reached for his cell phone, wondering which young lady he might favor this afternoon, feeling especially generous after his total domination of the once tough ex-cop. And that thing with Jimmy, dear Lord, he'd never done anything like that before in his life! Pulled the guy right out of the car, and Jimmy had been too afraid to stop him.

He was aware that in such a euphoric state, he might do something precipitous, such as putting a pair of diamond earrings into a champagne glass, while sitting at a table at Charlie Trotter's, while his date was in the toilet. Horwitz held the phone in one hand, rubbing his cheek with it, wondering who he should call. Smiling at the thought of it, seeing it in his mind's eye, the woman drinking down the wine, while he—and everyone seated around them—caught the look on her face when she spotted the sparklers. He had to make certain that he called the sort of woman who would know how to properly express her gratitude at his generosity . . .

A MATTER OF HONOR

As it turned out, he would not be drinking champagne in Charlie Trotter's this evening, after all. Because in just over two hours, Horwitz would be right back in the parking lot he'd just pulled out of, called back there by the police in an attempt to help them put a name to a body they were almost certain they'd already identified.

CHAPTER

46

Gerald Podgourney stood in the hallway, next to tall windows that were already going dark, purposely trying to mark the marble floor with the heel of his boot, waiting for his lawyer, wondering what was taking him so long. The fluorescent lights high overhead were on, casting shadows about the hallway. Gerald could step back, and be ten feet tall; move up, and be a midget. His fate was in his own hands. He liked it better that way.

The hearing was scheduled for four; it was five minutes till right now. Gerald lifted his foot, let it drop, over and over, while maintaining eye contact with the shine down the hall, the janitor who was giving him a badass look. Gerald gave him an insolent smile, silently daring him to say or do something nasty. If he did, Gerald would go over there and kick his ass.

It was good to feel confidence, after all these months of fear. Even without any weapons on him, Gerald felt secure, strong. The world was about to be handed to him once again, and this time around, Gerald didn't plan to let it slip from his grasp. This time, he wouldn't let his greed fuck everything up.

Gerald's paranoia was gone. He knew he was safe in here, knew he had another lawsuit if anyone even opened their mouth to him. Right behind him, in the city council's chambers, fifty aldermen—as well as the mayor himself—were voting approval of Gerald's settlement. Gerald could have held out and gotten a whole lot more, but Horwitz had patiently explained a great number of things to Gerald, and one of them was that the process for doing so would have taken years and years. Gerald did not have years and years. Gerald was hard up for money.

Hard up hell, he was flat broke. So rather than waiting years for a potential million dollars, he would settle for the maximum that could be approved by the city council without having to take the case to court.

A hundred thousand dollars.

He would be ripped off for more than a third of that, after Jew-boy took his piece and expenses off the top.

At least he wouldn't have to wait for any government checks to clear. Horwitz had told him that he'd have a certified check with him, made out in Gerald's name. Sixty thousand dollars even, drawn off Horwitz's client account. The shyster would take acceptance of the city's check, and would keep it all. He had also informed Gerald that there was no tax due on insurance settlements such as this one. So Gerald would take Horwitz's check, Horwitz would take the city's, and that would make them even, free and clear of each other. It was the deal the two of them had made. Gerald wouldn't tell the cops what he knew about Rita Cunningham's death, and Horwitz wouldn't represent him anymore, no matter what happened, no matter what Gerald threatened him with in the future.

That was all right with Gerald; he could live without the Jew-boy's services. Mr. Big Shot. He'd been mostly keeping his nose clean, doing low-exposure, low-risk scores, and was planning to keep doing so in the future. And there was another sucker just as rich as Horwitz, who Gerald was planning on paying a visit to, just as soon as all this lawsuit business was over, and Horwitz was out of his life for good. He had waited as long as he had for a reason: Gerald needed Horwitz to get this business out of the way before Gerald made his move. Gerald wouldn't be needing Horwitz anymore, after today. He could make his move on the other guy without any outside interference.

He wondered how long sixty thousand would last him. At his present standard of living, it could get him into the next century. Gerald didn't plan on maintaining his present standard of living. At least he could get out of the neighborhood he was in; shit, since the riots, the city hadn't been the same, what with the jigs lighting white people on fire, everybody copping attitudes, talking in whispers about conspiracies.

The government and the cops, as usual, had used the riots to take away even *more* of the people's rights. Stop-and-frisks on the street were the order of the day, if you looked poor, or like you didn't belong in the neighborhood . . . Nothing was going to be the same, ever again, Gerald knew. The riots had changed everything, had caused the white people to be even more distrusting and intolerant of blacks, and it had caused the blacks to become even more radical and self-pitying than they had been

301

before. He was glad that it was wintertime, he wanted to be living in an all-white neighborhood before summer rolled around. Gerald thought that Edmund might have had the right idea all along. But Edmund was gone, Gerald had to come up with scams all on his own.

Gerald looked up at the sound of footfalls, and he hid his fear at the sight of the cop, that son of a bitch who had kicked down his door and whose subsequent actions had wound up costing Gerald his apartment, his girlfriend, and very nearly his life. Gerald fought his fear, and grinned. The cop stopped a few feet away. He stood staring at Gerald, his hands in the pockets of a shiny, double-breasted overcoat.

The cop said, "You're a hard man to find."

"For you, I bet I am; I live in a pretty white neighborhood." The cop actually smiled at him. Gerald, thinking of sixty thousand dollars, smiled back. "Why you been looking?"

"There's something I been wanting to tell you."

"What's that, how sorry you are?"

The cop shook his head and did not respond, just stood there looking at Gerald, as if lost in heavy thought.

"Thought you could get away with it, didn't you?" Gerald said. The detective just shrugged.

Then, after thinking it over, the cop said, "There're a few uniformed officers who got five days off without pay because of you. I just thought you should know that, Gerald. They'll be looking for you, wanting to make it up out of your hide."

"Is that a threat? Are you threatening me?"

The spade cop pursed his lips and shook his head. He had to be wearing a couple of thousand dollars' worth of clothes; Gerald felt painfully aware of his own, far cheaper clothing.

"I'm trying to educate you," the copper said.

"That's why you were looking for me? Wanting to know where I lived? So you could threaten me? Man, you'd think you'd done enough. Caused enough grief for everybody. Seems to me even *you* could get that through your nappy head."

"That wasn't what I was looking to tell you. I just thought I'd mention that, in passing, so you'd continue to cover your ass." He smiled. "We wouldn't want anything to happen to you."

"It's all right. I'll get a business card, with my address on it. They can come kick my ass anytime; I could always use an extra hundred grand."

The cop said, "There is something you should know . . ."

"Yeah? I don't think there's anything you have to say that I want to know about." The cop once more did not respond, just stood there, patiently waiting, now rocking on his heels. Last summer, Gerald would have had no second thoughts, he would have felt confident that he could have won a fistfight with this cop; now, after all he'd been through, he wasn't so sure.

Resentful now, thinking of what the cop had said, Gerald spat out, "Educate me," spitefully. "Don't worry, I know enough. I know about my rights. I know you people ain't got no goddamn business kicking in people's doors and then pounding the shit out of them. I know that much."

"*Don't have* any business, Gerald. Not *ain't got*."

"Go give your English lessons to your kid."

Gerald waited while the cop closed his eyes, waited while the cop took in a couple of deep breaths. Finally the cop opened his eyes, and didn't seem surprised to discover that Gerald was grinning at him, broadly.

The cop's voice and manner were quite calm when he said, "You ought to be grateful we were there. Here's what I been wanting to tell you: There was an assassin outside your apartment the day all this happened, waiting on the sidewalk. There was a report made of it, you can look it up, I can even get a copy of it for you free, if you want me to. Guy with a gun, outside in a suit, wearing a hat to cover his face, waiting for you to come home. He was planning to kill you, Gerald."

"And who was this mystery man, another nigger cop?"

"No, he was Italian."

"A guinea?" Gerald laughed, relieved. "The one race you could name that I *don't* have trouble with." He said, "I never had any dealings with any guineas, I always stayed away from them."

"Yeah? I know somebody who didn't. Someone who did some business with them just the day before your surgery." The sound of hurrying footsteps came to them, echoing down the corridor.

"Is that right?" Gerald said, not believing him for a minute, but still curious, "and who might that be?" He leaned forward a little bit, and said, as if anxious for approval, "Did I say that right? Is it *who* might that be, or *whom*?"

"You had it right." The cop turned toward the footsteps, as a shadow fell across them. "Ask your lawyer," he said to Gerald, as Horwitz came and stood beside his client.

"Ask me what?" Horwitz said curtly, then said, "Come on, let's get inside. We're cutting it close."

But Gerald was just standing there looking at him, with an expression of dawning wisdom. He looked over at the cop, then back at Horwitz.

"He harassing you?" Horwitz turned toward the detective. "Officer Turner, when are you going to learn your lesson?"

"How'd Del Greco make out?"

"Piece of cake; five-minute acquittal."

"You ever wonder why he came to *you*?"

"Because I'm the best there is. People get in trouble, they want the best in town, and they don't care about personality conflicts." Horwitz paused. "You should have talked to me instead of the PBA rep. I'd have gotten you off scot-free."

"It would have presented a conflict of interest."

"You ready, Gerald? Or you want to stay out here and shoot the shit with this guy?"

Gerald's voice was tight when he said, "You got my check?"

Horwitz patted his breast pocket. "Right in here. But let's get the papers signed first, shall we? You never know, the mayor might have decided that you aren't worth a hundred grand."

"We're mighty chipper today, aren't we, Counselor?" the black cop said, and Horwitz turned to face him.

"Why shouldn't I be? I'm batting a thousand. Got my young friend here a hundred grand, got your old partner off the inciting to riot and official misconduct charges, and I got a new employee." Horwitz smiled thinly, grabbed for the heavy brass door pull.

"And who might that be?"

"Ask Del Greco, when you see him," Horwitz said, then pulled open the heavy wooden door leading to the chamber and ushered his client inside. Turner had to hustle to grab the door, caught it just before it slammed shut in his face.

What had he been talking about, ask Del Greco when he saw him? Turner wondered about that, sitting in the spectator's gallery, unarmed and resentful that they'd taken away his weapon. All fifty aldermen could carry concealed weapons, by city ordinance, even the ones who were convicted felons, it was one of the perks of the job. But honest, hardworking city cops had to give up their weapons, put them in a locked vault if they wanted to view the proceedings.

Turner watched, bored, as the resolution that had already been accepted in committee was passed on the council floor. He listened to the end of the vote, knew that it would be unanimous. He felt an inkling of joy at the thought that he'd cost these fat cats a hundred thousand dollars. That joy was daunted by the thought of who the money was being handed over to: Gerald Podgourney and Arthur Horwitz. Two men who deserved a bullet more than a city check.

Although it was good to see that Gerald had gone downhill. Turner was pleased by the sight of him, the weightlifter's physique barely suggested now, his clothes hanging off his back. He must have lost fifty pounds since that awful July afternoon.

Turner hadn't sweated the five-day suspension; he was aware of how close he'd come to getting charged with involuntary manslaughter. Although he hadn't laid a hand on the man himself. Although he had even ordered the cops who were doing so to stop. The woman had seen it, Amy, but she wasn't talking, nobody could even find her. She had left her parents' home for parts unknown, and Turner didn't blame her; in the aftermath of the riot, the media had been turning over every rock available, and Amy would have been under one of them. She'd been smart enough to see that, and to get out before the locusts descended.

Gerald had contracted peritonitis, had nearly died in the hospital, they'd been pumping him full of antibiotics when the riot had broken out. There he'd been, a martyr, and he hadn't even known it, had been in a coma by the time the reporters finally pieced together what had happened. Turner hadn't been in any coma; he'd had to face them or lose his job. With his own son in the hospital, near death, when it could have gone either way, Turner had to stand in front of the still cameras and the Minicams, had been forced to endure the microphones thrust into his face, the print reporters with their notebooks out, scribbling shorthand notes of what he was saying so they could mix their own words in with his later on.

He wondered now why they'd bothered; they hadn't published a word he'd said. They'd misquoted him, they'd attacked him, one editorial had called him a rabid dog. They would probably have cut him some slack if he hadn't gone public at Rita's funeral, if he hadn't been so widely known as Marshall Del Greco's partner.

Ellis Turner sighed. There wasn't anything he could do about that now. It was over, and he still had his job. Surprisingly enough, he had Laney to thank for that. Turner was still shocked at the way she had leaped to his defense.

The mayor slapped his gavel down twice. Turner was surprised to discover that he'd been wrong, the vote had not been unanimous—Alderman Billy Charge had abstained. There were a few words spoken for the media's sake, how the city was sorry for what had happened to Gerald, how they were in his debt. Turner felt his lips twisting down in disgust. These pigs would do anything to get themselves reelected.

And then it was over, Gerald and Horwitz were walking out of the room. None of the politicians who'd voted to give him money were applauding. The TV camera lights were fading out, the reporters were chasing Horwitz and Podgourney. Horwitz was a media sensation today; Turner couldn't wait to get home and find out what the man had said about Del Greco's acquittal. He would call Quentin, have the boy tape the news for him. He would wait a few minutes before going out to make the call, though. He didn't want to be anywhere near the cameras, the reporters. He'd had enough of them to last him a good, long time.

Turner had known about the acquittal, of course. It had been announced over the car radio, with speculation over whether it would cause another riot. Turner knew that wasn't likely; it was too cold to riot, such things generally only happened in high summer. Besides, he'd been following the case. It had gotten heavy play in Chicago's media, but no community groups were in the courtroom, there were no organizations calling press conferences, demanding Del Greco's head. Del Greco and Turner were old news. The riot itself was old news, even though its aftereffects were still being felt, like those of an earthquake.

Turner's beeper went off, and he fumbled for it, stared at the readout. Since the riot, he always checked his beeper as soon as it went off, always kept it turned on audio, never switched it to vibrate. Since the riot, he changed the battery on the first day of every month. Since the riot, Turner kept it on his headboard when he slept. His family would never need him again only to discover that Turner was busy.

Laney's phone number floated up at him. What did she want now? Probably wanted to know if Podgourney had gotten his pound of civic flesh. Wanted to know how Turner felt about that.

She could be a pain in the ass, but one Turner could live with. She had his best interests at heart, she'd proven that repeatedly in the months since the city had burned.

Turner looked around him, at the now near-empty audience gallery. He nodded at the sergeant at arms, who was looking at him angrily. Maybe you weren't supposed to carry beepers in the gallery, either. Turner decided that enough time had passed, that it was safe for him to leave City Hall. The reporters would have gone back to file their stories, would want to get them on the four-thirty news, with film of Podgourney and Horwitz.

Ellis left the auditorium, walked down the hall to the bank of pay phones. The reporters never used these phones anymore, they were all equipped with cellulars. He dialed Cheryl's number, was trying to think of something funny to say to her, when her voice came on the line, breathless and shocked. Turner felt a moment's terror at the thought that something had happened to a member of his family.

"What is it!" He barked the words, expecting the worst, and Cheryl gave him the news.

"Marshall Del Greco just killed himself," his sergeant told him. "They found his body in his brother's car, in a parking lot a couple of blocks down the street from the criminal courts building."

CHAPTER

47

The responding officers had cordoned off the entire parking lot just as soon as they'd run the license plates on the dead man's car. There'd been a moment's confusion after the registration record had come back from the DMV. The car was registered under the name of an Angelo Del Greco; the stiff in the front seat was carrying ID identifying what was left of him as Marshall Del Greco, the ex-cop, the guy they'd tried to lay the blame for the riot on, and who'd just earlier that afternoon walked out of court, a free man. The officer who'd pulled the wallet out of the body's pants was white-faced from more than the cold, and he was sitting in a squad car, head back and eyes closed, a cup of coffee in his hands, taking deep breaths.

Yellow crime scene tape was strung up everywhere, layered over itself at waist length, taped to light posts, to the grilles of cars, stuck around the little shack where the parking attendant tried to stay warm. The attendant was being questioned now, they had taken him back to headquarters.

There were uniformed officers everywhere, wearing their heavy leather winter jackets, wearing their hats against the cold, bulked up by long underwear and their mandatory Kevlar vests. One of them decided to break established procedure, went into the little guard shack and told the detective in charge that it was getting to be a pain in the ass; the courts had closed, the ME had left, and people who wanted to get their cars out of the lot were bitching. The detective stopped talking to the lawyer who claimed to be the last man to have seen Marshall Del Greco alive long enough to tell the officer to keep the civilians out of the lot; to get out there and do his fucking job. The detective turned back to the ashen-faced lawyer, hiding his distaste at the fleck of vomit that had splattered onto the lapel of the man's expensive overcoat.

"You're absolutely certain that's him?"

"He wore the same clothes to court four days in a row. The same coat, shirt, tie, everything, shoes. I'm telling you, those are the same clothes. The build's the same, the wedding ring, even. What I *can't* tell you is that I'm *absolutely certain* that—thing out there is Del Greco. I mean, I'm sure, but I'm not gonna bet my kids' eyes on it; his fucking head is blown off."

The detective did not care for the man's attitude. Just a couple of minutes ago he was standing out there next to the car, puking his guts out on the frozen pavement. Now, all of a sudden, he was acting like a tough guy.

With this in mind, the detective said, "Maybe we should go out there and take another look." That got Horwitz's attention.

"No!" He shouted the word before he could stop himself. The detective gave him a blank-faced stare.

"That's him, I'm sure of it. There should be a thousand dollars in hundred-dollar bills in his—right—coat pocket. Unless somebody grabbed it."

"Excuse me?"

"It was a joke."

Not to the detective, it wasn't. The detective knew who Horwitz was, and knew he would have to tread lightly. Still, there was only so much you had to take.

He touched Horwitz's arm lightly. "Come on, I need you to show me *exactly* which pocket. I don't want to get all that blood and brains all over me digging around in the wrong one."

Horwitz pulled away. "I am *not* going back out to that car."

"Listen—" The door to the attendant's shack opened, and Ellis Turner strode in, leaving the door open behind him.

"What happened, Horwitz!" Turner was staring hard at the lawyer, blaming him for something that the detective knew nothing about, his anger barely under control. The detective had eighteen years on the department, and knew how to act. He walked the two steps to the door, pulled it shut.

If Turner went off on the lawyer now, there would be no civilian witnesses. As soon as the door closed, Turner moved in fast, and Horwitz backed up in response, raising his arms in a protective gesture, showing the first signs of panic.

"Get away from me!" Horwitz turned to the detective, and when he spoke, his voice was a high, tight whine. "Get this man away from me!" The detective looked back at Horwitz, lifted his eyebrows and shrugged, puzzled. This wasn't the first self-styled tough guy he'd ever seen fold, though most of them didn't do so with such little pressure applied.

"The man told me he gave Del Greco a thousand dollars."

"Is that right?" Turner answered the detective, but did not look at him, his attention was focused entirely on the lawyer, he was right in his face, their bodies inches apart.

"What did you give him that kind of money for?"

The lawyer didn't answer. Turner put his face right next to his, and shouted, "*HUH?*" The detective watched Horwitz shrink back, felt the structure shake as the lawyer's ass hit the wall.

"Don't you think you can—"

"I asked you a *question,* motherfucker!"

"He was coming to work for me!" The detective began to get worried; the lawyer looked to be on the verge of a nervous breakdown, was waving his hands around his face, all that muscle action going on in his cheeks, around his wide-opened eyes . . .

Turner didn't seem to care, though, he just kept bearing down.

"You had to take it all away from him, didn't you?" Turner reached out with one leather-gloved hand and shoved Horwitz, not hard, but enough to rock the building again. Horwitz cowered. The detective could not believe what he was seeing.

"Pussy motherfucker. What'd you tell him, you'd let him work off the bill, take it out in trade? You were going to show him off, your own personal fucking ex-cop, gonna put him on a leash and let everyone see how powerful you are. What's the matter, the high media profile wasn't good enough for you? You had to take his last fucking shred of manhood away from him, you had to break him down." Turner shoved him again, and Horwitz yelped as he fell against the wall. The detective took a step toward them; there were reporters out there, and they would want to know why the building was shaking.

"Hey, Ellis, come on . . . " the detective said. Turner didn't move. The detective walked toward him, reached out and touched his arm lightly.

"The guy's a piece of shit, granted, but he's a *lawyer,* Ellis." He watched as Turner nodded.

"You see anything? You hear anything?" Turner stood in front of Horwitz, but he was speaking to the detective.

"Me? Didn't see anything; didn't hear a word."

"Good. Here's something else for you to not see or hear." The detective winced, thinking that Turner was about to punch the lawyer, but Turner didn't; in fact, he lowered his voice.

"Someday, sometime, when you least expect it, Horwitz, you're gonna come out of one of your girlfriend's houses, or step out of your town-house, or a restaurant, or a bar, maybe even a fucking Blackhawk game, and I'm gonna be there. When it happens, I'll leave my gun at home. It'll be just you and me." The lawyer was nodding rapidly, eyes wide, and the detective felt disgusted. The last time he'd seen a man act like this, it had been a prisoner he'd been picking up from the County—a guy who had spent the night getting gang-raped by members of the Gangster Apostle Nation. The lawyer reminded him of that guy, eager to please, ready to do anything just to make sure that the man in front of him wouldn't cause him further harm.

"You through with this asshole?"

Turner still hadn't turned to the detective.

"I guess I am now, shit."

Turner said to Horwitz, "Now get out of here, before I lose my self-control." He said it and made the lawyer squeeze around him, the little weasel whimpering, shaking, skitting around Turner and running for the door. Turner spun slowly, watched with the detective as the lawyer pulled the door open and ran through it, then across the pavement. Cold air whipped in around them, stealing what warmth was being provided by the little electric space heater that was on top of a filthy desk.

The detective watched Turner use his teeth to take off his right glove, watched him reach into his inside breast pocket, pull out cigarettes and a lighter. Turner's hands were steady as he lit a Kool, then put his cigarettes and lighter back. Turner sucked in a deep drag, then nodded at the detective.

"Thanks."

The detective shrugged.

Turner said, "The wagon's here, they're about to take him away. Del Greco and I were together for seven years before—all this shit happened. Okay if I take a look at him, say good-bye?"

"If you're sure you want to." The detective paused. "You know how it happened, though, right?"

Turner was walking past him, said over his shoulder, "Head's gone, over and under, Italian-made shotgun, right?"

"Part of the head's still there; looks sort of like his hair is growing out from between his shoulders. The face is totally gone, Turner. He had a pocketful of ID on him; driver's license, social security card, credit cards, union card from the Hod Carriers'. Pictures of the ex in the wallet. There was a pack of Lucky Strikes in his shirt."

"That was his brand."

The detective followed Turner down the row of cars, toward the blue vehicle that was parked near the end of the row.

"We found ten hundred-dollar bills in his right-hand pocket, where Horwitz said he put them. I didn't mention finding them in front of the shyster, he had just gotten out of line with me when you walked in."

"Blood money."

They were at the car now, right beside it, and the uniformed officers and detectives surrounding it stepped back in respect, aware of what was happening, respectful of the concept of partners. They waited quietly, watching, hands stuffed in their pockets, stomping their feet to ward off the cold.

The inside of the car was a gooey mess; the rear top of the car's roof had been blown out by the force of the blast. The steel looked peeled back, like the bottom of a soup can that kids had blown up with a fire-cracker. The officers made a point of staying away from the back of the car, not wanting what was on the ground back there to get all over their shoes. Parts of Del Greco had ended up on a number of the other cars in the lot, were now frozen onto metal.

There was a frozen puddle of vomit on the pavement, next to the driver's side door. The detective warned Turner to watch it, Ellis stepped around it, and thanked him. He seemed to steel himself, set his shoulders, took a breath, then bent over and looked inside.

The shotgun was still where Del Greco had propped it, between his legs, pointing up. Del Greco had taken off one of his shoes, had pulled the trigger with his toe. Red had sprayed everywhere. Turner looked at the body, at what was left of the head. There was no face left, just bone fragments, and, as the detective had mentioned, hair. The shotgun was short, what was it, a .410? Del Greco wouldn't have had to use his toe; he'd chosen that manner, for some reason.

In a soft voice, the detective said, "We don't believe he put the barrel in his mouth. From what we gather, from the length of the weapon, the position of the body, the pellet pattern, what was—shot off—and the angle it took, we think he sat back a little and faced it, looking almost down on it, with the barrel five or six inches away from the center of his face."

"It's the way he'd have done it; Del Greco would have wanted to face it head on, to see it coming."

The detective was surprised by the normality of Turner's voice. He knew what Turner had been through in the past five months—there wasn't a cop on the department who didn't—but still, there was a difference between being tough and being a stone, cold hunk of marble. The detective thought that some sort of emotion was called for when you were looking at your partner's body, when he had his face blown off.

Then Turner surprised him. He leaned deep into the car, disregarding his fine, shiny coat, his expensive pants, and hugged the body close to him, one arm around Del Greco's shoulders, the other somewhere in be-tween them. Several cops turned their heads away; others moved in closer to get a better look. Turner seemed to be squeezing the body, almost frisking it, and the detective looked away, giving him his privacy, shooting a sharp, angry look at the officers who were gawking.

After what seemed like a very long minute, Turner let go of the corpse, moved back out of the car, and nodded at the meat wagon crew. He sniffed. There was blood all over his coat, covering his tie, smearing Turner's white shirt. The detective had a moment of suspicion. He was unsure whether Turner's eyes were wet due to the cold wind blowing into them, or if the man was actually crying. His voice had been hard, matter-of-fact . . .

Testing him, the detective said, "You gonna be all right?"

"I'm fine," he said, and he was. Turner kept his face stern, but there wasn't even a hint of passion in his voice. The detective looked at him, frowned at the blood that was covering the gloved right hand, smeared all over the palm. The coat, the pants, the shirt and tie he could understand, the man had just hugged what was in the car, his clothing would have *had* to have blood on them. But how had that happened with the palm of one glove? What had Turner done?

The detective decided that it wasn't the proper time or place to ask that sort of question.

The detective looked back at the body, just as the meat wagon guys were gently pulling it from the car. They were being careful because of all the blood, didn't want too much of it on them. They were dressed out with surgeon's gloves and wearing those clear, plastic suits. The body bag was already opened up, lying flat on the ground.

The detective noticed that Del Greco's shirt was open. The tie was pushed to the side, the middle buttons of the shirt looked to have been torn off. The detective would have noticed if he'd been that way when the body had been found. That shirt had been closed, buttoned up; there'd been not even the slightest hint that this was anything other than a suicide. The detective looked back at Turner, who was already walking away.

"Hey," the detective said weakly, and Turner, walking into the wind, dropped his gloves to the ground as he lighted a cigarette. He did not answer, the wind no doubt whipping the detective's voice out of range.

Or maybe Turner was just ignoring it.

CHAPTER

48

From outside, the bar looked warm and inviting. Then again, on a night like this, a funeral parlor would have looked warm and inviting. The tall, slender man had this thought as he stood outside on the shoveled, salted sidewalk, looking in. There were cursive letters spelling out the tavern's name: December's Mother. What sort of woman would admit to having giving birth to the ugliest month of all twelve?

The man was shivering, but he wasn't ready to go inside just yet. A cautious man by nature, he had grown even more so over the last several months—judged by normal standards it could be said that he was paranoid. His clothes were new and expensive, the hem of his lined coat fell past his knees. He wore heavy gloves on his hands, and he had a thick, wool stocking cap pulled down low, covering his ears and the back of the head. The collar of the coat was turned up against the cold.

Still, he was freezing.

He felt uneasy, even in a safe, upscale South Loop neighborhood such as this one. There weren't many people on the streets tonight, strolling. Two weeks before Christmas, and the weather was keeping everyone in. The man heard barking, turned.

There was a little postage-stamp-sized park across the street, an empty lot that had been paved over. The man could see two small, thin trees, and a short, green wooden bench. Somebody had strung Christmas lights over the bare limbs of both trees; there were small, round garbage cans wired to the trunks. A woman in a thick, hooded coat was walking a small dog on a leash that played out like a tape measure. She had an

inverted Baggie over the glove of her free hand. The man watched the dog defecate, watched the woman lean down and pick the mess up. The dog leaped into her arms, and she hurried away. The hood on her coat blocked her vision, would allow muggers to sneak up on her. The little dog was effectively useless for defense. No wonder violent crime was on the upswing. The woman dropped the Baggie in the garbage can attached to one of the trees, walked to the building next to the park, then went inside through well-lighted glass doors. Taking a ring of keys out of her pocket, she unlocked an inner door. The man turned back to the tavern.

The weather might be too cold to go out walking around in, but it wasn't stopping people from drinking; it never got cold enough to stop people from doing that. Some of them were even stupid enough to believe that drinking brought you warmth, rather than sapping it from your body.

The gaily lighted bar was about half-filled with people, all of whom appeared to be much younger than the man. There was a long L-shaped bar, and tall, four-legged stools had been set against the walls, with small square tables between them. There was no music playing. There was a Bulls game playing on the TV set hanging from the ceiling at the far end of the bar. The place seemed to be all red leather and brown wood. The bartender was a pretty, blonde young woman wearing jeans and a tight T-shirt, with a pleasant smile that seemed permanently etched on her face, and a lithe, youthful body that was being ogled by several of the male patrons. The bar was only a few blocks away from the Chicago Board of Trade, and it looked it; the place was filled with well-dressed, younger men and women, relaxing, winding down in the company of their own. A handwritten sign—black oil pencil on lined white plastic—was leaning against the glass. Written upon it were December's Mother's rules and regulations:
No Cigar Smoking
No Cubs Fans Allowed
No Whiners
December's Mother Is An O.J. Free Zone

What was someone like Gerald Podgourney doing in a place like this? the man wondered. Winning the crowd over, by the looks of things, charming them. A haggard, slim young waiter, carrying a pitcher of beer in one hand and a tray of frosted mugs in the other, was making his way over to the table where Gerald was holding court. Gerald was seated on one of the tall stools, surrounded by four other men. Gerald looked thin, but fit. A couple of the tables had been pushed together, to accommodate them. An overflowing ashtray sat in the middle of the table, surrounded by empty beer mugs. The waiter put the pitcher of beer and the new mugs down on the table, put the used mugs on his tray, wiped what little table surface there was available down with a bar rag, slapped the rag across his arm, and dumped the ashtray onto the tray. He grabbed the empty pitcher, and Gerald put a bill down on the tray, in the middle of the ashes. The man could not see the amount of the bill, but he saw Gerald wave away the change, saw the smile of thanks on the young waiter's face.

The man saw two women get up from the table beside Gerald's, both of them looking hostile, as if the men had somehow offended them. Or maybe they didn't care for the smell of cigarette smoke. The women grabbed their coats off the back of their stools, put them on, and left a couple of crumpled bills on the table. The man stepped to the door and held it open for them, heard them whispering to each other, angrily. He slipped into the bar, welcoming the warmth, and sat down at the table they'd vacated. He looked over at the TV, watched a slim, muscular, young black kid leap into the air and dunk a basketball. The people at the bar roared approval. He glanced over at the men sitting beside him; most of them had been cut from the same mold.

Dressed in casual but expensive sweaters that had bizarre designs on the front. Dress pants over expensive shoes. Hair expensively saloned, blown-dry, moussed into place, bald spots covered over as best as a costly foreign hairdresser could manage. Gerald, in contrast, had a bright blue ski jacket hanging off the back of his stool, was wearing a Northwestern University sweatshirt over loose, faded blue jeans. He had a pair of black, heavy work boots on his feet. The men at the table were laughing it up, having a good time, as Gerald entertained them now by pulling his shirt up, showing them an ugly scar that stretched from one end of his abdomen to the other; the belly of Frankenstein's monster.

The man was finally beginning to feel warm. He took off his gloves, put them in his coat pocket, and slipped out of his coat, was hanging it over the back of the stool as the waiter approached him, his smile wavering slightly when he looked into the man's face. The man ignored the look, cleared his throat, and said, "Large tap, please." He laid a five-dollar bill on top of the tip the women had left for the waiter. The waiter got his smile back in place, wiped down the table, took the glasses and money away. The man listened to the men at the next table as they oohed and ahhed and made other sympathetic noises over the slash and the accompanying staple marks that stretched across Gerald's stomach. Gerald was drinking his beer, proud of having shown off his battle scars.

"Here you go, sir."

"Thank you." The beer had come in a frosted mug. The man sipped it; it seemed watery, almost tasteless. He could not remember the last time he'd sat back and enjoyed a beer. He could not remember the last time he had sat back and enjoyed anything. He had not removed his wool cap, though he'd rolled the sides of it up, over the tops of his ears. He lit a cigarette, blew the match out with his first exhale, and played around with the plastic ashtray as he listened to Gerald explain to the other men at his table how he'd managed to get the scar.

"So I will *not* spend a night in the hospital. Not with all the stuff they got floating around in the air in those joints, viruses and shit, can get into your incisions and infect you. Hottest day of the year, can I enjoy it? Can I go to the beach? Not me; I got to have surgery. And then, I got to go home.

"And I won't let the broad who's living with me drive my car, either, on account of she's such an airhead. So I end up taking a cab home. I made the nurse wait, with me sitting in a wheelchair, cause I was trying to get one didn't have a fucking Iranian driving it. Shows how naive I can be. I'm minding my own business, in pain, but it was a hernia opera-tion, it's not like they cut off my dick, and I had painkillers, so it was all right. I get home, get into bed, and I have Amy—my broad—running around in the kitchen, making me a pot of chicken soup—" Gerald paused, half-drunk, basking in the laughter of the men at the table, before he continued.

"Then what happens? There's a pounding at the front door, I think it's these mopes from across the hallway, always slamming their door, coming over to fuck with me after they noticed I was laid up. I hear Amy yelling, 'What do you want?' Hear them tell her it's the police, they got a warrant.

"I says to myself, oh, shit.

"Soon as I hear this, I'm out of bed, one hand holding my stitches in, the other reaching around for a baseball bat, a barbell, some fucking thing to defend myself with. I hear Amy tell them to go away, that I'm sick, and I wonder what's wrong with her, I mean, that's *all* they need to hear. Next thing you know, *BAM,* they kick the door down."

The man sat back and turned in his chair, looked over at Gerald, who was taking another drink of his beer. The man smiled, so Gerald would know he was listening as an admirer, that his intentions were friendly and nonjudgmental. Gerald caught his eye, looked away, then brought his gaze quickly back to the man, Gerald now squinting, half-smiling in surprise.

"I had too much to drink, or don't you have any eyebrows?" All five men from the table were looking at the man now, two of them with serious expressions, the other two, like Gerald, seeming bemused. The man shrugged harmlessly.

"Alopecia."

"Ala—*what?*"

One of the serious-faced men softly said, "It's a disease, takes all the hair off your body." He said it as if he knew better, as if he knew the truth, but was going along with the man's deception to help him save face.

"Your parsley gone? That alo-whatever disease make you lose your pubes?" The man turned, looked down at his beer. He heard someone mutter something to Gerald, then there was silence, then Gerald said, "Ah, fuck it," and picked up where he'd left off.

"I'm standing next to the bed now, with a T-shirt on, in my undershorts, and here's this big—" There was a pause, then Gerald said, "—*black* dude, surrounded by a lot of coppers in uniforms, racing towards me. I drop back down on the bed, with my arms up in the air, so they can see I ain't got a weapon, and Amy—genius that she is—shouts out, 'Be careful! Don't hurt him, he just had *hernia* surgery!' "

Gerald's tone became ironic. "Smart fucking move, Amy. Good piece of ass—she'd do anything I wanted in the sack—but stupid? Let me tell you, like a *rock*."

The man now thought he understood why the two women had left their table. He used the butt of his cigarette to light a fresh one, stubbed the spent one out in the ashtray.

"I shout out, 'Amy, you dumb cunt, shut the fuck *up!*' " Gerald had hollered it, and the man looked up, saw the pained expression on the bartender's face, the look of concern on the waiter's. Most of the bar's other patrons were looking over at Gerald, most with undisguised abhorrence. The men at Gerald's table seemed taken aback, but Gerald himself was oblivious.

Gerald ordered another pitcher of beer, and did not lower his voice—in fact, he raised it—in order to be heard over the uncomfortable laughter of two of the men at his table. The man looked back down into his beer, and patiently listened.

"Sure enough, what do these morons do? They'd flipped me over onto my belly, so they could cuff me from behind. Now I got a gun in my ear, my stitches are split open, I'm bleeding all over my satin sheets, there are cops going nuts, shouting and cursing, and here's Amy, Little Miss Concerned, Florence Nightingale, all of a sudden going, '*What* did you just call me? *What* did you just call me?' I can picture her, with her hands on her hips, tapping her fucking toe.

"The cops flip me *back* over, onto my back, and by now I'm getting dizzy from the pain, the loss of blood. I look into this motherfucker's eyes, and they're *wild,* man. He punches me in the gut, and I can't see his eyes no more, all I can see is this red film, like somebody poured a bucket of paint over my face."

No one at Gerald's table was laughing anymore.

"But I can hear him," Gerald said. "He makes his voice all high pitched, like a girl's, making fun of Amy, and he goes, 'You just had *hernia* surgery?' and he punches me again. Now, I hear the nig—the *black* guy, screaming for the guy to leave me alone, which is a crock, like this macho-ass street copper's gonna listen to some stiff detective. The copper, he's still making fun of Amy, and now Amy's screaming her head off, and he says to me, he goes, 'Poor little Gerald just had *hernia* surgery?' and I guess he whacked me again, I guess, cause I passed out.''

There was a stunned silence at the table, in the bar. The man heard one of the announcers of the game inform the audience as to which team had the better halftime statistics. He heard the announcer say that they were going to a local news update.

At last, one of the other men at the table broke the unpleasant silence. "That's the story, and you settled for a hundred thousand *dollars*?''

"My lawyer said to take it. He said it'd take years to get any more than that, and there weren't any guarantees.''

"Then you should sue him for malpractice. Even if the cops tried to cover it up, you no doubt have a doctor's report concerning the new wounds, right?''

"Report, hell. I nearly died of peritonitis.''

"You've got a witness—what's her name—Amy.''

"Well . . .''

"She split on you?''

"Nobody can find her.''

Another of the men said, "That makes things more difficult.''

In spite of the sign in the window, the man smelled cigar smoke. He didn't turn around again, did not want to be the butt of any more of Gerald's jokes.

"Who was your lawyer?'' someone asked, and Gerald told him: Artie Horwitz. There were grunts and sounds of assent. The first man said, "A shark like *Horwitz* advised you to settle?''

"That's what he told me he was one time; a shark. He says to me, 'Cause I'm sleek, deadly, and I never stop moving.' I told him he was more like a jellyfish: Small brain, no spine, and I could see right through him.''

"You said that to Artie *Horwitz*? What'd he say?''

"What's he gonna say? He can drive around in the big, new car, dress in the fancy suits, and play his little word games in the courtroom all he wants. He can run on one of the treadmills at the East Bank Club until his heart explodes. I'll *still* take his ass outside and stomp it.'' There was an embarrassed silence at the next table, the man could actually feel the tension.

Relating humorous tales of police brutality was one thing; macho posturing, insulting one of their own kind, was another. These were men who knew Horwitz, who probably worked out beside him at the East Bank Club. One or all of them might have skied down Wisconsin or

A MATTER OF HONOR

Michigan slopes with the lawyer. Men such as these would find Horwitz a far more acceptable social companion than Gerald Podgourney.

But Gerald was not picking up on their silence, had seemed to have decided that it was caused by their awe at his toughness.

Which encouraged him to say, "You want to know what he does? He hires these kids fresh out of law school, and makes them go out to teach nig—*black* kids—over at Cabrini-Green how to read and write. He gets himself a big tax write-off for their billable hours, and at the end of the year he sends a press release out to the local columnists, pointing out all the good deeds his firm did over the year. I know, I used to work for him. I'd hear the new guys bitching all the time, but they'd never quit." Gerald's next words were bitter. "They had to stay on that fast track with Artie Jew-boy Horwitz."

The man was watching the TV news with interest, watched as a picture of a young man identified as Randall Montague—known by the street name of Big Gangsta Rap—appeared on the screen. The man strained to listen as the newsreader spoke of the gang leader's shotgun death. Big had tried to take control over what was left of the Gangster Apostle Nation *and* King Youngy's gang after the deaths of Youngy and Crocodile Berkley. A homicide cop was now on TV, saying that the word on the street was that Terry Glover had personally ordered the death from behind prison walls.

The man at the table heard one of the men next to him excuse himself abruptly, and he looked down at his beer, saw a flicker of the man's legs as he walked past the table. The man felt the freezing air come in when Podgourney's companion opened the door and left. He looked up briefly, saw the waiter coming toward Gerald's table.

"Another pitcher, gentlemen?"

"I don't think so." Gerald's voice was hard now, challenging and tough. "Unless one of these yuppie assholes is gonna pay for it." The man looked up at the TV screen. Gerald said, "Hey, Pierre, where's the shithouse at?"

The little boy was lying on the sidewalk, on his back, his face frozen in a look of surprise, of shock and horror. A frozen string of tears ran from either eye, down to his chin. It was so cold outside this evening that his blood had crystallized around his head, it stuck up out of the crack in the sidewalk like a full glass of red pop that had been left in the freezer too long. It was a good thing it was winter; in the summer, the killers pissed on the corpses, as further evidence of their disdain. Turner did not wish to see urine soaking such a young, hapless victim.

Ellis Turner wished that he hadn't dropped his gloves in the parking lot after viewing the body in the car. He put his mind off it; he did not want to think about that—he did not want to think about Del Greco right now. Turner was less than three blocks from his own home, and he was looking down at the still, lifeless body of a child who couldn't be a day over ten years old, the child dressed in the best clothing his parents could afford, his blood frozen in a red halo that surrounded his head.

Turner did not want to think about that right now, either. But he had to. It was his job. This was his neighborhood. This boy was of his village, of his tribe. One of Turner's neighbors' children. Turner wanted to go home. Wanted to look into a few things on his own time, without the constraints the department placed on him, the limits, without having to account for his time. But first, there was the little boy.

The little boy's shoes were missing.

Turner heard an expulsion of breath, saw the cloud of condensation before he heard Cheryl Laney's voice. "My God." Spoken almost to herself, Cheryl expressing abject disappointment, almost wonder at the sight. In the five months since the riots, Turner had taken Del Greco's place in Laney's heart. He considered her his confidante, had been her shoulder to cry on, late at night, after working hours, in bars away from police stations, as Cheryl spoke of the pain of her divorce. Her experience, although horrific for her, had been good for Turner; it made him appreciate Claudette more, made him work harder at maintaining his own marriage.

Cheryl raised her voice slightly to say, "They're getting younger and younger." Turner had to fight down the urge to respond with an angry remark. This wasn't some empirical *they,* this was a little boy without shoes on his feet, lying dead with a bullet hole in the center of the top of his skull. He told himself that Cheryl hadn't meant anything by the remark; she was not being specific, she was commenting on the age of recent homicide victims in general, as well as on the age of the offenders.

Turner was standing with his hands deep in his coat pockets. A cigarette was smoldering in the corner of his mouth. He heard Cheryl start, heard her intake of breath.

"Is that—from *him*?"

Turner looked at her; Cheryl was looking down at the blood that covered the front of Turner's coat, his pantlegs. He shook his head. "It's from—earlier," he said.

"You want me to assign somebody else to this? You shouldn't be working tonight."

Turner agreed, but for reasons different from Cheryl's. He said, "I can handle it," and looked back down at the child's body, his mind making rapid connections.

There was a razor cut part down the left side of the boy's hair, an inch above the ear. His hair had been cut very short. He was neat, not dressed in gang colors, but in older, out of fashion, but clean, clothing, more than likely handed down from an older sibling, or bought at a used clothing warehouse. A kid this age, this size, he'd grow out of whatever clothes were bought for him new before he had a chance to break them in. There was a hole in the big toe of the boy's left sock. Turner saw that the child had an ingrown large toenail. He looked away.

"The shoes were new; they were his pride and joy." Turner did not realize that he had spoken aloud. "They didn't hurt his feet, like the last pair, the pair he'd outgrown."

Cheryl said, "I mean with the city settlement, what happened with Del Greco, and now this, so close to home . . ."

Turner looked at Cheryl Laney, somewhat touched. He said, "I can handle it," again, then nodded, as if confirming his words to himself. He had cut off all other sights and sounds, was staring down at the boy with a near tunnel vision; his world consisted of himself, the child, and his boss, hovering protectively, worrying about him. Turner appreciated the concern. He did not wish to hurt her, so he wondered if he would be able to manipulate her, later, without her getting wise.

There were no reporters out here this evening, no Minicams rolling, as there had been in the parking lot, earlier, down the street from the criminal courts building. This was an all too common death, a gang shooting in a South Side neighborhood. The rich white people who watched the news and read the papers had nothing to fear or to worry about. Even the uniformed officers at the scene did not seem too surprised or affected by what had happened. Turner shut them out; they only existed to him as a means of keeping civilians from the neighborhood away from the child's body. Cheryl touched his arm. Turner absently patted her fingers, nodding. He stepped away, took the cigarette out of his mouth, put one hand on Cheryl's shoulder as he lifted his right foot, then crushed the cigarette's ember out on the bottom of his shoe. Turner rubbed the filter around in his finger, making sure he'd gotten all the hot ash, then stuck what was left in his coat pocket.

The evidence techs hadn't come yet, the scene was fairly recent, fresh. There were only a couple of sets of footprints marring the snow. Turner wondered if he would solve this crime before the men and women with their heavy black cases even finished processing the scene. If he did, he knew, he could call it a night, go home and talk to Quentin, have him go to work on his computer, do a search for his old man . . .

Cheryl was looking at him strangely. Turner saw her eyes widen.

"You know this boy. You know him, don't you, Ellis?"

"Shoes were his birthday present, I'd bet." Turner moved back over to the body carefully, stepping into his own footprints, and stood looking down at the body from less than a yard away. "That, or he got them as an early Christmas present. From a relative from out of town, say." He was aware of the blood on his coat, on his pantlegs. Knew that some of the other officers on the scene would leap to assumptions, as Cheryl had done, would think that the blood belonged to the child. They would think that Turner was taking this case personally. They would be correct in that particular assumption, though their reasoning would be skewed.

Turner had never seen this child before, though he'd seen others like him. Innocents, caught in the cross fire. And he was in fact taking it personally.

Quentin hadn't done anything wrong, either, other than being in the wrong place at the wrong time. He wondered how it got to be that way, instead of the other way around. Citizens should be safe anytime, and anywhere, in any neighborhood of the city. And when young, innocent boys were shot in the back and survived, they were supposed to consider themselves lucky.

Aloud, Turner said, "Seems like yesterday, this was the right place to be, and there wasn't any wrong time to be here."

"Pardon me?"

Turner waved his arm, made a rolling gesture with his wrist, encompassing the neighborhood.

"You could walk down this street at midnight, you'd never have a problem." He looked over at Cheryl, as if she might have the answer, then looked away, back at the body, at the footprints in the snow . . . He closed his eyes, raised his face to the dark night, puffed out his cheeks and blew out his breath.

"He was giving them up," Turner said.

"Pardon me?" Cheryl Laney repeated. Turner looked at her, lips pursed, nodding sadly.

"The shoes. We're looking for kids, at least one, probably two. Wanted the shoes for himself. At least one punk approached him, pulled his shit, and told this boy he wanted his shoes. He was taking them off when one of them shot him right in the middle of the top of his head."

"*Why?*" Cheryl's voice was soft but urgent, as if she were consulting a psychic she was afraid to bring out of his trance.

"To prove how tough he was to the gang elders. Maybe he was impatient, and the boy wasn't moving fast enough. Maybe he wanted to untie them first, didn't want to step on the back of them and scuff them, in case he somehow got them back. Or maybe they just felt like killing him. I don't know anymore."

"No one does, Ellis." There was concern in her tone, not a warning exactly, but enough vague distress within it to set off Turner's highly developed emotional alarm system.

Turner walked quickly away from the body, looking down at the ground, walking on the street, close to the curb, following the footprints that were in the small patch of snow that covered the grass between the curb and the sidewalk. The dead child was a snow angel, crying death tears. Turner walked toward the crime scene tape, marked police vehicles that had their engines running and their heaters on high, Mars lights flicking off buildings, still looking down, stepping past the laughing, joking uniformed officers, Turner ignoring them as he walked toward the gawking crowd that stood just outside the tape.

He abruptly jerked his head up and glared intensely at the crowd, saw the one boy jump, then try to catch himself, trying to recover the pretense that he was nothing more than an interested observer who was wondering what was happening. Ellis glared at him, saw the boy look away, then back, then quickly away again.

The boy couldn't have been more than eleven or twelve years old. Turner did not look down at his shoes, but continued to glare into the boy's face, silently challenging him. The boy turned and began to run, and Turner took off after him, ignoring the shouts, hollers, and surprised cries of the people in the crowd, of the other officers, of Cheryl Laney.

Please God, Turner thought, let him run into a house, let him do that while I'm in pursuit.

Which was exactly what happened, which meant that the subsequent apprehension was legal.

Or so Turner hoped. You never knew how an assistant state's attorney would act, what was acceptable, what wasn't. Particularly three months away from citywide elections. In any event, apprehending a fleeing suspect did not automatically give Turner the right to search his home. Which is what he'd have to do; the gun wasn't on the kid.

Turner stood over the boy in the living room, holding his finger toward him as a warning for him to keep quiet, to sit still on the couch with his mouth shut. The mother was nearly insane with concern, worried about her child, but—thank God—somewhat respectful of the law. The situation could become problematic if she had just told Turner to get out of her house.

"I didn't do nothin'." The kid was petulant and whiny, no longer afraid now that he was safe inside his mother's apartment. Maybe he had burned off his fear in the short, fast run home. Turner raised his finger higher, gave the child a stare that shut him up. He was breathing heavy himself, trying to catch his breath. Meat was frying somewhere. There was a layer of smoke in the air. The apartment was freezing cold, the paint on the walls peeling, but the room was spotlessly clean. Turner could see that the end table in front of the boy had been recently polished; the couch was covered with a plastic fabric protector.

"Ma'am," Turner said, "we've got us a problem here."

"What problem! What are you talking about!" Turner was concerned; he did not know where the weapon was, though he had patted the boy down before sitting him down on the couch. He did not want to look away from the child, but he wanted to get the mother's respect, he needed her in his corner. He might be able to get her there more quickly if he was able to look her in the face while he spoke to her.

But he couldn't bring himself to do that, not with her son glaring at him, wishing Turner dead.

So he said, "You hear the gunshots outside a little while ago? See all the police cars?"

"What'd he do now?" The woman ran to her son, stood close beside him, looking down at him, torn between wanting to help him and wanting to punish him. Turner was relieved; he could see them both now, and the boy wouldn't be able to make any sudden moves that Turner wouldn't be able to notice. The woman was wearing her winter coat in the house; their heat had no doubt been shut off. The ghetto was moving closer and closer to Turner and his family, would sooner or later engulf them.

There was a sudden pounding at the door; Turner had no idea how it had wound up closed and locked.

"I don't want them in my house, tracking mud in!"

Did she think they were there to accuse her son of vandalism? Turner, still unsure of his legal status, said, "There's a woman there, white woman, mid-thirties maybe, short hair, got a dark blue coat on. Would you let her in, please?"

"Only her?"

The boy said, "You got a warrant? Mama, they ain't got no warrant, you ain't gots to let them in."

"I'm telling you, son, shut up."

"I ain't your son." The boy spoke these words with emotion, glaring at Turner.

"Lady . . ."

"Shut *up,* Donell!" The boy turned his glare on his mother, and Turner closed in a little bit as the woman went to answer the door. He could hear her, upset because he and Donell had tracked wet footprints into her house. He vaguely remembered seeing a plastic runner on the carpet next to the door, with several pairs of women's shoes lined up on them, in a row.

No gym shoes, though.

"You can make this real easy for yourself, Donell."

"I'm a juvie." The arrogance in the boy's tone caused Turner to take a deep breath. He heard the boy's mother talking loudly, heard Cheryl ordering the other officers to stay outside, she and Turner had the situation under control. Cheryl would know as well as Turner that they were on slippery legal ground. They could drag the kid out of here . . . but if he kept his mouth shut, then what? Cheryl would know what to say to calm the woman down. Turner heard her speaking softly, comfortingly, heard the woman—the mother—begin to cry as she tried to speak. Heard Cheryl's voice comforting her, softly, gently.

Turner never took his eyes off the boy, who was now sitting on his spine on the couch, looking up at the ceiling as if the events that were occurring around him had no connection to himself. Turner knew that appealing to the boy's sense of family would do no good. He was not sure if anything he said or did to the boy *would* do any good.

So he said, "Where's the gun, and where're the shoes." The boy glanced at him briefly with reptilian eyes, grunted, then looked back up at the ceiling, as Cheryl explained things to the mother, who cried out loudly at the news. Turner decided to jump while emotion was still running strongly, before the woman had the sense to calm herself down and call a lawyer.

"Ma'am, I'd like permission to search Donell's room."

"He wouldn't kill anyone! He wouldn't!" The woman pulled away from Cheryl Laney, her face streaked with tears, a woman in her mid-twenties, in way over her head. "He's out of control, there ain't nothing I can do to make him listen anymore!" Cheryl was now close to the child, watching him, and Ellis turned his gaze from the boy and looked hard at the young mother, at a devastated woman who had been pregnant in her mid-teens, and who was now all alone, watching as the street geared up its juices to digest her only son.

"May I search his room, ma'am?" Ellis Turner said, and the woman turned her gaze toward her son and back to Turner, two or three times. The woman bit her lip, rubbing her hands together. She looked to Cheryl Laney for guidance, but Cheryl knew better than to give it outright. Cheryl put her arm on the woman's shoulder, rubbed it, her compassion for the woman obvious on her face, in the gentleness of her touch . . .

Turner hid his relief as the woman lowered her head, and nodded.

CHAPTER

50

The man moved into an open spot down at the end of the bar, right below the television set; he had to crane his neck to see the screen. He watched the local news coverage—taped footage of a bloody downtown sidewalk—heard a newsreader's offscreen voice tell him that a seventeen-year-old student from Jones Commercial High School had been shot down in broad daylight, killed right there in the South Loop, not four blocks away from December's Mother. The man sat up, winced, got himself under control, then looked up at the TV again. Now they were running a tape of a high-ranking police official, the man decked out in full uniform, looking like the dictator of a small South American nation. The officer was standing in front of a podium. He looked directly into the cameras and said that it was a planned shooting, a continuation of an argument that had begun in the high school, several hours earlier. He told the citizens of Chicago to remain calm. He emphasized the fact that this was not a random shooting; it was still safe for suburban Christmas shoppers to come downtown.

The man heard the door to the men's room open, looked over his shoulder, and was face-to-face with Gerald Podgourney.

"Why don't you let me buy you a beer, Gerald?" Gerald looked at him, puzzled. He looked back over at the table where he'd been sitting, and the man shifted his gaze, saw that the table was now empty.

"How you know my name?"

"I saw you on the news."

Gerald glanced up at the TV. "They showed me again? Damn. I only set the VCR for four, six, and ten."

"Beer?"

"Might as well." Gerald stood next to him, leaning on the bar. The bartender did not seem pleased to see that Gerald was still in the place. On the screen above them, the announcer was saying that the fourth deliberate burning of the month had occurred that afternoon, at the height of the rush hour. This time, the victim was a middle-aged, suburban male. His coat had been destroyed, and he'd received first- and second-degree burns on his neck, as well as on the back of his head.

"Can you believe this?" Gerald said, shaking his head. "What's the world coming to?" He lowered his voice so only the man could hear him. "One shine walks up behind a white man, squirts lighter fluid on his back, another one comes by in the opposite direction, lighting a cigarette, and flicks the match at you, sets you on fire. Some sport, huh?" Gerald grunted as the bartender put his beer down in front of him. "Supposed to make the white man live in terror. I hear Christmas shopping is down something like forty percent from last year. The white man figures that every jig with a cigarette in his mouth is his potential assassin."

The man had just lighted a cigarette, himself. He shook out the match, looked at the cigarette, and said, "Well, they say it's bad for your health."

Gerald grinned at him. "Makes your hair fall out?"

"They're not connected."

"And everyone in this bar gets mad 'cause I said the word 'cunt.' People like this, they don't live in the real world. I was walking up the street, not a block away, they got this thing called a Juice Bar. They use a machine, squeezes all the good shit out of carrots and celery, you're supposed to drink it."

The man nodded. "It costs more than Jack Daniel's."

"They also got what they call 'smoothies.' Same principle, I guess, but only with fruits." Gerald paused a second, then said, "You're not a fruit, are you pally? Not buying me a beer because you think you're gonna get lucky tonight?"

"I'm not a lucky man."

"No?" Gerald said it as would a man who didn't give a shit either way. He said, "You come here a lot? I'm looking for a guy, maybe you know him." The man stiffened slightly, then caught himself. Gerald hadn't seemed to notice.

"He owe you money?"

Gerald stood still, tilted his head.

"What made you say that?"

The man shrugged, looked into the mirror behind the bar. "I was just wondering. Neither one of us seems to be at home in a joint like this."

"Yeah, you're bald and old, and I ain't what you could call politically correct."

"What happened to your friends?"

"Never saw them before in my life; they recognized me from TV as soon as I walked in the door."

"Wanted to be with a celebrity."

Gerald drained his beer, put the glass on the bar. "Wanted me to invest my settlement with them, is what they wanted. They said my man comes in here almost every time the Bulls are on."

The bartender had worked her way to them, had overheard.

"Guy you're looking for hasn't been in in a few days. You might want to check Kasey's, it's a block south, on this same street. In the Donohue building. You get to Polk Street, you've gone a block too far."

Gerald grinned at her. "I didn't tell you his name. You trying to tell me something?"

The young woman looked him in the eye. "I heard you talking to the other guys." She paused for effect, then said, "And yeah, now that you mention it, we like to try and maintain a certain level of clientele."

The man rolled his hat down on his head, almost covering his eyes. He rolled it past his ears, stood, and put on his coat.

Gerald said, "Let me buy you one before you go; I don't like owing people."

"You don't owe me anything." The man watched the bartender walk away, then turned, moved in close to Gerald. When he spoke now, his voice was low and hard.

"You tired of cleaning out apartments? Leaving circulars outside of doors and waiting to see if they get picked up, going in if they don't? What do you get for a TV set, a stereo? Hundred dollars? Looking at ten years in the pen over small-time shit like that." Gerald was staring at him, open-mouthed. "Yeah, I know about that. And the pizza delivery gig, setting scores up that way. And pimping the homeless. Gerald, I know *all* about you." The man paused, watching the shock and fear in Gerald's expression turn quickly to suspicion.

"I want you to do a job for me," the man said, and Gerald held up both his hands, palms out.

"Whoa, slow down, big boy. I came in here looking for a friend of mine, and to have a few drinks, that's all. I'm celebrating, not job hunting."

"You got a hundred-thousand-dollar settlement. Horwitz would have taken a third of that, another ten off the top for his expenses. Doesn't leave you with much of a retirement nest egg."

Gerald stiffened, thought about what the man had said, then relaxed. "You pay attention. So you're offering me something more, is that right?" Gerald was eyeing him up and down now. This close, the man could see that the sleeves of Gerald's sweatshirt were very tight at the elbows, the fabric distorted, pushed out. The man looked up, inclined his head, and nodded.

Gerald said, "Look, you think I'm stupid? Go find a coffee shop, eat a doughnut, pull Rodney King out of his car and kick his ass, whatever it is you coppers do when you're not hanging around in gin mills, trying to entrap innocent citizens."

The man smiled. "You think I'm a cop?"

"Let me tell you what I think: I think you're bald, and got a limp, which don't mean you ain't a cop. I think I beat the city out of a hundred grand today. I think the city ain't pleased about that. I think the cops who put this scar on my belly would just *love* to see me get pinched. They'd like it so much, they might even go to a lot of trouble to set it up."

Gerald pushed off the bar as the Bulls took the court for the second half of the game. "You asked me what I think? I think it's time for me to go home."

"You don't even want to know the name of the guy I want you to take care of?"

"All right," Gerald said, as if humoring the man. He was smiling when he said, "Who might that be?"

"Arthur L. Horwitz." The man saw Gerald's smile waver, watched him catch himself and get it back. "And there'll be a lot more in it for you than you got from the city today."

Gerald walked over to the table, plucked his jacket off the stool. The man turned forward, looked at the mirror again, watching Gerald in the glass. He saw Gerald put on his coat. Saw Gerald shoot a withering glare at two of the men he'd been sitting with earlier, men who were now sitting at the bar. The man saw them look away from Gerald. When he saw Gerald begin to walk back toward him, the man averted his gaze, and watched himself in the mirror.

"You a guinea?" Gerald asked. The man looked at him in the mirror, with no expression on his face. "You like to swim?" Gerald said to him, switching gears in the happy bar, with the sound of laughter around them, Michael Jordan above their heads, passing the ball to Scottie Pippen, and men and women all around them gushed as Pippen jammed it through the hoop.

A wino had wandered into the bar. The bartender was looking at him with distaste. He came to the end of the bar, stood in front of Podgourney, looked from him to the older man. They were the only two men in the bar who didn't seem to belong there.

He said, "You got a dollar?"

Podgourney didn't even bother to look at him when he said, "Go get it from O. J. Simpson, motherfucker."

A MATTER OF HONOR

The bartender ordered the bum to leave, and he shambled away from them. Gerald had never stopped staring at Del Greco's face.

He said, "I asked you, do you like to swim?"

"When it's hot out." The man felt the cold as the door was opened, as the wino exited.

"You know where the Swissotel is?"

The man hesitated. " . . . East Wacker?"

"The big, tall, glass building. The last one on the block. We're going to walk outside together, partner, and you're going to get into a cab. This is a one-way street. I'm gonna wait a few minutes, and if I see another vehicle following your cab—particularly a Chevy or a Plymouth—I'm bailing out, and it's been nice talking to you. If I don't, I'll meet you in the lobby of the Swissotel. You go there and wait for me. If I'm not there in fifteen minutes, you can find yourself another boy."

"We going swimming?"

"What's your name?"

"Del Greco," the bald man said, holding out his hand. Gerald looked down at it, nodding, thinking. Del Greco could see it on his face: the man had never heard the name before. He had confidence in Gerald's ignorance, but hadn't counted on getting this lucky. Gerald finally took the offered hand, and squeezed, looking into Del Greco's eyes.

"Angelo Del Greco," the man said, squeezing back.

CHAPTER

51

Turner called home from the car, to warn his family of his appearance. He wanted to go home and change his clothes before going to the station to interrogate Donell. Claudette listened silently, then told him she'd get the kids out of the living room, she didn't want them to see their father covered in blood.

"It's white man's blood," Turner said, wincing and shaking his head before the words were even out of his mouth. What had made him say something like that? What was he trying to prove?

There was a hurt pause, and then Claudette informed him that the sight of *any* blood would disturb Anne and Quentin.

There had been some changes made in the household over the course of the last several months. A ramp had been installed, from the sidewalk to the front door, to accommodate Quentin's wheelchair. The downstairs bathroom had been enlarged, and long metal bars had been installed beside the toilet and the bathtub. The Turners had taken Claudette's downstairs study and turned it into Quentin's bedroom. They'd had to enlarge the doorframe.

Other changes were less overt, but with more powerful, lasting effects.

The TV was never turned on during school nights, for a couple of reasons. Quentin had been "lucky" enough to have been accepted for home study for the duration of his recovery, with the bill being picked up by the school system. Claudette would not allow him to fall into the habit of watching TV, did not want him lacking discipline or getting lazy. And when the TV *was* turned on, there were definite restrictions on what could and couldn't be watched. There were no dramas taped for later viewing in the Turner household, unless they involved African-Americans in a positive, constructive manner. No vapid sitcoms were watched, with black or white stars. The cable box had been returned. The children were never allowed to watch the news. The stereos had been taken out of both the children's rooms; Quentin's Walkman had been appropriated. He'd get it back when he turned eighteen. He had his exercise, his recovery to worry about. And his computer took the place of the television set.

Claudette ran the family with a firm hand, these days.

"Hi," Ellis said, fake-shivering as he entered the house, rubbing his hands together and motioning for Claudette to follow him into the kitchen.

"Where are your gloves?"

Turner removed his overcoat and suit jacket, draped them carefully over a chair, bloody-side out. He could hear voices from a black talk radio station, two men shouting at each other over twin speakers, coming from the kitchen radio. Claudette turned her lips down at the sight of her husband's bloody clothing, then looked up at him, puzzled and concerned.

"Oh, Ellis, I heard about Marshall on the radio . . ."

Ellis waited, but she didn't say more. He turned the radio down, and when he spoke it was in a low, quiet, conspiratorial tone. He told Claudette what he suspected, and what he planned to do.

Ellis had to swallow hard when Claudette asked him how she could help. At last, he was able to thank her.

"There's nothing you can do right now. I've got to get out of these clothes, then I've got a—suspect—I've got to interrogate."

"This suspect involved with the shooting down the block?"

Ellis kicked off his shoes, was looking down at them as he nodded.

"My God, Ellis, my dear God in heaven, when is it going to end?"

"I don't know," he said.

Claudette walked over to him, pulled him close to her, and hugged him tightly. Ellis held his hands out for a moment, his face grim and pained, wanting to warn her about the blood Claudette didn't seem to care about. He hugged his wife, held her, rubbed her back, feeling her sobs, but not hearing them; she would not want to upset the children.

At last she pulled away, as if embarrassed by her breakdown. Claudette wiped at the tears on her face, shaking her head at their inconvenience. She moved quickly to the chair, picked up Ellis's coat and jacket. "Get the rest of them off, I'll take it all right down to the basement, so the kids won't see it. Drop everything off at the cleaner's on my way to work. I'll wait for you upstairs." She was speaking too quickly for Turner's liking.

"Claudette?" She stopped at the doorway, stiffened, then slowly turned and looked back at him. "I said I don't know when it's going to stop. It's probably even going to get worse. That doesn't mean we have to accept it. It doesn't mean we can stop fighting it every single goddamn day of our lives."

"I do it my way, and you do it yours."

"I don't do it for the Man."

She looked at him as if she didn't know what he was talking about. Perhaps she didn't. Perhaps Turner was hanging on too hard to angry words that should have long ago been forgotten.

His voice was shaking when he said, "I love you."

"I love you back," Claudette said. She bit her lower lip, and nodded several times, then left him standing in the kitchen, listening to muted voices coming from stereo speakers turned down low. Ellis walked over to the radio and turned it off.

Turner knocked on Quentin's door before entering. Quentin looked at him from his position on the floor, the boy's arms crossed over his chest, doing sit-ups, the tight, hard abdominal muscles gleaming with sweat, in the glow of the computer that was on the metal desk.

"I write down a few names, can you look them up for me in the papers?"

"For the past ten years, in the *Tribune*." Quentin stopped doing sit-ups, was glaring with wide eyes at his father's trousers. "What happened! Is that yours!"

"No, no, don't worry, it's somebody else's." Turner spoke hurriedly, wanting to reassure his son without telling him where the blood had come from. Maybe he wouldn't find out. "I've got to go back to work for a little while, but I'm going to be taking a couple of days off. I think." Turner walked over to the desk, grabbed a pen and Quentin's legal pad, and wrote out the names DEL GRECO, ANGELO AND MARSHALL—CUNNINGHAM, RITA AND CHARLES.

"Can't you find out about them from work?"

Ellis paused before saying, "I don't want to use their equipment right now. It might come back to haunt me. Though I might run Angelo's and Charles's names on the MDT in the unit, if their addresses aren't in the papers."

"You want their addresses?"

"Can you get them?"

"Get them? I can get you a copy of their driver's licenses, if you want it."

"No, no, don't do that." Ellis rubbed his jaw with his hand, thinking. "Just get what was in the papers, and the addresses, if you can."

"When will you be back?"

Ellis thought about the child killer who was now down at the station, more than likely asleep by now, or asking for his phone calls. He did not want to tell Quentin about that, either.

"Couple hours. Can you get that for me in that time?"

Quentin grunted. "Go change your clothes. I'll have it before you get back downstairs."

Ellis apologized to Claudette before he left the house, and she looked at him oddly as he did so, then she swallowed, and nodded her acceptance, no doubt having figured out that it was a blanket apology, for everything that had ever happened in the history of the world. Turner took a step toward her; Claudette moved toward him. He nodded; she gave him a sad smile.

"We'll never stop fighting," Claudette said, and Ellis nodded in agreement, before taking her into her arms.

"Never."

CHAPTER

52

"**I** ain't got to tell you shit."

"No, you don't, that's true." Turner sat on a molded plastic chair on one side of a small table that was bolted to the floor, looking over at the handcuffed murder suspect, eleven-year-old Donell. The two of them were awaiting the arrival of one of the assistant state's attorneys who specialized in juvenile cases. The ASAs who specialized in the prosecution of youth had been particularly busy these days.

Due to the change in the laws after Del Greco's shooting, boys like Donell could now be prosecuted and detained until their twenty-first birthdays. Before the law had been changed, the state could only hold them in a secure facility for sixty days.

Still, Donell's case would not be an automatic transfer to adult court, Donell was still a few years too young for that. But upon conviction he would be sent to one of the state's six juvenile detention centers, more than likely, due to the heinous nature of his crime, to the single maximum-security juvenile prison in the state, down in Joliet. While awaiting trial and after incarceration, the boy theoretically would be tutored. Turner knew that his tutoring would take more than one form. At eighteen, Donell would be transferred to one of the state's adult prisons; they would send him there at seventeen, if he posed a problem in the juvie jail. The three or four years he would languish there would more than likely be spent lifting weights in the yard.

Donell would be loosed upon society at twenty-one.

"I tole you, man, I want my lawyer."

"I'm not questioning you, Donell," Turner said. Cheryl Laney opened the door, looked inside, saw Turner's face, then hurriedly stepped out again, pulling the door shut behind her. Turner thought Cheryl's concern toward him could be used to his advantage. He knew a way to get a couple of days off, with pay.

Turner looked back at Donell, and said, "Nothing you say to me in this room can be used against you in court. Look, I've got you cold. I found the murder weapon in your bedroom, along with the bloody gym shoes. You're going down, Donell; we got you."

There was no more expression on Donell's face than there was on a ventriloquist's dummy's. Turner had the feeling that he could turn off the lights and leave, and the child would simply close his eyes; everything he needed was within him, along with all that he loved in the world.

Still, he had to try.

He leaned forward, looked Donell in the eye, and said, "If I can help you out, Donell, I will. But you'll have to meet me at least halfway. If I can get you special treatment, say, private psychiatric counseling, a guy who comes in to see you three times a week, rather than the guy who comes once a week for five hours, to counsel fifty kids, would you take it?"

"Ain't nothin' wrong with me. I'm going to jail 'cause I'm young and black."

"You're going to jail because the boy you *killed* was young and black."

"I ain't did shit."

Turner lit a cigarette and took a deep drag. He left the pack on the table.

"This is the only place I'm allowed to smoke anymore, in an interrogation room." Donell was eyeing Turner's cigarettes, but he would not ask for one. Nor would Turner make the offer.

"Let me ask you a question: Pretend that chair you're in is a time machine, and you can go back a few hours, to right before the murder. Is there anything you'd do differently?"

Donell looked up at Turner with a thoughtful expression on his face. He looked at the wall, at the ceiling, silently mouthing words, repeating the question to himself. He looked at Ellis just as Turner was putting out his cigarette.

"I'da dumped the gun and cleaned the shoes."

"I'll see you later, Donell." Turner left the room.

Cheryl was on the phone, hearing ghastly news. She looked up at Turner as he walked out of the interrogation room, watched him lean his back against the door, close his eyes, and just stand there for a moment. She looked back down at her desk, continued scribbling notes concerning an atrocity, not wanting Turner to see her watching him.

He was in trouble, and he didn't even know it, he wouldn't seek her help, nor would he accept it were it offered. Laney had seen this before; it was called burnout, and denial.

There was a high rate of burnout among African-American detectives, and an even higher rate among women. Laney's personal opinion was that the smarter you were, the more likely it was to get hold of you. Attempting to hide your stress and pretend that the job wasn't adversely affecting you would do it, too, every time.

Cheryl knew all about stress; the job had cost her her marriage.

Daniel had told her that he did not believe that Cheryl should have been promoted to sergeant before him, thought that it was a setup, even though he knew how well she'd tested on the sergeant's exam, the son of a bitch. Cheryl had divorced him, and she could live with it; it wasn't the first time a man had believed that she wasn't worthy of her job.

When Cheryl Laney had shown up at her first roll call, she'd been the only woman in the room. The sergeant had stood at his lectern, straight-faced, delivering his orders in a normal voice, while the men in the room tried not to snicker, and failed.

The front of the lectern had been nearly covered over with taped-on Tampons, which some wit had covered with ketchup. Welcome to the district, Officer Laney. The only veteran officer who would ride with her was a drunk who had thought she was a whore, and had tried to prove it. His wife had written dozens of letters to the brass, demanding that "that bitch" be transferred out of her husband's car, as if Cheryl had been waiting her entire life to seduce an overweight, ugly, middle-aged, drunken, Polish loser from Hegewisch. The desk sergeant in Cheryl's district had refused to take the woman's calls. The woman had then begun calling Cheryl at home, berating her, making accusations, calling her a lesbian and demanding that Cheryl leave her husband alone. Cheryl could not change her number, it had cost a fortune back then, and besides, the department would have to have it, and her partner would definitely need it. Cheryl would listen to the young women in the department today, the rookies. Who had their own locker room, their own showers, their own space. Who had laws to protect them, lawyers lined up to file sexual harassment charges against the city should one of them feel slighted, and she would keep her mouth shut, would not say a word about the way things used to be. The one good thing about what she'd been through was the fact that it had been excellent preparation for her acceptance of the most ghastly news, whether in person or discussed over the in-house departmental phones.

Cheryl knew about pressure, knew what it could do to you.

She was seeing what it was doing to Ellis Turner right now.

Turner, who was walking slowly toward her desk. Who plopped down in the extra chair as if he weighed twice as much as he did. Cheryl said into the phone, "FBI called in?" listened, then said, "I'll send somebody right over to keep them honest. See if we can keep the press off it for as long as possible." She listened, said, "Yes, sir," hung up the phone, and looked over at Ellis. She had already decided she would not give him this case.

Had he stopped working out? He seemed to be gaining weight lately. There were dark circles under his eyes. His dress was nowhere near as meticulous as it had been earlier that day, it looked as if he'd grabbed whatever had been in his closet.

"Joint case with the FBI, and you want a wall of silence with the media? Good luck. What have we got that's got to be kept away from them?"

"You're not waiting for the state's attorney?"

"They approved charges. What's left? Taking Donell to JDC? A uniform can do that, drop him off with the paperwork." Cheryl shuffled the papers around on her desk, and Turner stopped her.

"Don't be looking for an easy one for me. Don't do me like that. What was the call about? What's up with the FBI? How you going to keep things quiet with *those* media whores involved?"

She gave him what she hoped he would take to be a sardonic look. "There *are* no easy homicides, Ellis." Turner waited a moment, then nodded his head.

"I was in the house, asked Donell's mom if I could use the bathroom? I wanted to see what was in the medicine cabinet, basically. The sink and the tub were filled with frozen water, the toilet water had a layer of ice over it, but it broke up when I flushed it. The woman and the boy slept under about a dozen blankets apiece, but the house was *clean*, you could eat off the floors." Ellis paused, thinking back. He said, "I asked the boy, Donell, what he would do differently if he had to do it all over again. You know what he said?"

"Hide the gun and the shoes better?"

"Close enough. He did it all alone. You believe that? Eleven years old. I thought for sure it'd be two. One to pull the trigger, the other to give him the guts to do it."

"Ellis . . ."

Hadn't he realized that he'd been holding his head in his hands? He jerked his head up and looked at Cheryl, as if surprised to hear her voice.

"What's next up? I want that call."

Cheryl hesitated, looking around the near-empty room. All right, he wanted it? Let's see how badly. Let's push the envelope. She said, "There's a call in the Wentworth District, a couple of miles from the last one. Two verified dead, one uncertain, one child missing. Report is that a fetus was cut out of a woman's womb . . ."

"Was she one of the dead, at least?"

"We don't know yet, it just happened." Cheryl looked down at her handwritten notes, trying to decipher her own handwriting. "White woman, mixed-race kids. Five- and four-year-old females dead; two-and-a-half-year-old male toddler missing."

"They cut it out of her *womb*?"

"Sergeant Laney?" The woman had walked up on them quickly, dressed in a long, black cape, wearing sneakers. She'd come up behind Ellis, and when she'd spoken, he'd leaped to his feet. He sat down slowly as the woman looked at him oddly and softly excused herself, shooting a worried glance at Cheryl.

Turner had his head in his hands again. The three other officers in the room were watching it all, waiting to see how Cheryl responded. The woman said, "I'm Loretta Hutchins, from the state's attorney's office."

Cheryl nodded toward the door and said, "Kid's in there."

"Restrained?"

"Ellis?" Turner looked up quickly, wildly.

"Hunh?"

Hutchins said, "The murder suspect. He restrained?"

"Would you excuse us for a minute, Ms. Hutchins?" Cheryl said, and waited as the young woman gave them a look, opened her mouth, closed it, then turned and toted her briefcase into the bathroom. Cheryl turned to Ellis and softly said, "You need to take some time off, Ellis, starting right this minute."

He looked up at her as if they'd never been interrupted.

"They cut the fetus out of her womb."

"That's right. And it's not the first time it's happened, and it won't be the last. Now, do you want to take comp time, vacation, or administrative leave? I'll leave that in your hands." She did not belabor the fourth option, which was totally out of his hands: She could suspend him, and she would do so in a second if he chose to argue.

Turner blew out his breath, looking at her, thinking. He said, "Let's do comp time; that way, there's no written record. I'll get Donell down to JDC, first, finish this deal up." Turner nodded at her gratefully, and Cheryl, expecting an argument, was surprised. He said, "I could do with a couple days off."

In the car two hours later, Donell wanted to know what had taken so long. He asked Turner when he was going to get something to eat. He asked Turner what was in the large manila folder on the front seat. He demanded to know if what was in the folder had anything to do with him and the phony case the white police state was trying to hang on him.

Ellis did not bother to answer any of Donell's questions.

CHAPTER

53

"We're going to the penthouse," Gerald said to Del Greco, as they rose quickly in a hotel elevator that had smoked mirrored walls. "I used to work out here, had all the conventioneers' daughters and wives checking me out from the swimming pool while I pumped iron. Now I put the fucking chlorine in the pool for them, and they're pretty tough about the rules; no fucking around with the big shots' families." The elevator was fast. Rather than pushing a floor button, Gerald had used a special key to start it moving. "Elevator won't go up to the gym once it's closed down for the night."

"But we can get in."

"I work there. I'm a personal trainer now." The self-pity dripped from every word. Del Greco wondered who Gerald had blackmailed to score the job.

"So we'll be alone?"

"We're not, I'm out of here. Maybe do it another time."

The elevator stopped, and Del Greco stepped out while Gerald removed his key, then followed. They were in a long, dark room. Del Greco could make out a sharp curve in the hallway, just a few yards away from where he stood. He had no idea where it led.

"Hang on a minute." Gerald walked behind the counter, flipped some switches, and fluorescent lights began to flicker overhead. He fumbled with several buttons on the wall, and country and western music filled the room. Gerald turned it up. He said, "We're forty-two floors above Lake Michigan. Come on, you can gawk at the view in the locker room."

Del Greco did not gawk. He got out of his clothes while Gerald stood watching him, holding his hand out for each piece of clothing as it was removed. Gerald felt through the pockets, took out the wallet, checked the driver's license. Flipped through the wallet quickly, found no pictures, nothing of consequence. He did a quick count of the hundred-dollar bills he found in Del Greco's pants pocket, then put the rubber band back on, acting unimpressed. He hung Del Greco's clothing in an open locker.

When Del Greco was naked, Gerald handed him a thick white towel. "Here, put this on if you're shy." Del Greco wrapped the towel around his waist as Gerald began to undress. Gerald turned his back on Del Greco, blocking his view as he worked the combination on his locker. "Go on out into the pool area, settle down in the water, it's heated." But Del Greco hesitated, watching Gerald closely.

He'd been right, earlier, about Gerald's elbows. The man had heavy leather elbow pads attached to each arm. The pads were studded, as were the kneepads worn on both legs. Legal weapons that could withstand a pinch. Gerald stripped the weapons off as if they were a normal part of his wardrobe, then tossed them inside his locker, as if Del Greco hadn't seen them. Del Greco looked at Gerald's boots, saw that, as he'd suspected, they were steel-toed. Not Doc Martens, but rather steelworkers' boots, a working man's boot that, to a police officer's quick glance, would not be obvious weapons of assault. With the knee and elbow guards, the boots, Gerald would be able to stand up to a frisk without worrying about getting pinched. Del Greco was not surprised to see that Gerald had a pepper spray keychain.

All of which told Del Greco that Gerald wasn't anywhere near as fearless as he'd spent the evening pretending to be.

Del Greco quickly inspected Gerald's naked body. There didn't seem to be much collateral damage due to the beating, his hospitalization. Gerald had muscle tone, he was tight, but his size was gone. He seemed to have lost bulk, rather than strength. The scar across Gerald's abdomen made it seem as if parts of two different men had been stitched together, creating Gerald. The scar was white and brutal.

Gerald turned to face Del Greco and said, "You worried about your money, or did you lie to me in the bar? You're not a queer, are you?" Gerald turned sideways, giving Del Greco his profile, was now slipping into a pair of Speedo swimming trunks. "Go on, I'm flush. Your money's safe." The hillbilly music was getting on Del Greco's nerves. He suspected it would be even louder in the pool, sound waves bouncing off water. "Through that door, and up the stairs, the lights are on, go ahead."

The view was, indeed, breathtaking. Del Greco looked at it from the swimming pool room as he stood against one glass wall, the view to east and south, Del Greco seeing the frozen lake, the lighthouse beacon, the vast park with the kids still out there playing hockey in the circular rink, the headlights from the cars heading north on Lake Shore Drive . . .

"Jump in, what're you waiting for?"

"We can't talk in the lounge chairs?"

"You want to talk to me, you got to get in the water."

"Naked?"

"As the day you were born."

Del Greco did not hop in. He walked down to the shallow end, carefully made his way down the stairs, putting both feet on each step before moving one gingerly down to the next. When his knees hit water, he tossed the towel behind him.

"It only goes to four feet, it's not like you have to worry about drowning."

"No one else comes in here at night?"

"We got free use, employees. For working out. But nobody but me ever comes here at night." Gerald spoke while he watched Del Greco walking toward him, trudging slowly through the water. He had already jumped in, was standing with his back to the tiled wall, elbows resting on the pool's ledge, closely watching Del Greco's progress with a half smirk on his face.

"Sometimes we get celebrities staying here, Tom Selleck, Robert Conrad, they want to bring broads down here, or work out with their own personal trainers after hours, once everybody else is gone and they won't be bothered by autograph hounds."

Del Greco reached him, stopped, self-conscious now, vulnerable. The water surrounding him was warm. He stood in it up to his navel, watched Gerald take a deep breath and lower himself down. Del Greco stood still, unmoving, as Gerald swam around him, touching Del Greco's legs, looking up from beneath Del Greco's scrotum. Gerald's head broke the surface. He let out his breath, threw back his head, used both hands to wipe the water out of his eyes.

He said, "Where'd you get the scars?"

"Those are from shanks. I was in St. Charles when I was a kid."

"You were? I thought Charlietown was newer than that."

"I'm not as old as you think."

"And if there's a wire up your ass, it's hidden pretty good. It won't pick up much through the water."

"You're paranoid, Gerald."

"I get the feeling someone's watching me. You knew about the apartments, the circulars; you were watching me."

"It proves I'm not a cop."

"How?"

"You took three apartments down this month. Never a place with a doorman. You wait until someone's walking in, then you hurry after them with your keys in your hand and your hat pulled down, smiling thanks. You're either taking your circulars in, or checking up to see who hadn't picked them up. I can even tell you what you've scored, and where you laid it off. If I was a cop, you'd be under arrest by now, wouldn't you?"

"You been watching so you can do me a favor; make me rich."

"I was right. You're paranoid."

"Let me tell you something, Angelo, I'm always cautious around people who've lied to me."

Del Greco didn't say anything, just stood there, the water calm around him, warm and inviting. He could barely hear the music in here, Gerald must have just had it turned on in the locker room, the weight room, and the lobby, to cover what was said in those rooms. The water would do the trick in here.

Gerald said, "You got red Magic Marker lines running up your inner thighs, on your ass, pointing under your balls." Gerald fingercombed his hair back, leaned on the pool's ledge again, smiling now, having a secret. "You get that from alo-whatever?"

"I've got cancer."

"Guy in the bar pointed that out to me. Said he could smell the chemo; I didn't believe him."

"It has a scent."

"So why'd you lie?"

"It's not the sort of thing you discuss with strangers."

"You got any other secrets?" Gerald lowered his eyelids, relaxed his face. After a time, he said, "Since the operation, that beer runs right through me." Del Greco stepped back.

"That's it," he said, walking back toward the stairs. He heard the sound of water breaking as Gerald pushed himself out of the pool, heard Gerald's soft chuckle.

"Sit down on the top step, that way your booty'll still be in the water."

"I can't sit on concrete." Del Greco mounted the steps, grabbed the towel, and wrapped it around his waist. "You don't want to think that you're the only man I could get for the job."

"But I was first choice. I wonder why that is."

Del Greco approached slowly, and Gerald stood his ground. He saw Gerald avert his gaze, appraising Del Greco's body.

"You stay in pretty good shape, for an old guy with cancer."

"Good-bye, Gerald," Del Greco said, shaking his head, as he limped toward the door.

"Wait a minute . . ."

Del Greco said over his shoulder, "Wait a minute, my ass."

A MATTER OF HONOR

"What about Horwitz?"

Del Greco kept walking. He saw Gerald's reflection in the glass, saw him hurrying to catch up. Del Greco stood still, made loose fists with his hands, ready to turn and fight if he had to. Gerald must have noticed the move. He stopped several feet short of Del Greco. Del Greco turned to face him.

Gerald said, "You watched me for a month, came looking for me. Talking big about getting more money from Horwitz than I got from the city. Now you're taking off, just like that."

"Hang onto whatever the city gave you, Gerald." Gerald did not seem so confident now, seemed almost afraid as he watched opportunity slipping away.

"Why's that?"

"Because once I get what I want accomplished done, I'm going to have something to sell you."

"What's that?"

"Videotapes. Of you talking to your boss." He watched Gerald's face fall as he realized what Del Greco was saying.

"You didn't know he taped your conversations? He's got his office and conference room wired. Every word's down for posterity, every image captured. For all time." Del Greco smiled softly, watching Gerald's range of emotion change from cocky to uncertain to afraid, and at last to dawning terror. "There a few conversations you had with him that you wouldn't want the police knowing about?" Del Greco dropped the smile. "Once you're in prison, they take away your leather elbow and knee protectors. Won't let you wear steel-toed boots, or carry pepper spray around." Del Greco took a step toward the younger man, half-turned, fists loose. He watched, aware and pleased that Gerald was wondering if Del Greco was going to hit him, and was slightly afraid of the prospect. Del Greco widened his stance, and the towel fell away from his waist.

Del Greco's eyes were narrow and his voice was low as he said, "In prison, it's never one on one, either. It won't be like this, two men in a room, ready to go at it. It'll be gangs, Gerald. Black gangs coming at you, sizing you up, picking you out of the herd. And I'll bet you don't have a lot of friends left in the Aryan Christian Kinsmen movement these days, ready to back you up inside. Am I right, Gerald?"

Gerald was looking from Del Greco's hands to his face, he half-flinched as Del Greco twitched one of his fists, moved it fractionally. He looked up into Del Greco's face, and held his gaze. Del Greco could smell his fear, could taste it. Podgourney's fear calmed him; he allowed his muscles to relax.

"What did you want me to do, kill him? Is that it?"

"I can tell you how you can be richer than you ever dreamed. I can

345

show you how to get those tapes, so they won't come back to haunt you. I can give you those things, and what do you do? You make fun of my cancer, you call me an old man. You tell me I'm a liar. You piss in the fucking pool, like a little fucking kid."

"I—"

"You nothing." Gerald opened his mouth again, and Del Greco told him to shut the fuck up, then waited until Gerald closed his mouth. Del Greco nodded. "Maybe you're learning."

"How do you know this? How did you find out about these tapes?"

"I've been making even more of a study of Mr. Horwitz than I've been of you. You could say he's been my personal project for the last five or six months."

"He screw you around?"

Del Greco kept it simple. It would be easier with someone like Gerald. "He killed my brother."

Gerald became animated. "Killed your brother? *Horwitz*?" Gerald paused, thinking. Del Greco could see how hard it was for him. He patiently waited. "He had it done, you mean." Gerald's eyes lighted up with his insight. "Sure. He had somebody do it. He'd never have the balls to kill anyone himself." Del Greco opened his hands, relaxed his stance, turned so that the two of them were standing face-to-face.

"You have an interest in getting your hands on those tapes. I have an interest in seeing Horwitz get what's coming to him."

"Can I ask you a question?"

"You don't want to get into the pool first, piss in the water? You don't think I've got a wire up my ass?"

Gerald held his hands up, not wanting to go through this again. He said, "Listen," and Del Greco held up his own hand, stopping him from going any further.

"What's your question."

"Why don't you do it yourself?" Gerald waved his hand toward Del Greco's body. Del Greco could hear the bass of the music playing in the weight room next to the pool. Gerald said, "With your clothes off, you can see, you got the muscle left, cancer or not. You come off in the bar like a sissy, but in here, you're a fucking tiger. I've been around tough guys before. I can see it in your eyes, you could handle Horwitz."

"You don't know yet what I want you to do."

"I know I'll be the one who'll take the fall for it."

"There won't be a fall, you won't get caught. Not if you do exactly as I tell you."

"So you've—done this sort of thing before?"

"I've patched up loose ends before; that's all this is."

"And you'll be somewhere else, you'll have an alibi."

"No, I'll be right there with you. I'll be"—Del Greco once more smiled softly—"let's say, your backup."

"No offense, Mr. Del Greco, but I'd have to know more than you've told me so far if you want me to get involved with this."

"Call me Angelo," Del Greco said, still smiling. "Now, do you want to get back into the pool, or can we sit in the lounge chairs and get to know each other a little bit better?"

CHAPTER

54

Alderman Billy Charge strode into Minister Africaan's reception room with all the dignity he could muster, which was a considerable amount. He was freezing, but he would not show it. He was frightened, but he would not show that, either. Although he had come to Africaan's mansion, he was there at the Minister's request, the invitation having come in the form of a personally written note, which had been hand-delivered by four shrouded African-American women, who had averted their eyes when they'd brought it to his doorstep earlier that morning. Charge appreciated the gesture, as he appreciated the Minister's intelligence. The alderman would not have come to the mansion had the invitation been brought to his home by members of the Seeds of Africa. Charge would have taken it as an act of intimidation, and would have resented it. Which Africaan had not only anticipated, but averted.

Charge had suspected that the invitation might be coming; he had been warned about it, in fact. But even after thinking over what he'd been told and accepting it as a possibility, he had not expected that the invitation would come so soon. He hadn't thought it would happen until after the holiday season.

He had been hoping it would never come.

One of the four Seeds in the hallway accepted the alderman's coat, but none of them made a move to search him for weapons. Another thing that had been predicted. The man who had spoken to Billy Charge was turning out to be quite a prophet; it was a shame that he was dead, Charge could have used his talent for clairvoyance right about now. He would appreciate somebody telling him whether his heart was going to burst in his chest. It felt as if it were about to.

But nobody could tell that, he was certain he was exuding an aura of strength, appearing to be a serious man, one who had only bothered to come here today as an act of courtesy. Charge spoke to none of the Seeds, and they were silently respectful, keeping their distance. Charge's presence at the mansion this morning had obviously been expected.

Now Charge stood silently in the waiting room, his hands behind his back, waiting, hearing the footsteps walking quickly down the marble hallway on the other side of the door, the sound of footsteps growing louder as the Holy Reverend Minister Africaan got closer to the reception hall. Charge kept his eyes on the center of the wide wooden doors, was feeling incredibly nervous in spite of his resolve that he would not show his fear. With his back to the Seeds, Charge licked his lips. One of the doors flew open, and the Minister was standing there, beaming. Charge looked at him blankly, half hearing the Islamic greetings spoken in awed whispers by the security forces around him; half-hearing the phrase that Africaan spoke in return. The Minister never looked at the Seeds, his eyes were riveted on Charge.

Minister Africaan stepped forward, took Alderman Billy Charge into his arms, and hugged him. Charge put his arms awkwardly on Africaan's broad back, patted it, feeling the man's power, his raw, savage strength. "Brother," Africaan said into his ear, his voice thick with emotion. "How did it ever come to this?" He pushed away, held Charge's arms and looked him over, a forlorn look on his face, the Minister's eyes shining.

"Come in," Africaan said, and waved Charge forward with a sweep of one hand. He used the other to remove his glasses, then wiped at his eyes with his sleeve.

The red-veined marble floor of the vast living room was highly polished, shiny and slippery. Charge had removed his shoes as soon as he'd entered the room, had replaced them with a pair of soft slippers, choosing his selection from the dozen pairs that were lined up just inside the door, expressly for that purpose. Africaan had left his shoes on; they weren't covered with snow or salt. The two men sat across from each other in comfortable, brightly designed chairs, at a small tea table, with the silver service between them. A barrier which offered both men a small measure of emotional protection. Charge fought to keep his expression neutral, though the Minister was obviously touched at the sight of his old friend, was smiling sadly, eyes shining behind the glasses.

"It's been too long, William."

From where Billy Charge sat, it hadn't been nearly long enough. But he didn't articulate this, he merely nodded thoughtfully, pursing his lips.

"I understand you've been busy in the community."

"I want to get as much good done as I can before the March elections, Minister."

"Are the rumors true?"

"I won't be running for alderman again."

"Are you aware of the most recent polls? The media's gotten off you. They're reporting you could win aldermanic reelection without opposition, should you choose to run." Charge had not known that. The Minister added, "Your community work is finally being recognized. They're saying that with the right people behind you, you have a good chance of winning the Democratic nomination for the United States Congress."

"I'm not running for Congress, and I'm aware of the polls. The media can't *not* report them." Charge was careful in his response; the same polls that reported Charge's public support in his ward had also reported the Minister to be the man most of them felt to be primarily responsible for last summer's riot.

"As they have not reported your recent good deeds?"

"It doesn't matter, Minister; I don't do it for them."

"Do you realize what a great loss it would be to the city if you gave up your city council seat?"

"I've devoted most of my adult life to the betterment of this city. That's long enough."

"And you have lost your ambitions to be a congressman?"

Charge kept his tone soft now as he said, "All things considered, it would have been too expensive."

"You mean financially."

"I mean in every possible way." The Minister waited, but Charge merely lowered his head and sipped at his tea.

"You can't be feeling responsible for the uprising . . . ?"

"I created the climate. As did you."

Africaan was looking at Charge softly, with compassion. Out of touch with him these many months, Charge had nearly forgotten the power of the man's charisma, how seductive he could be, how he could charm you without even saying a word. He was either a true man of God, in touch with the powers of the universe, or a raging psychopath who could expertly mimic the strongest human emotions. Either way, the man was dangerous. Charge kept telling himself that, thinking of his wife now, of their future together. They were happy. They hadn't been happy when Charge had been overwhelmed with political ambition.

"The white snake created the climate, my brother. Marshall Del *Greco* created the climate." Charge held Africaan's steady gaze, and the Minister shook his head, and sighed. "But I didn't ask you here to give you a sermon." He flashed his huge smile. "And you wouldn't have come if you'd expected me to be giving one, would you?" Charge found himself smiling back at the man. He told him no, he probably wouldn't have.

Africaan's expression was sober as he said, "We need to resolve what happened between us last summer, William. The night before the uprising. We need to put it behind us."

"What's done is done, Minister. I bear no grudges against anyone. I have no hard feelings. Crocodile Berkley's dead, along with dozens of other young black men. I'll have to carry that weight for the rest of my life—snake or no snake."

"We fought right here, in this very room." The Minister was thinking back, looking away from Charge, speaking in a low, faraway tone. "I remember Berkley was out in the waiting room. When you two left, the Seeds reported that he had been acting exceptionally hostile." The Minister turned back to Charge, looked at him with a sincerity that touched the alderman's heart.

"I yelled at you that night." His voice was filled with disbelief. "I treated you as a servant, instead of a brother." Africaan leaned forward, placed his fingertips on Charge's forearm. When Charge didn't pull away, the Minister inched his fingers further on, until he was grasping Charge's arm.

"I am so sorry for that, my brother. My strong, proud brother." Charge was nodding, looking into the Minster's eyes, mesmerized by the man's words, relaxed by the great man's touch. It felt good to hear this from such a man, from a man so strong and powerful, a man so incredibly wealthy.

"The coalition that you and I had built together was destroyed by the uprising, by all the in-fighting afterwards. Did you ever wonder, William, in all the months that have passed, how there just *happened* to be a convoy of white racists heading downtown, at the exact same moment that Crocodile's men were going there themselves?"

Charge knew what was coming, another conspiracy rap. The Minister seemed to have forgotten that he had only met Crocodile Berkley for the first time just a few days before the riot. Did he think that the government had a permanent watch on the house, put a surveillance team on everyone who came and went? Just following all the Seeds of Africa around would deplete the ranks of the FBI. And logic obstructed the belief that the government had any control over a group such as the Aryan Christian Kinsmen. Still, Charge did not respond; he had not come here to argue. He still wasn't exactly certain as to why he had accepted the invitation to visit the mansion. But it wasn't to argue. He'd done enough fighting to last him a lifetime. Let somebody else carry on the battle.

Yet it was all he had ever known. Charge had spent countless hours these past several months, pondering his future, wondering if he could live without being at war with someone.

He said, "Minster, it doesn't matter. It's over."

"For you and me, perhaps," Africaan said. He was still leaning over the table, relaxing in the company of a man he saw as his friend, still holding Charge's arm. Now he squeezed it for emphasis. "You and I, we've lived important lives, but we have more years behind us than we have ahead. We're older men, men of comfort. Safe, secure. We have some measure of wealth.

"What about the other ninety-nine-point-nine percent of our people? Are we to abandon them now, leave them without any true leadership? Give up the battle, because of what happened last summer? We've lived through worse times, the both of us. We've suffered and struggled, drunk from fountains down south that were marked for Coloreds, or—if we were lucky and the townspeople men of compassion—Negroes." The Minister laughed softly.

"I can feel it within me, the need to give a sermon." Self-deprecation was in his tone as he said, "I was about to tell *you* what our struggle was like, how hard we had to work to achieve just a tiny fraction of the justice we've got coming. How far we had yet to go, and how powerful were the forces that were aligned before us, wishing to prevent our rise." Squeeze.

"I don't have to tell *you* about that, do I, William?" The Minister patted Charge's arm and sat back in his chair, relaxing. "No, I don't have to tell you about that. Any more than I have to remind you about the hard struggle ahead for the rest of our brothers and sisters, those who haven't been as fortunate as we have. The young ones, who have no hope."

"Minister, I work with them every day."

"I've heard of that, my friend. I've heard you're working harder than you have in many, many years."

"It's easier to do when you don't have to worry about fund-raising, about getting reelected. About appeasing someone more powerful than you, down at City Hall."

"And when you're seeing your own young brothers and sisters shot down in the street like rabid dogs. That should make it easier, shouldn't it, William? And when you see racially based murders brought down upon their heads by a white snake of a racist policeman, then see it twisted around by the media, until they're blaming *us*. That makes it easier, too, doesn't it?" Charge shook his head in frustration, looking away quickly, so as not to show the Minister disrespect, then deciding, to hell with it, and looking directly into Africaan's eyes.

He said, "What do you want from me, Minister?" His tone was respectful, yet strong. "You want to put what happened last July behind us? All right. It's behind us, I've told you that. What else? Are you telling me you want me to run for reelection? Is that why you asked me here?"

A MATTER OF HONOR

"No, no, I'm not interested in your running for alderman."

"Thank God," Charge said, but did not mean. He knew what was coming next, and was doing everything he could to prevent it.

"Praise Allah." The Minister and the alderman smiled politely at each other, and Charge was trying to think of a respectful way to take his leave when the Minister said, "I asked you here today to try to convince you to run for Congress."

It took Charge a moment before he was able to say no. He thought again of the man who had visited him last month. This was the third prediction he'd made which had now come true.

Africaan said, "The city is crumbling around us, coming down on *our* heads, not on the heads of the snakes, but only upon those of the brothers and sisters. The politicians have destroyed all the social assistance programs; entitlements have been abolished because of the state's block grants that wound up going into the pockets of the greedy politicians who would like nothing more than to see us all die: Starve in the streets like dogs, or get shot down by their police, or wither away in their penitentiaries. You were a Panther, the snake almost killed you. I don't have to tell *you* what's going on."

Charge wished somebody would tell him what was going on.

Yet somebody had tried to tell him, last month, but Charge hadn't believed him. And now the man who had come and talked with him was dead, had killed himself in his car yesterday afternoon, after being found innocent of any crimes stemming from the events that had led up to the riot. Marshall Del Greco, whom the Minister had just referred to as a snake, had predicted this meeting, had told Charge that it would be soon in coming, and had even told him what would happen when it came, but Charge had not believed him.

Charge believed Del Greco now.

But he still could not accept Del Greco's notions as to what Charge should do next, after this meeting. The man had to have been insane to come up with such madness, to expect so much of Billy Charge. Still, Charge had scoffed at the idea of a conciliatory meeting with Africaan, and yet here he was, sipping tea with the man.

Del Greco and Africaan had more in common than either man might have thought; they shared strong, charismatic natures, made you believe in your heart what they were saying, even as your mind was telling you that they were speaking the words of madmen.

The Minister brought Charge out of his thoughts by saying, "You talk about appeasing people at City Hall who have more power than you. You wouldn't have to worry about City Hall, ever again. What would you do, William, if you were the most powerful man in the Congress? Wouldn't your political enemies then fear *you*? What if those political enemies, anyone who spoke strongly against you, woke up one morning and found a thousand proud black men standing in their front yards, chanting your name? I could give you that." Charge was envisioning it; it was a beautiful sight to behold, even if it was only a fantasy.

The Minister said, "You talk about fund-raising. I could take care of that, as well. How many millions of dollars do you need to become a congressman? I can have it funneled to you, William. TV saturation, radio commercials every fifteen or twenty minutes, on both white *and* black radio stations. Posters, billboards. You think of it, we can get it. We can run tapes of your call for conciliation down at Eleventh and State, the day before the uprising."

"I was calling for Del Greco's head."

"*After* that. You *begged* the people not to riot, you shouted it through a microphone, implored them not to leave there and go out and destroy their communities, or get themselves hurt."

"This wouldn't be a local election. There are limits to how much any individual can donate."

"What is it, a thousand dollars per person? I have over ten thousand people who can donate a thousand dollars apiece. The money can be handed to them, and they can send you a check and write it off on their taxes."

Ten thousand people? Had it been a slip of the tongue, or had the Minister lost half of his believers? Or perhaps the man had inflated the number of true believers all along, had doubled the number to make himself look more powerful. Charge didn't know. What he did know was that Del Greco's idea was sounding better and better to him. It could, at worst, cost him his life, and at best it would cause him vilification within his community, lifetime ostracization, but it might be worth it, in the long run. Charge would have to think it over, run it by his wife, and see what she thought.

Africaan said, "That's a minimum of ten million dollars, William. Could *that* buy you the district seat?"

Charge looked at Africaan, who was no longer self-deprecating, whose eyes were no longer wet. He was all business now, the niceties out of the way, the zealot, the despot speaking, staring at Charge in a harsh, demanding manner.

"Could it?"

Charge looked back at the man, biting his lower lip. He felt a surge of strength coming up from within, from down deep, in his balls, telling him the right thing to do.

He said, "I believe it could, Minister Africaan," and watched as the man smiled his broadest smile, then added, "But I'd have to be in on every move, we'd be equals, all the way. Everything that happened, every dime spent, I'd want to know about. No more secrets, no more shouting and yelling."

"Would that partnership extend to your congressional office, my friend?" The statement stopped Charge, gave him a moment of doubt. Africaan said, "Would we be equals on the floor of the Congress, William? With me as a silent partner?"

"Co-congressmen . . ."

"Would we?"

Charge did not trust himself to speak. He averted his gaze, lowered it, then began to nod his head.

"So be it," Africaan said, and startled Charge by slapping the table, making the tea service jump, the cups rattle in their tiny saucers. Charge looked up, saw Africaan coming toward him, and stood, then found himself once again in the man's powerful embrace. This time, he hugged him back, with manly poise.

"We started with Chicago," Africaan said. "And we're putting people in place to try and take over Illinois. With you, we're moving on to Washington. After that . . . ?"

Charge knew exactly what to say. Holding Africaan tightly, he whispered, "The world."

CHAPTER

55

The health club was nearly empty. Arthur L. Horwitz preferred it when the place was packed, jumping with excitement, with young and healthy women all around him, whispering to each other, telling each other who he was. He could not understand what prevented people with money from going to their health clubs simply because it was bitterly cold outside. Was it their fear of catching frostbite while waiting for their cars to warm up?

Horwitz was running hard on a treadmill. There was a heart monitoring device on his right index finger, attached by an alligator clip. The other end of the slim electrical cord was attached to a plug on the front of the treadmill. It told him how many beats per minute his heart was pumping. He had punched in his vital statistics (taking five years off his age), and the monitor would warn him if his heartbeat moved beyond what the machine calculated to be 90 percent of his maximum training capacity.

An acre of empty treadmills surrounded him, there were only four other people in the entire, cavernous room. Horwitz was wearing a tight gold silk tank top and spandex shorts. He was wearing three-hundred-dollar shoes while he ran six-minute miles, attempting to outrun his fear, to burn off the enormous amount of nervous energy that had kept him awake for most of the night.

What had the man been thinking of? How could *anyone* kill themselves?

Horwitz did not like to think about death. He always told himself that it was too far off in the distant future for him to concern himself with it on a daily basis. Wishing to deny its certainty, he had turned death into a mere probability, had convinced himself that in his lifetime doctors would find a cure for everything from cancer to AIDS, and those remedies would be readily available to those few who could afford them. Death would come to the wealthy well beyond their hundredth birthdays, was as unimportant to him in the here and now, as was, say, hair loss. When he had begun to go bald, Horwitz had paid fifteen thousand dollars to a man who had implanted titanium snaps into his skull. Horwitz's natural-hair wig was attached to those snaps in five spots, and looked more natural than his own hair ever had, and it only needed weekly cleaning. He had the hair replaced every three months, custom-built wigs replaced with exact replicas, colored to perfection.

Death was at that level. Something he might be at risk of, but surely something that could be put off indefinitely if one had the wherewithal to do so.

He was thinking about death now, though, his heart rate steady, one hundred and fifty-five beats per minute, and holding.

Eternity.

Looking it in the eye and not blinking, welcoming it with open arms. The possibility was unimaginable to him, something Horwitz could not comprehend. He himself was an atheist, and now he wondered what Marshall Del Greco had believed in, if anything. Italians were Catholics, and Catholics were taught that suicide precluded them from ever going to heaven. Any other sin, it was presumed, could be forgiven by their merciful God.

What could beat a man down so far that death would appear to be a viable alternative to life? Beatings did different things to different people, Horwitz knew. Another thing he did not like to think about, but which was now in his mind, like a tune from a childhood TV show—hear it once, and you were stuck with it, you couldn't get it out of your head for the rest of the fucking day.

Horwitz had taken his share of beatings; bullies—beginning with his father—had taken their daily pound of flesh. He had been in law school before he had stopped flinching in fear at the sound of an anger-raised voice. He could remember other kids in grade school who'd been picked on unmercifully, and they had gone on to become ferocious warriors, some of them had even become bullies themselves. Was it in the way the beatings were refined in the brain? Was it a matter of processing? Why did some of the kids who were treated harshly become heroes, and others cowards?

"God*damnit!*" Horwitz pressed his finger to the Slow button, held it there and ran more and more slowly until he was moving at a fast walk. Sweat poured freely from his chin, onto his chest. He was breathing in quick, hungry gasps. He could feel his pectoral muscles, straining at the silk. He could look down and see his abdominal muscles, defined, stretching the fabric. His arms were strong and firm—not too big, not too small—a runner's body, not a muscleman's.

But inside Horwitz was quivering, was a frightened child again, with his father chasing him around the house, holding his belt in his hand.

Jesus.

It was the spade, Turner, who'd done it to him this time. Horwitz was convinced of that, believed it with all his heart. Shoved him against the wall of the little shack, who did the bastard think he was? Abusing the power of the state like that. Some men, you gave them a badge, and they started to think they were God. Horwitz couldn't even file a complaint against him, or a lawsuit. He'd heard the other detective in the room promising to back Turner up. He hadn't seen anything, hadn't heard anything. The code of silence was in force here, working its magic even against a man as powerful as Arthur L. Horwitz.

Horwitz hit the Stop button, stepped off the treadmill, stood beside it while he wiped his face and arms with the small towel that had been hanging from the thin, round, pebbled handlebar that surrounded the treadmill's circuit board. He let the towel drop to the floor; there were people who got paid to clean up after the club's clients.

He decided he would go to the locker room, get one of the large bath towels, wipe himself down with that. Then he'd go to the health bar, have a carrot juice or something before heading into the boxing room. His personal training appointment wasn't until eleven, and the large, round clock that was hanging on the wall said that it was only a little after ten-thirty now.

Horwitz blamed the emptiness of the health club for the darkness of his thoughts. He walked into the locker room, letting the door swing shut behind him. If there were more people around, someone to talk to, laugh with, a woman to kid around with, maybe hit on, he'd be all right, wouldn't be replaying all those ghastly memories inside his head. If Del Greco hadn't killed himself. If Turner hadn't shoved him around. If Jimmy hadn't called the office three times already, threatening him . . .

Horwitz saw a white blur as the twisted towel came around his neck from behind, felt it pull tight and drag him nearly off his feet, felt himself being dragged backward, Horwitz pulling at the towel now, unable to breathe, eyes wide and looking at the ceiling, gasping for breath, and then there was darkness. Horwitz heard a door close, knew he was in a closet. The towel around his neck came loose as something hard slammed into his stomach. He felt a sudden stinging pain in his head, realized that his hair was being pulled, his head being violently raised.

"A hundred thousand dollars, motherfucker, do you hear me?" The voice was a rasp, low and tight, a male voice that Horwitz was unable to recognize. He was holding his throat with both hands, gasping for breath, feeling a hot pain in his belly, radiating outward, as if he'd swallowed a hot charcoal. Horwitz could not catch his breath. The man slapped Horwitz's face, and the lawyer whimpered, put his hands over his head, fell to the floor, and cowered. The man followed him down, slapping at the top of his head.

"A hundred thousand dollars. Do you hear me?"

"*Please*! I hear you—*I hear you*!" Horwitz sobbed the words, curled up into a tight ball, his ropy muscles useless now, his legs made of water, unable to allow him to rise even if he had wanted to. He breathed rapidly through his mouth, chin in his chest, covering his face with his hands, expecting a foot to come crashing down on his kneecap at any moment. There was a flash of bright light, which receded, then darkness again. Horwitz opened his eyes, could see light filtering in through the crack at the base of the door.

He was in a linen closet, and he was alone.

Trembling legs beneath him, Horwitz reached shakily for the wall, grabbed a stack of towels and nearly fell again, got hold of a piece of shelving, and somehow managed to get to his feet. He waited a moment, listening at the door, one hand on the knob, the other rubbing his stomach. A hundred thousand dollars. Someone wanted a hundred thousand dollars from him.

Gerald Podgourney, it had to be him.

Unless it was Benny, someone Benny had sent in anger. Horwitz felt a moment of paralyzing fear, before he calmed himself. Benny would not allow anyone to come after him for a mere hundred thousand dollars, even though he'd been quite angry when he'd discovered that a cop—Turner—had been watching Podgourney's apartment on that day last summer, when Benny had sent his own nephew over to do the number on Gerald. Horwitz told himself that he had made things right, had convinced Benny that he hadn't known about the cop. Benny and one of his closest associates were now on Horwitz's client list, and they were sent hefty monthly bills, which were never paid. Horwitz had to pay taxes on the full amount billed, however, as if it had indeed been collected. Representing a couple of clients for free—while at the same time laundering a little money for Benny—was Benny's idea of Horwitz making things right between them.

So it had to be Gerald Podgourney. Horwitz had just seen the young man yesterday afternoon, at City Hall. Podgourney had lost weight, he was thin now, no longer had the steroid-headed, weightlifter's physique. His diet would be horrible. And he was dumb enough to think that a hundred thousand dollars would last him forever. Dumb enough, too, to have gotten drunk and started bragging about his score to his racist pals, who would have convinced him that he had a lot more coming to him than what Horwitz had negotiated on his behalf. A man such as Podgourney might seethe with anger, now that the money was his, would resent the fact that the city had settled with him for a hundred thousand dollars, while Los Angeles had made Rodney King a millionaire. And King had taken far less of a beating, all things considered. And it might not have even been a demand for money, it might well have been a chastisement, Podgourney or one of his lowbrow cronies saying the number aloud as a curse.

It had to be Gerald Podgourney. Horwitz thought that he could handle Gerald Podgourney.

Horwitz threw the door open, waited a second, then rushed into the locker room, fists up, snorting through his nose, scared, but ready for battle. But the locker room was empty and silent. There wasn't even an attendant anywhere in sight.

"Hey!" Horwitz barked the word, then waited, looking around for a fire extinguisher or something else he could use as a weapon. There was no sound, no response. He skirted the edge of the lockers, careful as he passed each row, not about to allow himself to be blindsided again. He saw no one; he heard nothing. He came to the row that held his own personal locker, turned the corner quickly, moved toward his locker, and was stunned to find it open. He saw his combination lock lying on the tiled floor, the thin, curved, steel bar snapped cleanly at the point where it met the lock's thicker rounded body. His clothing was where he'd hung it, each piece suspended on cedar hangers the club provided.

Horwitz grabbed his pants, found his wallet, riffled through the bills. His money seemed to all be there, none of his credit cards were missing. Paranoia gripped him, and he pulled his clothing from the hangers, began to search each pocket, fingers digging deeply and feeling around, Horwitz now convinced that someone had planted drugs somewhere on his clothes.

But he found nothing, could detect nothing wrong or added to his suit, his coat, his shoes, his socks, his gloves, his clean underwear . . . Everything seemed the same.

Could it be that the two incidents were not related, the break-in and the choking, the mention of money in the closet? No, they had to be related, no man could have such a bad run of luck. Horwitz patted his coat pocket again, puzzled, his brow furrowed. He patted his right leg, as if checking something, turned slightly to the left, then to the right, hands reaching as he re-created a scene from an hour earlier. He stopped, reached into the locker, grabbed his coat, and quickly patted down the pockets again.

A MATTER OF HONOR

His keys were in his left pocket, nestled next to his glove.

He grabbed them out, looked through them, counted them. Was one missing? Christ, was the lockbox key gone! No, there it was, between the key to the town house and the one to the office bathroom. Arthur Horwitz was right handed. It was the middle of the winter. This morning was one of the coldest days in Chicago's recorded history.

Horwitz thought back, wondering, remembering. He'd been preoccupied, thinking about what had happened with Del Greco, feeling poorly because he hadn't had the chance to celebrate his win-win day. He'd parked the car in the club's lot, carried the gym bag in his gloved left hand.

He remembered pulling his right glove off with his teeth, as he stepped in front of his locker, working the combination with his right hand before ever taking off his left glove. He'd tossed the right glove onto the tin shelf at the top of the locker. It was still there, turned inside out from Horwitz's search for planted drugs. He'd put his bag down on the bench, removed his left glove, shoved it inside his coat pocket.

Horwitz was certain he'd had the keys in his right hand, had stuffed them into his right coat pocket when he'd needed his hand to spin the dial of the combination lock.

So why had they been in his left-hand coat pocket?

Horwitz said, "Fuck me," then slammed his locker door closed and raced out of the locker room and out to the front desk, having a vague memory of having seen a security camera suspended from the ceiling somewhere in this club, and hoping now that it was near the entrance door.

If it was there, and Podgourney was on it, the punk was going down, no matter what he knew.

CHAPTER

56

"**D**on't tell me I got to go out in this weather."

"*Have* to, Dad; not *got* to."

"Whatever."

Quentin, sitting in his wheelchair in front of his computer, did not stop to look at his father, but he was smiling when he said, "That's what I'll say to you the next time you correct *my* language."

"Got to; have to," Ellis Turner raised the pitch of his voice and affected a British accent. "Oh, dear heavens, I mustn't be getting me bloomers froze by heading out into this horrible weather, now, must I?"

"Frozen."

"You're sitting there telling me that you can't crack the recorder's office?"

"It can probably be done, but you don't want me to do it, and we both know it." Quentin interrupted his typing, logged off the computer, and spun the chair around to face his father.

"Watch this," he said. Quentin stood up, walked to the door, turned stiffly, walked back, and sat back down in the chair with an audible, painful breath. "Ta-dah!"

The boy would never know how hard it was for Turner to keep his composure; to even smile. Ellis nodded his head several times, then shook it, as if surprised.

"You're getting it down, Quentin."

"Be good as new by summer."

Good as new. Ellis swallowed, nodding.

When he was able to, he said, "I'm going to run down to the recorder's office, while it's still early."

"The clippings help?"

Turner held up the thick file he was holding, shook it. "Oh, man, did they ever. Particularly that *Chicago Alive* piece by Dabney Delaney-Hinckle, profiling the tragedies in the Del Greco brothers' lives. I didn't know Angelo had cancer."

"I read it after I downloaded it, before you got home. She vindicated Marshall and put the blame on the 'climate' created by people like Africaan, Berkley, and Charge."

"She was right."

Quentin said, "Mom wanted to use the phone, and I was on-line," sheepishly. Ellis smiled, knowing what he was working toward.

"It's all right, she's your mother, and it's her phone."

Quentin tried another tack. "There were over a hundred different hits in the *Tribune* with the Del Greco name in them, most of them about Marshall. Not to mention today's front page. I skipped through all of the repetitive stuff from last summer, but still, I tied the line up for a couple of hours. Mom was pretty upset about not being able to use the phone." Quentin shrugged. "You know Mom. She likes me to get off the computer by the time she gets home from work."

Ellis gave in. "I'll get another phone line installed, just for you." They already had two; one for regular use, and one for emergencies only. Quentin called the phone that was never used "The Batline." It was programmed, in consecutive order, to dial 911; Ellis's beeper; his desk in the squad room at the police station; the car phone, and, if for some ungodly reason he couldn't be reached at any of those numbers, *5 would dial Cheryl Laney's beeper number. Cheryl was as paranoid about keeping her beeper in good working order as Ellis was himself, but for a different reason. She was only concerned about it because of her career, she did not want to miss any calls from her superiors, which they could then use as an excuse to prove that she wasn't a competent supervisor.

"My own *line?*" Quentin's eyes were wide.

"Your own line. I'll talk—speak—to your mother about it. *Don't* tell your sister."

"Dad?"

"Yeah, Quentin."

"It's *have*. You'll *have* another phone line installed; not *get*."

"Thanks for pointing that out, son."

"Will you be coming home, or are you going right to work?"

Ellis hesitated for only a moment before saying, "I've got some things to do. But I should be home early."

"People don't get murdered a lot when it's cold out?"

Ellis thought about a little boy, lying in the snow, with two trails of tears frozen to soft, chubby cheeks. He thought about a young woman who'd had a living fetus cut out of her womb with a hunting knife.

To Quentin, he said, "Not a lot." Then forced himself to smile. "And I want you to think about that last sentence you spoke. I can think of three separate points that were ungrammatical."

"Whatever." Ellis smiled at his son, who said, "Be careful." Quentin spoke the words that Claudette said to him every day, and Ellis's response was automatic.

"Always," he said.

Turner used his badge to get to the front of the line at the recorder's office, and he was soon disappointed to find that he'd gone out into the cold on a hunch that had been so easily proven wrong.

Marshall and Rachel Del Greco had indeed gotten divorced. Turner had a copy of the decree in his hand, proving that the marriage had been dissolved.

Turner sat in one of the hard plastic chairs that were set back from the wooden railing that separated the general public from the slow-moving, arrogant bureaucrats. It was slick enough to have been a Del Greco move, to have only pretended to divorce Rachel in order to win some sympathy from the potential jurors' pool; to have Artie Horwitz spread the lie until it became a part of their consciousness; ingrained, public knowledge. One of those "Everybody knows" statements that were so often made on talk radio, spoken by people who actually knew nothing at all. What was it called? The Big Lie Theory, Ellis remembered. Tell a lie long enough, and loudly enough, it will soon become part of the fabric's coloring, rather than an ugly stain.

It was hot in the room, and Turner had removed his knee-length, down-filled coat, sat with it across his lap. There were two thick Federal Express mailing envelopes balanced atop the coat. The first was filled with the newspapers and magazine articles that Quentin had printed out for Turner, the second had the police case files that were pertinent to the Del Greco case, including the files pertaining to the riot. Turner's long underwear was itching his legs. He ignored the angry discussions around him, the grumbling about the government from the citizens in the other chairs. He was used to that, it was background noise. You could not last as a policeman without becoming somewhat immune to the unhappiness and hostility of a percentage of the people you served.

Turner had spent part of last night and most of this morning reading the files, and he thought he knew all there was to know about the Del Greco brothers, more than he ever wanted to know. The stunner was that Angelo had cancer. Turner didn't think that the man was fifty years old.

He thumbed through one of the files on his lap, and discovered that Angelo had been forty-six when his daughter had been shot down. He had not only lost his only child, but he had a debilitating disease that could kill him.

Would that drive him over the edge, make him kill himself? Or kill somebody else? Take the people he thought were his enemies into hell with him?

Rita Cunningham's case file was stamped Closed Exceptionally. Which meant that the case was officially closed; the department thought they knew who'd killed her, and the killer had died himself. Without further evidence, proof that they were wrong, the file would never be reopened. Rita wasn't talking, and almost everyone involved in the case was now dead, either shot down in cold blood, or killed during the riot. The powers that be—in the department and among the elected officials—wanted to keep the citizenry happy; they did not want this particular bucket of shit to be stirred up again, racial tensions were already high enough without another ugly reminder of what had happened last July.

Turner didn't know how he felt about that. He lived with a young boy who was a constant reminder of the riot. He did not want the people to forget.

Still, Del Greco had shut him out from the beginning, and the two men hadn't spoken since the day of Rita's funeral. Turner knew something was wrong, out of whack. He thought about it as he looked through his files and clippings, as he placed the divorce decree in the back of one of the mailers.

Maybe he should go see Cheryl Laney, tell her what he suspected, and see what she thought of it all. But she would then know that he'd scammed her into getting some time off, that his head-hanging nervousness had been nothing more than an act. After what Del Greco had pulled on her, Cheryl would not take that lightly. But what else could he have done? The opportunity had been right there for him to exploit, she'd been giving him the opening for months. Hovering over him, looking out for him since Quentin had been shot. Showing him more attention than she gave to anyone else in the squad. Turner had even wondered about her intentions, when they got together socially after work, when she'd been working through her divorce. He had wondered if her concern for him was more than career related. Before the divorce, he had only picked up bits and pieces about Cheryl's personal life, short statements spoken in a terse voice over the phone, but he had suspected all was not well within his sergeant's marriage. He had been surprised when she had turned to him for a sympathetic ear, had wondered what she'd *really* wanted . . .

But he'd quickly torn his mind away from such dangerous imaginings.

What was wrong with him? he'd wondered. Thinking about Cheryl like that. It wasn't because she was his boss that stopped him from thinking she was coming on to him, or the fact that he was married. What bothered him was the fact that Cheryl was white, and he was black. In today's racially charged climate, that wasn't a mixture that people their ages could logically consider. The kids, they didn't pay as much attention to the social taboos, but people heading into their forties, people like himself and Cheryl, they were older, set in their ways . . .

"Jesus Christ."

Turner hadn't realized that he'd spoken aloud until one of the other people in the room said, "What are *you* carping about? *You* got what you wanted without even having to take a number!" Turner looked over at the man, saw a middle-aged white guy, wearing a heavy green parka that had a thick, red-lined hood. There were deep lines in the man's face; accusation in his eyes.

Turner offered the man a small smile. "You're right, my man," he said, and stood up, placed his mailers on the chair, and threw on his coat. He looked back at the man as he zipped up his coat—looking down at him now—and said, "Thank God for affirmative action, huh? Really changed things for me."

Turner pressed the buzzer and waited, stomping his feet, his gloved hands stuck in his pockets, his scarf up around his nose, nearly meeting the wool cap he was wearing on his head. Only his eyes were exposed to the cold, and some skin around and under them. The wind whipped around the side of the house, coming at him from the unprotected side, from around in back, by the forest. He reached out again, and this time gave the doorbell a good, long ring. He was standing at the side door of the large house, looking through an outer screen door that was more of a burglar repellent than a barrier to the cold. The door was heavy, made of steel, with thick glass molded between a heavy, barred grille. Turner thought the glass was more than likely bullet resistant. He could see that the knob of the wooden inner door was hidden within a thick, steel depression that had been built into the outer door. Turner couldn't see the wooden door's lock. A burglar wouldn't even be able to see what type of lock it was, let alone be able to pick it. There was a small window built into the wooden door, however, a lacy curtain covering leaded glass. Turner saw it pulled back, saw Rachel's eyes looking out at him, quizzically. He pulled down his plaid scarf, pulled back the front of his wool hat. "It's me, Ellis Turner, Rachel!" Turner saw Rachel's eyes widen, then saw something else; complete, total shock. The curtain fell, and for a moment he wasn't even sure that she was going to allow him inside. But then the wooden door opened, and Rachel was fumbling with the lock of the outer door, shaking her head in frustration because she couldn't get it to turn.

"Is it frozen? Want me to go around front?" Rachel heard him over the driving wind, looked at him behind the Plexiglas.

"Don't bother," Rachel said. "You won't be staying long."

Should he hug her? Shake her hand? Turner didn't know how to act. He was standing in the kitchen of a North Shore mansion, with his hat in his hand, looking around at the hanging pots, at thousands of dollars of stainless steel and copper. There was a huge, double-doored refrigerator built into one wall, just the doors and the handles sticking out of the wall. On the other side of the room was a huge, restaurant-type, eight-burner cast iron stove. A pot of something was simmering on one of the front burners. The floor was made of large, square, black and white tiles, and it was spotless, except for the area in which Turner was standing, dripping melted snow from his winter boots.

Rachel hadn't invited him any further into the house, hadn't offered to take his coat. She stood looking at him now through wide, frightened eyes, as Ellis fought down a bubble of resentment over the way he was being treated. He was angry with himself, as well. Why had he gone to the side door, instead of to the large, double doors out in front of the place? The driveway went all the way to the delivery door, whereas the circular front driveway did not; you either had a garage remote, or you had to walk a couple of dozen feet from the drive to the front door. Ellis had chosen the more convenient route, due to the weather, that's all. He told himself this now, and tried hard to believe it, as he looked down at Rachel, who stood in front of him, holding a sweater closed with both hands, as if hiding her breasts from Ellis.

She didn't have to worry about her breasts, but she was hiding something else Turner wanted, and he didn't plan on leaving until he had an idea as to what that might be.

"Rachel—" he began, but the woman cut him off immediately.

"If it's about my ex-husband's suicide, I don't want to discuss it. Not with you, or anyone else."

"Anyone else?"

"The reporters were camped outside most of the night, waiting for a statement."

"Can I ask—did you make arrangements for the funeral?" Rachel's eyes softened. He could tell that she was wondering if she'd judged him too harshly. He quickly added, "We were partners for seven years, Rachel. I'm not here to judge you, or to talk about what happened." She was nodding rapidly, and Ellis wondered if she realized she was doing it, or if it was an unconscious reaction. Her eyes seemed suddenly wet. Ellis stood, waiting.

"I can't—I won't . . ." Ellis wanted to take her into his arms, wanted to comfort her, but her body language was telling him not to dare. He waited, trying to communicate compassion and understanding through his expression, through his stance. Rachel said, "I called Angelo and told him about it; he's taking care of it all. I think he had—the body—shipped to Scottsdale."

"That's where Angelo's living now? Arizona?" He said it and watched Rachel's eyes narrow; she had lived with Marshall long enough to have acquired a devious mind.

"If you want to discuss Angelo, or what happened yesterday, with me, you'll have to take me in and question me."

"I don't know what you're—"

"I don't have anything further to say to you."

"Are your parents here? Servants? Anyone?"

"Why?" Rachel was frightened, Turner could tell. Of what? He hadn't made a threatening statement, hadn't put any force into his words. What did she know that he didn't? And could he get it out of her without causing problems with the department?

He said, "I'm worried about you. You're upset. Maybe you shouldn't be alone at a time like this."

"I'm not alone."

"Then there *is* someone else here."

"Listen, Ellis," Rachel said. Her eyes were cold now, dry. He saw her swallow. "It's another life now. Another time. I divorced Marshall. You don't have any idea what happened to him, what he turned into." She paused, looking at him, and Ellis waited, nodding his head, patiently, wanting to hear whatever she was willing to tell him.

But she was shaking her head again now, as if she had thought it over, and had talked herself out of going any further.

Rachel said, "The fact is, it's over. Marshall's gone. He was dead for months before he killed himself." Rachel's tone turned bitter as she spoke these last words.

Ellis took a shot, and said, "Do you want to talk about it, Rachel?" in his softest, most persuasive voice. Rachel looked up at him, imploringly, as if she desperately wanted to talk to him. Turner had seen this before, with guilty suspects he was questioning. Rachel wanted to expiate her guilt. Well, if she was willing, he'd certainly let her. He reached one gloved hand out tentatively, and touched her shoulder.

"I was *your* friend, too."

Rachel broke eye contact and looked away from him, looked down, then shook her head, hard.

"There's nothing else to say. It's over, goddamnit, Ellis. Marshall's dead now. All I can say is I hope he's at peace."

Turner did not remove his hand from Rachel's shoulder.

"Is that all you want to say? Are you sure?"

Rachel pulled away, shook off his hand. She took a step back before she looked up at Turner, and there was a hardness in her voice when she said, "If you have anything else to ask me, Ellis, get a warrant." She walked around him, put her hand on the doorknob, reluctant to open it in the unbearable cold. "You're way out of your jurisdiction," she said.

"Are you sure we aren't both getting in over our heads?"

"What's that supposed to mean?"

"Rachel . . ."

Rachel pulled the door open. Turner felt the temperature in the kitchen drop sharply, even through the heavy outer door.

"Good-bye, Ellis," Rachel said, firmly.

CHAPTER

57

Arthur L. Horwitz sat in his chair, swiveling back and forth nervously, thinking, his mind connecting him to images he'd rather not be seeing. He could justify and rationalize things in his head all he wanted, but the truth was, he was in deep, he owed the outfit now, instead of them owing him.

Or at least in Benny's mind he owed the outfit, which made it one and the same thing.

He wished the state of Illinois would be as progressive as half the other states and would allow people who didn't have criminal records the right to carry concealed handguns. As things stood now, carrying a pistol in this state was a felony. Horwitz knew he would not do time if he were caught—there wasn't enough room in the prisons for all the violent criminals in the state as it was—but he would surely be disbarred should he be caught packing heat.

Yet he didn't have a lot of other options open to him.

He could call Benny and have him send some people around. The people Benny would send would be good, solid, and tough, and they wouldn't waste a lot of time worrying about the consequences of being caught carrying pistols. On the other hand, the men Benny would send would no doubt have criminal records, felony convictions. You could not win the trust of a man like Benny without having served time somewhere and keeping your mouth shut while you served it. Getting caught with a gun would cause such men to serve an automatic two years in a federal penitentiary. Benny's code of honor would demand that Horwitz pay them for their time, look out for their families, educate their kids.

Horwitz couldn't turn to Benny. And everyone else was gone, all the other old-timers, the stand-up guys. Death or prison had claimed them, and the Young Turks who had replaced them were no more trustworthy than the gunslinging gangbangers.

Jimmy would have taken a bullet for him, but he'd tossed Jimmy out of the car when he'd thought he'd found the man's replacement. Jimmy felt betrayed. Jimmy kept calling, demanding to see Horwitz. The doorman downstairs had been put on notice not to let Jimmy up, to dial 911 at the sight of him. Aggie, Horwitz's personal secretary, was keeping the door locked today, checking out everybody in the hallway through the closed-circuit camera before letting them inside the offices. Inconvenient, a hassle for everyone, but necessary. Particularly today.

They'd be making their move soon. These would not be patient men, these friends of Podgourney. All that was left to wonder about was the avenue they would use to approach him.

Either way, he was prepared for them; Horwitz had a pistol. A lightweight Glock, with a fifteen-round clip. Most of the people he knew had pistols, too. A lot of them lived in the city but had addresses in the suburbs—offices or PO boxes, a Mail Boxes, Etc. Suite, or some other forms of mail drop—where their Illinois Firearm Owner Identification cards could be sent to them by the state. They would then go to suburban gun shops, where pistols were easily procured. Chicago had banned the ownership of handguns back when Jane Byrne had still been mayor. City residents could legally own longguns—rifles or shotguns—but not pistols. Which didn't stop half the people who attended Bulls games from packing them for protection against the disadvantaged youth who lived in the West Side neighborhood that surrounded the United Center. The law didn't do much in the way of stopping those disadvantaged youths from carrying pistols, either. They were shooting each other in record numbers.

The cops didn't have time to waste with an armed lawyer.

Even if they didn't, Horwitz couldn't afford to be caught carrying a concealed weapon. He would just have to make certain that he didn't do anything that would cause him to be caught.

Should he shoot someone in his own home, he'd be okay, he could get away with it. And if he were alone on the street when it happened, he could probably get away with that, too. Tell the cops he'd taken the weapon out of the hands of his attacker, twisted it out of his hand, turned it around, and shot the guy down in self-defense. They would have to prove anything else, Horwitz would not have to explain why the attempted assassin had been carrying two guns. The more he thought about it, the more it sounded like an attractive idea.

He'd prefer that Gerald Podgourney end up dead.

Gerald, living, might convince someone in authority that Horwitz had put out the hit order on Rita Cunningham. Horwitz had kept the tape, had direct evidence of the conversation between the two of them, last July. Would Gerald have figured out who Rita was? Hell, he'd been in the hospital; he might not even know that Rita's death had been the beginning of a series of events that had set off the riot. Horwitz doubted that Gerald had figured anything out for himself. Podgourney had never been much for thinking, always needed someone to do his thinking for him, to guide him, to tell him what to do.

Which was what had frightened Horwitz the most about what had happened earlier that morning, at the gym. Podgourney would never have thought that stunt up by himself. He would have come straight at Horwitz, grabbed him by the shirtfront and shouted in his face. Somebody else had told Gerald what to do, or was working with him.

If it was actually Gerald.

Horwitz had seen the surveillance tape, had seen two images of a shadowy, heavily dressed figure, first coming into the club and heading toward the locker room when the counter clerk had gone into the back—the guy claimed he'd had to use the bathroom. Precisely thirty-four minutes and seven seconds later, the same shadowy figure, head down, hood up, hands thrust in pockets, had left the club, eliciting no more than a bored look from the idiot behind the desk.

Horwitz had filed a formal police complaint, leaving out some of the details—what had been said, and how he'd reacted to it—so he would have some justification and legal standing should he wind up shooting Podgourney down in the street. There were red burn marks in a ring around his neck. The police hadn't doubted Horwitz's story, but they hadn't seemed overly concerned about what had happened to him, either. They no doubt believed that all lawyers had a good choking coming to them.

The health club management, on the other hand, had been greatly concerned. Horwitz had no interest in suing them, but he had not told them that, had wanted them to sweat. Maybe they would be more careful the next time one of their minimum-wage imbeciles decided he had to take a piss. The shadowy figure on the damn videotape could have been Podgourney, or anyone else. The surveillance tape couldn't even establish the perpetrator's race, for God's sake . . .

Horwitz sat upright in his chair, white-faced.

What if it hadn't been Podgourney at all? What if it had been Ellis Turner who had assaulted him? Turner doing it just to fuck with him, to scare him, pushing him into making a mistake that would bury him in prison due to Turner's anger at the way that Horwitz had treated Del Greco.

Whoever it had been, he had made copies of Horwitz's keys. What else could he have been doing in the thirty-four minutes that he'd been inside the club?

Horwitz grabbed the phone, then put it back, unlocked his Rolodex, and looked up the number of the company that had installed his burglar alarm system. He picked up the phone again, punched in their number. Within seconds he had established his identity—told the rent-a-cop on the other end of the line his name, where he lived, his social security number, what his mother's maiden name was—then told him that he wanted to change the security passcode on his alarm. Moron that he was, the security company man waited Horwitz out, listened while Horwitz told him his code—the day, month, and year of his birth—and gave him the new number he wanted—his license plate number. The man then told Horwitz he would have to change the passcode himself. It was fully explained in the instruction manual, hadn't Horwitz given it a thorough reading? The man couldn't help him, unless Mr. Horwitz wanted to change his emergency pass*word*. That, he could do for him.

Horwitz hung up on him.

He didn't even know if he still *had* the goddamn manual.

He dialed information to get the number of the locksmith firm that was closest to his home, got connected, and got into another argument when the woman who answered the phone said it would take three days for their company to come out. Horwitz told her it was a goddamn emergency, and she told him that it was fifty below zero outside with the windchill factor; every call that came *in* was a goddamn emergency.

This time, he got hung up on.

There was a light tap on the door, and Horwitz jumped, gasped, and reached for the pistol on his desk. He shook his head in disgust—who would be stupid enough to try and hurt him here? Besides, nobody could get in—and he lowered the weapon, held it under the desk. He hollered for Aggie to come in.

Aggie brought in a stack of pink message slips, arranging them in order of importance—the highest-billing-hour customers on the top, the lower on the bottom, no matter whose call had come in first. Horwitz thanked her, ignored her look of concern, the way she was staring at the marks around his throat. He noticed her little shrug as Aggie turned and left the room. She wasn't that good a piece of ass to begin with; he wondered now if she were thinking the same thing about him. Horwitz shook his head, trying to clear it, he had to stop thinking like this, had to get himself under control.

He'd been letting things go today, was not on top of his game, or of his current situation, positions he hated to be put in. He could go home, claiming he had the flu; the bug was going around, half the city was sick. Or he could sit here and wait, let his imagination run wild. How difficult could it be to change the number on his alarm? He could go home and do it, call another locksmith, get them to meet him at his house while he looked over the alarm booklet. His mind made up, he buzzed Aggie, told her to cancel his appointments, and to rearrange his calls, he was going home early. He was sick, he told her, and she seemed to understand.

Horwitz put on his coat, put the pistol in his pocket. He looked down, saw the way the weapon dragged down the right side of his coat. He reached into his pocket, grabbed it by the grip, lifted it a little bit. There, that looked better, and if he had to he could fire right through his coat, without having to fumble for the damned thing, let some Aryan assassin get the drop on him while he played around looking for the trigger.

Unless it was Turner who was after him.

Horwitz would prefer it to be the Aryans. He was a Jew, and he might be able to get away with killing a couple of fringe, racist maniacs. He could even become a hero, a role model, for killing them. One lone man, standing against the hatemongers. He would have support from around the nation. Nation, hell, from around the world.

Even though there was a pattern of bad blood between him and Turner, Horwitz was under no illusions that he'd be able to get away with shooting the cop.

He walked past his secretary without saying good-bye, holding his left hand to his stomach, as if he were having a hard time trying not to vomit. "See you tomorrow, Aggie," he said. "Call me at home with emergencies *only*."

Ellis Turner wasn't having much luck today. First he'd struck out at the recorder's office, then Rachel had refused to speak with him, and now here he was, freezing his ass off while he pounded on the front door of Charles Cunningham's condominium. Charles lived in the corner section of a large triplex that was set within a walled community in the heart of the Near North Side. There was a spiked iron fence around the entire three-family building; someone had left the gate open. Ellis had walked right in. There were burglar bars on Charles's windows, on all three floors. A light was burning somewhere inside, in one of the rooms around back, casting shadows into a living room that Ellis could see through the bars of the front windows. He could feel the fence behind him, sensed it, could feel it closing in on him. How could anyone live like this?

Turner wasn't sure what he was going to do, what he would say to Charles should the man answer the door, he had only the most vague excuse for being here. The fact was, there were only two places for Ellis to go: here, or Angelo's condo in Marina City Towers. Rachel had told him that Angelo had had Marshall's body shipped to Arizona. It was a story that could be easily verified, and Turner would indeed check it out, later, after he left here. The way his luck had been going, Angelo would have had the body cremated by now. There was no point in Turner's going to Marina City until after he'd checked Rachel's story, and he would only go there if there were holes in what Rachel had told him. For all Turner knew, Angelo had sold the place.

The condo door next to the one he was pounding on opened an inch, and Ellis turned wet eyes toward a young white woman, glimpsed her through the crack. She appeared to be wearing just a flimsy nightgown.

"What the *hell* are you doing, beating on the door like that?" Turner noticed a slim security chain obstructing his view, bisecting the next-door neighbor at the neck. Did she think those skinny little links would protect her from anything stronger than a child?

He said, "Police. I'm trying to find your neighbor."

"My *neighbor*?" The woman's face was puffy, her cheeks pillow-marked. It was getting on in the afternoon. Turner wondered if she was just waking up for the day, or if she'd only been taking a nap when he'd started beating on Cunningham's door. He nodded at her, watched her shiver, keeping his eyes on her face, not allowing his gaze to wander downward. The nightgown seemed incredibly sheer; he glimpsed skin without trying. The woman hugged herself, then said, "Shit. I thought you were pounding on *my* door." She closed the door in Turner's face.

"I—" He lifted his hand, ready to knock on her door . . . But what would he do then? What could he say to her? If she called 911, it would be all over for him. Turner knew that he was dancing on pretty thin legal ice as it was, coming over here with only the slightest idea as to what he might say to Cunningham.

Who didn't appear to be home, anyway.

Turner walked around the back, edged his way in past the tight iron fence, feeling claustrophobic, with the stone wall directly behind him now. Charles would be able to look out his third-floor windows and see the street, but on the first or second floors, he'd see only steel and brick. The man lived in a quarter-million-dollar urban prison.

It was darker back here, no sun reflecting off the snow, obscuring his view into the kitchen. Turner looked inside and immediately saw the mess: the refrigerator and table were overturned; what appeared to be dried blood was all over the floor, leading in a trail from the kitchen into the living room.

Turner started. He looked around the backyard area and was relieved to see no footprints other than those he'd made himself. If a crime had been committed, Turner hadn't screwed up any evidence. He stood there shaking in the cold, wondering what to do next.

The mess in the kitchen gave him probable cause to effect a search. But he was supposed to be on comp time, recovering from the psychic pain of losing his ex-partner. Turner could not bring himself to walk away, to call 911, and let whoever responded investigate the crime. Besides, the neighbor had seen him, spoken with him. The woman might be able to identify him.

Slipping away silently was out of the question. It wasn't his style, and besides, Turner had to be a part of this, had to find out what had happened.

As he retraced his steps back to his car, heading for the cell phone, Ellis Turner fleetingly wondered about the manner Cheryl Laney would choose when she handed him his ass. But there was nothing for it; he had to call her. He might be able to schmooze Cheryl, might be able to get her to see this from his own, personal point of view. Anybody else would immediately take him off the case, might even suspend him for sticking his nose into official police business. That wasn't something Turner was about to let happen.

Turner was wincing from more than the cold while he waited for his call to be connected.

CHAPTER

58

The cellular phone rang, and Horwitz reached down for it, had the built-in car unit up to his ear before he realized it was the private line. He swerved slightly, put the other phone down, and grabbed the larger, scrambler phone.

"Yeah."

"You get our message?" The voice seemed frightening, eerie and tinny, somehow otherworldly.

"Who is this!" The icy street was dangerous; there seemed to be traffic cops on every corner. Horwitz had been heading for his Central Station town house. He glided to a stop at the traffic light on Balbo. He turned the CD player off with his free hand.

"What do you want!"

"It's not what *we* want, it's what *you* want." The voice speaking to him didn't seem human—its pitch and tone had been electronically altered. Whoever was calling him had one of those devices that allowed you to change your voice.

The voice said, "Let me ask you a question, do you want to stay a free man? Or do you want to spend the rest of your life in Stateville, with niggers fucking you up your Hebrew ass?"

"Who the hell is this!" A horn blared behind him, and Horwitz, enraged, shot up his arm, shot the guy behind him the finger. He saw the traffic cop in the middle of the street, saw her mouth working angrily. Saw her begin to stride determinedly toward him. He thought about the gun in his pocket. Horwitz put his free hand on the wheel and hit the gas.

377

The voice said, "Let's get back to the first question; did you get our message?"

Horwitz breathed through his mouth, forced himself to calmly answer. "Yes."

"You know we can find you, anytime, anywhere."

"That appears to be the case." He'd call Benny. Fuck this son of a bitch. It didn't matter what it cost him, didn't matter what Benny wanted. Whoever this was on the other end, he was a dead man, he had to die.

"You sound pretty calm, Artie."

The inflection, that couldn't be changed. The way people spoke, the cadences, no machine could alter that. He thought for sure it was Podgourney now. He thought he'd only need to hear a few more lines before he could be absolutely certain.

"What was it that you wanted?"

"A hundred grand, and a certain videotape, that's all."

"That's absurd."

"Or we go to the cops, tell them all we know about Rita Cunningham's murder."

"You can tell anyone anything you'd like. It's a free country, we have free speech." Horwitz paused, amazed at how good he felt with this, how strong. He was smiling as he said, "The First Amendment guarantees you the right to speak. It doesn't guarantee you the right to be heard, or that what you say will be taken seriously, *Gerald*."

There was a sharp intake of breath on the other line, as Podgourney no doubt tried to control his surprise over the fact that Horwitz had found him out, had called him by name. He'd be angry, too, over what Horwitz had just said to him.

Then the voice said, "What makes you think you were the only one who recorded the conversation?"

Horwitz felt his mouth drop open. He nearly cruised through the light at Roosevelt Road without waiting for the arrow that would allow him onto the semiprivate street that led to his residence. Horwitz slammed on the brakes. A group of black teenagers were standing on the corner, waiting for the bus. They looked over at the sound of screeching tires, began to taunt and scream at Horwitz, making fun of him. He held the phone to his ear and looked at them, ready to run the light if even one of them moved toward him.

There would be no car in prison; no place to hide from animals who would be far worse human beings than these kids could ever imagine being.

He said, "What do you want."

"Not much. We want to see the tape destroyed. We'll send one man. You and him can torch them both in your fireplace."

A MATTER OF HONOR

"What makes you think I have a fireplace?"

"Come on . . . You have the Fitzpatrick prints hanging over the mantle. There's a zebra-skin rug in front of the fireplace, a leather chair a few feet in back of that . . . Let's see, a little table next to the chair, where you put the book you pretend to be reading—there's a pipe rack on the table."

"It *is* you, isn't it, Gerald, you son of a bitch."

"We want to see the tape burned, and we want a hundred grand. No negotiating. The bank's still open, you can get the tape out today."

"You think I can just walk into a bank and take out a hundred grand without attracting any attention?" Horwitz got the arrow; he turned onto East Roosevelt Road.

"I don't care what kind of attention you attract, and we both know you've got that kind of money in your box. I'll call you in one hour, and you better have the tape. If you don't answer, the price goes up to two hundred grand. I'll give you another hour, and if you don't answer, it goes up to three."

"And what if I tell you to go fuck yourself?"

"Then we take the tape to the cops. All it has on it is talk. Our associate can say that he took your money, then didn't do the job. I can spit off a building in this city and hit ten lawyers better than you, who can get him off the hook if he gets pinched. But *you,* Artie, you'll be going down."

Horwitz pulled into his driveway, stopped, put the car into reverse, and backed out again. He parked on the street. He hated winter; it got too dark, too early. He could see the moon in the sky already, hanging high above the lake even though the sun was still shining.

He patted the gun in his pocket for reassurance, then said, "You'll call this same number in an hour?"

"Good-bye, Artie," the voice said, then disconnected the call.

Cheryl Laney was standing by the front door in Charles Cunningham's living room, talking to three uniformed officers and one detective from the homicide squad, and every so often she would shoot a withering glance Turner's way. It didn't do a lot for his confidence. But he still had his ace in the hole, would lay it on her as soon as he had the opportunity to get her alone.

He had told his story three times already. The condo was smaller than Turner had imagined it, seemed filled with uniformed and plainclothes officers, technicians, and paramedics. There were maybe ten people in the place—a typical crime scene—but in such close quarters, the place seemed packed. There was even a guy there from the state's attorney's office. Although there were signs of foul play, a search hadn't turned up a body. Rumors were rampant that the FBI would be getting involved.

379

Turner hoped they wouldn't want to interview him. He hoped that Cheryl hadn't called in the prosecutor for Turner's benefit.

Cheryl broke away from the crowd. Turner got one more scathing look before she mounted the stairs. The uniformed officers stayed by the door, but the detective that had been with her came toward Ellis, nodding his head as he looked down at his notebook, biting his lower lip, as if he only had one problem with Ellis's statement. The man's name was Hernandez; he and Turner had always gotten along, so what was with the perp look?

"Fuck that," Turner said, as soon as Hernandez was close enough to hear him. "Don't you start playing Columbo with me."

"What?"

"You got a problem with what happened, talk to me, but don't play me, Ernie. I've done it too many times myself not to recognize it when somebody else tries to run it down."

"Come on, Turner. We're on the same squad, for God's sake."

"Yeah? And where's the homicide? What are you investigating? And since when does being on the same squad make us asshole buddies?"

Hernandez shook his head, and said, "You stated that you wanted to come over here and warn"—the detective looked down at his notebook, as if he'd forgotten who lived in the condo, then looked back up at Turner—"a Mr. Charles Cunningham that he might be in some sort of danger?"

"That's right. Marshall Del Greco died yesterday, under suspicious circumstances. Cunningham was married to Del Greco's niece. She was killed last—"

"I know when she was killed."

"Then what's your problem?"

"Del Greco didn't die under any suspicious circumstances; he killed himself. You were one of the guys who identified the body. The detective from the scene is upstairs right now, talking to our boss." The statement gave Turner pause, he hadn't seen the lead detective from the parking lot enter the premises. Hernandez looked up at Turner with pleading eyes.

"Come on, Ellis, give me a break. The guy said you hugged your pal good-bye, got blood all over your snazzy outfit."

"What do you mean by that remark?"

"I mean what I said. The entire department knows how you like to style. You wouldn't have gotten your suit all fucked up if you had thought Marshall had died under 'suspicious circumstances.' You'd have demanded an investigation. You'd have gone to Laney . . . She'd have done whatever you wanted."

"What's wrong with you? Are you trying to get me to swing at you? Is that it, Ernie?"

"If you're froggy, leap. Everybody knows you took Del Greco's place in Laney's heart after he got the ax."

What was the man saying to him? Turner could only bring himself to say, "He resigned."

"Same difference." Hernandez gave Turner another pleading look. He said, "Now, you want to talk to me? Tell me what you're doing here? Or you gonna make we work to find out. Either way, it's no skin off my ass. It'll just make things worse for you."

Turner didn't say anything, but he didn't believe things could get much worse for him. He saw Cheryl Laney coming down the steps, saw the heavyset detective from yesterday afternoon following her. The detective looked at Turner the way detectives look at suspects. Laney's expression wasn't much kinder. He looked at her, raised his eyebrows.

It dawned on him then, for the first time. He was a suspect. Turner felt light-headed, felt the room begin to sway. It wouldn't be the first time a Chicago copper had killed someone, then wormed his way into the investigation so he could throw the investigators off course.

If the FBI came into this, he could be in a lot of trouble.

Cheryl came toward him quickly, clearing a path through the officers who had come inside to get warm. She stuck her finger toward his chest, inches away from touching him. Turner looked at her, wondering where all her great concern for him had gone.

She said, "OPS and IAD are both waiting for me to give them the okay to come into this one, Turner. Give me one good reason why I should call them off."

They thought he was having an affair with Laney? Turner looked around the room. More than one officer was smirking at them, waiting to see what happened.

Wait until they got a load of this.

Turner leaned in close, put his mouth right next to Cheryl's ear. "I need to speak with you alone, right now, Cheryl."

Cheryl pulled back, as surprised at what he'd done as she was at what he'd said. Turner saw her cheeks redden, heard muffled guffaws from some of the other officers in the room. Cheryl spun on her heel and walked toward the stairway. She didn't beckon him, or look at him, or induce him to follow in any other way. But he did follow her, walked quickly behind her, catching up with her on the stairs, ignoring Cheryl's harsh, whispered words, her pointing finger, as they mounted the stairs side by side. He did not want to interrupt her, could not afford to alienate her now.

Cheryl slammed the door of the second-floor bedroom and spun around to face him, her face aflame, her eyes slitted.

"That was a cheap shot, Ellis. A *cheap* fucking shot!"

Turner waited, expecting more. Laney seemed too angry to speak, waited, her body tense, her coat open, her hands on her hips. Turner could see the butt of her pistol, riding high on her skirt, turned toward her rear right hip.

"I can tell you something that might clear it up for you a little bit, but I have to be included. I won't tell you if you cut me out, I'd rather take my chances with the Rats."

"You have some fucking insight that's going to explain this all away, make things right. Justify what you did. And you've got demands before you tell me what it is? You think you're in a position to be giving me conditions?"

"I didn't mean to insult you, downstairs."

"I should have suspended you yesterday. I let you take comp time, and I did it in front of witnesses. Tongues were wagging before; now this confirms our love affair." Was she about to start crying? Turner wasn't sure. He wouldn't touch her, would not try to calm her or otherwise reassure her.

Cheryl said, "I've been hearing about it for months. Little snitch bastards, think they know what they're talking about, dropping accusations into my ex-husband's ear. First about Del Greco, now about you."

Turner thought he'd been wrong, Cheryl wasn't even close to crying. Her eyes were alive with anger, not wet with tears.

"And now you're going to whisper in my ear in front of half the fucking squad, like I'm your goddamn squeeze . . ."

"Can I talk to you?"

"Oh, why the hell not. I'm already fucking you, I might as well listen to what you have to say."

"That wasn't Marshall Del Greco's body in the car, yesterday, Cheryl," Turner said, and watched Cheryl Laney's mouth snap close, saw her drop her arms to her sides.

She said, "You've got my attention, Turner; talk to me."

CHAPTER
59

Del Greco had to show Gerald Podgourney several different forms of identification before he would take this any further, Podgourney had made that clear to him last night, as they'd sat chatting in lounge chairs, in a warm and comfortable pool room with a vicious and deadly wind trying to get at them through the forty-second-floor windows. Del Greco had brought his birth certificate. He had brought his driver's license. He had his social security card. A Citibank Visa with his picture on the front. He showed Podgourney the deed to his Marina City apartment, showed him the title to a car that was now in a city impound lot, having been towed there yesterday afternoon. He told Gerald he was leaving it there, told him the city was welcome to it. Del Greco had lain the documents out one at a time, displaying them for Gerald as they sat in the living room of Podgourney's apartment, which was a far, far cry from the apartment in which Gerald had once resided.

Gerald Podgourney had come down a long way.

Although the furnishings were good. He'd brought the stuff with him from the old place, after he'd gotten out of the hospital. The building manager from the Wacker Drive rental had kept Gerald's things in the storage room, though he hadn't wasted any time in evicting Gerald; the slick son of a bitch had rented the apartment out again before Gerald's stitches had even begun to heal. They couldn't have people like Gerald living in the building, the man had explained. He'd kept one hand on the phone as they'd talked, in case he'd had to call for security. In the meantime, we've kept your furniture for you. Would you like to sign this release? Or shall we sell your furniture to pay for the damages that the police did to your apartment when your girlfriend—whose name was *not* on the lease and who had no legal right to be living there—would not let them in to execute a legally sworn warrant. Gerald had been around slick sons of bitches all his life; he knew one when he came across him. He'd signed the piece of paper.

So he had ten thousand dollars' worth of furniture stuffed into a two-hundred-and-fifty-dollar-a-month, one-bedroom, South Side apartment. The cops had wrecked a lot of Gerald's stuff, the pillows, mattress, and box spring had been useless. But the rest of it was in pretty good shape, banged up, but it still looked good. The leather couch was now resting on a ratty, water-damaged carpet that looked as if it had once been red. The walls were dirty, with fingermarks still on them from the last tenants. The sinks were rusty, the kitchen faucet dripped, and the toilet never stopped running.

But it was better than a homeless shelter. And Gerald now had sixty thousand dollars in a brand-new bank account that he'd opened late yesterday afternoon; he had to wait the legal two-day limit that had been set for checks to clear on new accounts—cashier's checks, money orders, it didn't matter, the bank wasn't taking any chances. Gerald was planning on moving real soon. From what this Angelo guy had been saying to him, it might be to better digs than he'd expected.

But first, he had to make sure about the guy. This was a major, major piece of good fortune. Gerald Podgourney was a man who did not put much faith in fortune. And there was something wrong about his story, something Gerald could not put his finger on, but was bothering him all the same. It would come to him, sooner or later.

He said now, "What did you say you used to do again, Angelo?" Del Greco was sitting on the couch, still wearing his coat, as if not expecting to stay very long. His hat and gloves were shoved in his pockets. He was sitting forward, with his elbows on his knees, as if wanting to touch as little in the apartment as he absolutely had to. Podgourney was resentful, but at the same time grateful. He wanted to keep the man's hands in his sight at all times.

"I told you last night, I ran an electronics store." Podgourney knew that; he'd seen the ad in the Yellow Pages, when he'd been on hold with one of the local hospitals.

"And your brother was a cop."

"He used to be."

"He killed himself."

"It was in today's papers, all over the TV news last night. It was Horwitz's fault. He caused it. Read the papers, Gerald."

"You can't believe a word those fuckers print. I haven't picked up a *Jews*paper since the day the cops came in and nearly beat me to death."

"Horwitz was my brother's lawyer. My brother beat a case, and Horwitz was the last man to see him alive. He stuffed a thousand dollars in my brother's pocket, an advance for the job *you* used to do. He insulted Marshall, took away the last bit of pride my brother had."

"Your brother blew his own brains out, and you blame Artie."

"It's his fault."

"And you want *me* to kill Horwitz."

Del Greco held up a hand. "I never said those words to you. All *I* want you to do is to go over there tonight and get two different, specific items from him. Horwitz knows you, he'll let you in. He won't suspect you're a part of—something else I've been setting up. You'll be surprising him, Gerald, when you drop in on him, when he finds out why you're there. He'll be shocked to see you, let me warn you about that up front."

Del Greco said, "First, there'll be a tightly wrapped, plastic garbage bag, around the size of a brick, that'll be covered in duct tape. You take that over to the kitchen, drop it out the window to me. I'll be waiting for it in the backyard. Then, more importantly, there are videotapes. I want every one that hasn't got you on them; you can burn your own tapes, keep them, make copies of them for all I care."

"Drop a bundle to you, then get the tapes, right. I got it. And that's gonna somehow magically make *me* rich . . . " Gerald paused, and Del Greco waited, knowing there was more to come.

Gerald said, "Let me ask you a question, Angelo. Where were you taking your chemotherapy treatments at? No disrespect intended, but I spent the entire goddamn morning calling every hospital in the Chicago phone book. You discount the maternity joints and the rehab centers, there's seventy-five of them in this city, can you believe it?" Podgourney paused for effect. "And guess what? You ain't a patient at any one of them."

"You spent the morning calling the hospitals."

"Oncology wards, pretending to be you, trying to change my chemo-therapy appointment. Most of them don't even have one. Saved me a lot of trouble, all things considered."

"And you would have changed my therapy date on me?" Del Greco was not smiling.

Podgourney quickly said, "I'd have hung up the second somebody confirmed you as a patient."

Del Greco nodded his head, thoughtfully. He said, "I've been in Scottsdale, Arizona. I lived in an apartment complex on Thirty-second Street. I received treatment at the Mayo Clinic, on Shea and a Hundred-and-twentieth Street."

"The Mayo Clinic? Even *I* know that ain't in Arizona."

Del Greco flashed a brief, sour smile. "There's one in Scottsdale. You want to call and confirm it, you'll have to use my cellular phone."

"Yeah? And why is that?"

"Think about it. Your phone already has a record of calls to seventy-five hospitals. I don't think even the Gee could nail down what department you called—that would go through the hospital's own service. Should you become a suspect for anything, you could tell the police you were looking for a friend of yours, someone you heard got shot, whatever. How would you go about explaining a call concerning *me* to Scottsdale, Arizona?"

"Wait a minute! " Gerald was thinking furiously. "Why would I *have* to? What's with this my-becoming-a-suspect shit?"

Del Greco smiled a knowing smile. "I expect the police might be wanting to have a little talk to you, should anything happen to Arthur Horwitz."

"That didn't get mentioned in our little talk last night."

"Because I didn't tell you everything."

"What were you holding back?"

Del Greco reached into his coat pocket, took out a slim, streamlined cellular phone, a single, standard, grey music cassette, and a thick wad of what looked like legal papers that had been wrapped up and stuffed into a fake-leather pouch. He put the phone and tape on the table, handed the papers to Gerald.

"What are these?" Podgourney unsnapped the pouch, and a bunch of papers that had been folded over three times rolled out into his lap. He began to thumb through them. "Some kind of—what—insurance policy?"

"There're only three things on there you have to worry about, Gerald." Podgourney looked up, puzzled. "And they're on the cover sheet—the application form stapled on the front."

"What's this?" Podgourney was looking up, then down, back at the application form. "Farmer's New World . . ."

"It's a whole life insurance policy."

"But it's dated last *May*."

"On the day you went to work for Horwitz."

"And he *signed* it?"

"That's his signature."

"How did you—?" Podgourney squinted, read the application again, more slowly, then looked up at Del Greco, as if slapped.

"A quarter million *dollars*?"

"You read the beneficiary?"

"It's me," Gerald Podgourney said, his mind racing, trying to sift through all the details, figure out what Del Greco had done. "Angelo, God, I'm the first guy they'll *look* for."

"I told you last night, Gerald, I needed something taken care of. The tapes, the garbage bag, those are all I need." Del Greco shrugged once-thick shoulders. He said, "I also told you I could get you more money than you ever dreamed of having." He pointed at the insurance policy. "There it is. Whether you decide to collect it or not is your business, not mine."

"This is legitimate?"

Del Greco gestured toward the cellular phone. "You want the number for the Mayo Clinic in Scottsdale?"

Gerald looked down at all the forms of identification on the table. He put the policy back on the table, and Del Greco picked it up and snapped it shut, put it back in his inner coat pocket.

"What are you doing?"

"Come on, neither one of us is stupid. This stays with me. You hand over the brick and the tapes to me, and I put this in Horwitz's file cabinet in his office, with the rest of his insurance papers. You can come with me, if you want."

"He's got an alarm on the office."

"I told you I used to own an electronics company."

Gerald couldn't let it go. He said, "How did you *get* that?"

"I went to a great deal of time and trouble to get that, Gerald. And it cost me more than you'd believe. It's legitimate. Predated insurance is the newest underground scam, all you have to do is know the right people. It started with AIDS. Sympathetic insurance agents got AIDS victims onto policies so they wouldn't die *and* go bankrupt; it was only a matter of time before somebody started doing it with life insurance, too." Podgourney was looking at Del Greco, disbelieving what he was hearing, afraid of it.

Del Greco smiled, and said, "You ever hear of the National Viatical Association?"

"No."

"I can give you their eight hundred number. It's a place that buys up your life insurance. Yuppies like your friend Horwitz invest in these groups, and get a ten to twenty percent return on their investment."

"What investment?"

"It's for people like me, who're dying, Gerald. We get proof of it, take it to the association, and get eighty to ninety percent of our life insurance policy's worth, right there on the spot, to do whatever we want with."

Gerald realized his mouth was open, and he quickly shut it, shaking his head. "What is that, they bet on how long it's gonna take for you to *die*?"

"Basically."

Podgourney felt his mouth twisting into a smile.

"I'll bet once you get into that, you learn a whole lot more about the way to play the angles than you ever knew existed." Del Greco nodded, once. Gerald thought he had him figured out.

"And you took your benefit money, found some wise guy son of a bitch in the insurance agency, and gave him your money to rig up this policy, right?" Del Greco looked at him, but did not speak. Gerald said, "Why didn't you get one in your own name?"

"I wouldn't live long enough to enjoy it."

"And you couldn't pull the trigger, either." Gerald was smiling now. "You need *me* to do that for you, don't you?"

"Did you know Horwitz had an outfit contract out on you?"

Gerald stopped smiling, shocked. The nigger had said that a guinea had been waiting to kill him. What else had he said?

Del Greco said, "Now the only question we haven't answered is, can you work up an alibi you can count on for tonight?"

"A quarter of a million dollars . . ." There was a faraway look in Gerald Podgourney's eyes. He had forgotten all about his niggling doubts.

"After you take care of the first piece of business for me, you hand that tape to Horwitz. You don't let him play it until I have the bundle, though, you understand?"

"What else do you know you ain't telling me about?"

"Neither one of us will live long enough for me to recite that list." Del Greco said, "He'll be anxious for that tape, waiting for it, he might get pushy about it, but it's important that he wait, that he doesn't hear what's on it until you make the first drop." Del Greco paused, then said, "And if you want to take care of that other problem we were discussing . . ."

Del Greco reached inside his coat, in around behind his back, and Gerald's eyes widened as he took out the large, long pistol. He said, "Hey, Angelo!" and watched Del Greco smile. He turned the gun butt-first toward Gerald, handed it to him.

"This should do the job."

Podgourney looked down at the large pistol, read the words *Sig Sauer* stamped on the side.

"You ready to get it done?" Del Greco said to him, and smiled. "Got a big, heavy coat to hide that in? Go ahead, get it. I've got to use your bathroom."

"It's—"

"I know where it is."

CHAPTER

60

"**D**o you have what we told you to get?"

The electronic voice made Horwitz angry. "Gerald, quit playing games. I've got the tape with you on it, and I've got the money. You bring *your* fucking tape over here, we'll have a bonfire together. If you made a copy of it, I swear to God, I'll hunt you down and shoot you myself."

There was a pause, and Horwitz thought he detected a smile in the electronic voice when it said, "Would you believe me if I told you that Gerald knows nothing about this?" Mocking him.

Horwitz was terse. "No, I wouldn't." The gun was on top of the coffee table in front of the couch that Horwitz sat on, the Glock pointed toward the door, within easy reach. The money was in a briefcase, every dime of it, next to the weapon. It wasn't even five o'clock yet, and it was already dark outside. For all Horwitz knew, the son of a bitch was right outside on the street, calling from the car. He could be walking in here any minute now, using the copies of the keys he'd stolen . . .

"I want the money in a garbage bag, stacked tight, the plastic wrapped around it, then wrapped with duct tape."

Did he have duct tape in the basement? He didn't know . . .

"How do I know you didn't make copies?"

"How do *I* know *you* didn't make copies of the video?"

"That wouldn't do me a lot of good, would it?"

"Or one of your outfit friends could be waiting for us."

"Would I do that to you?" The gun in front of him gave Horwitz confidence. In here, within these walls, nobody could harm him, he could literally get away with murder. Let Podgourney think what he wanted. As long as his friends understood that there could be no copies of that tape. He would pay after he listened to it, but he would not pay twice. And he *had* made another copy of the video. Although Gerald wouldn't need to know that. He said, "How many of you are coming over?"

"Just one."

"And you'll use your own key."

"I don't know what you're talking about." Then, impatiently, "Just have the money and the video ready, Counselor. We'll be seeing you in a little while."

The body in the blue automobile did not have a chest scar. Turner had stood riveted to the sidewalk a year and a half ago, had watched the kid shoot Marshall Del Greco, had seen Marshall fall into the boy, had seen Del Greco wrestling with him. He'd visited his partner in the hospital, had spent time with him during Del Greco's recovery. Turner knew that there was a large scar on Del Greco's chest.

He'd searched for that scar yesterday, had wrecked a suit, shirt, and tie, as well as his good topcoat while doing so. The corpse in the car didn't have any scar on its chest.

"You didn't go see him during his trial at all, did you?" Cheryl Laney was on hold, sitting in the squad room. Around them, detectives were working other cases, homicide cases, while Turner called around to the hospitals, trying to locate Charles Cunningham. This was Cheryl's way of punishing him for not coming to her with what he'd known sooner than he had. She'd given two other detectives the fun jobs.

Hernandez had a call in to O'Donnell's funeral parlor; Turner had told him to use his name. Mr. O'Donnell himself might not remember Turner, but Turner would bet that O'Donnell's young assistant would have no trouble remembering not only Turner, but Marshall Del Greco, as well. Valencia had already told them that they couldn't get near Cunningham's bank accounts or investment portfolios until morning, and maybe not even then, as an assistant state's attorney had informed him that there was "as yet insufficient probable cause to procure the appropriate warrant." Valencia was now on the phone, trying to get a court order that would allow them access to Ameritech's cellular records concerning Charles Cunningham's phone calls. The calls from the regular line would take a couple of weeks to get hold of, even with a warrant. But cellular records were immediately accessible—if you had the legal authority to get them.

Three homicide detectives and a supervisor were working a case without a dead body. Laney would play hell explaining this to the lieutenant. Even if she found a way to cover it on her report, either Valencia or Hernandez would drop it in his ear, let him know what was going on, paying her back for cutting them out—they had been told what to do, but not what it was about.

The secret was between Cheryl and Ellis, and neither had any intention of giving it up.

"I didn't go to court," Turner said, to Cheryl. "The papers said he was in Minnesota, working construction. His father-in-law would have done that for him, as sort of a divorce present."

"You sure they're divorced?"

"Got a copy of the paper in the car." Turner did not look over at his sergeant when he told her this.

Cheryl said, "Yes," into the phone, and Turner looked up, saw that she was sitting straight in her chair, writing something down on a sheet of paper. "Thanks a lot, Sergeant," she said. "Would you do that? That'd be great. You ever get out to Chicago, you give me a call; I owe you a steak."

"What do you have?"

Cheryl held her finger up, punching numbers into the phone, using the back end of the pen she'd used to write down a Scottsdale, Arizona, phone number. She waited, letting the phone ring, and hung up when she got the answering machine. "Shit." She picked up the phone and hit redial, gesturing to Turner. "Pick up six; see if you recognize the voice on the machine."

As Turner waited through the rings, Cheryl said, "The only reason he'd move to Scottsdale would be to receive therapy at the Mayo Clinic. Sergeant Walter Gaites is checking there for me, first. He says he can have one of his men check every hospital in Arizona, if we need him to—"

"I thought the Mayo Clinic was in Minnesota," Turner said, and immediately regretted interrupting her. The look on Cheryl's face shut him up, and he was grateful to be able to hold his hand up quickly and look away, as a semi-familiar voice came over the phone, telling the caller to leave a message.

Cheryl said, "Is that Angelo? The phone number's unlisted, under the name of A. L. Del Greco."

Turner waited for the beep, and said, "Angelo, are you there? It's Ellis Turner, in Chicago. Call me as soon as you get this, it's urgent." He left his phone number and extension, hung up the phone, and leaned back in his chair, thinking.

Cheryl said, "Sergeant Gaites is sending someone over to the apartment complex, to see what he can find out for us."

"There must not be a lot of crime in Scottsdale."

Neither Cheryl nor Turner paid any attention to any of the ringing phones in the squad room—the only calls they'd concern themselves with would be the ones that came over their personal extensions. So Turner was surprised when one of the detectives in the room called his name.

"Turner! Some FBI guy's on three."

"Tell him I'm not here."

"*You* lie to a federal agent." The detective hit the hold and transfer buttons, and hung up.

"You better take it, Ellis." Cheryl's look and tone were both warnings.

"Fuck him, let him wait."

Valencia said, "I got authorization for access!" and hung up his phone, immediately began to punch in another number. Turner could hear him talking as he picked up his own line then immediately hung up.

"Whoops," Turner said. "The bugs in this phone system . . ."

Valencia was giving the Ameritech rep the order number.

Hernandez hung up his phone. "O'Donnell cremated the body this morning."

"What?" Laney said, as the phone on her desk rang.

"They got a call yesterday, from the brother, Angelo, in Arizona, they said. No wake, no memorial service, no nothing. Just wanted the remains shipped to him at an address at—"

Cheryl said, "The Arabian Apartments, Thirty-second Street."

Hernandez did not seemed surprised that Cheryl had said this. He said, "Right. Guy paid in full with a Visa, I'll run the number right now."

"Don't bother, it's Angelo."

Turner said, "Or in Angelo's name, anyway."

Cheryl lowered her voice and said, "What are you saying?"

Turner had left his hand on the phone as he'd sat back, listening and thinking. He was trying to put something together, something that should have been obvious to him, when the phone rang under his hand. He looked down at it, knowing who it was, seeing the phone light ringing, the phone . . .

"You gonna answer that?" Cheryl asked.

The phone.

Cheryl's extension rang. Turner took his hand off his phone. He knew from the expression on her face what Gaites was saying to her. He heard her thank him, watched her hang up.

"Angelo's gone; his neighbors are worried. Says he's a good neighbor, a quiet guy. The manager let an officer in; there's no sign of him. No suitcases, either."

"Mayo?" Turner asked.

"He stopped his therapy two days ago, hasn't shown up." She paused, looking at Turner. "Gaites talked to one of the nurses, who told him it was too late, they were only buying Angelo a little time." She frowned. "You going to answer that phone?"

"No." Turner got up from his desk, walked quickly over to Cheryl's, leaned down and spoke softly and hurriedly.

"I think that was Angelo in the car yesterday. He had terminal cancer, what did he have to lose? That means Marshall's running loose." Cheryl leaned her head forward, listening intently. Ellis said, "At Cunningham's house, there was the phone, that oversized cellular?" Laney didn't answer, just nodded her head; she remembered the phone. "Guess who has another phone, just like that one?"

"Who?"

Valencia said, "We got a list of numbers coming at us over the fax. Eleven in the last three days to the same number." He rubbed his hands together as he dialed the 976 number that would tell him the name of the party that number was listed to.

"He's Cunningham's lawyer," Ellis said. "And Gerald Podgourney's too."

"Podgourney?"

Valencia was still holding the phone to his ear as he announced in a triumphant voice, "Arthur L. Horwitz, Esq." Cheryl and Ellis both looked over at him. "You need the address?" he asked, but they were grabbing their coats and heading for the door before he even hung up the phone.

CHAPTER

61

He didn't know what Horwitz was talking about? Had somebody *else* broken into the locker? No, Gerald was only trying to throw him off base, fucking with him.

Horwitz sat in the darkness of his town house, wired, the weapon in his hand, ready. The only light came from the blazing fire that he'd started after the last phone call. The flames leaped behind the glass shield, throwing shadows around the room. Horwitz jumped at some of them, pointing the pistol the way he would a flashlight, the way he'd been taught by the firearms expert at the range down in Calumet City. He shook his head at himself, disgusted at his nervousness. The alarm was on, the passcode changed. A good thief might get past the new locks, but he'd play hell beating that alarm system, and even if he did, there was one more little safety measure that nobody else in the entire world knew about but him.

Horwitz checked the pistol for the thousandth time, hefted it, took out the clip, slapped it back in, hard. There was a small, slim, second trigger sticking out of the first one, that was considered to be a safety. All he had to do was draw in the slack on that little clitoris of a trigger, then squeeze the real one, and *boom*. What happened, happened. The videotape would be burned up in the fire before the neighbors even had a chance to dial 911. Horwitz took in deep breaths, let them out slowly. He could do it if he had to. He was sure of it, as certain as he'd ever been of anything in his life.

That certainty redeemed him; the knowledge that he could kill a man made Arthur L. Horwitz feel strong. Like a man. He could do it, he knew he could do it—but only if he had to.

It might not come to that. This could go smoothly. Listen to the tape, make the exchange, get a promise that there would be no further contact of any kind. Gerald's friends were not that smart, not anywhere near as smart as they thought they were. They knew he had Gerald on tape, visual image and sound, knew that Horwitz had his office wired.

But they weren't bright enough to figure out that he'd done the same thing to his home.

There were two cameras, actually. One in the bedroom, and one down here, hidden inside the large-screen Mitsubishi TV. The camera was fixed, immobile, and pointed downward, to record anything that happened on the rug in front of the fireplace. Horwitz had seduced more than one young woman on that rug. *Those* tapes he kept in a safe upstairs, he didn't put them in the FirstChicago vault, with the others. The machine could even record when the TV was running. Though the setup had its limitations, it also had a full view of the area, for several feet all around. Horwitz had set another chair across from his own, one each on opposite ends of the zebra-skin rug. He'd set the small table on top of the rug, with a cassette player on top. He would get whoever came over to sit in the chair, would have a picture of the son of a bitch relaxing while Horwitz pretended to be listening to the tapes. There were people he knew at the DMV who could match a still picture with a driver's license photo . . .

The cellular phone rang, and Horwitz almost shot it.

He looked at it as it rang again, slowly raising the pistol toward the ceiling, trying to regulate his heartbeat. He picked up the phone with his free hand.

"Hello?"

"You sound out of breath."

"Quit fucking around. Let's do it."

The doorbell rang.

Horwitz jumped to his feet, frantically, the phone to his ear, eyes searching, weapon pointed.

The voice shouted into his ear. "What was that!"

"My—my doorbell!"

"You son of a bitch, you called the FBI, didn't you! God*damn* you, Horwitz!"

"I didn't . . . !"

The doorbell rang again.

The voice said, "You want to fuck around? You can fuck around in prison!" The phone went dead in Horwitz's ear. He dropped it to the floor, then walked to the door, slowly, the gun held in both hands now, the barrel shaking, Horwitz hyperventilating, terrified, alone, not knowing what was going on anymore, ready to shoot through the door if he had to, ready to do anything to get them to leave him alone.

He stood to the side of the door, thrust his head quickly toward the small window set in the wood, too small and high up for anyone to break the glass, reach down and unlock the dead bolts. Horwitz peeked, then brought his head back quickly.

Gerald was out there, smiling at him.

Horwitz leaned against the wall, trying to calm himself down. So it was Gerald. But where was the phone? It didn't matter. Horwitz knew what he had to do now. He stepped away from the wall, punched the alarm passcode number on the keyboard attached to the wall, right beside the door. He saw the red *armed* light go out, saw the green *unarmed* light come on. He punched in the number again, saw the red light flashing. He'd have twenty seconds to let Gerald in and close the door before the alarm went off, summoning the police.

"How does all this fit in with Del Greco, Ellis? What do you know that you're not telling me?"

"Angelo owned an electronics store. He'd know how to clone cellulars, he'd get Horwitz's number without a problem. Cunningham's, too."

"That didn't answer my question." There was a stern warning in Cheryl's tone. Turner could tell she was fighting to remain patient, to not go off on him. He knew he had to tell her something.

"We're almost there."

"Ellis, goddamn you . . ."

"Cheryl, you'll just have to trust me."

"What are we walking into? Will we be needing backup?"

Turner didn't bother to think before saying, "You should get on the horn, send a couple of units over to Gerald Podgourney's apartment." Turner paused. He said, "Electric or gas company should have an address. Or the phone company."

"When we get back to the station, I'm handcuffing you in an interrogation room, and I'm not letting you out until you tell me what you know, even if I have to pistol-whip it out of you."

Turner felt himself smile, shot a glance at Cheryl, and said, "You promise?" as he turned off Michigan and onto East Roosevelt Road, the access road that led to Arthur Horwitz's expensive town house.

"How's it going, Artie?" Gerald said, as he entered the town house. He stopped as soon as Horwitz opened the door, looking down at the gun in the lawyer's hand. He slowly took both hands out of the comfort of the pockets of the long, down-filled Chicago Bears coat he was wearing. "Whoa," he said. "Are we a little jumpy today, or what?"

"Where's the phone!"

"*What* phone?"

"Where *is* it?"

Podgourney stopped, at a loss for words. This wasn't the way it was supposed to be going. Horwitz waved the gun barrel, and Gerald stepped inside, waited while the lawyer closed and bolted the door. Gerald watched him, hands open, out from his sides, not exactly raised above his head, fingertips held up about shoulder level, palms outward. Horwitz moved in a jerky manner, stepped into the middle of the room.

"You're alone?"

Goddamnit, the man was supposed to be shocked to see him. Surprised, Angelo had said. Maybe Horwitz had figured things out for himself, maybe Angelo wasn't as smart as he thought he was. Gerald nodded his head. He'd made Angelo give him the keys to the car, they were in his left-hand coat pocket. The pistol was in his right, he could feel its weight, dragging the coat down. It wasn't supposed to be like this, Horwitz was supposed to be surprised, not prepared.

Still, the tape-wrapped plastic bundle was on the table, and there was a videotape right there next to it, a single one. Angelo had said there'd be a bunch of tapes. A boombox was on the table, too. A briefcase was on the floor. The other tapes must be in there.

Gerald said, "Well, we gonna do this, or what?"

"Give me the fucking tape!"

Gerald had to screw up the courage to say, "Not a chance. Not until you put that gun away."

Horwitz lifted the pistol, pointed it straight at Gerald's head, and Gerald somehow forced himself to keep his eyes open, to not close them in fear. Horwitz seemed as frightened as Gerald was himself. Gerald had never seen him like this before, not even when he'd been with him every day.

"You've got it on you?"

"I look stupid to you? It's nearby, and I ain't getting it until you *put that fucking gun away!*"

"I knew it was you all along, Gerald. You weren't fooling anybody." Horwitz backed toward the two chairs that had been set up near the fireplace, on opposite sides of the zebra-skin rug. He sat down in one of the chairs, put the pistol in his lap.

Gerald had never shot anyone before, and he hoped that his maiden voyage would be going a lot smoother than it was. He'd have to get the guy to put up the gun. His own weapon was too big, he couldn't shoot through the coat, he'd just blow off his own damn leg.

He said, "Knew *what* was me all along?"

"Yeah, keep fucking around. Now, let's get something straight. You and your friends, whoever talked you into this, are *not* going to get another dime from me. Is that clear?"

"I don't know what you're talking about."

"You're repeating yourself. You just said that a little while ago, when you were trying to convince me you weren't you, and you didn't have a fucking key to my house."

Was the guy on drugs? Gerald couldn't tell. He'd never seen Horwitz take any coke, or anything stronger than a mild tranquilizer, a little booze now and then after dinner. He'd drink beer at his luxury skybox at the United Center, when he was trying to be one of the guys.

"Sit down, Gerald."

"I think I'd rather just get what I came for."

"And drop off what you came here to give me. I swear to God, if you duped that tape . . ."

"I didn't dupe anything."

Gerald lowered his arms, left them hanging loose at his sides. He raised his eyebrows for permission, and Horwitz nodded. Gerald knew he had to be careful here. He'd known tough guys and he'd known cowards, and he believed that both types of men were of an equally dangerous stature.

It wouldn't take much to make Horwitz pull the trigger.

"What was with that last call? Were you just being cute? Fucking with me?" Horwitz was trying to smile now, pretending he was in control. Gerald walked over to the table, saw the lawyer's hand tighten on the pistol. Gerald leaned down, touched the package, looked at Horwitz, and raised his eyebrows again.

"Go ahead, I don't see why not. As long as you don't think you're walking out of here with that before I get the tape."

"I won't be going anywhere." Gerald straightened. "Except to the kitchen." Gerald said it and waited, saw the smile twitch its way onto Horwitz's face.

"Get whatever you want. Bring me a beer on your way back." Gerald walked toward the kitchen, stepping wide past the lawyer's chair, seeing Horwitz raise the pistol, seeing the barrel following him, tight on him, dead on target, as he walked out of the room.

Horwitz moved several steps away from the chair and stood waiting, pistol ready, in both hands, pointed toward the kitchen door. He knew what was happening. Thought he did, anyway.

Gerald would come flying through the door with a weapon in his hand, trying to take Horwitz out. If he did, it would be the last stupid move he'd make in a lifetime filled with stupid moves. If he came walking back in with a couple of beers in his hands, Horwitz would let him live. For a little while, at least, until he was sure that there were no other copies of the tape. He heard a banging sound, heard Gerald curse. He tightened his grip on the pistol, pulled the slack out of the clit on the trigger. He waited, smiling, afraid, but fully alert and alive.

Feeling that way for the first time in his life.

Gerald took his pistol out of his pocket as soon as he was out of the lawyer's sight. But now what? he thought. Go back in there, and the two of them could point their guns at each other? This was hurting his head. Bothering him. Horwitz with a gun out there, Angelo waiting outside—for what? For the package.

What was in the package? It had to be money. Felt like it, anyway. Gerald's mind, driven now by adrenaline and fear, was working overtime. He was seeing things more clearly, having what Edmund's daddy Adolph would have called a Vision.

He had finally begun to figure out what had been bothering him about Angelo.

He had to put the gun on the counter so he could lean over the sink and unlock the window. He could see Angelo waiting, the man shivering out there in the cold, his coat collar up, his wool hat pulled down low on his forehead, covering the spot where his eyebrows should have been . . .

Gerald frowned. What had Angelo said to him? He'd been making a project out of Horwitz for five or six months. And he knew all about Gerald, what he'd been doing, robbing apartments. And it would have taken some time to get that insurance policy set up, to somehow get a valid signature.

But Marshall had only killed himself yesterday afternoon.

What the fuck? Gerald thought, as he opened the window, and the alarm went off.

As soon as Horwitz heard the alarm, he knew he had underestimated Podgourney. The son of a bitch, he'd gone into the kitchen to open the back door, to let his cronies inside.

It was a hit; they were going to kill him.

He charged the kitchen, pulling the trigger before he even turned into the doorway, firing again and again, seeing Gerald turn, seeing Gerald's look of horror and surprise, seeing Gerald jump as the bullets slammed into his chest. Horwitz followed him down, shooting him over and over, ran to the sink and slid in the blood, fell down, smacked his knee, got up with a few rounds left over for Gerald's friends. He turned to the door.

The door was still dead-bolted. What were they going to do? Come in through the window? *What was going on here!* He heard Gerald making moaning sounds, saw Gerald's gun on the counter. Shaking, near hyster ics, Horwitz looked around for the money, but couldn't see it; perhaps it was under Gerald's body.

Horwitz slammed the window closed, the alarm going off in his ears, deafening him. He never even heard the sound when his front door was kicked open; never even knew that Turner and Laney were in his house until he felt something cold and hard smack into the back of his head, saw a woman moving quickly, coming around to the side to twist the pistol out of his hand.

CHAPTER

62

"**H**e broke in." Cheryl stood in the living room, not about to touch anything more than she already had until her detectives and the crime scene technicians got here and got a murder book opened up, got everything dusted.

It was obvious there was nothing to be done for Podgourney.

Arthur L. Horwitz sat on the edge of his chair in front of the fire, with his hands cuffed behind his back. Ellis Turner sat across from him, legs crossed, glaring. Horwitz was crying, trying to convince them that this was all just a big mistake.

Turner wasn't buying it, Cheryl could see it on his face.

"He came in here to kill you with an empty Sig Sauer." Her words dripped sarcasm, as her earlier statement had done.

"Why would he do that?"

Turner sat, silently watching.

Horwitz said, "I'm *trying* to cooperate! I don't even have to talk to you! I'm just trying to clear this all up!"

"What was he doing in the kitchen?"

"He came in through the window!"

"And you closed it *after* you shot him?"

"I was *trying* to lock it when you two came in! I didn't know what was going on, how many more might be out there!"

"Where's Charles Cunningham?" Cheryl said. And the lawyer looked confused, surprised at the question.

"Charles? I do business with Charles; he's one of my clients. I haven't spoken to him in—" Horwitz closed his mouth, sat there thinking. Cheryl looked from him to Turner, trying to figure out what was going on between them.

Horwitz said, "That's it, I'm not saying another word until I speak with my attorney."

Cheryl watched Turner shrug, as if he'd been doing the questioning.

Outside, they heard the sirens winding down. Thank God it was as cold as it was; the neighbors would be hidden in their houses, peering through their windows. The mayor lived just a few blocks away. The neighbors would probably not be coming out until they saw their chance to pose for the TV cameras.

Turner finally spoke. He said, "What's on the videotape, Counselor?" and Cheryl saw Horwitz start, saw him look guiltily down at the tape that was on the table.

"That's privileged communication between a client and me."

"Sure it is," Turner said, picking it up, hefting it in his hand. "Says 'Gerald' on the side."

"Ellis, let's wait for the state's attorney . . ." Cheryl said.

"It's a murder scene, Cheryl, we have the right to investigate it."

"Ellis . . ."

Turner looked at her, then shrugged again, put the tape back down on the table, then smiled at the lawyer.

"We've got you, Counselor," he said to Horwitz.

"TV stations are doing live remotes from the scene. We had to arrest some asshole cameraman for trying to go around back."

"What's out there?" Cheryl said.

Valencia said, "A bunch of tracks in the snow; we'll get good prints if the techs don't rush through it just to get back in here where it's warm."

"Here" was the town house, which was now filled with brass, milling around and acting important, in the middle of a high-profile, heavy-media-involved case. Cheryl was staying out of their way, had made her statement while sitting at a desk in the upstairs den. Horwitz had demanded his medication. His request had been refused. With any luck he'd get desperate for it, and they could make a trade, say, a half of a tranquilizer for every page of his confession.

He'd killed Gerald good. Hit him six out of eleven times, all in the chest, as if he'd had a lot of practice.

They would eventually discover that to be the case.

But at the moment there were dozens of questions; this wouldn't be an easy case, no matter how cut-and-dried it appeared to be. The killer had money, and—after his first frightened, feeble attempts to create an alibi—knew enough to keep his mouth shut. God only knew who a man like

A MATTER OF HONOR

Horwitz might be connected to. God might shudder at the thought of what Horwitz was probably involved in.

Lieutenant Foster snuck up on Laney from her blind side; she'd been able to avoid him for much of the time that he'd been in the house. Cheryl fought to keep her expression impassive; she thought she pulled it off.

Foster said, "The ASA said it's legally permissible to view the tape—but *only* the one we found on the table, with Gerald's name on the side." *We?* Cheryl thought, but put a pleasant, inquisitive look on her face. The lieutenant could be coming down on her with both feet right now, and had every right to do so. Instead he was being pleasant, was acting almost friendly.

Foster said, "They're checking precedent for the ones we found in the safe, or anything we might find in the office. The tapes in the safe upstairs all have women's names on them."

"That should get a few chuckles out of the crew."

Foster shook his head. "The captain already issued the order: only supervisors will view them, at my office back at the station; we'll understand if you want to pass."

"I will. What about the cassette we found on Podgourney?"

"It's blank, there's nothing on it. The keys are to a stolen hunk of metal that's outside, at the curb."

"He won't beat this, will he? The Sig Sauer was empty."

"There's two sets of shoeprints from the car. One—Podgourney's—leads to the front door; the other goes out back."

"So he had an accomplice."

"Or came in with Horwitz, or they came in *together*, and Horwitz somehow got him to go around back, talked him into climbing in the window."

"There were no marks on the sink, the counter."

"And Podgourney's shoeprints don't match the prints in the snow, around back."

"It was a murder," Cheryl said.

"They're talking manslaughter, at least."

"Gonna plead it out."

A voice behind them said in an urgent tone, "Captain, Lieutenant, did you see *that*?" There was a stunned pause, as whoever was holding the remote rewound the tape a few feet. An excited babble of voices broke the sudden, shocked silence.

"Watch, he's ordering the son of a bitch—"

"Who's Rita Cunningham—?"

"You nuts? She was Del Greco's *niece*—this mutt, he—"

A laugh preceded the statement: "Hey, what do you think's in the envelope?"

There was a smattering of applause as the police officers in the room cheered Horwitz's stupidity.

Foster said, "Then again, maybe they *won't* plead it out." He looked back at Cheryl.

"All right. Good work. Now, the FBI's pissed, they need to debrief Turner, yesterday. I've been a cop long enough to understand why you gave him comp time." Foster was smiling, conspiratorially. His voice was lower when he said, "That was good work, too, Sergeant. Didn't waste homicide man-hours on a closed exceptionally case. Put the best man in your squad on comp time, so he could investigate without investigating."

Cheryl nodded her head at the compliment, accepting it without question, grateful now for a story she could stick with no matter how things turned out.

Foster said, "I promised the feds I'd have Turner in their office at nine tomorrow morning. I can't find him anywhere; you know where he is, Cheryl?"

Turner walked through the security cage and waited for the elevator with what looked like a bunch of college students. Standing next to them, he felt old. He told himself that he'd be feeling old even if the students weren't there. The elevator came, and they all packed into it at once, Turner shoved into the back, wrinkling his face as one of the kids sneezed without covering his damn mouth.

"Hit thirty-two, would you?" he said. The kids were all gone before the twentieth floor. Turner played with it while the last of them walked out, thought he had it figured out before the door closed on the last kid's back.

Their parents would buy or rent them condos in this building, at relatively low rates. The higher the floor, the more it would cost them. The older tenants, they'd live up high. Some of them would have been here since the time the building had first opened, back when it was a state-of-the-art, architectural wonder, and Chicago's highest-ranking gangster had lived in the penthouse with his trophy wife.

The elevator doors opened on thirty-two, and Ellis walked out, looking at the door number across the hall, trying to get his bearings.

Though he needn't have bothered. Del Greco was walking toward him, a suitcase in either hand.

If he was surprised to see Ellis, he didn't let it show on his face.

Turner said, "That's right, just like that. Keep those hands occupied."

"Ellis," Del Greco said.

"Marshall." Turner nodded his head, looking Del Greco over. He said, "Nice haircut." This time, it was Del Greco who nodded.

"I'm glad you came alone; I've got something for you. You'll save me the trouble of mailing it out; it'd cost a fortune in stamps." He looked at Turner. "Can I put them down?"

"Go ahead."

Del Greco did so, carefully bending his knees and placing both suitcases down at the same time. He knelt down on one knee before them, zipped open a side pocket of one of the suitcases, and took out a manila envelope that seemed ready to burst open. He stood, handed the envelope to Turner. Turner looked down at it, saw that his name and home address were printed on the front, in Magic Marker, in large, block lettering.

"What's this?"

"For your kids; their education."

Turner fell silent, glaring.

Del Greco said, "You want to pinch me, pinch me. But don't pretend I'm dumb enough to try and bribe you."

"Where'd you get this from?" Turner lifted the thick package.

Del Greco shrugged.

Turner hit the button. The doors slid open. "Well, come on, don't be expecting me to carry your bags for you, too."

In the elevator Turner said, "You got this from Horwitz, somehow, didn't you?" Del Greco looked up at the ceiling, and Turner's gaze wandered upward; he saw the camera mounted in one corner, the lens sticking out through the mesh of the protective cover. He waited. The elevator made several stops before finally hitting the first floor. The lobby was long and wide, with tacky old couches and chairs in the common area that led to the street. Del Greco picked up his bags, followed Turner across the dirty carpet, past the security desk, and stopped when Turner did, in front of one of the couches.

"Sit down, have a smoke."

"I have a plane to catch."

"Sit down."

Del Greco sat down, crossed his legs, and lighted a Lucky Strike. He dropped the match in the standing ashtray beside him, watched it burn itself out. Ellis lit one of his Kools, let the smoke out through his nose, nodding at his ex-partner, trying to figure him out.

"Am I under arrest?" Del Greco said.

"We're just talking here, is all."

Del Greco turned marble eyes on Turner. When he spoke, his voice was a hiss.

"They had to pay for Rita."

"It was Angelo in the car, right?"

Del Greco glanced at his watch. "I told you, I have a plane to catch."

405

"You didn't kill anyone yourself. Just tell me that, Del, and I'll let you go. Give you a ride to O'Hare."

"*I* didn't personally kill anyone, no."

"But you—facilitated—a couple, am I right?"

"Let me ask you a question: of the two men, who do you think would have a tougher time in prison; Horwitz or Podgourney?"

"That's no question."

"Then I'm free to go?"

Turner saw Del Greco look past his shoulder, saw Del Greco's eyes narrow, saw him nearly snarl. He saw Del Greco look back at him, his expression now flat, neutral.

"And you didn't know anything about this, did you?"

Turner chanced a brief look over his shoulder, saw Cheryl Laney heading toward them quickly, her hand now coming out from the folds of her heavy winter coat, her weapon clearing wool and pointing directly at Del Greco.

She said, "Keep your hands where I can see them."

"Hello, Cheryl," Del Greco said.

"Shut up, Del, just shut up." Laney turned to Ellis. "You were—doing what? Shooting the shit? About to let him go?"

They were drawing a crowd. Del Greco looked around, saw the people stopped, watching. He stood up; Cheryl stepped back.

"Freeze, Del Greco, goddamn you!" The warning in her tone sounded ominous, even to Turner.

Del Greco dropped his cigarette to the carpet, stepped on it, then leaned down and grabbed his suitcases, one in each hand. He straightened, looking at Laney.

Who said, "I said *freeze!*"

The crowd was watching, gasping, some of them running away, others cheering Del Greco on: Go, mister—fuck those po-lice.

Del Greco turned his back on Laney, and began to walk away.

"Goddamn you, stop! You're under arrest!"

Turner saw Laney pull the hammer back on her .38. "Not one more step!"

Del Greco kept walking; Laney's finger began to tighten on the trigger; Turner saw her close one eye, draw a tight bead on Del Greco's back.

Turner leaped to his feet and began to run toward Del Greco, in Laney's line of fire. He tackled him, received no resistance. The crowd was screaming now. Laney was there, above Turner, her knee in the prisoner's back, her weapon tight against the base of Del Greco's skull. Turner spoke to her reassuringly, as he clamped the cuffs on Del Greco's wrists.

"Take it easy, Cheryl, it's all over, he's down, he's under control, you've got him . . ." He pulled Del Greco to his feet. Del Greco seemed calm, his face without expression, breathing normally, there wasn't even a single drop of sweat on his hairless head.

"What's the charge, Detective?" was all he wanted to know.

"Suspicion of first-degree murder."

Del Greco looked surprised. "Suspicion?"

Cheryl was putting her pistol back in her purse. She spoke under her breath. "You heard me, you son of a bitch," she said.

"You were going to shoot me over your *suspicions?*" He was speaking loudly enough so the crowd could hear him. Turner heard many of the people watching gasp in surprise and shock.

Behind them, someone said, "Excuse me."

Turner spun around, frightened, hand fumbling for his weapon. A small, older black man was holding the manila envelope out toward him.

"You left this on the couch," the old man said, and Turner took a deep breath, accepted the package, and thanked the man.

"Turner, grab the bags," Sergeant Cheryl Laney ordered, and Ellis shoved the envelope under his arm, leaned down, picked up Del Greco's suitcases, and began to follow his boss as she led Del Greco out of the building.

CHAPTER

63

"**I** want to know what you know about this. How deeply are you in this, Ellis?" They were in the lieutenant's office, waiting for him to finish his press conference. Turner looked at Laney, still not fully believing not only what she had done, but what she had been willing to do.

"You were going to *shoot* him? In the back? While his hands were in full view, without any evidence that he was involved in anything illegal?"

"He's involved up to his ass in two homicides. It's just a matter of time before we find out how deeply."

"Two homicides."

"The stiff in the car, and Podgourney."

"The stiff in the car *still* could be a suicide, and *Horwitz* shot Podgourney."

"Oh, bullshit. Del Greco's part of this, Ellis. And I'm trying to find out if you are, too."

"Me? I haven't spoken to Del Greco since the day of his niece's funeral." He suddenly understood why he hadn't; Del Greco had planned ahead, had thought that something might go wrong. Now Turner was not a part of it, could honestly give the answer he just had.

"And you can pass a polygraph, if you had to?"

"I won't take a polygraph."

"It could mean your job."

"It could have meant yours, an hour ago, if you'd have shot an unarmed man in the back on your gut feeling." Turner waited, but Laney did not reply, so he said, "If my boss thought I was a crook, a killer, the job wouldn't be worth having."

Laney shook her head and walked behind Foster's desk, sat down in his chair. She began to play with a pencil, turning it around and around on the large calendar-blotter. It reminded Turner of an adult version of spin the bottle.

"How long do you plan to hold him."

"We can keep him for 'a reasonable period of time,' according to Illinois law. Precedent's set that at seventy-two hours, unless we can come up with more during that period."

"And you hope to find enough evidence to charge him with murder in that time?"

"Operative word 'you.' *Me. I* hope to have enough, that's right." Cheryl looked up at him. "You're not a part of this, you won't investigate this, you won't even take a phone call concerning it; I mean it, Ellis."

"You don't think I was a part of it."

Cheryl shook her head. "I can't believe Del *Greco's* a part of it. There's no way I can square you being in on the deal."

"Thank you."

"Now go home. Get some rest. The FBI wants you down on Dearborn at nine in the morning; you make it to that appointment, Ellis." She reached for the phone on the lieutenant's desk, dialed in an extension number.

"Ernie? Do me a favor, get Del Greco out of the tank. Put him in One. I want to talk to him." She hung up, looked up, and seemed surprised that Turner was still in the room.

"Can I take him his cigarettes?"

"I don't want you anywhere near him." Cheryl paused. "Good*night,* Ellis."

"Maybe you shouldn't be interrogating him, either. There could be a conflict there. He was on your squad. And you've obviously got feelings"—Turner was careful here—"a sense of betrayal against him."

"I know him better than anyone else. Except you, and you aren't a part of this."

"Cheryl—"

"*Goodnight,* Detective Turner. You dodged one bullet tonight, let's not press your luck."

Turner carried the envelope into the house, tossing it up and down in his hand, wondering about it, about all the tape wrapped around the top. Was it evidence? Del Greco had said it was for Turner's children's education. He'd said it wasn't a bribe. So it had to be money. From where? It must have come from Horwitz. But how did Del Greco scam it out of him?

He heard Claudette's voice in the kitchen, thought she was on the phone, but then she came into the living room, saw him standing there, and he caught the concerned, worried look on her face right away.

"What's wrong." Turner was cold and hard, immediately expecting the worst.

"We have a guest," Claudette told him.

Alderman Charge rose and shook Turner's hand as the detective came into his kitchen. He saw the coffee cups laid out on the table, saw that Claudette had favored the alderman by bringing out the good china. Turner put the envelope down on the table, eyeing Charge suspiciously. He looked at Claudette, then back at Charge. He sat down at his table, leaned back in the chair. He hadn't bothered to take his coat off, even though he'd unbuttoned it, could get at his weapon quickly if he had to.

"What can I do for you, Alderman?" Turner's tone was harsh.

Charge said, "You know about my plans to retire from the city council?"

"I know nothing about you. I turn the page when I see your name in the paper."

If Charge was insulted by the statement, he kept it out of his expression, and out of his voice when he said, "Minister Africaan wants me to run for Congress. Wants to funnel ten million dollars my way, launder it through his congregation. He wants to be a co-congressman, draft legislation with me."

"Why are you telling *me* this? Go to the FBI, they'll know what to do about it."

"FBI doesn't want any part of Africaan. And they'd make me look like a publicity hound, a traitor to my community."

"*Community.*" Turner spat the word out. "We're twelve percent of the population, Charge. Hardly a mere *community.*"

"I think you know what I mean." Charge began to reach into his jacket pocket, and Turner's stare stopped him. He paused, his hand inside his suit coat, and said, "Marshall Del Greco paid me a visit last month."

"Did he now?" Turner's eyes were on the alderman's hand. He watched as the alderman brought out a regular, white, number ten business-sized envelope. There was a small bulge in the middle of the envelope. Charge placed the envelope on the table.

"Del Greco told me Africaan would call. Said the man had taken too much heat over the riot, he would need me, would summon me, and would offer me a seat in Congress. Would buy it for me."

"And you said?"

"I was taken aback; I had attacked him, I was part of the reason he'd lost everything. But when he came to my house he was friendly, outgoing, acted as if we were old friends."

"Alderman, why are you here?"

"I met with him because I was sick over what I'd done to him. I thought he'd come in, vent his spleen, maybe hit me, then go on about his life. Yet he told me a story. And everything Del Greco said would happen in that story, happened. So far."

"What's the rest of the story?"

"That's what I'm here to find out."

"Meaning?" Turner felt Claudette's hand fall on his shoulder, and managed to hide his surprise. He hid his gratitude, as well.

Charge said, "Three years ago, Africaan's top advisor taped a conversation—"

"Mallik, I remember."

Charge began to spin the envelope on the table. It reminded Turner of Cheryl Laney and her pencil, an hour ago, at the station. Both people had used the device to stall for time as they thought.

Charge said, "Mallik was doing it from an answering machine. The clarity was for shit"—Charge looked up at Claudette—"Pardon me," he said, and looked back at Turner. "There was no time-date stamp, and Africaan's voice was muffled. Mallik had an extensive criminal record. The tape was inadmissible as evidence. And even if it hadn't been, it would have come down to Mallik's credibility versus Africaan's. There was no indictment. But it shook Africaan. It was the last time he spoke on a telephone."

"So how did you tape him?" Turner gestured to the envelope.

Charge smiled in appreciation. "Nagra wire, on my chest."

"Recorder?"

"In my car, out front."

"Clarity?"

"Crystal clear. I identified myself before going into the mansion, with the date, time, and street address. Spoke to myself all the way up to the time that I was allowed into the entry hall with the Seeds of Africa."

"And you brought *me* the tape."

Charge pushed the envelope toward him.

"Del Greco said I should bring it to you, that you could put it to its proper use."

Turner reached up absently and patted Claudette's hand. He looked at Charge, nodding. He said, "Claudette, would you please get me an ashtray?" Then said to the alderman, "Would you care for another cup of coffee, Alderman Charge?"

"I just spoke to your brother Angelo," Cheryl Laney said. She was leaning with her hips against the windowsill, arms crossed. Del Greco was looking straight at her, in that way he had—the look that he always used when he wanted to make suspects afraid of him. She said, "He was crying, he was so glad to find out you were alive."

Del Greco now seemed puzzled. "I didn't know I was supposed to be dead."

"You didn't watch the news, didn't see any newspapers."

Del Greco's expression was earnest as he said, "Listen, I beat a court case a couple of days ago that's been hanging over my head for months. I went to my brother's condo, took a shower, and passed out on the bed. I only got up to go to the bathroom."

"For thirty-six hours."

"You know how cold it was yesterday? Angelo's junkheap wouldn't start. My lawyer dropped me off at the lot, I got in the car, it wouldn't start. I took a bus from Twenty-sixth Street to downtown, went home, and went to bed."

"That's your story."

"Cheryl, what does homicide want with me?"

"You may call me Sergeant Laney."

Valencia said, "Do you know Gerald Podgourney?"

Del Greco said, "Who?" He seemed puzzled, then widened his eyes, looking at Laney. "Isn't that the guy Ellis was looking for, the day you and I went to breakfast—"

"That's him."

"He got killed? And that surprised you?"

"Why'd you shave your head."

"There a law against that?"

"Where's your wallet?"

"My *wallet?*" Del Greco shook his head in exasperation. "Goddamnit, that's the problem with this department; one hand never knows what the other's doing." He glared hard at Laney. "A pickpocket grabbed my wallet over a week ago, at O'Hare, when I came back from Minnesota for the trial. I filed a report right there at the airport."

"And that's your story. The car wouldn't start, you shaved all the hair off your body just for the hell of it, and your wallet got stolen at O'Hare airport."

Del Greco shrugged, elaborately. "Listen, I've been patient enough, just for old time's sake. If you're not going to tell me what this is about, at least let me call my lawyer." Del Greco paused for just a moment, then said, "Arthur Horwitz."

Valencia and Laney looked at each other, then Cheryl looked back at Del Greco.

"I'm not buying any of it. I think you're responsible for two murders, Del Greco."

Del Greco spread his arms out wide and opened his hands, and Cheryl would forever believe that there was a flicker of triumph in his eyes as he said, "Prove it."

SELF-FULFILLING
PROPHECIES

CHAPTER

64

"**Y**ou can go on in, but we got to search the stranger," the Seed of Africa said to Charge and Turner. Turner looked at the young man in front of him, then lifted his hands, as if acquiescing. The young man opened Turner's coat, saw the mark on the belt where the holster generally hung. Turner had left his weapon in the car. The young man was patting him down, not being at all careful about the weapon that was hanging from his own belt. Turner looked at the other two young men in the room, and couldn't help himself.

He plucked the weapon from the man's belt as the Seed stood, then swept the younger man's ankles out from under him with a low, fast kick. As the young man fell, Turner pointed the weapon at his companions.

"You want to take your weapons out *real* slowly," he said.

When the Minister opened the wide double doors, he found three of his men sitting against the wall, with their hands on their heads. His eyes widened, and he turned to Charge. He looked at Turner with real fear.

"I'm not here to harm you, Africaan," Turner said. "But you could use some better bodyguards."

Turner had to hand it to him, he got his composure back quickly. "Perhaps you'd like to apply for the position."

"I've got a job," Turner said, and Africaan turned to Charge.

"It's late, and I rise early. Why don't the two of you come inside and tell me what this is all about?"

Turner watched the Minister's face as he listened to the tape, seeing the loathing there, the betrayal-driven rage. He looked up at Charge and demanded, "How *dare* you!" Charge did not respond. The three weapons were unloaded, were on the table between them. It would take a few seconds for even a young and fast man to pop a clip into one of the guns, pull back the slide, and fire. Africaan was no longer young and fast. Turner was almost hoping that the Minister would make the attempt.

Turner said, "Save it for the mosque. And this is just a copy, so don't get any ideas in your head." Africann was glaring at him now. Turner made a point of smiling. He said, "We've got you on tape, breaking half a dozen laws. Conspiracy, trying to rig federal elections—a half-bright U.S. attorney could probably make a case for treason."

"What do you want."

"This afternoon, at your second meeting, you offered Alderman Charge ten million dollars for a run at Congress."

"You're my Judas," Africaan said to Charge, who averted his eyes.

"No he's not," Turner said. "He's as black as you, and I'm even blacker. Now I told you, save the bullshit for the masses. You want to cut a deal, right here and now, or do I go to the U.S. attorney and the media?"

"Who *are* you."

"The alderman told you my name; Turner." Ellis spelled his last name out for him. "Ellis, with two els." When the Minister didn't respond, Turner said, "There're laws against handing out more than a thousand dollars to any candidate for federal office. There are no such laws concerning city office."

"What do you want from me?" Africaan said, at last getting down to business, and Ellis Turner told him.

CHAPTER

65

They tried again in the morning.

Del Greco looked rested, with a stubble on his face and head. He rubbed the spot where his eyebrows should have been, as if the area itched.

"You get hold of my lawyer yet?" he said.

"Tell me about the phone calls you made from your brother's phone."

Del Greco appeared to think that over. He said, "What, the phone company won't turn over the records?" He thought this over, as if wondering if he should tell them to get a warrant. "I called my brother when I beat the case, told him the good news." He nodded, then said with conviction, "That was the only call I made."

"No local calls?"

Lieutenant Foster walked into the room, stood against the wall, observing the interrogation, but watching Laney just as closely as he was watching Del Greco. Del Greco, looking at the lieutenant without acknowledging him, said, "Come on. You can check the records. I don't know what your problem is. But I have to tell you, I'm getting more than a little pissed off about all this."

Valencia did not know why he was in the room; it was obvious that whatever was happening, it was between Del Greco and Laney.

"And, *Sergeant Laney,* I think you should know, I have every intention of filing a complaint and a lawsuit against you for the manner in which I was arrested."

"It was a lawful order to stop." Laney was appealing to Foster as much as she was answering Del Greco.

"You were going to shoot me." Del Greco looked around. "Where's Ellis?" He looked at Lieutenant Foster. "Ellis Turner'll back me up on that. The woman wanted to bring me in for questioning, she didn't have to pull a gun, cock it, and nearly shoot me. There were witnesses, too." Foster looked concerned. Even Laney frowned.

"Can I go now?" Del Greco asked. "Or will you at least let me call Horwitz?" Del Greco looked around the room again. "He's gonna be pissed," he said.

Laney ignored him and said, "We found an insurance policy someone put on the toilet lid at Gerald Podgourney's apartment. It was in the amount of one hundred thousand dollars." Laney paused. "It was taken out on the life of Rita Cunningham, with her husband as the beneficiary."

Del Greco paused before saying, "If I were you, I'd want to talk to Charles Cunningham about that."

"There was a page ripped off, a little corner was left hanging on the top, caught by the staple. You have any idea what might have been on that page, Mr. Del Greco?"

"No, Sergeant, I don't." He looked at Foster again, raised his hands, pleadingly. "Would somebody please tell me what this is all about?"

"Sergeant? Could I speak with you a moment?" Foster said.

"Take him back to the cage, Vince," Laney said to Valencia.

Foster waited until Del Greco was out of the room before he said, "We've got eight complaints at OPS, Cheryl." His voice was weighty, concerned. "People from Marina City, who're claiming you used excessive force in the arrest." He paused before saying, "I don't have any choice, you're off the case."

"He set it up that way, he waited for us to come before he even tried to leave Marina City. He was watching the lobby on the fucking closed-circuit channel, left the apartment when he saw Ellis Turner."

"There's no way we can connect him to Podgourney's death."

"What about Cunningham? You *know* that was him in the car!"

"We *don't* know that. Whoever it was in the car can never be identified. And we've got witnesses, solid, reliable people, who gave us statements that Podgourney was in a South Loop tavern, looking for Charles Cunningham just two nights ago."

Cheryl slammed the palm of her hand against the wall. "Goddamnit, you *can't* take me off this case!"

Foster reached into his inside jacket pocket, took out a folded fax sheet, opened it, and handed it to Cheryl.

"This is from the FBI lab. They worked all night for us." Cheryl read it, then looked up, shaking her head in disbelief. "The blood found in Charles Cunningham's kitchen belonged to Gerald Podgourney; there's no doubt about it, Sergeant." Foster paused, then said, "You're barking up the wrong tree."

"Give me another day. We've got forty-eight hours—maybe thirty-six now."

"We don't have that much time. This isn't some black kid from Englewood, it's a white ex-cop whose name is known by every reporter in town."

"Which is why you want to cut him loose. Because the media's in a feeding frenzy. He made us look like fools! First, we pronounce him dead, then we drag him in as a suspect in—shit—his own murder!"

"You don't have any evidence to hold him, and the state's attorney won't approve charges based on what you feel."

"Lieutenant, he's playing games with us. You see how he's acting? He didn't refuse to answer any questions, he didn't clam up and demand an attorney. He *wants* to talk to us. Another couple trips in here, I'll get him to slip up, on camera." Laney gestured to the video setup hidden behind the one-way mirror.

"We both know better than that. I reviewed the tapes from last night. The man didn't even acknowledge that he knew he was supposed to be dead."

"His wallet, his clothing, they were on Cunningham's body!"

"And his wallet was reported stolen, as he told you, last week. I've got a copy of the report. We checked the car at impound; the battery was dead. And we don't have any proof that it was Cunningham in that car." Foster paused. "Cheryl, you've got nothing to hold him on."

"If he walks, we'll never get him back in here."

"Don't be so sure."

"Who ordered the body released?" Cheryl was livid, stalking around the little room. "Who okayed it to go to the funeral parlor? Jesus *Christ,* why wasn't it printed, at least?" She stopped pacing, looked at Foster.

"And what did you think would happen to a ten-year-old car that was left in impound overnight, on a night like we had? Of *course* the battery would die."

"Nobody checked the corpse for keys, either."

Cheryl straightened up. "Did we do that now?"

"Personal effects were sent on to the brother."

"Get a warrant for them."

"Based on what? That Del Greco shaved his head?"

"So what do you think? Somebody who stole Del Greco's wallet snuck into his brother's car, dressed in Del Greco's clothes, then, after the car wouldn't start, blew his own head off with a shotgun?"

"I think you're right, I think it was Charles Cunningham. And I think Del Greco killed him. But we can't *prove* it."

"We were so glad to think it was Del Greco, we got sloppy."

"That, or we're always sloppy, and a razor blade like Del Greco was able to cut his way right through us."

"I can't cut him loose, Lieutenant. I just can't do it."

"I can," Foster said. "Cheryl, you're off the case."

Turner waited outside the waist-high wooden fence in the detective squad room while Del Greco checked out his bags. He didn't open them up and look through them, just grabbed the handles and pulled them off the counter, turned, saw Ellis, then stopped. He nodded, got himself under control, and began to walk toward the fence. Turner held the gate open for him. He heard heels clicking, looked up and saw Cheryl Laney striding quickly toward them. Del Greco stopped when he saw her. She came to within inches of him, glaring.

"I told you in Lou Mitchell's, I thought you were capable of shooting a man down in cold blood."

"Excuse me," Del Greco said, and walked past her, through the gate, saying "Thank you," to Turner.

"You want a ride to the airport?"

"That's all right. Thanks anyway."

"I'll give you a ride to Marina City."

"I can hop a cab, but thanks for the offer, Ellis."

"Come around back, at least. My car's in the alley. There're a thousand reporters waiting downstairs."

That stopped Del Greco. He silently followed Ellis through the halls, past doors that Ellis had to open with keys. He stood next to him in the prisoner transport elevator, not saying a word, looking straight ahead. When the elevator opened, Turner took one of the suitcases, and Del Greco nodded his thanks, used his free hand to hold his coat closed against his throat when the cold wind hit him as they stepped through the outer door.

In the car, Del Greco remained silent for a time, until Turner took out a piece of paper and handed it over to him, told him to take a look. He heard Del Greco take in a breath, but didn't look over at him, kept his eyes on the road.

"I'm not wired, and the car isn't, either. Besides, we both know whatever you say to me can't be used against you, not at this point."

"What do you want?"

"Answer one question."

"And you forget about this?" Del Greco rattled the paper.

"I was the only one who thought of it, and, truth be told, I never saw it before in my life."

"It proves nothing, you know."

"It could get the media riled up. The feds."

"It's a list of cellular calls to Horwitz's private number, that's all it is. Calls, and how long they spoke. For all I know, Rachel was calling him to see how I made out in court."

"Could be," Turner said, reasonably, then said, "You're right, it proves nothing." He paused, then added, "Except that you told me yesterday you had a plane to catch. It didn't take a lot of work to find out who was sitting next to you, in first class."

Del Greco remained silent.

"Couple more calls, I found out Rachel's entire family was heading out to Vegas on the same plane."

"Now that I'm not living in fear of being a convicted felon, I'm free to accept a job at Bally's. Chief of security. They want me working ASAP. New Year's Eve's a problem, they tell me."

"Got the reception room all ready for a party, too."

"There a law against a man remarrying his ex-wife?"

"I wish you both a lot of luck."

"Thank you." They were coming to the bridge now, Marina Towers was straight ahead.

"Pretty smart of you, using Horwitz as your lawyer."

"We always got along," Del Greco said, and Turner grunted a laugh as he pulled into the drive, stopped the car at the residents' entrance.

"The envelope last night, we're going to use it as a campaign donation."

"You get Africaan to kick in a few bucks?"

"He yelled and screamed, hemmed and hawed, but it was worth a couple million to him to not spend a few more years in Marion. And Charge won't have to be co-*any*thing with his sorry ass." Turner paused, then said, "I know just the woman to be in charge of the new campaign."

A valet was walking toward the car now, and Ellis waved him off. The young man walked off, angrily. Ellis didn't hold his resentment against him, it was too cold to be working outside.

Del Greco said, "Can I take the paper with me?"

"Just answer one question."

"What's that?"

"How did you get Podgourney's blood into Cunningham's town house?"

Ellis watched Del Greco tear the computer printout into pieces, saw him stuff them into his pocket.

He said, "Rachel got it, the day of the funeral. Snatched his bloodwork out of the hospital lab." Ellis laughed out loud.

When he stopped, he asked, "How'd you know that Africaan would call Charge *before* the holidays?"

Del Greco shrugged. "Nominating petitions have to be turned in before the first. If I was right about him calling, I would have to be right about when. The only question was, would Charge stand up to him, or revert to his old ways."

"Charles was a better actor than I thought. At the wake, the funeral, he acted all broke up. That was a good touch, taking a dive on the casket."

"It wouldn't take a good investigator long to find out that he was in financial trouble. And that his lawyer was Arthur Horwitz."

"So Angelo killed Charles, right? He wasn't at home, nobody saw him around for a few days. Dressed him in your clothes, put your ID on him, put him in the car . . ."

"You said I only had to answer one question; I answered two." Del Greco opened his car door, and the freezing wind assaulted them.

"That or you were lying to me yesterday, and you killed Cunningham yourself."

"You want to pop the trunk, please?"

"You got them all, didn't you? Edmund and Crocodile died in the riot. Podgourney and Charles are dead now. The best lawyer alive today might be able to plead Horwitz out to twenty-five years. You even got Africaan."

"Africaan's like the Ebola virus; nothing can wipe him out, and he multiplies."

"You hurt him where you could; in his pocket."

Ellis leaned over, opened the glove compartment, and pressed the button that popped the trunk open. He said, "How'd you know what *I'd* do? How'd you know I'd go to Africaan? Am I that predictable?" Del Greco did not answer, just quickly got out of the car.

Turner walked around to the back, helped Del Greco pull out his luggage. The suitcases were on the frozen pavement; the two men faced each other.

"I'm gonna miss you, Del. You were fun to watch."

Del Greco put out his hand. Turner briefly considered hugging him, then put the thought out of his mind. He shook Del Greco's hand as the wind tried to push them off their feet, the two men ending an eight-year relationship, looking each other in the eye, Turner smiling, Del Greco grim. He was white, brilliant, and was pledged for life to a beautiful, wonderful woman whose parents would someday leave them millions. But Del Greco was lacking certain, basic things.

He had no passion. He could not trust. Perhaps he could not even truly love.

Turner wouldn't change places with him for all the money in the world.

He said, "You think Rita has more peace now?"

"I do. Angelo does."

"Give my best to Rachel."

"And to Claudette," Del Greco said, leaning down to pick up his bags. "And to Anne and Quentin," he added, before turning away, and walking off to begin his new life in Las Vegas.

CHAPTER

66

It was hot, but nowhere near as hot as it had been last summer. Just a normal Thursday at the end of August, in the eighties, with high humidity. Ellis Turner drove the shiny, new, black Lincoln Towncar, with Claudette and Quentin already in back. He pulled up in front of Charge's home, nodded at the policeman sitting in the marked squad car parked in front. There was another vehicle, just like this one, parked in the alley, the car running so the air conditioner could cool off the inside. Quentin adjusted the lapels of his suit, straightened out his tie. Turner got out of the car and waited, saw Charge hurrying down the stairs toward them, and he held open the back door. As soon as Charge was inside, Turner got in, closed his own door, and hit the button that locked all the doors.

Turner heard Claudette and Quentin welcome Charge, heard Quentin's awed voice telling Charge how much he appreciated what he was doing for him, calling him Mr. Mayor, until Charge told him to just call him Billy.

"Your Mom and Dad made me mayor," he said. Quentin would never know how much truth were in those words, though he'd left out one name. Del Greco'd had something to do with it, too.

"You nervous?" Claudette asked, and Quentin said, "Mom . . ."

Turner drove down Twelfth Street, pulled over at the curb, put the car in park and turned to face his son.

"Knock 'em dead, champ."

"Good luck, son," Claudette said, hugging him.

Turner watched as Quentin formally shook the mayor's hand, then waited as Mayor Billy Charge stepped out of the car, and held the door open for the young man. Turner kept his eyes on his son, saw all the young kids turning in awe, gaping at the mayor of the city of Chicago, dropping off one of their classmates. He felt around in back until he found Claudette's hand, and held it tightly, sniffing, hearing his wife sob, as their son strode quickly away from the car.

Charge was surrounded by kids, signing autographs. Turner found his voice and said, "Shit, I better get out there."

"There aren't any assassins out there, Ellis. It's our son's first official day of high school, wait a minute," Claudette said, and Ellis did, clinging to Claudette's hand, fighting tears, as Quentin, with hardly a limp, strode tall and proud through the doors of the St. Ignatius College Preparatory Academy.